SOUL SURRENDER

Also by Katana Collins

SOUL STRIPPER

SOUL SURVIVOR

SOUL SURRENDER

A Soul Stripper Romance

KATANA COLLINS

APHRODISIA
KENSINGTON PUBLISHING CORP.
www.kensingtonbooks.com

APHRODISIA BOOKS are published by

Kensington Publishing Corp.
119 West 40th Street
New York, NY 10018

All Kensington titles, imprints, and distributed lines are available at special quantity discounts for bulk purchases for sales promotion, premiums, fund-raising, educational, or institutional use.

Special book excerpts or customized printings can also be created to fit specific needs. For details, write or phone the office of the Kensington Special Sales Manager: Kensington Publishing Corp., 119 West 40th Street, New York, NY 10018. Attn. Special Sales Department. Phone: 1-800-221-2647.

Aphrodisia and the A logo Reg. U.S. Pat. & TM Off.

ISBN-13: 978-0-7582-9015-1
ISBN-10: 0-7582-9015-2
First Kensington Trade Paperback Printing: May 2014

eISBN-13: 978-0-7582-9016-8
eISBN-10: 0-7582-9016-0
First Kensington Electronic Edition: May 2014

10 9 8 7 6 5 4 3 2 1

Printed in the United States of America

For Eliza: Soul mates come in all forms, including best friends

Acknowledgments

Despite most people's concept of a writer's life (you know, alone in a dark room, the door closed, eight empty coffee cups strewn about the floor), the fact is no writer creates a book entirely on their own. There have been so many people from all walks of life who've offered their invaluable assistance, knowledge, advice, and support through this book and all others.

Thank you to my first (and only) writing professor from undergrad, Heather Dune McAdam. Without her fabulous tutelage and guidance, I may have never known all that I could achieve. It was only one class. But it changed my life forever.

Special thanks go out to Eliza Lamb—my best friend who not only came up with the series title but also lent me her surname for Monica. Thank you for your love, your support and, most important, your friendship.

To my amazing editor, Martin Biro—you never fail to turn my words into something more succinct and sensical. Thank you for deciphering my crazy brain. Also, many thanks to everyone on the Kensington team who works so hard to put these books out!

Many thanks to my agent, Louise Fury, and her fabulous team. My critique group—Krista Amigone, Derek Bishop, and Shauna O'Garro—thank you for helping mold my book into something cohesive!

Many thanks to my family, Mom, Dad, Bo, Bridget, Adam, Adelynn, and Harrison. I promise to lift my nose from my laptop long enough for a bite of turkey and some green bean casserole this year at Thanksgiving!

And to Sean. I love you. Thank you. Tonight we drink a glass of wine (. . . or, you know, a bottle) and toast to *Happily Ever After*.

1

This wasn't my first time riding a mechanical bull. But it was the first time I'd done so while in a wet tank top, cowboy boots, and a thong. I was still surprised I had talked Lucien into replacing the stripper pole with the bull for the night. Then again, my ArchDemon of Las Vegas had deep pockets and shallow morals, so perhaps it shouldn't have been such a shock.

The spotlight on center stage warmed my mostly bare flesh. With the bright lights and pulsating bull between my legs, it should have been hard to see the sea of spectators ogling the stage. But my succubus vision was sharp, and each face was clearer than high definition television.

The tank top clung to my hard nipples with a damp chill, and bills rained onto the stage. One of the greatest things about being a succubus is the fact that I can shift into any look I want: man, woman, or creature. With one hand in the air and ass cheeks slamming onto the moving leather bull, I slinked one leg over the side and did a back bend off of the moving centerpiece.

Sitting front and center, chin at stage level, was Damien. My elemental . . . friend? Boyfriend? Fuck buddy? It had been months since our first hookup in Salt Lake City, and we still couldn't define what the Hell we were to each other.

A smirk tugged my eyes, and I fell to a crouch in front of him. With a finger, I stroked the length of my sex over the gauzy cotton panty (also shapeshifted to be wet) and then plunged that same finger into his mouth. His tongue slid over my nail, nibbling the edge, and his moan vibrated through me.

Jutting my hip forward, I paused, holding his steely gaze.

His eyebrows climbed higher. "You've got to be kidding me."

"Can't give you any special treatment, Detective Kane." My voice had a humorous lilt to it. "You sit in the front row, you cough up the dough."

Grumbling, he reached into his back pocket, crinkling a five in his fist. He hooked the bill into the G-string along my hip and curved his finger in as well. It slid down the length of my panty, brushing the smooth skin inside. My pulse jumped with the wicked gleam he flashed at me. "I'll see you after, then?"

The thumping bass beckoned me back to the performance to center stage. Damn this job. With a wink, I pranced back to my duties. I tore the tank top from my body, ripping it with the ease and strength of any supernatural being. The dank club air swirled around my naked breasts, and I shimmied out of my thong as well, two-stepping about. With one more spin, I stopped dead in my tracks. There, at the back of the audience—in the midst of blended bodies writhing together—was Drew. My Drew—my best friend and human boss at the coffee shop. Drew—the man I loved but could never have. Part of the succubus curse was an eternity sleeping with humans and taking some of their life to sustain my existence. It pretty much took any sort of real human relationship out of the equation.

I blinked once. Twice. Was it actually him? I couldn't tell. Not only was it weird to see Drew here, because the man wouldn't be caught dead in a strip club, he'd also been missing for almost eight months after learning that his friends, girlfriend, and ex-lover were all either angels or demons. Then add to that his leap into an abyss of Hell to save all of us from an angry elemental family—well, no wonder he didn't want to come anywhere near us.

Sea green eyes locked onto mine, and for a moment there was no one else in the room. No assholes whooping and hollering for me to shove my tits in their face. No groaning mechanical bull. No boyfriends or girlfriends, current or ex, in the front row. It was just him and me.

And then I blinked—and Drew was gone. Or the man who *looked* like Drew was gone. I felt empty and abandoned all at once. Did I just imagine him there? My eyes cruised the crowd once more.

"Mirage! Mirage! *Monica!*"

"Huh?" Someone was calling for me . . . by both my real and stage name. Stage name . . . shit, I was still onstage. It had only been seconds, but for this crowd, seconds of not shaking my succubus ass was grounds to be deported back to Hell.

My eyes found Damien's, and his were wide, concerned. "Are you all right?" he mouthed rather than said.

I didn't bother answering; instead I slid back into my routine. The chorus of assholes booing quickly morphed into whistles and hoots. It didn't take much to please the deviants that hung around Lucien's strip club, Hell's Lair. And as much as I loathed being a stripper, it provided me access to some of Vegas's worst souls. The kind of guys from whom I didn't mind stealing some life energy. Most of the losers who slipped in here every night after work had it coming.

After my set I shifted into jeans, but kept the wet tank top, and took a seat at the edge of the bar. T, our bouncer and bartender at Hell's Lair, slid me a scotch and water. My favorite after a rough night.

"Hey, kid," he said, even though we both knew I was decades older than him. Two meaty elbows leaned against the bar, and though he didn't smile I could sense the warm grin in his eyes. T rarely smiled. I could count on one hand the number of times I'd seen his dimples. He was a massive man, easily taller than six feet. His weight was entirely made up of pie and burgers. It only took one out-of-line customer to learn that T didn't need bulging biceps to assert power. He was strength personified and acted like a bulldozer to those needing to be bounced.

"Everything all right?"

I brought a shoulder to my ear. "Oh, sure. Just another night, you know?"

"Yeah, I know." He stared wistfully at one of our other dancers and a fellow succubi, Janelle.

"What happened with you two? Things looked like they were going well."

"They were." His baritone voice licked my skin, rough like a cat's tongue. "Until they weren't."

It was probably all I'd get out of T, I realized, and so I sipped my scotch and water instead of pushing him further. "Where's Lucien tonight?"

"Around. He's always around."

Two arms curled around my waist, and I found myself lost in someone's muscular chest. "I've missed you." My skin tingled and I gasped at the low voice. *Drew.* I sighed into the embrace, dropping my head back against his chest, and glanced down at the arms enveloping me. Only they weren't covered in blond hair; they were dark. Damien. Shit. Was I totally losing it?

"How can you miss me when you saw me onstage just a minute ago?"

He chuckled, released his hold, and slipped onto the seat next to mine. "Because you're addictive. You of all people should know just how much."

I rolled my eyes. "Yes, but we both know *your* kind is immune to my poison."

Damien dipped his finger into my scotch and let the droplets fall onto my palm. After using his finger to swirl the tiny bit of liquid like a whirlpool, he raised my palm to his lips. His tongue flattened to my hand in a tortuously slow lick. "I like my liquor stirred." He ran a hand through his dark hair, which was trimmed in layers but still long enough to dive my fingers into.

"Show-off."

I never knew how powerful Damien's elemental magic really was, until his mother and brother, infamous elementals from my past, came back to seek revenge.

His eyes darkened and he trailed a finger down the side of my face. "Let's go back to my place." His voice was raw. Husky. I inhaled his scent—it was earthy, like his magic.

I curved my fingers onto his clean-shaven jaw and ran a thumb across his full bottom lip. He nipped the edge, his lips sliding into a smile. Man, that smile is hard to resist. "I can't—I wish I could, but I have to recharge first."

The sexy smolder immediately wilted into searing anger; his darkened gaze took on a whole different tone, and he jerked away from my touch. Instead of curving those talented fingers around my body again, he gripped my glass of scotch and tipped back a loud slug.

The sudden shift lacerated my already bruised ego. This wasn't a life I chose for myself, and yet at every turn judgment slammed into me. Impatience and pain collided against my heart, but as always, I pushed my battered soul to the side. "Damien, this is part of the deal. Elementals can't give me power—and luckily in return, I can't take your life. You know that. Or would you prefer I never fuck another man again? Recede into nothing and allow my soul to fall away into a tortuous Hell?"

His jaw clenched, teeth grinding away at the top enamel.

"Well, at least then you could be with your precious Drew." His words were cold, and they speared me like an icy dart.

"Fuck you," I spat. "And for your information, Drew's not in Hell. He's just not *here*." My fingers twitched, and I resisted the urge to run my hand along the postcard Drew had sent me from Alaska months ago. I carried it as a constant reminder that he was out there. Somewhere.

I finished the rest of my drink with one swallow and slammed it down before pushing the stool back. His hands darted out, one grasping me behind the waist, the other behind the neck. His fingers laced into my hair, tugging it into a knot at my nape.

"Let me go, Damien."

"Not a chance, angel."

I gulped. "Don't call me that." I shuddered remembering the man who instituted that nickname long ago: Lord Buckley. He, along with a vampire named Dejan, had been responsible for my fall from angel to succubus.

There was a hurricane of emotions swirling in his eyes. "Dammit, woman. Do you know what you're doing to me? I never used to give a shit about who my lovers were fucking in their off time, so long as they were safe. But you—you . . ." He hissed an exhale, sloping his lips over mine. His tongue stroked my own in soft, needy glides. Arousal flared in my body, and I hated myself for being so quick to respond.

"Damien," I said against his lips. "Stop. This—us . . . we fight all the time," I said on a moan as his lips trailed kisses down my neck, nipping my collarbone. "This is why I don't *do* relationships. My lifestyle is not an easy one to accept. And I don't blame you if you decide it's too hard."

"No," he growled. "I'm not ready to give up yet." His hand glided to my lower back and cupped my ass. "I'm sorry," he added.

"Why don't I finish up work tonight, then tomorrow we

can pick up where we left off?" Our mouths met in unison and tongues twisted in an intensely emotional kiss that I felt in every area of my body. His erection was denim-clad steel pressed between my legs.

"I'll leave you to it, then." He stood and tossed some bills onto the bar. With a wave at T and another smacking kiss on my lips, he slipped out the door.

The air in Damien's absence was clearer and my lungs seemed to work easier without his looming gaze on me.

"Monica!" I recognized Lucien's growl immediately. I'd already dismantled one bomb tonight—I wasn't sure I had it in me to do another.

Like a rat running from a flood, T bolted to the other end of the bar. Lucien was the only man I'd ever seen T afraid of. He was our boss not only here at the club but in the Hell-realm, too.

"Tell your boyfriend that if he doesn't back off, he won't be allowed in here anymore."

"Back off of what?"

A string of long, black hair escaped its ponytail and fell into Lucien's equally dark eyes. "What the fuck do you think I mean? *You.*" He shoved it behind his ear, then slapped a palm down on the bar top. "He might as well lift a goddamn leg and piss all over you. No guy will dare buy a private dance if it comes with a risk of getting his ass kicked."

"They might. The thrill-seeking sort . . ."

"You're fucking hilarious."

My eyebrow curved into an arch. "Jeez. What's got you so grumpy?"

"I run this damn place on my own. I'm ArchDemon over the entire Southwest region. I'm investigating who the fuck is stupid enough to put a bounty on you. And on top of all that, I'm searching tirelessly for your missing human. The latter would be a lot easier if you would just tell us what you know about him."

"I told you already—stop looking for him. He'll come back if and when he wants to." I slid a glance over my shoulder, scanning the crowd for Drew. I could have sworn that was him in the audience. Attention back on Lucien, I opened my mouth to mention my sighting. But as Lucien's gaze narrowed, assessing my every move, I chickened out and instead grasped my glass, slugging the rest of my drink in one gulp.

"I would *love* to stop looking for him. He's clearly no longer in Hell. I know enough people down there that I would have at least had confirmation of that by now. But no one will release the information about where he is or what he is doing. Not to mention that angel of his is pretty damn insistent. She finally caved and hired Kayce to find him."

The bags under Lucien's eyes were blue and heavy. His skin lacked its usual luster. He raked a hand down his face. Emotion knotted in my stomach. He was worried about Kayce. Of course.

"Lucien—"

"Shut up," he grumbled.

"I didn't even say anything yet!"

"I don't care. Unless it's about where Drew is, I don't want to hear it." His gaze slid over me, taking in everything from head to toe. "Where's your gun? And the holy water mace I gave you?"

"Oh, um"—I looked down and put a hand to my pockets, something we both knew was bullshit since these jeans may as well have been painted directly on my body—"they're back in my dressing room, I think."

"Monica." Lucien's face dropped with his sigh, a defeated sound that made me instantaneously regret not being more cautious. "Do you know how expensive it is to get bullets blessed in holy water for a demon? You should at least keep the mace on you at all times."

His full eyebrows creased in the center, and he glared at me with more sorrow than anger.

"You're right. I'm sorry."

Shock registered on his face before his eyes dropped into a narrowed gaze. "You're not disagreeing with me? Not taking the moment to fight me?" Like a dart to a bull's-eye, his hand shot to my forehead. "You're not sick, are you?" he asked with a smirk.

I slapped his hand away with a playful grin. In the 250 years since I had fallen from angel to succubus, there has been one consistent rock in my life: Lucien. He found me when I fell from being an angel. He guided me. Taught me the rules of being a succubus. And never once allowed himself to be relocated without bringing me with him. "I can admit when you're right." My smile slid wider. "It's not my fault that it just doesn't happen all that often."

Hooking an elbow around my neck, Lucien pulled me in for a hug and pressed a kiss to my temple. His cheek rested on top of my head, and his breath was heavy, laden with stress.

"You know," I said, "Kayce acts tough and all. And she in no way *needs* a man in her life. But that doesn't mean she wouldn't enjoy having one. . . ."

Lucien's eyes slid to me, pupils dilated, and he pulled back from our embrace. "She said that?"

No. "Yes." A pause swung between us like a noose. "Not in those exact words . . ."

He shoved off the bar to his feet. "Go make me some money, Monica. And if you decide to cut all of us a break, and want to tell me where Drew is, you know where I'll be." He stalked two steps before looking back over his shoulder. "For your sake, make tonight's conquest someone good. I can tell you could use the energy."

I caught my reflection in the mirror behind the bar. The draught menu and various specialty drinks were painted over the top, obscuring my reflection. My lack of energy radiated from every aspect of my features. The lower my powers, the more beautiful I became. Saetan's own little insurance policy on us succubi. My skin shimmered like dew. My nails were long and glossy. Overall, it looked as though my body glowed; I was a lighthouse beckoning the strongest and most virile sailors. My body was compensating for what my soul lacked.

With a deep breath, I released my succubus pheromone into the club. It billowed out like cigarette smoke, swirling above the crowd. T rushed back to me, his eyes glossy. "Another one?" He shook my empty glass. The question was simple, but his lovesick gaze was not.

"No, thanks, T. Janelle seems to want something, though." I inclined my chin in her direction. She glowered at him, and my scotch and my pheromones were quickly forgotten.

It didn't take long for heads to turn in my direction. My scent was powerful to begin with—and the more a succubus needs energy, the more potent the scent.

"Excuse me," a familiar voice rumbled beside me. "Are you available for a dance?"

The bar stool nearly tipped out from under me. "Drew?"

2

Confusion marred his rugged face. No—not Drew. His aura wasn't right. But holy damn, did he look like him. Chiseled bones and a strong chin peppered with reddish-blond stubble. He even had a similar scar on his lip. Were dopplegängers possible? My hand twitched to reach out and feel him.

"No," he said. "I'm Ryan."

I nodded, my pulse slowing to its normal rate. He wasn't my Drew. His soul wasn't perfect . . . not Heaven-bound. He was the ideal candidate for a one-night stand. Slowly, carefully, I extended a hand, curling it into his and lacing our fingers. His hands were softer than Drew's, not so calloused. My eyes fluttered shut and I inhaled, lost in memories of Drew on top of me, his face between my legs, palm against my trembling breast.

"Um, are you okay?"

Arousal pulsed between us, and I raised my eyes to his emerald green irises again. "More than. You sure you're ready for me?" I pressed a hand to his chest and slid it down to taut abs.

"Oh, yeah." He grinned. One dimple creased at the corner of his mouth.

I searched the room for Lenny, the horrid manager Lucien had hired to run this pit.

He caught my eyes, and I gestured to Ryan. Like the little weasel he was, he scurried over to us, his obnoxious clipboard clutched tightly in his clawlike hands. Beady black eyes and an awful comb-over made up most of Lenny's appearance. Other than that, he bought button-down shirts two sizes too small, and his belly always spilled over the top of a pleather belt. I'd seen more style waiting in line at McDonald's.

Ryan held my gaze, full lips slipping into a soft grin. His eyes slid down my body like a gentle kiss. Goose bumps rose, nipples hardened, and my breasts were heavy with need. He hadn't even laid a hand on me yet and I was squirming to slide on top of the man. He was a darker souled Drew. Hell-bound and deadlier.

"It'll be four hundred fifty—and that doesn't include a tip for the lady." Lenny's nasal voice broke the moment, pulling me back to the present.

From his back pocket, Ryan opened an expensive-looking leather wallet and pulled out a fistful of cash. He held it out for Lenny, still not tearing his eyes away from me. "Not to worry," he said, his green eyes twinkling, "I'll take good care of the lady, too."

Everything inside me clenched. Leaning into his chest, I ran both palms down his arms and grasped his hands. With a tug, I directed him to one of the private rooms in the back. For one of the first times working here at the club, I was nervous. Guilt gnawed deep in my belly. This is a job. He is a necessity to keep on living.

The wooden legs of the chair scraped across the floor as I placed it in the center of the private room. His saunter was slow, with one hand tucked into his front pocket. The other brushed along his top lip. He flicked a glance at the chair. "I'd rather stand, if that's all right with you."

"Sure. Of course." In all my years dancing, I'd never once

had a client want to stand during my dance. With a little re-mote, I set the music low, the vibrations pulsing through my body. He closed in, backing me against the wall. What was that smell? His scent was so familiar.

His breath was hot, and the itch for his life force flared in-side of me. Between my legs the ache was so agonizing, I didn't know if I could make it through an entire dance.

"Let me help you," he rasped, curling his fingers under my still-damp shirt and lifting it above my head. Blood rushed be-hind my eyes, roaring in my head. "In fact"—his fingers skimmed the curve of where waist meets hip, and he popped the button on my jeans—"what are the chances we can skip the dance?"

The breath hitched in my throat—why did this guy affect me so? Sure, he looked like Drew, but I was supposed to cloud *his* thoughts, not the other way around. He tilted his lips, cov-ering my mouth in a scorching kiss that resonated between my legs.

I slid my palms under his jacket, and impressive shoulders clenched under my touch. The jacket fell to the floor, and I popped his shirt buttons open, one by one. A silver cross gleamed around his neck. I immediately withdrew, snapping my hands back to my sides.

"What's the matter?" Despite the question, something knowing gleamed in his eyes, and I narrowed mine to slits.

"Nothing." I went back to undoing buttons, careful not to touch the cross, and he shuffled his arms out of the shirt. His chest and abs were marble—pure chiseled rock.

His thumbs hooked into my jeans and I shimmied out of them. One hand cupped my sex through my damp panties, and his thumb pressed into my clit. With flattened palms shoved against the wall behind me, my trembling knees gave out and I fell back, allowing the wall to absorb my weight.

His chuckle was a practiced lullaby, and he caught me around the waist. "Easy, there." Sure, easy for him to say. Two muscled thighs flanked either side of me like two columns. The cross around his neck winked at me in the soft lighting, and a lump lodged in my throat.

"Could you take off your necklace?" The interruption was an odd one, sure. But I doubted I could enjoy myself knowing at any moment the holy relic could scald my skin. Branding me as Hellspawn.

He quirked an eyebrow. "Why?"

I sidled closer, my ache deepening with each passing second. "I just . . . prefer not to have a constant religious reminder for the duration of our time together."

He didn't respond right away. His face was masked with stern lines and a gritted jaw. "What if I don't want to take it off?"

I snapped my eyes back to his. Why wouldn't he want to remove a cross? Unless he knew . . .

The pregnant pause was unnerving. From just outside the door, the bass thumped under a low hum of chatter and laughter.

"Or," he continued, "I suppose I could just get a refund." He peeled away, and the absence of his touch flamed on my skin.

"No." I loathed that the word escaped my mouth as almost a whimper. I clamped his hand tighter in my fist and tugged him toward me once more. "It's fine."

Fire danced in his eyes. I shivered, not quite understanding what this raw and exposed feeling was about. He made me feel—alive. Desired. Grasping at my hips, Ryan spun me and nudged my body onto the sofa that flanked the corner. The leather whined, cradling my weight.

I stole a peek over my shoulder just as his pants dropped, and my mouth dried at the sight of his long, hard dick. Arousal was thick in the air around me, and it flooded any ounce of rational thought that might have been left.

His fingers dove into my hair, and he jerked my head back so I could look up at him. The tight pull was deliciously rough, and my sex tightened with the act. His mouth moved over mine. His scent was fresh and clean, as though he'd just stepped out of the shower. Even his smell was similar to Drew's

From behind me, his thick erection cradled into my backside and he ran the head of it along the length of my sex. He tugged away my panties and with a palm between my shoulders pushed me onto my hands, bent over on all fours, exposed. Adrenaline swelled, and my pulse jumped into my throat.

He caressed a path down my back with careful fingers and then curled one inside of me. Moisture gathered along my lips, my skin all too sensitive. Each touch flared my heated flesh. There was a shuffle from behind me, and his other hand trailed along my ass. I arced into his touch, nipples pressing into the cool leather couch with tortuous friction.

The hand on my ass slid up my torso and palmed my breast, flicking and teasing the nipple. The fact that the actions were so focused on me—attending to my desires and my bodily needs—was an odd sensation here at the strip club. Most men don't pay $450 to do the majority of the work. I closed my eyes and relished the pleasure.

I was lost in a swirl of lust as his fingers nimbly tweaked and twisted my clit and nipple. His finger filled me, stretched me, before he withdrew entirely. I cried out, frustrated, my skin flaring impossibly hot.

Tension swirled through me and I was lost in sensation. A deep inhalation came from between my legs, and I realized he'd dropped to his knees, his nose buried deep in my cunt. With a flick of his tongue, he claimed my pussy with his mouth, suckling and nibbling me to the very brink of orgasm. A trembling tightness tugged inside of me, my lips swollen and throbbing. Fisting the leather in my hands, my body clenched in result—just as he pulled back, blowing cool air on my sex instead. The orgasm faded, leaving me a panting mess in its wake. As my breathing returned to normal, his tongue darted out again, running along my entire length.

He repeated this technique twice more—pushing me to the

edge of climax before stopping. If women could have blue balls, mine would have been turquoise. On the third time, I darted a hand to his head, twining my fingers through his hair and squeezing his face into me. "Are you fucking kidding me?" I rasped through ragged breath.

His low rumble of laughter vibrated through the air and tingled a path into my sex. He nipped my clit, sliding away from my grasp. He was purposefully denying me, teasing me—torturing me. I both hated and loved him for it.

His shaft pressed between my thighs and his hands gripped my hips, squeezing the flesh. His cock stroked my wet heat without yet entering, and my arms trembled, still bearing the weight of my body on all fours. "Please . . . oh, Hell, Ryan . . ."

"Take it easy." He chuckled. From between my legs, I could see his fist clenched around his shaft, directing it between my swollen flesh.

He plunged deep inside of me, not giving my body the time to adjust to his girth. I cried out, and he, too, moaned with the impact. Each thrust was a wild, grinding dance, and I lifted my hips to give him the access needed to fill every depth.

His grunts were animalistic and wild, as were mine. No words were needed; no eye contact necessary. He needed my cunt and I needed his orgasm to survive. It was an even trade. His hands roamed my body, kneading my full, aching breasts as his cock dragged inside of me. I tightened myself around his shaft, my muscle pulsing and the orgasm beginning to bloom yet again. This time, I refused to let it slip away. The luscious euphoria was too close. I bit my lip and, using the leverage of my arms, pushed against the couch, impaling myself on him. He ground into me harder, the ball-slapping thrust sending us both over the edge. I stiffened, fastening down on his steel-like length, and splintered into fragments around him. My orgasm trembled through my body, tensing each limb until the shudders slowed.

Ryan's grunt exploded and quivered with his own release. He nipped my shoulder, burying himself deeper into my contracting sex. Hot, white ecstasy jettisoned into me, and his soul flooded my mind like sunshine.

With bated breath and closed eyes, I waited for the vision of his death, the moment when I get to physically see just how much life I've actually taken from my conquests. From behind me, a foreign language sprang from his lips, and I recognized the chant immediately as the ancient Indo-European language of witchcraft.

I yelped, and the smell of burnt flesh sizzled in the room. His palm, cross in hand, flattened into the small of my back, shoving the holy relic into my skin as the chant finished.

I thrashed from below him, doing my best to fight him off, wriggle from his grasp. But the combination of his weight, the spell, and my body absorbing his life force was too much.

White flashes darted across my vision, popping like lightening. Ryan's face flickered between the flashes and then faded into . . . John? Lord Buckley?

"What the fuck?" I finally shoved him off of me, twisting and falling back onto the sofa. His life force radiated through me—I was strong, virile, and more alive than ever before. "Buckley?"

Ryan's grin was sly as it stretched across his face. He dropped his head into his hands, his appearance flickering. His sated dick hung in that limbo stage—not hard and yet not quite flaccid. Within seconds, his blond hair changed into a curly brownish-red. His stubble disappeared and his features morphed into the man I most despised from my past. He grinned. "Hello, angel. You've learned some new techniques in the last couple of centuries."

3

I trembled with the betrayal of the moment. He remembered my body well . . . remembered what I responded to and the kind of touches I craved. His juice dripped down my leg, blanketing my sex in the shame of who I am. Monica, the sex goddess. Useless save for one thing.

"How could you do this?" I jumped to my feet, shifting into normal clothes—jeans and a fitted cotton tee. The shift came on quickly, and the power of the life force he had given resonated in my body. I was strong—yet, I *knew* Buckley. He was anything but a glowing soul. His life force should have barely given me enough to make it until tomorrow. "And what did you do to me?!" I craned my neck, the flesh at my lower back blistering and angry in the shape of a cross. It was the world's worst tramp stamp. I closed my eyes and shifted the third-degree burn away, only it didn't disappear. The pain flared across my back. "What the *fuck!*"

Snatching his pants from the floor, he shoved a leg in. "I'm sorry," he said as he zipped his fly, his boyish grin spreading wider. "Was it not good for you?"

Asshole. He *knew* it was good for me. He had a damn good memory for a man that hadn't fucked me in almost three centuries.

His saunter was slow, and his bare feet scuffed along the floors. My back was against the wall again, and before I had the sense to stop him, his breath was on my lips. "I can try again, if you'd like."

A retort strangled on my lips as he slipped a hand into my pants. My knees buckled and he caught me around the waist, plunging a finger inside my dripping sex.

"No!" With both hands, I shoved his chest. He shifted back, not stumbling in the slightest, but his gaze lifted with humor. I advanced on him with lightning speed, shoving my forearm to his throat and slamming him into the back wall. "What was that spell? What did you do to me?"

"Spell?" He cocked his head as amusement flashed in those emerald eyes of his, and he peeled my arm off. "All right, then." He bent slowly, back muscles rippling as he snapped his shirt off the floor. He took his sweet time buttoning it. "I only released what was already inside of you, my angel."

"Stop *calling* me that." I gnashed my teeth together.

He glanced at an expensive watch. "Sure you don't want to go once more? I've got some time to spare." His eyes flashed, one side of his mouth lifting into a smile. "I want to taste every ounce of flesh on your body," he whispered. "I love the taste of you."

"Me and every other woman, isn't that right?" The bitter words tumbled from my lips and I clamped my eyes shut, but still seeing visions of Buckley cheating on me, his face buried between some other woman's thighs. The recent memory of his tongue flared scorching desire through my body.

"I can smell your arousal, Monica. I would pleasure you until you were completely satisfied, my angel."

"With you? I'd use the term *satisfied* very loosely."

His mouth split into a full-on grin. "That's because you can't get enough of me."

I held my steely gaze and crossed my arms, cleavage pressed toward my chin. "Oh, I've had enough of you to last an eternity. What are you doing here, John?"

"Where's your sense of nostalgia?"

"Apparently lost with your rationality." I paused, soaking him up with my eyes. It had been a while since I'd seen him in his true form—the man I'd known in my angel days. "Well, at least one good thing came from tonight. You'll die a little sooner thanks to me."

His eyes flashed. "Will I, now?" His bottom lip was fuller than the top, resulting in a pout that supermodels would envy. One side of his mouth lifted in a grin that didn't quite reach his eyes. "But what a way to go," he said, his voice dropped, low and husky.

"You never answered me. What are you doing here? And why won't this burn shift away?"

Adjusting his watch, he put his appearance back in order and took two steps closer. "Did you ever imagine how we would be together?"

I couldn't even pretend to placate his thoughts. Instead I snatched the remote, turning off the mood-inducing music.

"You want Drew?" he continued, ignoring my obvious dodge. An incantation trickled out of his lips and he transformed into Drew before my eyes. "I can be your Drew." His voice had a different croon to it. Drew's voice. I shook my head out of its daze. Do not get sucked in by his magic.

"Not a chance. Your ugly spirit will shine through every time." I pushed past his shoulder, gripping the lock on the door.

"Well, that's a shame. It's just too bad he doesn't crave you the same way you crave him." Buckley took his time buttoning his sleeves, and I spun to face him.

Anger trembled low in my core and the doorknob pressed

into my lower back. "You forgot to tip." I cocked a hip and held out a hand.

"But, of course. Silly me," he replied, and reaching back into his wallet he pinched a folded hundred between his fingers and advanced with a casual gait. Twisting my hair into a fisted ponytail, he yanked my neck back, exposing taut flesh. The edge of the folded bill traveled over my tight nipples before he tipped his fingers into my jeans, leaving it pressed up against my drenched clit.

His grip loosened at my neck, and I hissed an exhale. Leaning past my shoulder, he reached for the doorknob, his leering smile hovering above me. Without thinking, my arm sprung out, stopping the door with my weight. I shoved a hand down my pants, balling the bill in my fist, and tossed it in his face. He barely blinked as it bounced off his cheek and hit the floor.

"On second thought, I'd rather starve in a box under the highway before spending another penny of yours."

He chuckled, and an auburn curl sprang into his eyes. "I always did love your spunk, angel." He bended to lift the bill and slid it back into his pocket. He slapped a postcard in my hand instead. "My new show," he said. "Now that we both know Drew is safe . . . and you're not gunning to kill me, why don't you come check it out."

"Who said I wasn't gunning to kill you still?" Damn. Now I wished I had listened to Lucien and had that damn gun on me. I glanced at my palm. "Raul's Rogue Angels," I read aloud. "Catchy. Using your alias still, I see?"

He grinned. "Well, Lord Buckley doesn't quite have the same ring to it."

"So what is it? Some kind of musical revue?"

"Don't be ridiculous. It's a magic show, of course." He leaned a shoulder against the dusty black wall and crossed one leg over the other. "You could join me—be my partner in the act. With your newly developed witchcraft, think of the crowds we'd draw."

Heat flashed through me. I had gotten the witchcraft when Adrienne, Drew's ex-girlfriend and a detective, died saving me. I had accidentally ingested her blood and power. She had since turned into an angel, and I into some crazy ass succubus-witch hybrid. Over the past year I had managed to refine the power into something I could control.

"No, thanks." I flipped the flyer back at him. His hand hovered above the card, and it floated back up into his palm. "Remember that whole 'I'd rather starve' comment. It applies here, too."

"Just come check it out. I'll get you in for free. Bring your friends, too. It's at the Wynn. Tomorrow night."

Curiosity spiked in my chest, and his eyes twinkled knowingly. "Where'd you find your rogue angels?"

"Heaven, my love. Where else?"

4

The drive back to my apartment was a short one. Drew's café is only a couple of blocks away from home, and as I passed, I swung into the parking lot. As the acting manager, I had extended our hours on weekends to cater to the late-night crowd. Business grew exponentially with the change. With a quick look at the clock, I figured the doors were already locked, but Genevieve, now my assistant manager, would be there counting the cash box.

Sure enough, the lights were on. I dug in my purse, yanked out my set of keys—which was increasingly looking like a set of janitor's keys—and unlocked the door. "Hey, G—how was tonight?"

With a glance up, she shook her head. "Can't you ever just go home and take a break?" Her face split into a grin.

"If only," I muttered to myself, and mirrored her smile. Genevieve had an infectious personality: When she was happy, so were you. If she was crying, your eyes welled up with just as many tears. She was genuine. Sweet. "You just seemed so tired when I left tonight. I wanted to make sure you're okay."

Her smile wobbled before she firmed it back into a tight-lipped grin. "I'm . . . fine." Despite the calm smile she sported, her voice wavered, her aura changing to a dark blue. Sadness.

"Genevieve." I rushed to her side, guiding her by the arm to a seat. "What's going on?"

Her face was so tight, it appeared as though it could shatter at any given moment. "I—Adam and I, we've just been trying for so long to have a baby."

A gasp caught in my throat and I choked it back, my hand instinctually flying to my own barren belly. "It can take a while, G."

"No—you don't understand. We, I'm—I can't." Her chin dropped to her chest, trembling. "You know . . . low egg count or something." With her index finger, she swiped at the one escaped tear traveling down her cheek.

I clasped a hand over hers, squeezing. "Oh, Genevieve. I'm so sorry." The air conditioner hummed around us, offering its own condolences. Her palm was clammy and chilled compared to mine. "There are lots of options, you know?"

"I know, I know. I just really wanted to experience pregnancy."

"I know. You're going to make an amazing mother."

She sniffled, eyes rimmed red. I sandwiched her palm between both of my hands and closed my eyes. In my mind, I thought of the words to the guardian incantation I had learned, the ancient language becoming second nature. I pulled her in for a hug, kissing her temple. A zap shocked my lips, and I pulled back just as quickly.

The fastest flash of her life reeled in my mind. Shit . . . had I just stolen some of Genevieve's life? It's supposed to happen only when someone reaches orgasm at a succubi or incubi's touch. But her face—no, a baby's face—flashed in my mind with the same white lightning breaking up the images, just like with Buckley.

I released my hold on her, doing my best to procure a shaky smile. "You'll be okay, girl. Trust me—I know."

How much life had I stolen? Most likely only minutes, but it was still too much.

She returned my smile, hers looking stronger than mine at the moment. The irony of that resonated deep in me, and I couldn't help but scoff at myself. "Why don't you go on home. I'll finish up here."

"Oh, no . . . I couldn't let you do that. You worked all day."

I shrugged, mouth tilting. "So what's another hour? It's nothing, I promise. Go give your husband a night to remember." I winked at her and she laughed, her hand flying to cover her mouth.

"Thanks, Monica." She gripped me in another hug before untying her apron, balling it at her side. Grabbing her purse, she gave another wiggle of her fingers before slipping out the front door.

Forty-five minutes later, I had finished the books for the night and cleaned the shop. With the counted cash in hand, I entered Drew's office, blinking with the flickering fluorescents. I spun the lock to open the safe and stuck the money inside. I wouldn't have time to get to the bank until next week. A sigh crept up on me as I stood, hands on hips, looking around Drew's office. A hoodie rested on the back of his office chair, and I hesitated before sliding my arms into it. The fleece lining cradled my sensitive skin, and I hugged it tighter around my body. With closed eyes, I inhaled. His scent was faint but still lingered, a freshly sweet smell of arabica beans and soap as though he had climbed out of the shower and brewed a pot of coffee, allowing both the soap and brew to permeate the soft cotton. The fading memory swirled about like a long-lost friend.

But when I opened my eyes again, I was still alone. Clutching a shirt that wasn't mine in an empty coffee shop with a hollow heart. Drew and I could never be; I knew that. Even one night with me would result in Drew losing time off his life. No—it wasn't worth the risk. We'd crossed that line once, but never again. He would find a woman to love and grow old with. And then, someday far in the future, he would pass on to Heaven. Without me.

Emotion rolled through me like a wave lapping over my body. After one last, deep breath, I dropped the sweatshirt back onto his chair as I had done almost every night the past several months. The shirt would lose its scent soon enough. But until then I would relish every aromatic breath I could take.

I made sure to shut off all the lights and lock the doors behind me. The night air was dry and warm. That was the beauty of the desert; once that sun dropped, you had a reprieve from the heat.

I walked to my car with keys in hand. When it was only steps away, footsteps crunched in the gravel behind me. I forced my breathing to remain regular. As I approached my little Toyota, I saw the briefest reflection of a body in the mirror behind me. Someone was definitely on my tail. And for a girl with a bounty on her head? That was a bad sign.

Faster than the human eye could register, I lifted a hand in the air. "Ailukah!" I shouted the enchantment and, using my witchcraft, threw the person onto the hood of my car. The crunch echoed through the parking lot and a startled cry shattered the quiet evening.

I was on top of her in moments, hand crushing her windpipe. I hovered my other palm atop my purse, and the can of holy water mace flew into my hand. Her fear caught in the back of my throat and tasted like bitters and lime.

Her body thrashed beneath mine, and yet I stayed strong, pinning her down with my knees. "Monica!"

I stilled. "Kayce?"

"Yes! Fuck, let me up!"

While the rational part of my brain knew that Kayce was my best friend and would never hurt me, the suspicion from Salt Lake City remained. She and Lucien were supposedly acting under cover, attempting to find out who was the boss in charge of my bounty—only it didn't make sense why they couldn't tell me about that plan from the beginning.

Kayce was a killer. An assassin by trade. And I couldn't shake that uneasy feeling of knowing my best friend, whom I admittedly loved very much, wakes up each morning, has a cup of coffee, and goes to work slicing jugulars and strangling strangers. A shiver tickled my spine.

"Monica?"

Shit. I shook the thoughts away and pushed off of Kayce's windpipe, grasping her hand and pulling her to a standing position. "Sorry," I mumbled. "What are you doing here? *Lurking* behind me."

"Lucien said you'd be home by now. I waited for a while, and when you didn't show, I came looking for you here." She brushed her clothes back into place. "Jesus. Twitchy much?" She glanced at my hood, dented in the shape of her slender body.

"Yeah, I tend to be a little on edge these days." I did my best to hide the bitterness in my voice. The whole bounty thing was getting old fast. Every strange noise in my house was enough to send me running for my cabinet of weaponry. Which admittedly was growing larger and larger with each passing day.

With my hand on the dent, I incanted a quick spell and it popped out.

"Damn," Kayce hissed. "How do you do that?"

"You kill a witch. Eat a bitch," I bit back, Adrienne's face popping into my brain.

She tugged her curtain of jet black hair over one shoulder and dropped her neck to the side. "Okay, what flew up your ass today?" Even though succubi and incubi can shapeshift, most tend to stick with one body at a time. For as long as I've known Kayce, she's pretty much had the same look. It just makes life easier and gives us a semblance of normalcy. Kayce's chosen body was svelte and Asian, and she wore lots of leather . . . even in the scorching Vegas summers.

"Where are you off to tonight?" Her jumpsuit looked more like a costume than an outfit.

She glanced down, hands on hips, and laughed, shifting into tight jeans and a low-cut top. "I just finished up at a *Star Trek* convention." Geeks and social pariahs were Kayce's favorite targets. "You should have come. There were plenty of good targets there. There's another one in California next month."

I quirked an eyebrow in her direction. "*Star Trek*? No, thanks."

"Oh, come on! You never come out anymore. Not since you took over Drew's stupid business."

I shrugged. "I just want to make sure he has something to come home to."

The silence between us crackled in the air. "You really don't want to help us find him?"

"I want him to come home on his own accord. I'm sure Hell is an awful place to visit—and who knows what he experienced while there."

Another pause. "I've been hired by Adrienne to find him."

"Lucien told me," I said. "Why didn't she hire some angels to get him?"

"Oh, she tried. Nobody on her side will help. They adopted the same mind-set as you—that he'll come home when he's ready."

"But shouldn't San Michel be able to just sense where he is . . ." The sentence strangled in my throat. I didn't let myself think of the ArchAngel very often anymore. Hell, he was more than an ArchAngel—he was the boss over all ArchAngels. And the man who made the final call on my banishment from Heaven. "Oh, shit." The curse was merely a whisper.

"What?"

"If Drew was still a Heaven-bound soul, San Michel should be able to sense him wherever he is."

"Don't jump to conclusions. You have no idea. . . . Maybe he just chose not to tell Adrienne."

I nodded, but that wobbly feeling in my gut didn't go away. "Where are you off to now?" Kayce's eyes flashed with a knowing gaze I had seen all too many times. She was on a job.

"I have a lead—about your bounty."

My heart hammered against my ribs. "Who is it? Where?"

Kayce looked around us—she was smart to do so. Just because we couldn't sense anyone around didn't mean prying eyes and sensitive ears couldn't listen in on what we were saying. The damn supernatural world had hearing better than you could even imagine. "Does your car have enchantments?"

Faster than she could finish her next thought, I had my little Toyota unlocked and slid into the driver's side. "Okay, spill. No one can hear us in here."

"Okay—you know the Suck 'n' Swallow?"

"Isn't that one of Mia's bars?" Our Succubi Queen owned establishments all around the world, though to my knowledge she rarely frequented the notorious succubus haunt herself. It was dank and the perfect spot for demon-folk to let loose.

"Exactly," Kayce said, voice hushed even though we both knew no one could hear a thing we said. "The bartender there, Ink, said he knows most of their clients. But this one demon has been coming the same night every month. She slips into the back and Ink hears someone else teleport in—and then she leaves."

"But—you can't teleport into Suck 'n' Swallow . . . not unless . . ."

"Unless you work for the higher-ups." Kayce fell back onto the seat, folding her arms and smiling.

"So, what? People visit Vegas all the time. What's the big

deal that some random demon has been making an appearance?"

"Well," Kayce continued, "last time she was there, she left her purse on the counter while Ink made her a drink. He caught a glimpse of the Eden stone inside."

I shivered, remembering that damn stone—which could essentially turn a succubus or incubus into a mortal, making them easy to kill. "How does *he* know about the stone?"

"Mon, everyone knows about that stone now. You weren't the only succubus targeted last year, remember?"

How could she even ask me that? Of course I remembered. I'd done nothing but remember for the last year and a half. "So this demon will be there tonight?"

"You got it."

A shaky breath caught in my chest. "I want to come."

Kayce shook her head with an eye roll and a snort. "Not a chance, Monica. They'll recognize your aura immediately."

"No . . . they won't." A smile curved on my lips as I whispered the incantation I'd been practicing for months. I imagined the bubble surrounding me, masking my powers, my aura. Once the spell was secure, I shifted into a dark-haired, shorter, curvier girl. My smile split into a full-on grin at Kayce's dismayed face. "Not bad, huh?"

She blinked. "I can't sense you at all. You read just as . . . as a mortal would." Her face fell. "One problem, though. Just how are we gonna get you into a demon bar?"

"Easy." The engine purred to life as I turned the keys. "I'll be your conquest for the night."

I fishhooked my car into a parking spot outside Suck 'n' Swallow, clicking the engine off. As we made our way to the front door, Kayce slid her palm into mine, lacing our fingers together.

A bouncer stood flanking the doorway, arms folded and face

covered in stern authority. As we approached, I could feel the hum of magic as Kayce shapeshifted just her eyes. The bouncer nodded and inclined a chin to me. "Who's your pet?"

"Oh, you know." Kayce ran a knuckle down my jaw, and I nuzzled into her neck. "Just a little snack for later." She winked at the bouncer, whose grin twitched in response. With a jerk of his head, we were in. So far, so good.

The bar was busy for a Thursday night, but not uncomfortably so. It was apparently eighties night: Toto blared through the speakers, and a bunch of demons danced in neon-colored clothing and teased hair.

"Want a drink?" Kayce's eyes were wide, and she slid a glance to the bartender, who gave a less than subtle nod in our direction.

"Gin and tonic, please."

With a tug on my hand, she pulled me toward the bar. "Hey, Ink. Two gin and tonics." Her eyes flashed, and he glanced at the clock.

"We missed it?" Kayce's jaw dropped.

"Not yet." His voice rumbled as though he'd smoked a few too many packs of cigarettes in his existence. His long, jet-black hair, braided in one section, fell past his shoulders. A tribal-looking tattoo started near his hairline and swirled down one side of his face to his temple. "Any minute now."

"Well"—Kayce glanced at the front door—"when that minute arises, let me know what I owe ya for the drinks."

He nodded and, in one fluid movement, mixed up two tumblers for us. The tart lime flavor bubbled on my tongue and tickled my throat. I was used to smooth liquor, not the carbonated stuff. But like anything else, it just took a moment to acclimate.

"So where's George tonight?" I said over the music.

Kayce rolled her eyes. "God. That boy works way too much."

I curved a brow at Kayce. Who was she kidding? With a laugh, she nodded. "Okay, fine. Yes, we all work too much."

"I talked to him a few days ago. It sounds like the film is going really well, at least."

Kayce played with her glass. "I hope he isn't gone the entire length of the shoot like last time."

I nodded in agreement as my eyes flitted around the room. Most of the faces were familiar, even if I didn't know any of them specifically. But one face particularly stood out. Buckley stood by the jukebox, strumming his fingers along his whiskey glass.

5

Fear was cemented in the pit of my stomach until it finally softened into something else—something more resilient.

"Oh, yes," I said more to myself than Kayce. "This could be fun."

"Huh?" She absentmindedly sipped her gin and tonic, eyes zeroed in on the unmoving front door. When she finally tore her gaze away, I nodded in his direction. "What is he doing here? Wait—he couldn't be—"

I shrugged. "I don't know." Was he capable of killing me? He already had in one sense. "Hey, Ink." I held a finger up to signal one more gin and tonic.

Like a vice, Kayce clamped onto my wrist. "He can't know who you are."

I nodded, sliding out of my chair, and swung my hips to the jukebox. Buckley leaned against the jukebox, his brown hair perfectly disheveled and clutched his drink in the other hand. His grip tightened as I approached, as though he could sense me before I reached him. He spun just as I tapped him on the shoulder. Our eyes locked, and for all of one second, panic set in my chest. Did he recognize me?

His glare softened and his eyes licked my body, flickering like the center of a flame. It made sweat surge to the surface of my already heated flesh. His nostrils flared as he eyed my drink. "Well, well, well . . . what do we have here?" His voice was barely a whisper. And it could melt the pants off of any woman. I should know—it had happened to me once already in this existence.

"I thought you might like a drink." I held up the glass and clinked the ice against the sides.

"Thank you," he said quietly. "I prefer the amber liquids, though." He rattled his own glass.

I shrugged and sipped my drink. "Too bad. Guess I'll just have to double fist it." After a pause, I continued. "So, what brings you to eighties night?"

With eyes closed, he inhaled deeply before looking at me again. His narrowed eyes creased his tanned face. "Who doesn't love a good Bangles song?" He quirked an eyebrow and shot another glance to the door. Who exactly was he waiting for? "And you? What brings such a lovely woman to such a bar this evening?"

"Oh, you know. Girls just wanna have fun. . . ."

Buckley chuckled at that. "Right. Of course."

The song "Heaven Is a Place on Earth" clicked on in the jukebox, and the crowd went wild. Succubi and demons jumped to their feet, rushing the dance floor in a blur of neon and crimped hair.

Moonlight sliced across the dark room as the front door opened, and Buckley's gaze flew to the movement. He spun his body around so that his back was to the door, becoming suddenly very interested in the music lists in the jukebox.

"That'll be fifteen bucks," Ink said to Kayce, his eyes wide. We both darted a glance to the front door.

The first thing I saw was auburn hair in a pixie cut and the loveliest porcelain skin. Claudette, Salt Lake City's ArchDemon, walked through the door, eyes straight ahead. She ordered two martinis from Ink. With an elbow leaning on the gritty counter, she dropped a twenty and checked her buzzing phone while he prepared the drinks.

I inhaled sharply and eyed Buckley as he covered his face with a hand. When he glanced back up, his look was different. He glamoured himself not so different that a stranger would have noticed . . . but me, I knew that face really well.

"I'm so sorry," he said, extending a hand. "I have to be on my way. It was nice meeting you." He squeezed my palm and turned for the door, careful not to show his face to Claudette the entire time.

"Well, that was strange," I said to myself.

With a quick look around, I ducked into a little nook behind the jukebox and shifted invisible.

Then, slinking over behind Claudette, I peeked over her shoulder, careful not to make a sound. Though invisible, she could still hear me if I stepped too loudly. With two thumbs, she quickly typed a text message.

Just got here. Will be inside soon.

There was no name linked to the number, but as soon as her drinks arrived, she pinched them each in a hand and glided toward the back of the bar. With one more glance over her shoulder, she swung the back door open and I was able to slip in with her. The door slammed shut behind me, and both Claudette and I winced.

The room was simply decorated with black leather love seats and a couple of club chairs. In the center was a square glass table on top of a cream-colored rug. Claudette sank into one of the love seats, setting one martini glass on the table and tipping the other to her perfectly rouged lips. Svelte legs crossed at the knees, and she bounced one foot up and down.

I barely moved; didn't dare breathe or take another step for fear of a creaky floorboard. After what felt like an eternity, a *crack* sounded through the room, sizzling the air with sparking electricity.

"There you are." Claudette took a bored sip, slowly savoring the smooth gin sliding down her throat.

Directly in front of where I stood, she materialized before me. A gasp strangled in my throat, and I clapped a hand over my mouth to stop the cry from escaping. Her long, fire-engine red hair fell in Veronica Lake waves down her back and over one eye. A tight, black dress hugged her endless curves in a way that was sexy and still classy. There directly in front of me was Mia—my Succubus Queen.

My boss.

My killer.

6

Mia walked in a circle around the perimeter of the room, her three-inch heels clacking against the hardwood planks. Her hard eyes scanned the room as she rounded the back of the couch.

"Good evening, Mia." Claudette smirked, berry lips curving on one side. "Your highness," she added with a tilt of her head.

Mia's hand shot up, halting all conversation. As she drew nearer and nearer to me, she inhaled deeply, pausing just a few feet in front of me. Her eyes circled the general area I stood in, and she sniffed a handful more times, eyes flitting around my face. Even though I knew in all rational parts of my brain that she could neither see nor sense me, panic rose in my throat. Did I wear too much perfume tonight?

She closed her eyes and released a sigh, her ample chest deflating with the breath. "Was anybody else in here prior to your arrival, my friend?"

Claudette appeared genuinely concerned by the question. After a pause, she shook her head. "I don't believe so, Mia. Why?" Her eyes narrowed, and with a gentle touch she brushed her bangs from her curled eyelashes.

Mia's eyes narrowed, and her gaze drifted down my body before circling the surrounding areas. "No reason."

As much as I wanted to exhale when she moved on, I stifled it, knowing my Queen would have been able to hear. And even though I was invisible, she could still reach out and touch me if she wanted.

"How is business going in your sector?" The leather groaned as she sank into one of the club chairs, lifting the martini glass without even asking whom it was for. She was the Queen—without a doubt, it was always for her.

"Business is well. The girls managed to bring down a pastor just recently."

Mia's eyes fluttered closed as she sipped the martini, swishing the gin in her mouth before she swallowed. "Ink bruised the gin this time."

Claudette raised an eyebrow. "Still so particular, I see."

"You'll learn, my friend, that that's the only way to achieve greatness. If you wish to convince Saetan to promote you to ArchDemon of North America, you should *learn* to be more particular."

We don't have an ArchDemon of North America—the regional managers run their sections and report to Saetan's VP of sorts. Unless . . . was Claudette trying to create a position? Just for herself?

Claudette curved back into her seat, seemingly deflated by the comment. "I *am* particular. Just not with gin."

"You should be so with *everything*." Mia paused, spearing the olives and rolling one over her tongue. "If only you weren't a silly demon . . . you could be one of my succubi. Be my number two."

"I was never any good at seduction. Besides, angels don't become succubi—even if you were only an angel for fractions of a second. We turn into demons when we fall."

Mia clicked her tongue. "Yes. All but one."

Claudette was an angel first? A fallen angel—Julian *must* have known as much. How long had it been? She was an ArchDemon, so she must have been around longer than I was, for certain.

"And the stone? It is safe?"

Claudette's eye roll was accompanied by a derisive sip of gin. "Of course. Don't be ridiculous."

"Please tell me you took it off the sales floor finally."

"Yes. That was only for the succubus's benefit. She had to know just how easily I could smite her." Despite Claudette's simple, professional outward appearance, I knew that bitch was twisted. She was almost too collected. Like a sociopath ready to snap.

"You and your games." Mia's rose-colored lips curved, slicing across her smooth skin into a terrifyingly beautiful smile.

Diving her delicate fingers into her short auburn hair, Claudette fluffed the roots. "What of the human? He's seen Hell now—I'm still in shock that Saetan granted him his freedom."

My inhalation was sharp at the mention of Drew, but I immediately held my breath when both Mia and Claudette darted a look in my general direction.

Mia slid her gaze back over to Claudette. "Don't let that concern you."

"But it happened in *my* sector. How do you expect me to be promoted if I can't even control a damn human." She shook her head and pushed the sleeves of her cream blazer to her elbows. "I have to find him."

"Saetan has his reasons. You dare to question Him?" Mia snapped. Though the two were obviously friends, Mia was the boss here and she would never let Claudette forget that. With another laborious sip of her "bruised" gin, she huffed a final breath. "Very well. Go off and find the human. However, bring him to me before acting. You want to tread lightly, my friend."

Her fingers folded together in front of her full, moist lips. "What's next on the docket?"

"The sorcerer. He's finally out of my sector—in exchange for some of my girls, he moved back here to Vegas to start some ridiculous magic show. He will be Lucien's problem now."

"I must pay a visit to him. He is far too powerful to not be on our side."

Claudette nodded. "Powerful and filled with nothing but spite and vengeance."

"My favorite mixture." Mia dipped a finger into her martini, swirling it in the center. Leaning over the table, she placed the same finger on Claudette's lips, painting her with the liquor. "Tell me this is not a terrible martini." She was truly unable to focus on anything else. Note to self—never make the Queen a bad drink.

Claudette licked her lips, swallowing the drops of gin, and nodded. "You're right. It's terrible." She wasn't exactly convincing. Claudette looked cultured and smooth, but I doubted she could tell a cappuccino from a latte, let alone a bad gin martini from a good one.

Mia stood with a grace that came only from centuries of oozing sex. "Would you care to join me in paying a little visit to this magic show?"

Claudette shook her head. "I've seen more of that man than I care to in a lifetime."

Mia gave no indication if she was pleased or displeased with Claudette's decline of her invitation. "Very well. Take this swill back to the bar on your way out."

Claudette pinched the martini glass, nodding. "Next month?"

"Yes. Let's hope it will be the last."

"Surely, with the number of demons we have on her case, this will come to an end soon?"

Mia's heels were high enough to need an elevator to reach

the top and yet she glided across the room with ease, as though she were barefoot. With one last, narrowed glance around the room, she blinked before looking again at Claudette.

"Mia." Claudette's voice was soft and willowy. "I know I am not one of your subjects. But just know—none of my girls will ever bow to her if she takes your position. No one will issue her the same respect that they do you. Monica will never be the Queen you are."

My teeth sunk into the inside of my lip, a tiny bit of blood seeping onto my tongue. It took every ounce of willpower not to rematerialize and demand to know what they were talking about.

"Thank you, Claudette. But don't claim knowledge about that which you have no understanding. And don't make promises you cannot keep."

7

What? Me, the Queen? Dread rolled in my stomach and bile rose in my throat. It would have been laughable if not so damn terrifying. Me—the fallen angel—as Queen of the Killer Vagina? That made no sense whatsoever. I was the worst succubus in existence. I hated my job. Hated the entire demon realm. There's no way *I* was destined to be Queen. Then again, Lucifer and his first army of misfits were the original fallen angels. And look at him now, the patriarch of Hell.

I shook the thoughts away until I could tell Kayce and Lucien. Slipping through the crack of the door with Claudette was easy this time. I slid back behind the jukebox, shifting back into the smaller, curvier human I came in as. Cloaked powers? Check. Black hair? Check. Curvy ass? I stole a glance behind me. Definite check.

From behind the jukebox, I could hear Claudette lecturing Ink on the terrible martini—as if *she* was the one who'd discovered the bruised gin.

"How long have you been a demon?" Her voice was bitter, though still collected and poised.

Ink stood straight, a pole in the place of his spine. "Almost four hundred years."

"And how long have you been a bartender?" Her top lip curled under with the question.

"Thirty."

"You're telling me that after thirty years, you don't know how to make a martini without bruising the gin?" She was still calm, not screaming like some irrational customers I'd dealt with in my past. I watched on in fascination. There was a hard edge to her facade—and though I'd never seen Claudette lose her cool, she always looked like she was seconds away from cracking. As though her face would disintegrate into dust at any moment.

"My apologies." Ink dipped his head. She wasn't our ArchDemon here in Vegas, but I didn't blame him one bit. You don't want to get on *any* demon's bad side. "I'd be happy to make you another."

The saccharine smile she flashed lit her face. There was something innately evil about Claudette. Yes, okay, she's a demon, I know. But as proven by Lucien and George and . . . Hell, maybe even Kayce, "demon" is not synonymous with "evil."

"No. Just get it right for next time." She pushed off the bar and, with chin high in the air, exited amidst the crowd of demons and succubi dressed in eighties costumes.

A light, breezelike brush tickled one of my shoulders and a hand clamped down on the other. I screamed, flinching out of the grasp, whipping around to fight my attacker. Kayce snatched my wrist in midair, pressing a palm against my mouth to quiet my screams.

"Shhh! Calm down. It's just me!"

"Could you hear them?" I asked.

Kayce shook her head. "There were enchantments on the

room. Which was what I was expecting. The most I'd hoped to get out of tonight was a visual on who was coming."

I scanned the room; the sea of bodies clad in silver and sparkles and neon colors grinding on each other to Bon Jovi. Man, demons were a weird crowd. "We shouldn't talk here," I said. My eyes landed on Ink, busy behind the bar, pouring pint after pint of beer. Sweat descended the side of his face past his temple, and his eyes shifted about the room. They swept past mine before landing on Kayce's. She nodded as we headed for the door. Instead of acknowledging her, he simply went back to pouring drinks.

"Yeah," Kayce said, shouldering the door open. "Besides, all this hot pink is giving me a headache."

I managed to tell Kayce almost everything—except their mention of my being Queen. That fact nibbled at my brain all day at the café. I should have told her, right? She's proven herself; and I trust Kayce. But I knew that I'd feel a lot more comfortable confiding in her after I spoke to Lucien about it. If Lucien didn't know what they were talking about, he'd know how to find out the truth.

My shift at the café came and went with little excitement. Genevieve entered the coffee shop at seven to relieve me of my barista duties; there was more bounce in her step than before, and when I raised my eyebrows at her, a blush warmed her cheeks. She quickly glanced away.

I clocked out, eying the tip jar. Sure, those were my tips, but she could use that money more than me. Centuries of existing will give one a good nest egg, and the extra twenty-five dollars wasn't going to make or break me.

I slipped the apron from around my waist and untied the scarf from my head. After I slowly shapeshifted my hair back into place, blond curls fell below my shoulders.

I hiked my purse over a shoulder, and the Smith & Wesson

clunked against my shoulder blade. Though it didn't hurt necessarily, I grunted at the impact.

Exiting the back room where the barista lockers lined the walls, I ran flush into Kayce. Her leather pants brushed my jeans as she hooked an elbow into mine and guided me back out to the front. "Hey," she said, a tight grin clipping her cheeks.

"Uh—hi. What's . . . going on here?" When we reached the front, Lucien stood, latte in hand, and Damien was beside him, sipping an espresso.

My steps slowed to a stop in front of the group, and I eyed each person individually, finally resting on Damien's pewter gaze. His eyes flashed and a smirk quirked his lips upward. "Hey babe."

"What is this? Some sort of intervention?"

Damien's head tilted to the side. "Not sure what you mean."

"Come off it."

His grin widened, and from beside me Lucien slapped a flyer down onto the counter. The startling noise made me jump, and when I glanced down, between his fingers was Buckley's ad. "We're going," Lucien grumbled. "Tonight."

Folding my arms across my chest, I darted a glare at Kayce and then back again to Lucien. "Who's 'we'?"

Lucien rolled his eyes. "Oh, come on. Don't play dumb, Monica. You. Me. The gang. We're all going."

"Do I get a say in this at all?"

"No," everyone answered at once in varying degrees of passion. Lucien and Damien were, of course, the loudest.

"Fine. Then I will need some serious caffeine before we go."

Lucien took a final glug of his latte and tossed the cup into the garbage. "Me too. Damn those things are addictive." He slid me a look, eyes softening at the corners but not relaxing entirely. "I'll buy yours."

"Damn straight you will. Caramel mocha latte, please," I grumbled, and hooked my arm into his elbow. I leaned in, dropping my voice to a level that humans couldn't hear. I only hoped that Kayce and the rest wouldn't pay too much attention. "I need to talk to you about what Kayce and I found last night."

"I know. Kayce filled me in earlier." He barely glanced at me, pulling a ten-dollar bill from his leather billfold.

"Lucien—I *really* think I should tell you *exactly* what I heard myself." I stared at him pointedly and he finally looked up, catching my eye.

He nodded, understanding flashing over his deep brown gaze. "Of course." He kept his voice casual, but there was a new tension in his forehead. "After the show?"

Once we were all adequately caffeinated, Lucien and Kayce teleported to the Wynn. I, on the other hand, rode with Damien in his truck, as he was our lone group member who couldn't just appear anywhere he wanted.

"How's Baxter?" I asked. I never imagined myself a maternal kind of girl, but something about that damn yellow lab pulled on my heartstrings. Damien had adopted him when his owners tragically died and got blamed for a string of murders in Salt Lake City.

"Baxter's great," Damien answered, flashing me his stunning, pearly-white grin. "Misses his mommy."

I groaned. "Oh, Hell . . . do not call me that."

His grin widened. "Will he be seeing you after the show tonight?"

I nodded, my own smile quirking my lips. "If he'll have me."

"Baxter would never turn *you* away." Damien pulled into a parking spot off The Strip. "He's been keeping your side of the bed warm for ya."

We made our way into the Wynn. The area outside the theater was mostly white marble with red accents. Butterflies affixed to the walls and flew above us, and the entire hotel had a very Asian feel to it.

An usher showed us to our seats. Lucien hung back until the only person left not in the row was Kayce—at which point, he slid in between her and me. He and I had to have a chat about the art of subtlety soon. We all settled into our seats, getting comfortable, and I reached into my bag, pulling out a sack of chocolate-covered almonds.

"What are you, five?" Lucien sneered.

One aisle seat was empty and the lights blinked a few times, signaling to the crowd that we only had a few moments until show time. Kayce strained her neck to the door, completely oblivious to Lucien as he lowered his nose to her hair, inhaling. His eyes fluttered closed.

"Hey, Casanova," I whispered, tapping his knee. His neck swiveled to face me. "Go easy."

He sank deeper into his seat as the house lights dimmed. Spotlights zoomed about the audience in various colors. The curtain parted, showing a single spotlight center stage with no one in it. The music droned on in an eerie hum. A drum pounded and Buckley—or should I say Raul—appeared center stage with a *crack*. Within moments, he disappeared and teleported to the balcony, sitting on the edge. The spotlight followed him as he continued to appear and disappear in various areas of the theater.

His "angels," who appeared to actually be fallen angels—or demons as most of us know them—wore costumes sluttier than most things I wore onstage at Hell's Lair: white rhinestone pasties and a matching thong. There were only four of them, but one by one in a line, they teleported onto the stage in various sexual positions.

Buckley finally landed center stage with his arms to the ceiling, and the music crescendoed.

"Welcome!" The greeting was a demand—not a request.

Kayce leaned across Lucien to me, whispering, "Doesn't this go against every code of ethics sorcerers have?"

I rolled my eyes. "Buckley lives by his own code."

"He's gonna piss off the other sorcerers living quiet lives," Lucien said to no one in particular, hard eyes directed at the stage.

Lines etched across his face with the grimace, and though his eyes were still aimed at the stage, his attention seemed miles away.

I nudged him with an elbow, and he shifted his eyes to me without moving his head. Offering him a little smile, I squeezed his hand.

He grunted before turning his attention back to the stage. But not before the lines at the corners of his eyes softened slightly. It was barely noticeable, but it was there.

The show passed in a seamless array of glitz and glamour. Literally glamour—considering Buckley was using his glamour magic to look like an entirely different person: the made-up twin brother of his biological son who had died in Salt Lake City.

The audience was entranced by his performance and the way he wove together his legitimate magic with his flair for showmanship. Each trick escalated into something bigger and bigger until the audience was in an uproar, on their feet, clapping and shouting for more.

The "angels," as he called them, danced around the stage. A demon's job on Earth was quite different from a succubus in actuality. Demons had pretty simple paper-pushing gigs. They were in charge of getting humans to sign their souls over to Hell before death in exchange for material things.

I mean, sure . . . my job was bad. Taking part of a human's life and slowly corrupting them. But to condemn a soul to Hell for eternity? That was way worse. I examined the women on-stage. Their talent was limited and consisted of simply walking around the stage in their flimsy costumes. The brunette was the curviest. Her smile was blindingly bright and yet, behind her eyes, there was barely a dull light. What could have happened to them that they'd lost their humanity so quickly? It had been a little less than three centuries since I was an angel—and yet I still felt that tug of conscience each time I had to take a life.

"For my final trick"—Buckley's voice boomed through the theatre—"I will need a volunteer!" He levitated off the stage and floated into the aisle. Hands shot in the air, a tribute to how well he could fool people. Or perhaps a tribute to what fools people can be.

The beam of light followed him as he floated up and down the aisle, finally slowing in front of our row. The entire aisle of my people hissed, glaring up at him as his eyes fell onto me. They seared through to my soul. A *pop* sounded through the air and another spotlight flashed on—directed right at me.

"You've got to be fucking kidding me, right?"

His smile twitched, but he didn't dare break character. "I'm sensing reluctance." He spun to the rest of the audience. "Let's give this beautiful young woman a warm welcome, huh?"

The crowd exploded into clapping. When I looked back to the "angels" onstage, their smiles were sadistic and twisted into a look that should have been terrifying to anyone not glitzed by their fancy clothes and stage charisma.

My teeth gnashed into each other. "I don't have a choice here, do I, *Raul?*" I grumbled under my breath.

His eyes sparkled, and even though he was glamoured as Raul, for a flash I could see the Buckley that I knew and hated behind the mask. I braced my hands on the armrests and moved to stand.

Lucien's arm darted out, and before I could lift up he was on his feet, sliding out into the aisle. "Not a chance," he grumbled.

Buckley actually looked taken aback for all of a moment before he gained his composure once again. "I was actually talking to the lady, here." He gestured at me once more, sliding a greasy smile in my direction.

"Well, 'the lady' won't be going onstage tonight." Lucien folded his arms across a very broad chest, which puffed out even more with his inhalation. "It's me or no one."

"Lucien." I touched his elbow, and his gaze snapped down to me. "It's okay. I don't mi—"

"It's either *me* or no one from my group," he repeated, his voice serious. The sort of deadpan tone I'd long ago learned was not to be argued with.

I looked back to Buckley with a shrug. "He's the boss," I said with a smile.

"He sure is, isn't he?" Buckley's own predatory smile penetrated me to my belly and sent a shiver through my whole body. I didn't like the look he gave Lucien. Not one bit. "Well, let's get started then. Come up with me. What was your name?"

"Lucien," he said into the microphone and followed Buckley to the stage. Hesitation gnawed at my gut, and Lucien flashed me a wink along with the tiniest reassuring smile he could muster as Buckley led the way.

Buckley did a strange lunge and hand motion thing. "And Lucien—have you ever seen magic quite like this before?" With one hand in the air, sparks flew from his fingertips as though each nail were its own sparkler.

Lucien quirked an eyebrow and slid a palm over his black ponytail. "I don't know," he answered coolly. "That Copperfield guy is pretty damn good."

There was a hum of laughter through the audience as Lucien held Buckley's stare, unwavering. Buckley laughed right along with everyone else. "I think we've got our own comedian up here tonight!" He directed the statement to the audience. "A hand—for Lucien. I must confess, my assistant for this trick is almost always a woman. But this could be a fun twist. . . ."

His words drifted off and the music blasted through the speakers. Two of the rogue angels rolled out a long, white box. It almost looked like the sort of thing you could purchase at a certain Swedish store and put together yourself during the course of one episode of *The Bachelor.*

"As you can see, this is a simple box! Nothing more, nothing less." With one hand in the air, he levitated the box and brought it off the stage and over the audience. "Please, ma'am, in the front row—stand. Look inside and around back. Does this box appear to be anything out of the ordinary?"

A plump woman stood and knocked a few times on each side, shaking her head. "Looks normal to me," she shouted in a deeply southern accent.

With a flick of his wrist, Buckley had the box lowered center stage once more. With a flourish he danced around, and Lucien stood statuesque with arms folded across his broad chest. His narrowed eyes followed Buckley's fluid movements and yet he didn't flinch when Buckley appeared in front of his face with a *crack.*

"I think what we have here—is a doubter!" Buckley called to the audience. "What do you all say we try to make a believer out of him?" He turned to Lucien, gesturing at the box. "Please, sir. Enter."

I twitched in my seat and Damien grabbed my hand, circling his thumb over my knuckle. "It'll be okay," he whispered. "Lucien knows what he's doing."

I nodded but didn't quite believe it. None of us knew what we were doing—not when it came to Buckley and this damn bounty.

Lucien clomped with slow, deliberate steps into the box. His dark eyes met mine. Only this time, he didn't smile.

"This is the point in the show," Buckley boomed, clutching a hand to the door, swinging open on its hinges, "where every other magician you know would shut this. However, here at the Rogue Angels, we don't believe in closed door magic."

I snorted at that. I couldn't help it. His whole shtick was just so ridiculous to anyone who had the slightest knowledge of the arcane. Of course most people here thought these were just some amazing parlor tricks.

From the audience, I could see Lucien's jaw clenching and unclenching. He cracked his neck to each side.

Buckley began a chant, his palms in the air. Cool wind blew down on the audience from the ceiling, feeling as though a strong air conditioner had kicked on.

With one last *pop,* Lucien disappeared from the box in front of everyone's eyes. The oxygen caught in my lungs, and I held my breath while Buckley lifted the box to the audience once more. Damien squeezed my hand and I stole a glance at Kayce, who had blanched to a deathly pallor.

On the exhale, I directed my attention back to Buckley. Lucien was the ArchDemon of Nevada and all the Southwest. He could teleport anywhere he wanted. He would be fine. Because he had to be fine.

Buckley raised his hands once more, chanting again in a foreign tongue. Another *pop* sounded through the theatre—only this time, nothing happened. The box remained empty. Buckley's eyes darted to us and every muscle in my body tensed when his eyes landed on me. I flinched, ready to spring to my feet.

"Wait," Damien hushed, locking me in the seat by flattening his arm across my body. "It could just be part of the show."

I gnashed my teeth but stayed seated.

Buckley didn't look theatrical. He looked nervous. One lone bead of sweat dripped passed his temple. He gave a nervous titter, pushed his sleeves up beyond his elbows, raised his hands a second time. "Where do you suppose he's gone?" His voice was sharp, and I knew Buckley well enough to know that this was not part of the plan. With the second pop, the audience edged off their seats, waiting for Lucien's return. Again, nothing happened.

Lucien was gone.

8

New Jersey, 1776

"*M*onica, what are the chances that you will pay mind to me before the day is through?!*"

"Oh, for Heaven's sake." I rolled my eyes and straightened my petticoats. With a glance to my right and left, the prostitutes flanking me on either side snarled in my direction.

"Could you at least attempt to appear interested in bedding a man? Show some leg, calf? Hell, show your bloody ankle for all I care!" Lucien threw his hands in the air and brought them down onto his hips with a slap.

"Very well." I offered him an exaggerated smile and puckered my lips, shapeshifting them so large that they nearly consumed my face.

Lucien's face flushed to a scarlet, contrasting the white knuckles clutched at his waist. I looked comical with the new pout and I knew it. But it was simply too enjoyable to watch Lucien's face turn red like that.

"Out. Everyone out!" I followed the line of drabs when Lucien snatched my elbow, yanking me from the queue. "All except you, love."

"*Oh, dear. Have I been naughty?*" *I pinched the scruff at his jawline.*

"*Stop that!*" *he grumbled, and caught my hand in his.* "*The problem is you're never naughty enough.*"

I snorted at that. "*Clearly, my dearest brother, you've forgotten my origin story. I'm as naughty as they come.*"

With both hands, he kneaded his forehead and eyebrows as though they were rolls of dough. "*If that were the truth, then I wouldn't be under the scrutiny of Hell right now for low numbers.*"

I wasn't exactly shedding a tear for him. Lucien the demon wunderkind wasn't Saetan's apprentice any longer. Hatred flooded my chest. I hated everything about the man. His job, his duties, his black heart. Perhaps if he'd never found me there in the courtyard years ago, I could have fallen off the radar. Perhaps Hell would have never known of my existence and I could have simply perished then and there.

"*Do you need to give me a spanking?*" *I said with an exaggerated pout. Of course, I wanted his hands nowhere near me. The worst had been in our last home—we had to act as though we were wed. I shivered, grateful for the fact that Lucien, at the very least, always gave me the bed and slept in the parlor.*

"*Spank? Christ, Monica—we are brother and sister here!*"

"*Yes, yes. I recall. I am your sister. Mummy and father died in England. And we came here to help win the good fight. Does that about cover it?*"

He narrowed his eyes. "*I'm glad you are able to recite the plan. And yet when it comes to acting it out, why does it become so goddamn difficult?*"

I didn't answer. His angry gaze scorched my own and I lowered my chin to my ample cleavage, gritting my teeth. "*Easy for you to say. It's not your legs that are spread each night for Hell's sake,*" *I spat back.*

Lucien's eyes closed and his face slackened. "*This again?*"

"Again? Just because I stopped complaining for several years doesn't mean it's become any easier for me."

He reached out a hand to my back, strong and reassuring. "You hate this life so much?"

I wrenched away from his touch. "As if you didn't relish in every grimace. Every tear of mine. You're a demon—you must love watching the angel be defaced."

With that, his mouth hardened, pursing at the corners. "You ungrateful little sniff. Did your angel mentor coddle you so? That vampire should have done us all a favor and just done nothing," he added, and turned to stalk away.

At that, I lunged for his back, pelting my fists into his arm. "How dare you! I want away from you! Send me anywhere . . . anyone else would be better!" Tears choked in my throat, and a jagged breath escaped in tremors.

Lucien clamped down on each of my wrists, and I continued struggling against his hold. "Monica! Stop, calm down—bloody hell. I apologize, very well? Stop! I said, I apologize!"

"One bloody powerful sorcerer and a damn vampire—both of whom tricked me! I hate them both and I hate you!"

"Enough!" His voice was deep and boomed through our little brothel. For once, I actually listened to him and stilled beneath his grasp. It was useless, anyway. Lucien had some sort of power over me—he wanted to keep me for whatever reason, and Saetan allowed me to be his and solely his. I was property. Less than a person—again. Another sob rose to the back of my throat, and I swallowed it down.

Still grasping me by the wrists, he tugged me to a settee. He dropped over, leaning his elbows on his knees and looked up at me through thick eyelashes. "We aren't supposed to officially tell our succubi this—but most figure it out on their own regardless. You don't need Heaven-bound souls to survive. You simply need a soul. Any soul. You could read auras as an angel, aye?" I nodded, eyes narrowed, not sure I believed or trusted anything he spoke of.

"How is your ability now? To read auras?"

I shrugged, swallowing. "Nothing special. I see faint colors surrounding everyone."

He nodded. "Eventually you'll learn to refine that. I can help you. It will feel a little different than when you were an angel—but soon it'll be second nature to sense the auras."

"What good is any of this?" I snapped, hopping to my feet. I walked over to a stone hearth and ran my fingers along the edge. Dust pooled under my nails and I flicked it to the floor. "It's still murder. I'm still taking life."

Lucien's sigh was patient and quiet. "If you only have relations with the Hell-bound souls, you won't be condemning anyone, true?"

I hesitated before answering. "Well—yes . . ."

"So, by your own logic, you could still do your job. Without compromising your morals."

"That's true," His eyes burned into my back, and I turned slowly to match his gaze. "You would allow me this?"

He shrugged, falling back against the settee. His arms spread out along the back edge and he crossed one knee over the other. "Don't ask me why. If this messes with my ArchDemon status in any way, I'll revoke it in a heartbeat."

The shock of his admission resonated, numbing my limbs. "Thank you," I whispered.

"You can thank me by running the ladies at this establishment. Come now." He popped up from his seat. "Let's get ready for the tavern. Your job will be to flirt with the men—help get the word out that the brothel is opening tonight. You can choose which men you take and how often."

"Will men even be interested in our services? What with the war consuming everyone's time?"

Lucien chuckled. "You really don't understand men, do you?"

I should have been offended by such a statement. Yet I couldn't argue that he was incorrect.

He raked a hand through his raven locks and tightened his ponytail hanging at the nape of his neck. "Wartime is when brothels thrive most."

I considered this for a moment. "Will you be fighting with them or against?"

Lucien scoffed. "With, of course. Demons love a good rebellion." He winked and chucked my chin.

9

A low hum of chatter and speculation rolled through the audience, growing louder with each passing second. "Where the fuck is he?" Kayce asked in a shaky voice.

I shook my head. Buckley's eyes met mine; they were wide, fearful. His fingers twitched in my direction—subtly asking me to wait. Wait for what, exactly?

"Perhaps that little devil decided to discover his feminine side!" He walked over to the brunette rogue angel and, placing a palm at the top of her head, traveled his hand down the length of her body. As his hand dipped, the brunette morphed into Lucien.

Steam rose from my head, and I was certain at any minute my I might explode in anger. "Lucien" held his hands out, giant smile stretching across his sharp features. Lucien didn't smile that wide. Ever. I'd seen that trick done just last night in the private dance room—it was merely another one of Buckley's glamour tricks. The fake Lucien shook Buckley's hand and trotted back to the seat next to me. He scooted passed Kayce, falling beside me.

My eyes narrowed. "You can tell your boss he won't get away with this," I said to the disguised brunette.

She—he, ugh, whatever—leaned in closer to me without making eye contact. "You can tell him yourself after the show. He wants me to bring you all back to see him."

"Well, then, Buckley's a braver man than I gave him credit for," I sneered, folding my arms.

When we were brought backstage, the fake Lucien led us directly to Buckley's dressing room. He was no longer in the Raul costume, but back to being the boyishly handsome, emerald-eyed magician I knew and hated.

"Angel," he said, and held two palms up facing me—as if this simple act would stop me from ripping his throat out.

"Don't you 'angel' me." I advanced on him, snatching his tuxedo lapels in my fists and shoving him into his vanity. "Where is Lucien?"

"I don't know."

"Bullshit!"

"Monica, stop!" Kayce's voice was husky and yet still shaky. "Look at him—his aura. I don't think he's lying."

I didn't tear my eyes away from Buckley. His were wide, earnest. Coppery hair curled over his ears and flopped into his eyes. "Only an angel could know that for certain," I hissed. "And you don't know him, Kayce. He knows how to mask his aura." I angled my chin closer to his face, dropping my voice equally low. "Remember when you told me you loved me? Yeah—that was a good one."

With two fingers, he plucked my grasp off his lapel. "Angel," he started, and I growled in his direction. "Monica," he tried again, "I do love you. I did in 1740 and I still do now. Why on Earth would I take from you the one demon I know you care the most about?" His eyebrows arched along his smooth forehead, and he pressed his lips together.

"I don't know. Why on Earth would you ruin the life of the woman you love by damning her to Hell?"

He rolled his eyes and stuffed two hands into his pockets. "Not *this* again."

"Why you little—"

I lunged just as two arms caught me around the waist, lifting me off the floor. Damien bear-hugged me from behind. "Okay, Monica, enough! This isn't going to help get Lucien back."

"But it will make me feel a shit ton better!"

"Come on, Buckley. Cut the crap and tell us what you know," Kayce said.

He looked first at Kayce, then at me. "I'm telling the truth. It was just a simple disappearing trick—I haven't the slightest idea where he went."

"Well, let me tell you what I know," I said, shoving Damien's hands off my body. "You wanted *me* in that box. You wanted me to disappear. And considering there's a hefty price tag on my head right now, I'd say that might have landed you in the spot of 'number one suspect.' "

"I'm telling you, I had nothing to do with this."

Damien took a couple steps forward. "Walk us through today. Did anything out of the ordinary happen?"

Buckley seemed to think about that for a moment, then shook his head. "No. It was a normal day. I slept late. Enjoyed the, er, company of one of my angels." He shot an apologetic look to me, and I rolled my eyes. "Then I had dinner here at the casino and came in for my first show."

Oh, my Hell. Mia—I didn't even get to tell Lucien about the Queen information. "Wait, last night—Mia came here, didn't she?"

Buckley looked startled but regained composure quickly. "Yes. But that's nothing out of the ordinary. I have Arch-Demons, Queens, and even ArchAngels checking on me constantly. They like to ensure that my operations are kosher, if you will. In fact . . ."

Jules thundered through the door, Adrienne at his heels and San Michel right behind him. Time slowed to a crawl as Julian—my angel mentor, my friend—stopped in his tracks, light blue eyes locked intensely on my own.

"Monica?" His whisper was hoarse, and after clearing his throat he tried again. "Monica." This time it was a statement, not a question, and his blond wavy hair tousled as he shook his head.

I needed to talk to Jules. Needed to ask him about what Mia and Claudette had said. Not only about me becoming Queen but about Claudette seeking out Drew. My eyes widened, and I only hoped that after all these centuries he still knew me well enough to read my body language.

Straightening his shoulders, he stole a quick glance at the other angels in the room. Upon verifying their attention was on Buckley, not him, he twitched a nod. It was the sort of movement that, had you not known Jules, you might have thought was simply a tick.

"Ahhh, back so soon?" Buckley's eyes flashed as they bounced from angel to angel.

I immediately slinked back behind Damien at their grand entrance. San Michel was particularly unnerving. Considering he was the angel that was supposed to have approved my relationship with Buckley in the first place, all those years ago. And he was the leader of the council in charge of banishing me after we caught Carman. My face blazed with heat.

He towered over the rest of us—easily standing taller than six foot five. Though his wings were invisible, I could hear the slight rustling from his back, feel the gentle breeze created by the movement.

San Michel's ice-blue eyes fell on me, and even though every ounce of me wanted to avoid that glare, I was powerless. Against my will and better judgment, I brought my gaze to meet his. His stare was cold, arctic—eyes so pale, it was as if he were looking at me through a block of ice. "Monica." My name rolled off his tongue like a whisper and sent a chill tumbling down my spine. "I'm surprised to find you here. With this sorcerer. Yet again." Ebony skin made his fair eyes that much more disconcerting. "I thought you would have learned your lesson long ago."

Damien reached behind and, without looking at me, found my hand with one reassuring squeeze. "She's likely here for the same reason you are. Lucien's untimely disappearance."

San Michel's eyes widened, and traces of humor—if the angel had any humor that is—stretched across brittle features. "Is that so?"

Damien continued—brave for an elemental. Most demons and angels wouldn't dare go head to head with an ArchAngel. Then again, Damien doesn't really answer to anyone. "Which begs the question—what does Heaven care about a missing ArchDemon?"

"I wish to speak to Buckley alone," San Michel said, eyes cruising along the rest of my friends.

"We're not done here," I whispered to Buckley before exiting. His smile veered toward hostility.

"We never are, angel."

10

Kayce led the way through the casino. Bells rung as a payout on a penny slot was awarded. The smell of cigarette smoke and recirculated oxygen swirled above, fueling red-eyed humans who probably didn't know if it was morning or night.

"Why do you think ArchAngels care about your Arch-Demon?" Damien said, glancing between us.

There was radio silence from the group. Finally Kayce offered, "Maybe it's disrupted the balance?"

I shook my head. "But Buckley specifically said, 'Back so soon?' They were clearly there recently, before his disappearance, too."

"Well, what now?" Damien tucked a hand into the front pocket of his pressed gray slacks.

"What do you mean 'What now'? We find our Arch-Demon!" I snatched a glass of something that looked alcoholic off a waitress's tray and shot it down. The amber liquid burned my throat and sizzled in my nose. Tears watered my eyes, and I told myself it was from the whiskey. Unfortunately, we all knew better.

"We will, Monica." Kayce placed a palm on my arm. "I wonder if it's . . ."

"What? You wonder if it's what?"

Kayce pressed her lips together, a look of regret flashing across her face. "Damn," she said, clearing her throat. "I shouldn't have said anything. The Contenitore," Kayce repeated as if I should understand. "There's a new bounty hunter," she said. "We call her—or him—The Contenitore. The Vessel. The hunter captures rogue demons and brings them back to Hell. But she does it in a way none of us have seen before. There's no holy water, no blessed bullets. She just sort of—captures them."

Kayce also grabbed a drink off a passing tray. "She's taking jobs away from all of us."

An excited shout came from the craps table to my left, and a curvy blonde hopped up and down. "But Lucien's not rogue." I paused. "Is he?"

Kayce shook her head. "Not to my knowledge."

Damien curled an arm around my waist, tugging me in to his hip. "Let's reconvene tomorrow. I'll see if I can pull up anything at the department. Kayce, can you find out if there was some sort of reward for Lucien's capture? Anything official from Hell. Maybe George can do a little research while he's on set."

"And me?" I asked, one eyebrow arched delicately.

Damien sighed. "Our main job is to keep you safe. It's what Lucien would have wanted."

"What does *that* mean?"

The sudden aura of an angel pulsed through me.

"It means I will stay with you while we look around Hell's Lair." At the sound of Julian's voice, I swiveled, breaking from Damien's grasp instinctually. Jules took note of the contact, his eyes quickly flitting to my hip, then back to my face and Damien's. "Maybe there's something in Lucien's office that will explain where he was summoned."

A low growl rumbled in Damien's chest. The sort of grumble that most people wouldn't even notice. Except Damien was surrounded by a bunch of angels and demons with exceptional hearing. His arm darted out to my waist once more with a possessiveness that made me both want to slap him and tear his clothes off. "Then it will be your job to keep her safe."

Jules's smile was placating. The succession of rapid blinks he fired off were directed right to Damien and as close to giving the middle finger as he'd ever gotten. "I think I can manage."

"You sure about that?" Damien's chest was pure steel beneath his button-down cotton shirt, and it tensed even more with the question. "If memory serves, you didn't do such a great job when she was an angel."

While I didn't necessarily disagree with Damien's statement, his tone was irksome, like a cat being petted in the opposite direction of its fur. I pulled from his grip.

Julian's smile dropped, and for a second I saw a flash of sadness. "Let's leave it to Monica, then, shall we?" His aquamarine eyes landed on me, sparkling brighter than any gem. "Would you prefer to stay at the café all day tomorrow? Or come with me and be useful?"

"Oh, ouch, babe. He just said you weren't useful."

"Stop it, Damien." I wrenched my arm from his grasp. "Just, stop." I walked to Julian's side but didn't touch him.

One corner of Jules's mouth lifted into a smirk as he slid a gaze in my direction. He crossed two arms over his chest, and his heather gray T-shirt wrinkled beneath his tanned arms.

"I'm not going to sit around all day and do absolutely nothing while the rest of you put your lives on the line."

"We're all just worried for you. You've already got a target on your forehead. We're just trying to avoid a second one on your chest," Kayce offered.

Damien rolled his eyes, and two palms slapped against his thighs in defeat. "Fine. Jesus. Stop being so dramatic. Can we go home now?" He held a hand out to me—as if I would simply take it and fall into his bed after all this. I did a mental eye roll. Men are such morons sometimes.

"Great," I said sharply. "Glad that's settled."

Kayce nodded a good-bye and teleported home, leaving Julian, Damien, . . . and me.

"C'mon, babe."

"Why don't I just meet up with you later?"

A pause hummed between us. Julian's snicker finally broke the silence. I snapped a glare to him, and he immediately backed up a couple of steps. "I'll give you two a minute," he said, humor flashing in those angelic eyes of his. Fucking angels.

With Julian no longer hovering, Damien closed in, his large hands immediately pulling me toward him. They curled around my waist, and the heat from his molten-hot body warmed my flesh. "What's the matter?" Damien played the tough guy well, but beneath that exterior was pure cream in the center. He was soft. Sweet. And I wanted to lick every bit of that cream from him.

I crunched my shoulders to my ears in that way girls do when they want to talk about something but pretend they don't. His thumbs circled my hip bone, pushing the hem of my shirt up and revealing a bit of velvety skin.

"Don't like me playing the part of protector?" Damien raised an eyebrow; his lips were pouty and petal smooth.

I lowered my voice hoping to Hell that Jules wasn't eavesdropping. Oh, who was I kidding? Angels were nosy little fuckers. "I just thought I'd go home. It's been a long day."

Damien dove a hand through his perfectly styled dark brown locks, and the sight of his fingers combing through those strands made my own twitch, wanting to feel their silk between my fingers. "Is that just what you're saying? Is this that girl thing where you say you just need a night but you really want me to come and sweep you off your feet or some shit? I like you, babe—but I don't even sweep my goddamn *floors*. Let alone a woman."

I grinned and shook my head. I was sort of looking for a little Prince Charming romance. But I knew better than to ask that of Damien. White horses and glass slippers were not in his repertoire. Toe-curling orgasms on the other hand . . . I gave an inward sigh. Yeah, those he was a fucking master at. "No. No grandiose sweeping gesture needed." I said through my smile—and I was proud that I even meant it. "Though, Hell . . . if you're offering, my floors could use a good scrub—"

"I dunno about your floors, but I could clean your carpet," he said through a smirk, tightening his hold and crashing my hips against a growing erection. I gasped upon contact. My mouth went dry and my eyes raised to meet his. The smirk grew. Bastard. "If you change your mind about tonight—"

"—I know where to find you." I finished for him, barely able to squeeze the words from my cotton mouth. Damn that man. He could heat me up, turn me on, and piss me off in seconds flat.

A cough came from behind us, and being reminded of Jules's presence quickly snapped me out of my horny fog. For now, I wanted to get back inside that theatre and have a look around. Then perhaps later Damien and I could resume where we left off. After I moved myself off of him, he backed toward the front door, pulling a set of keys from his back pocket.

"Don't worry." Julian's voice, though soft, teetered on hostile. "I'll see to it that she makes it home just fine."

The metal keys clunked against each other as he tightened his grip on their jagged edges. "It's okay, D," I reassured him. "I'll catch up with you later."

He nodded and shuffled out the door without another look back. I swiveled to face the angel and slapped him upside the head. He flinched but spoke through a grin. "What?" He mocked innocence.

"Don't give me that. What's wrong with you? You're supposed to be one of the good guys."

His hands slid their way into his pockets and he shrugged, eyes piercing right through me. "You have a way of bringing out the bad boy in all of us."

"You're an angel. On your way to becoming an ArchAngel. You have no bad boy in you." But even as I said it, I knew that to be untrue. Sure, he wasn't as depraved as Damien, but Jules had an edge to him. A sadness that resulted in hardened anger when he released it. A sex drive that I'd seen only glimpses of over the past few centuries. The way he chewed his lip when his gaze drifted to my cleavage. His quickened breath when I would cozy up just a little too close. The occasional fiery glance—like the one he currently sported.

A shiver danced down my spine. "Well, then. I guess I better get home, huh?"

His smile curved higher. "We both know you're not going home."

"Oh?" My eyebrows climbed higher.

His chuckle was a sharp exhale through his nose. "I can see you're lying."

Damn. Stupid angel lie detectors. "Fine. I was going to have a look around, okay?" I said under my breath, knowing he'd still be able to hear each word clearly.

"Great," he said. His hand slid into mine, fingers grasping my own in a way that felt both natural and foreign. His warm skin was dewy and velvety soft as it pressed against my own.

He tugged me back toward the theatre, leading the way through the double doors. A few stagehands tidied the stage but didn't seem to notice our entrance. I caught the door with my free hand just before it slammed closed.

Still cradling my hand, Julian tugged me down the aisle. I didn't necessarily like being the sidekick—the damsel—the lady behind the scenes . . . but for the moment, it felt kind of nice. Oh, Hell, I needed to snap out of it. I tugged my hand out of his grasp and he stopped midstride, looking back at me. "Is something wrong?"

I shook my head. "No—I think I can take it from here."

His bemused smirk was haughty and sexy and annoying all at once, and I wanted nothing more than to smack it away. "Oh, you do?"

"Yes," I snapped.

"The fact that there is an ArchAngel running around here, not to mention some sort of magic in that theatre with the ability to send an ArchDemon somewhere without his consent doesn't frighten you in the slightest?"

"Maybe Lucien wasn't sent anywhere. Maybe he just teleported home." I raised an eyebrow, and Julian's cheek flopped to his shoulder.

"That's what you think happened?"

"Maybe." My ear itched and I resisted the urge to tug on it. We both knew that was crap. Lucien would never have left and not told one of us where he was.

We were in a stare down. "Listen—I know you were my leader at one point, but now—I don't answer to yo—mmph!"

Julian's palm clamped down over my lips and he pushed me down to the floor in the last row of seats. With a finger to his lips, he went invisible—I did the same, just as the door flew open beside us. I quickly masked my powers as best I could in such a situation, assuming Julian was doing the same. Of course, he didn't realize I had these powers yet and when my aura disappeared, his hand tightened around my mouth before letting go entirely. His palm traveled over my face—my nose, my cheekbones, down my jaw and neck, stopping just above my breasts with a sharp intake of breath. His weight continued to press into me, flattening me to the carpet. His slim hips shifted above mine, and the stirrings of an erection pressed between my legs. The itch flared in me and I swallowed a shaky breath.

Initially I tried to wiggle out of his grasp a little. Make it so his erection wasn't pressed flush against my dripping sex. Oh, my Hell . . . had I ever felt Julian's dick before? I racked my brain through the centuries—definitely not. Curiosity got the better of me and I relaxed my hips against him, rocking against the growing rod in his pants.

Quick, erratic footsteps hurried their way to the stage, while slow and calculating steps—high heels—definitely high heels, followed behind.

"It happened here . . . onstage, your highness." The voice was nasally. Almost whiny. It was a voice I knew and just couldn't friggin' place.

"You did the right thing by calling for me." Now that was a voice I knew immediately—Mia. "He disappeared during a show, you say?"

"Yeah. Some magic act by a fella named Raul. I think he had been to the club a few times. Wanted a lap dance from Monica."

Lenny! That sniveling little bastard. How did he know Lucien had disappeared so quickly?

Julian's hair flopped onto my cheek and I inhaled his peppermint scent. Spicy, cool. That was my Jules. The blood rushed to my pulsing sex, and I chewed my lip to stop myself from acting inappropriately. Because more than anything, there in that moment, I wanted to arch my back and press my heavy, aching breasts into his steel chest. I wanted to circle my pelvis from below his and satiate that raging desire I knew we both had had since our angel days.

"This is quite disconcerting." Mia's heels clacked in a circle on the stage, pacing in her own royal way. There was a pause as she stopped walking entirely. "Everyone else is accounted for? All my girls . . . ?"

"As far as I know, it was only Lucien."

Mia resumed pacing. "Very well. Thank you again, Lenny. Your loyalty will not be overlooked."

"Then you will put in a good word for me? I've been asking

Lucien for over a year to be made into a Demon. I'd be a good one, too. I would." He reeked of desperation—and no one wanted a fucking desperate Demon.

My gasp was barely audible; just the tiniest inhalation of air, but Julian's grip on my arms tightened all the same. The silence froze the air around us.

"Let's not get ahead of ourselves," Mia answered after what felt like an eternity. "Get out of here. Go take care of his club." Lenny's footsteps were loud and fast, heading straight for the door. And Mia's heels clicked down the stairs, off the stage. She walked up one audience aisle, slowly, stopping at the end and coming back down the other.

"Come out, come out wherever you are." Her singsong voice echoed through the theatre. "Lucien, if this is some elaborate plan to save that succubus of yours . . ." Her words dropped off. After some rustling and a keypad beep, she spoke again. "Claudette, it's me. Next month's meeting will most certainly be our last."

11

The door slammed behind Mia, and I moved to get up. Julian held fast on top of me and I stilled beneath him, remaining invisible. Could he sense Mia perhaps? In all these years knowing him, if there was one thing I learned, it was that Jules's instincts were almost always spot on. Except with me, of course. His index finger fell on my lips—the unspoken signal to hush.

A few minutes finally passed when we heard a *crack* from inside the theatre—right next to the same doors we'd entered in—and heard Mia exit out of. Julian lifted his invisibility and I did the same. However, neither of us moved to stand.

"That was close," I said.

Jules nodded. His breathing was short and heavy, and his erection nestled at the apex between my thighs. I studied his face—his high cheekbones, nose, and chin so chiseled that he could have been sculpted right from marble. His skin was tan; his hair golden and unruly. And every ounce of him was delicious.

Those blue eyes refused to look anywhere but into my own. They penetrated to my very core and left me at a loss for words. "Jules," I whispered.

His lips twitched, the corners pulling fractions higher. "I've always loved the way my name sounds coming from you."

I smiled at that. "Julian," I said again, teasing. His eyes fluttered closed, grin expanding in territory across his cheeks.

The room was suddenly hot and sticky. Sweat glistened at my hairline, and I shifted it away. "I've never minded your sweat." Julian's voice was laced with desire—and, if possible for an angel, lust.

"Because you've never seen me sweat."

"Sure I have." He grinned, and his pearly whites sparkled. "That summer we spent in the Mediterranean. The 1600s."

I chuckled, still lying beneath his concrete body. "That's right. Humans would have been onto us if we hadn't sweated. That summer was hotter than Hell—and I should know."

His smile dropped and he brushed a thumb along my cheekbone. "I'm sorry I didn't save you—from Buckley."

"Buckley hasn't been a threat for centuries—"

"That's not what I mean and you know it." He cut me off harshly before continuing. "I'm sorry. I should have laid out the rules for you sooner. You shouldn't have been kept in the dark. I think—I think it was unintentional, but I wanted you for myself. The more I kept you in the dark . . ."

I pressed my fingers to his lips, and his long, fair lashes fluttered closed. His full lips covered my fingertip in a lingering kiss that resonated down between my legs. "I'm sorry," he repeated.

I nodded. "I know you are."

"Well, then," he said, rolling off of me. "Let's get you home, shall we?" He stood, brushing nonexistent dust off of jeans that hung low on his slender hips, then offered a hand to me. My Jules. Ever the gentleman.

I took it and he pulled me to my feet, perhaps forgetting his own strength for a moment. I slammed into his marble chest, my soft breasts pressed up against his flexed muscles. Still-tight pants pressed into my hips, and our inhales and exhales matched. It was the damn hardest thing I've ever had to do, but I put a palm to his chest and pushed him to arm's length.

Damien. I needed to see Damien; feel his body and be reminded that there are men in existence whom I can be with without killing their souls.

A moment of surprise flickered in his face, then the mask set firmly back on and he regarded me warmly. Like a friend; not with the same intense sizzling gaze I'd been met with moments before.

I swallowed. "Actually—I wasn't going home. I-I was going to Damien's."

The warm gaze hardened to an icy anger. "Of course. I trust you can teleport there on your own?" Shoving his fisted hands into his pockets, his shoulders curled to his ears in a sulk.

"Jules, don't be like that. What do you expect me to do? Never date?"

"You can date," he grumbled. "Date men who *deserve* you."

"Like Heaven-bound humans? That's who you want for me? Or perhaps Hell-spawn demons? None of those are great options—you know that."

"But—"

"No buts. Damien is a good guy. He's a detective and always fights for the right team. He's a little rough around the edges, but Hell—who am I kidding? So am I."

Jules shook his head, blond hair fanning out at his shoulders, and turned away.

"Wait—Jules! I need to ask you . . . in Heaven, did you ever hear any rumors about me?"

His eyebrows dipped as he turned to face me once more. "Rumors?"

"Yeah. Just anything about what I'm going to become? Anything to imply why this bounty was placed?"

Worrying his bottom lip between his teeth, he paused, thinking. "To be honest, no one up there really discusses it much. They're not particularly worried about the existence of . . . well, you know."

"Right." My voice caught in my throat and I cleared it, hoping it wasn't too noticeable. Why would angels give a damn about a sex demon? "So, nothing being whispered about me becoming the next Succubus Queen?"

Julian's gaze narrowed. "No—why? What have *you* heard?"

I shrugged, trying my best to appear nonchalant. "Not much. I think that maybe someone's afraid I might be stronger than Mia."

His eyes flashed, sparkling with an urgency that wasn't there before. "Have you given any indication that you want that sort of power?" His face twisted.

"No!" I shouted a little too emphatically and darted a glance over my shoulder. I half expected a dozen people to pop out from the wings and stare at me. Luckily for us, no one did. "No," I said again, quieter this time. "That's my worst nightmare. Being the leader responsible for all those lost lives?" I shuddered.

He exhaled, and the worry lines around his eyes melted away with the breath. "Oh, thank goodness." He put a palm to his chest and with the other held mine. "Not even San Michel could pardon that."

"Pardon?" A glimmer of hope sparked in my belly.

Jules shrugged. "Don't get your hopes up just yet. But I'm working on it. As long as I'm in existence, I'll be working on it."

I squeezed his hand before releasing it. "It's a long shot."

"We'll see."

He jerked his head in the direction of the door. "Go. Go to your elemental." His smirk was tender. The same smirk I knew from centuries ago.

I elevated on my tiptoes and pecked him on the cheek. His muscular shoulder tensed at the connection beneath my palm.

With a *crack*, I appeared outside of Damien's door. The sweltering heat surrounded me like a bubble, and I shifted away the beads of sweat gathering between my cleavage. The magic shivered over my skin like a cool breeze, and it felt momentarily wonderful. But it passed as quickly as the air off an oscillating fan.

Damien lived in an adorable suburb of Vegas called Paradise. For a lot of folks, that was exactly what it was. And I had to admit, it was a great neighborhood with a diner that made the absolute best peach pie I've had in my life. And for someone who's existed for many centuries, that was really saying something.

Palm trees shaded the moonlight, and just as I raised a fist to knock, I heard a *crack* directly behind me. Someone had blocked their aura, and I scrambled for my gun, my pepper spray, anything. Before I could even get my hand to my purse, fire slashed across my back and a blast of pain slammed into my skull. Blackness tunneled around me.

12

New Jersey, 1776

"*I*'ll take her." *His index finger pointed in my face, and more than anything I wanted to bat it away. Of course, that would be bad for business. And how dare I do anything to hurt Lucien's precious business.*

I stood in the lineup with the other women. And in all my rational thoughts, I knew I had to recharge. My skin glowed, practically radiating with my need to feed. My hair was glossy, sparkling in its curled coif. I was essentially starving myself, supernaturally speaking—only in the succubus realm, lack of powers worked to my advantage. Nearly every man who came in took one look at the girls and singled me out. The other ladies were just as beautiful and could shapeshift any curves or lack thereof they wanted . . . but because of my abstinence, my pheromone was more potent. A lethal opium that attracted men faster than a horse to an orchard.

To be honest, there were far worse men who had asked for me before. I certainly couldn't complain about this bloke. He was older, with smile lines creasing his face, and the setting sun glinted off his silver hair, showing the reflection of what was once auburn. His golden eyes twinkled and his grin was wide as he held out a hand, palm up.

I hesitated, unfocusing my eyes as Lucien had taught me. I looked at the edge of his hair where it frayed out from his curls and met the orange sun edging past the horizon. It was faint, but I could just make out the sense that he was not going to Heaven. Death. I saw a lot of death in his aura. But what the Hell did that mean? It wasn't his fault if there happened to be a lot of death in his life!

"Well?" His brows crunched together and he tapped his buckled shoe impatiently against the wood plank floors.

The side door banged shut and Lucien entered, glancing up from a roll of parchment paper. He glanced from me to the client and back to me once again. His head twitched a nod.

Lowering my chin in a false display of modesty, I curtseyed to the man, gathered my layers of gown in my arms, and dropped my fingers into his palm. They clenched around my own in a way that conveyed ownership. The customer's leering grin widened and he directed me over to Lucien, pulling out some coins from his satchel.

Lucien tutted and twitched his fingers. "This one doesn't come cheap."

The man's gaze molested me from head to toe, lingering far too long at my breast line. "Very well," he said finally, dropping a few more coins into Lucien's palm. Lucien smiled at me.

"Monica, you may take him to the suite. You're a lucky man; this one here only gets the finest room in the house." His grin swept over me, and I wanted nothing more than to wring his neck until that smile was squeezed away permanently. This was a big fucking game to him, was it? Easy for a man to sell our bodies—it's not his essence he's giving away for twopence.

Had the man known his way to the room, I was certain he would have slung me over a shoulder and taken me there himself. But as it stood, I directed him to the proper bed. I opened the door and let him enter first. He threw me another raking glance over his shoulder.

"I have a feeling you will be worth it, luv," he said with an extended hand.

I took it once more and he yanked me into him, twirling me so that my back pressed against the front of his person. A thick shaft penetrated the layers of my gown, poking into my backside. Heat flared through my body and the damn itch ached in my core, threatening to tear me apart, rip me from the inside out.

My need for this man slammed into my body like a hard wave crashing over me. Salt lapping at my wounds, burning with the desire. His mouth dipped to the curve of where shoulder meets neck, and his moist lips laid a trail up to my ear. Blood pulsed through my body, and moisture gathered between my legs. His hand trailed down and cupped my dripping sex through the layers of my skirts. I didn't want to admit it, not even to myself, how damn good it felt. With gritted teeth, I asked, "What is your name?"

He paused, and his hot breath fogged on my neck. "What do you care?" I could hear the raised eyebrow in his voice.

I swallowed. "I just . . . do."

A few curls fell loose from my updo, and he twisted one strand around a finger, turning me to look at him. I angled my chin down, not wanting to see what was behind those eyes of his. He hooked a finger under my chin and lifted my deep blue eyes to his honey-brown ones. One hand slid from my lower back to my bottom, squeezing. I clenched my legs as the itch flared to an almost painful level, and I cried out as he pulled me harder into him.

"Well, well, well," he grunted. "Is it possible we have ourselves a virgin here?" I swallowed the laughter that rose in my throat.

But Hell. If a lash-batting virgin is what he wanted, I could give him that. I blinked, looking up through the feathery strands of painted lashes instead of answering.

His grin widened and the spear in his britches hardened even more. "Darling." He brushed the back of his knuckle down my cheek to the jaw until he was tracing my mounding breasts. "My name is Jack." He tipped my head back and lowered his lips just above mine, stopping a hair's width away. "And you're in good hands."

His mouth captured mine, and with that one kiss I was a goner. The itch ignited to a full-on blazing hearth and this man's soul—his life force—didn't stand a chance.

A deep breath made my already constricted breasts hitch even higher. Within minutes, we had each other's layers peeled and sprawled on the floor. I smiled—all those layers were covering an impressive body: strong, lean muscles, slender hips, and broad shoulders. His member pierced forward, long and thick. A little bit of fluid winked at me from the tip, and I salivated at the sight. I sank onto the bed, my nose level with his arousal.

Wrapping a firm grip at the base, I tugged him toward my parted lips and took the first taste of his salty fluid. The hot, bitter drop fanned out onto my tongue, exploding like a musket at the back of my mouth. His soul wasn't exactly sparkling, but if you feed a starving person bugs, it will still seem like a feast. I batted my eyes, angling my face up to his. "Is this how it is done, sir?" I whimpered, my lips brushing the smooth skin at his tip.

He grunted, meaty hands falling onto the back of my head. "Open wide for me, my pet."

It took every bit of my self-control not to bite down on him at that term of endearment. Pet. I snorted in my head and instead of coming down on him too harshly, I merely scraped my teeth along his shaft with a loud, slurping suckle.

He hissed an inhalation through clenched teeth. "Not so rough."

"Aye. Silly little me." I swirled my tongue around him, tak-

ing my time at his tip to tickle the underside. I wiggled from beneath him. "I am dripping," I said, and dropped my eyes, "below."

"Then I suppose you are ready for me." With a catlike grace, he crawled across the bed over top my body, and I fell to my back, stretching my arms over head. My breasts stretched with the movement, and my nipples hardened.

"How did I get so lucky to snag a doll such as yourself?" He stroked my cheek with gentle fingers, and I bit my tongue to stop from lashing back with, "You paid a week's worth of cobbling."

"I don't know what you mean. Surely I am the lucky one here." I lifted my bottom off the bed, catching his manhood between my thighs. It slid between my legs with slippery, delicious friction as I pulsed my hips. Up and down; up and down. Sweat trickled down Jack's face, and his lips pressed into a thin line. I, too, was panting from below—waiting for the moment. That delicious moment when he entered me. After several tortuous panting breaths, he finally gripped himself and pushed into my slick opening. I shapeshifted my body tighter, more virginal, and he groaned at the resistance my new body offered.

I whimpered as well, and I was proud to say that this time it wasn't for show. He was long enough to hit that sweet knot inside of me, and my whole body tensed with the contact. He paused, brushing a blond curl from my forehead. "Everything quite well? I would hate to cause such a pretty girl pain."

His smile was soft and his eyes kind. The warmth spread in my chest, and for all of a moment I doubted Lucien's aura tactics. This man—this sweet, handsome gentleman—didn't seem at all like a Hell-bound soul. Perhaps I had read him wrong? Perhaps Lucien, that whoreson, had taught me incorrectly on purpose as a way to push me further on to Hell's team?

A breath staggered in my chest.

"My dear, are you well?" He repeated the question, only this *time Jack's face wasn't sexy and sweet. Concern was etched with every glance at me. His eyes flitted to my breasts and quickly back to my eyes. At least he was trying.*

He abruptly pulled out, and though he was still veined and erect, he sat back on his haunches and regarded me with concern. The sudden emptiness made me cry out. I needed him filling my void. Without him, I wasn't sure I'd make it to my next fix. "How dreadfully inconsiderate of me. You probably have not ever experienced bliss yourself, have you?"

"Well..."

"Please, allow me. I do quite enjoy the taste of a fine woman." He ran a tongue across his lips, and I wasn't sure if it was unconscious or for my benefit. He placed a hand on the insides of my knees and pushed them apart. His face lowered, and he ran a tongue along my wet slit.

I gasped, and my fingers plunged into his silvery hair, tugging the strands from his ponytail. "Bloody Hell!" I hissed. Remaining coquettish in the throws of pleasure would without a doubt be difficult.

His tongue impaled me, darting in and out, switching between the wet thrusts and quick flicks at the sensitive nib at the crest. Within minutes, I was close. The tightness knotted in my belly. With a final nip, I cried out—that knot exploding like a cannon settled on my chest. I exhaled as the tremors subsided and relaxed my curled toes.

He popped up from between my legs, proud smile stretching from ear to ear. "I think you are ready now."

He knelt, throwing my legs up over his shoulders. My pleasure meant nothing to the forces of Hell. Until he spilled his seed, my service was not over. And my powers remained low. Which meant that painful itch flaring through my body would remain—and worsen with each passing moment—until he finished.

He slid into me, and I sighed right along with his moan. I bucked my hips once more and his springy hair brushed against mine. His hips circled with each thrust, and a fireball of frenzy uncurled through my body. Fists clenched the bed, and his tight sack slapped into my buttocks with each salacious plunge. One thrust after the other became more erratic and explosive, less rhythmic.

It wasn't long before he was trembling above me, spurting white-hot liquid gold inside me. Light burst behind my eyes, flickering, and Jack's life flashed before me. Born and raised in England, consorting with royals. Raping young girls. Jack fighting on the Tory's side. And, finally, as the inside man of an attack here in Trenton. He lived through the battle and died several years later.

With a gush of air, I fell back to the present.

I wanted to tear his throat out right then and there. He certainly did like his virgins, I thought with a sneer. Of course, I knew in the rational part of my brain that those fighting on the rebellion side of things would also be killing in the battles. But that battle in Trenton chilled me to my very marrow. How could one so frigidly turn his back on the area that took him in, the area he called home and where he went to church weekly? I shivered and goose bumps pebbled my arms.

Jack stood, slipping his britches back on and tucking in his shirt. "Cold?"

I wrapped the blanket around my torso and shook my head.

He dropped a quick kiss onto my forehead before traipsing out the door. "I hope to see you again soon," he said with a wink.

And finally, even though I wasn't Lucien's biggest fan, his tactics felt right. "Oh, I hope so," I whispered.

13

Yellow light filtered through my cracked eyelids. A throbbing vein at my temple pulsed like a drum beat . . . only the last thing I wanted was to tap my toe to the rhythm. My arm was a load of bricks as I lifted it and rested a palm to my aching head. I groaned and blinked my eyes open, forcing myself to wake up despite the painful, bright light flooding my eyes and head.

The walls were white with a large window shaded by simple white blinds. The wall in front of me was adorned with various framed and signed vinyl records hanging in a grid. My wrist was cradled in a large calloused hand, and as the bed creaked beside me, I looked over to find Damien taking my pulse. "Hey there," he said, his gruff voice not quite a whisper, but not at full volume, either. Something my pounding head greatly appreciated.

I was no longer in my own clothes but an oversized T-shirt and a pair of male boxers with little cupids all over them.

"What the Hell happened?"

Damien rolled to his side, grabbing for a tall glass of water as I hoisted my body to a seated position. Another blast of pain slammed into my brain even stronger than before, and my head fell forward into both hands. As if sheer pressure would make it go away.

He passed me the water and I took a sip.

"I don't know." Damien dragged a hand down his face, scratching at his stubble. "My plants and I are on good speaking terms and they didn't see anything, either." He puffed an exhale, and creases marred his beautiful, olive features. "I heard the crack of someone appearing, and Baxter barked like crazy. I went to the door, assuming it was you for a surprise nightcap. As I opened the door, I heard another crack and you fell forward into my arms." Anger clipped his words short. "You didn't see anyone, either?"

I hesitated before shaking my head. "No. No one at all." Damn. If he was obsessive before about my safety, Damien would be a downright lunatic now.

He hesitated, almost as though afraid to touch me, before taking my hand and lacing our fingers together. His thumb trailed circles along my heated skin. "Your shirt was ripped open in the back. A couple of nasty cuts there, too."

I twisted around to see. Tugging Damien's well-worn LVMPD shirt above my waist, I could just barely make out the open cuts. It looked as though someone had tried to slash through my crucifix burn—unsuccessfully so. It was still red as a new scar would be. But the gashes stopped where the scar started and began again at the other edge. No wound touched the holy burn mark.

Damien interrupted my thoughts. "I don't recall that scar from the other times we've been together."

"Yeah." I sighed. "It's a new one. A gift from—from, uh, the guy I was with last night."

Damien snorted and his face twisted—in jealousy? Pain? Who knew anymore? "You didn't think it necessary to tell me?"

I sat still as a deer in hunting season and held his gaze. "I didn't realize I had to give you a minute-to-minute account of my evenings."

His head flopped to a shoulder and he rolled his eyes. "C'mon, Monica. What's this about?"

I caved and told him about the other night with Buckley, intentionally leaving out the part of the story that described how much he looked like Drew.

He didn't comment immediately, simply chewed the inside of his cheek before finally answering. "So—this attack tonight. It obviously has something to do with this new scar. Can Buckley go invisible?"

"I don't know. Probably. But—I don't think this was him. Why would he scar me just to rip it right off? Besides . . . wouldn't he of all people know that it couldn't be scratched away?" I closed my eyes and shifted the wounds closed. Everything cleared up . . . except for the cross scar. Part of me kind of liked it; I couldn't wear a crucifix anymore—but now I can always sport the symbol of my original religion.

"It doesn't shift away, either?" Damien growled, eyes glued to my lower back. I shook my head in response. "Great. Just great." He mumbled more to himself than to me. "How's your head? You feel okay otherwise?"

I smoothed the back of my hair with a palm; a nasty bump creating a hill and valley on the back right side. "It hurts, but it's not bad."

"Good. That's good." His lips thinned, and he nibbled the blanched corner between two teeth.

I raised an eyebrow in his direction, waiting for the other bomb to drop. "And?"

"And what?" he snapped.

"And . . . aren't you going to lecture me?"

His face was tight; the corners of his mouth turned down in a tension-filled frown. Finally, he shook his head. "Nope."

After a pause, he continued. "I might kick that angel's ass for not getting you here safely, though."

I opened my mouth to speak when Baxter, the exuberant yellow lab, bounded through the cracked door and leaped onto the bed. His greeting consisted of slobbery kisses and a tail so powerful, demons should patent it as a weapon. A bit of gray peppered his face and around his eyes and nose. We weren't sure of Baxter's exact age, but we knew he wasn't a young pup.

All tension in Damien's face melted away and he grinned that panty-melting smile that hit me in the gut every time. "I told you he missed ya."

I wrapped my arms around the dog's neck and buried my face into his soft fur. "Hey, buddy," I said quietly, scratching his favorite spot under his front leg. Somehow a cute and cuddly animal made a throbbing headache easier to ignore.

Damien patted the dog's butt and scratched the sweet spot right above his tail. "Okay, Baxter. That's enough. Get down." The dog flashed his sad, brown eyes in my direction.

"Aww," I whimpered right along with Baxter, kissing his nose. A little zap stung my lips while I kissed him, and a flash of Baxter's puppy face spun in my mind. Shit, again? There was only one time in my existence that something similar to this had happened—and it was when Wills and Lexi were gunning for my life. Sucking my powers away with a stone from the Garden of Eden. But recently, these little zaps of power were becoming more frequent.

"Nuh-uh," Damien playfully growled. "Don't you fall for it." He flashed a disciplinarian look to the dog on final time. "Down, boy." Then he turned his attention back to me. "Can I get you anything? More water?"

I rubbed the back of my head. Though the throbbing was still present, it wasn't nearly as bad as it had been. "Could use an Advil. But other than that, I'm fine, I think."

He nodded and popped up, wearing only his boxer briefs

(how did I not notice that?), and padded his way to the bathroom. He hurried back and handed me a couple of pills, which I swallowed with a sip of water.

Baxter circled the floor on my side of the bed and curled into a big, furry ball. If I stretched my arm, I could just barely reach him with my fingertips. "What time is it?" I stretched to look past Damien at his bedside clock.

"Just past one."

An exhale breezed past my parted lips. At least I wasn't out for long. "Did you call anyone? About the attack?"

He chuckled once, lacing his fingers in mine and bringing my knuckles to his lips. "I barely had time. I brought you into the house and, after changing and cleaning the cuts, I ran out to see if I could catch the bastard. Of course, it only took seconds for them to be long gone. Then, I did the elemental thing—talked to the shrubs; my door. They knew about as much as I did. Whoever it was must have been invisible and masked."

"A higher-up?" I quirked my eyebrow. "So . . . should we call anyone?"

He shrugged. "That's your choice, babe. We'll need to tell them at some point, but if we call tonight, they're all gonna be over here in a second. And then you and I will have yet another night *not* alone together."

I exhaled, finally relaxing. "I'd rather have tonight be just the two of us." The Advil was starting to work, melting away my throbbing head. "Weird that they would try to slash the scar, right? Why not take me out then and there?"

"There's a whole goddamn slew of things worrying me—first and foremost the fact that someone attacked you right on my doorstep. If I hadn't been right at the open door, they probably would have taken you out right there. One second longer and they could have disappeared with your limp body." He twirled a strand of my hair around his index finger.

"Yeah, lucky." I meant it when I said it—but nothing about my existence felt lucky. I rolled onto my side, snuggling into that nook against Damien's ribs and underarm. A thick bicep curled around me, tugging me closer.

"Why do you think Buckley burned you with the cross? Seems weird."

"Because he's an ass, that's why." Buckley didn't need a reason to be a dick. He just was. It was his way of asserting that he still has ownership of me.

"Maybe. But that guy's smart . . ." he trailed off, absent-mindedly stroking my hair in thought.

My blood froze in my veins. "He was murmuring," I whispered. "When he pressed the cross into my back—it was a spell. The bastard put a spell on me." My spine stiffened and my fists curling around the comforter. I had known it was a spell, of course, but the reality of it was just sinking in. Nothing about myself felt any different . . . other than the scar that wouldn't disappear.

"Whoa, whoa." Damien's hands curved around my shoulders, holding me tighter against him. "There's nothing we're doing about that tonight. You need to rest. We'll take care of Buckley in the morning."

"Double-crossing piece of . . ."

"Well, that's not any new information, right? Didn't we always know he was one of the bad guys? Playing for the wrong team. . . ."

"Buckley makes his own team. He's the Green Party."

Damien's chest expanded against my cheek and collapsed with his breath. "Let's just make sure you're healthy again, okay?" His fingers brushed my hair and he tipped my face up to his, dropping a sweet kiss on my nose.

An erection twitched in Damien's boxer briefs, raising the cotton into a pitched tent. I grazed my fingertips down his abs, feeling each ridge ripple and tense beneath my touch. "Maybe it's time you have a little luck thrown your way," I whispered, looking up through a web of lashes into his eyes.

I curled a finger into the waistband of his briefs, toying with the sensitive skin there before gripping his thick cock in my palm. Heat flared through my body and my sex pulsed.

Damien's eyes had darted to mine and then clenched shut. "Monica—no." His voice was soft but firm. "You need to rest."

I clutched my hand around his shaft. If he wouldn't let me stroke, I could pulse and squeeze until he caved. With a groan, his head flopped onto the headboard. "What am I going to do with you?" His erection twitched in my hand, growing with each embracing pressure. "I'm serious, Monica. You need to rest."

"They say orgasms help a headache," I said with a smirk.

He rolled over me, holding his body up in a plank type of pose without placing weight anywhere on me. His triceps rippled with mountainous muscles, and veins throbbed in his massive forearms. "Then *you* will get an orgasm," he said, running his tongue along his bottom lip.

I shook my head back and forth slowly and trailed my hands along his arms. "Nope. Either we both get one, or I'll have to suffer with this headache all night."

Damien pressed a kiss to my neck, nipping the tender flesh there as he pulled away. "You're a difficult woman, you know that?" He slid down the length of my body and I caught him, cupping his face with both hands.

"Just where do you think you're going?"

"Don't worry—we'll take care of me later," he growled. Nudging away from my hands, he lowered his face between my legs, tugging the boxers I wore down. The silk brushed against my skin, and goose bumps rose all the way down to my ankles.

I raised my arms to the bedpost, locking my hands in a grip above my head. Damien pressed his lips to my dripping sex, his kiss lingering between my legs. He licked my length, swirling his tongue into my opening.

His mouth and tongue moved with a fluidity, and with each

lap, each flick, my muscles twitched involuntarily. The pressure inside slowly compressed little by little until it felt like a balloon about to pop. He nibbled on my clit, and my body jerked with the first contact of teeth on the sensitive nub.

He pulled back, sitting up on his knees and adjusting his massive erection. I reached out toward his waistband again, and he playfully slapped my hand away, his grin full of piss and pride. "Your rule—we both have to come. My rule, however, is that you must rest. Kind of leaves us at an impasse, huh, succubus?"

Tugging his boxer briefs down below his thighs, his erection sprang free, pointing toward me. He stroked his length with a gripping fist, eyes locked onto mine with the smallest smile tugging the corners of his mouth higher.

Every muscle in my body twitched at the sight. The sight of his head, dripping with his arousal, made my mouth drain of all fluid, as though every bit of moisture headed south. I parted my parched lips, hoping for a drink from his oasis, but Damien shook his head. "Tsk-tsk. I don't think so, babe."

I walked a finger down my stomach and fluttered it over my clit. Just as I teetered on the edge of orgasm, Damien lifted my hand and took my finger into his mouth. His tongue rolled over my skin. Tortuously slow, he removed my finger from his puckered lips, sucking the whole while. "I don't think masturbating qualifies as rest, either."

My breathing was a full-on pant at this point and I fisted my hand, slapping it down to bed next to me. "Then tell me—what does qualify as rest?"

He pumped his hand faster. "You—lying there. Doing nothing."

I raised an eyebrow. "Nothing?"

His grin widened. "Nothing." He brought his massive hands down onto my thighs, spreading my legs and licking his lips like a wolf about to feast. Diving in once more, my body bucked beneath his lips and I fisted the comforter, unable to stifle my cry.

He immediately pulled back, touching himself. "One more outburst like that and 'rest' will mean both of us completely clothed. Not touching." Fire sparked behind his eyes and the playful grin disappeared entirely.

His tongue swirled around my opening and finally darted in and out in thrusting movements. My hands cupped his face, angling his eyes up toward me. They gleamed with mischief, and the bedside lamp highlighted the gray color. A smile tugged toward his eyes. I nudged my neck back. "C'mere, elemental."

He crawled over top of me and yet again donned some sort of magical yoga pose wherein none of his weight landed anywhere on my body.

"I want you inside of me," I whispered, my voice a mere gasp from below him.

Damien shook his head. "That wasn't part of the deal," he whispered back, licking his lips.

"What if I promise not to do any of the work." I blinked slowly, the flutter of my lashes creating a crackled web through which I could see him. I raised my right hand. "Angel's honor."

His face split into a grin. "But you, succubus, are no longer an angel. What good is that honor?"

I matched his grin. "You'll just have to trust me, elemental."

"Trust." He rolled the word over in his mouth as if it were a new flavor he was testing. "You know me," he said finally. "Up to try anything once." He lowered his lips to my ear. His breath was hot and his lips wet. "But don't give me a reason to regret it."

His hand trailed up from the curve of my hip, over my waist and ribs, to cup my breast under the T-shirt. His capable hands kneaded my breasts, heavy with need, and his thumb and forefinger rolled the end of my nipple, elongating it. The delicious sensation buzzed between my legs, and I moaned, trying to keep still. Damien kissed me, his tongue against mine, muffling my cries. His lips were the mallet that shattered the mirror. My body convulsed against his—aching, needing. And I was so wet, I dripped down the insides of my thighs.

His fingers slipped down between my legs, circling my drowning sex, and the heel of his hand applied pressure to my clit. "My God," he hissed.

Licking his hand, he pumped his erection a few times before nudging my legs wider and sliding inside. His head threw back and his eyes closed, relishing my tight grip around him. He filled me entirely, his head nudging that tight spot deep inside. He eased his body back in exquisite leisure and thrust back inside, rolling his hips. I took him all and then some, crying out as his hip bone slapped the insides of my thighs.

I clawed at his chest, moaning, begging—unraveling there right before him. "Please, Damien . . ." I was a mush of nonsensical cries and words. "Please, faster."

One bead of sweat rolled down past his temple to his jaw, and I caught it with my finger, sucking the salty moisture onto my tongue.

His movements in and out were tortuously slow at first, and he thrusted with a rhythmic ease. As he sped up, he grasped my face with two hands, urgent but yet still gentle, and kissed me. His teeth tugged on my lower lip. I desperately wanted to match him thrust for thrust; I wanted to ram my ass off of this bed into his cock—but a promise is a promise.

"Can I—can I wrap my legs around you?" I panted and fingered his damp hair at his neckline.

His eyes creased with a smile. "Of course," he grunted.

I wrapped my legs around his waist, locking at the ankles and offered him deeper access—if that was even possible.

Oh, yes, it *was* possible. With the next thrust, his head massaged me deeper than ever before. A sheen of sweat glistened across my skin, and the dip in between my breasts gathered a tiny pool of sweat. Before I could shift it away, Damien's head dropped and he licked it up, moving first to one nipple, rolling the tip in his lips, then to other, repeating the technique.

I squeezed my muscles around him and I swear I could feel his dick grow in size inside of me. My stomach muscles quivered, and everything inside of me stiffened beneath Damien. His muscles were thicker than corded rope beneath my hands, and I dug in my fingers while gritting my teeth.

"Come with me, angel," he whispered, and despite the fact that we were both about to explode, his voice was composed, if not a little breathless. I unraveled at his words, like a rubber band stretched too far and snapping back into place. My strangled cry split the air around us, and I splintered into a million shuddering pieces beneath him. Dropping his head to my shoulder, he nibbled my skin there, convulsing atop me. With a final hard thrust, he emptied himself inside of me.

I was a panting, sweaty mess, and Damien had his forehead against mine, breath just as ragged and sweating far more than I ever allowed myself to. My hair was in disarray, heart thumping wildly as I took a deep breath, willing my rapid pulse to slow. Damien's eyes fluttered open and he dropped a kiss to my nose before easing himself out of me.

He lay next to me, propped on an elbow, and tucked my hair behind my ear, letting his fingers linger at my jaw. "You okay?" His eyes were demanding, and they seared my soul with a simple glance. He was frustratingly handsome with his tousled dark hair, serious expression, and narrowed gray eyes.

"Huh?" I ask, breathless.

"Your head," he softened, but the intensity of the question didn't dissipate in the slightest.

Oh, right. I thought for a moment and grinned back at him. "The headache's totally gone."

His carefree smile was back instantly, and it's enough to make a girl melt. "Just call me Doctor Penis."

I grabbed his cock, which was in limbo—not quite hard but not yet entirely flaccid. "Does the doctor do house calls?" I asked in a husky voice that I learned from years of watching Kayce.

"Whenever you want, babe." He leaned down and kissed me again, snaking his hand up the back of my neck into my hair. "But not tonight." He pulled away, handing me a glass of water. "Drink up, then get some rest."

14

_____

Morning light spilled into the room in slits through the flimsy blinds. I rolled to my right, throwing an arm, expecting it to land across Damien's broad chest. Instead, I was met with a body covered in soft fur, panting hot breath against my skin. I blinked awake, and Baxter ran a wet tongue across my face. If I didn't know better, I could've sworn the dog was smiling back at me. He looked—different somehow. More youthful, energetic—something.

"Morning, buddy." I scratched behind his ears, and he rolled onto his back offering me his belly instead. "Greedy motherfucker, aren't you?" I said with a giggle, hugging him and rubbing his belly instead. Sitting up, I kicked my feet off the edge. "C'mon, Bax. Let's go find Damien, huh?"

I slipped Damien's silky boxers back on, just in case someone had popped in bright and early. Ever since last year, that seemed to happen more and more to me. There was a buzzing surrounding the house, as if the walls around us were vibrating, and after a second, I relaxed, realizing it was just Damien talking to the elements.

"I told you—the door had nothing to say. The bushes didn't see anything, either. Read my aura, asshole. I'm not lying," said Damien.

He grunted and I froze in the hallway. Who was he talking to?

"Why didn't you call me?"

Julian. I sighed, my knotted back relaxing at his voice.

"I shouldn't have had to," Damien growled. "If I recall, you were in charge of her getting here safely. I should have known I couldn't trust you."

"Oh, please." Julian's eye roll could be heard all the way down the hall where I stood. "So, what do you know about the attack?"

"All we know is that something teleported here, hit her over the head, slashed at that burn mark, and left—"

"What burn mark?" Julian snapped.

"This burn mark," I said, lifting my shirt as I entered the room. Julian's eyes dropped to the cross.

Heat flooded his cheeks and I peeked at my behind, realizing I had tugged the boxers down a little too far, revealing a touch of ass cheek to the angel.

"I-It's new?" he stuttered, eyes fluttering around the room, finally landing on my face.

I tugged my clothes back in place. "Just a couple nights ago. Thanks to Buckley and a glamour charm. I think it's a spell of some sort."

Julian nodded, his face still beet red. "I will look into it."

"Any insight as to why the scar won't go away?"

"Or why someone would specifically try to cut it away?" Damien cut in, handing me a cup of coffee before pouring one of his own. Such a gentleman.

"Before I can answer that, I need to find out what it is."

"Bullshit," Damien grumbled, diving his hand into his already rumpled head of hair. He slugged his coffee down, damn near finishing the whole mug in one slurp.

Jules's eyes drooped as though Damien's outburst was nothing more than a tantrum, which to be honest was all it was. "You ready?"

I shifted into an outfit; a pretty blue sundress with a white belt and kitten-heel ballet-style shoes. "I am now."

"God, you suck," Damien grumbled, and headed back to the bedroom. "*Some* of us actually need to shower in the mornings."

I caught his hand as he passed me and pulled him in, placing a soft kiss on his lips. He tasted of toothpaste and coffee. "I'll see you later." I smacked him playfully on the butt, and he ducked into the bedroom.

"Never thought I'd meet anyone less of a morning person than you."

"Don't let this quick shift fool you." I gestured up and down my new look. "I've got a lump on my head, a burn on my back, and a grudge in my gut. And I'm not afraid to take it out on you." I spoke through a grin, but there was no hiding the truth in the words. There is a land called Displacementia—and I am their Queen.

"I know," Jules puffed through a breathy chuckle. "It's why I brought a peace offering." From behind his back, he produced a giant to-go cup of something caffeinated. I snatched the cup from him, wide eyed and salivating at the thought of a latte and energy. Yes, yes, I'm a junky. Admitting it is the first step, right? I sipped the steaming beverage with a moan of pleasure. "Caramel mocha latte," I said, closing my eyes and relishing the sugar-packed flavor. "It tastes just like how Drew makes it." The smile crept to my face before I could stop it. When I opened my eyes, Jules was grinning back at me.

"Don't tell me you thought he was the only one who could fulfill your needs?"

The question lingered, dangling in the thick air between us. There was no way I was answering that.

* * *

We arrived at Hell's Lair early—our hopes being that it would be well before anyone from the club woke up and came over. You could never be sure though, with demons. Tricky little fuckers.

"Where to first?" Julian's eyes twinkled, and he didn't bother squinting in the direct morning sunlight. I, on the other hand, shaded my eyes with a flattened palm.

Damn, I wish I had drunk that latte slower. I shook the empty coffee cup, then tossed it into the nearest trash can. Bummer. "Let's start in Lucien's office. If there's time, we'll check the girls' dressing room." Not that I thought we'd find anything with my fellow strippers. Lucien was one of the best ArchDemons a girl could ask for. Even Kayce could admit that. Any of his inferiors stupid enough to try to get rid of him would surely end up with a bitch of a boss—someone like Claudette.

With a *crack,* we each teleported into Lucien's office. Cherry wood and gray carpet gave the room a gloomy atmosphere, reflective of the feeling in my stomach. I half expected him to be sitting at his desk, going through paperwork when we arrived. Like it had all been one big, unfunny practical joke. But the joke was on me. The Newton's Cradle desk toy, which could detect the supernatural, swung wildly with Julian's appearance. The little silver balls cracked into one another with a deafening sound. Jules put a hand to them, and they stilled immediately.

"I'll take the desk," I said, sliding open the top drawer. There were two trays inside—one for paperwork marked "invoices" and the other, a smaller tray for pens. Black pens specifically. Damn, Lucien was organized. Why he couldn't have taken the time to instill that sort of skill into me back in the day . . . I could have really used that, as well as learning how to seduce men. I smiled. He probably *did* try. I was likely too damn stubborn to listen.

The invoices were standard. Liquor distributors. Electrician—probably to get that damn mechanical bull installed. Independent contractors. Lenny . . . wait. What was Lenny giving Lucien an invoice for? It was for fifteen hundred dollars, and under the description it said "freelance work." I took a picture with my phone and added it back to the stack.

The middle drawer of his desk held a receipt book. And blue pens. I rolled my eyes. Separating the different color pens? Who knew he was such a geek. I'd have to get him a pocket protector at the next holiday party. I swallowed, a lump gathering in my throat. If he was even here for another holiday.

I shook the thought away as I flipped through the receipt book. Sure enough, each month, there was a paid invoice to not only Lenny but also to Mia and Claudette. Mia made sense— Lucien might be giving her kickbacks from the succubi he made money off of. But Claudette? And Lenny? That douche was on the payroll as it was. *And* Damien discovered months ago that he was skimming money off the top. I snapped a few more pictures and tucked the book back in the desk.

I moved to open the bottom drawer. *Clunk-clunk.* Damn— locked. That meant something juicy was in there. Holding my palm over the lock, I whispered an incantation, sneaking a sideways glance at Jules. He stiffened, and though he wasn't looking my direction, I knew he could sense the magic—neither Heavenly or Demon. As the spell ended, sparks flew from the lock, zapping my fingers and sending me back, flat on my ass.

I sat up, a bit dazed, rubbing the back of my head, which, even though I had shifted the lump away, still bore a bit of the ache from the blow last night. "Mother of Hell, Lucien." I whispered, pushing to my feet. Jules was at my side, helping me up.

"It's an enchantment," he said, hand lingering around mine.

I tugged it away before I did something stupid. Like pressing his erection against my hip. *Again.*

"No shit, Einstein," I muttered back. Jules stepped back,

stuffing his hands into his worn jeans. His tight, gray cotton shirt clung to his chiseled chest, and I swallowed as I lifted my eyes to his.

He raised an eyebrow, a breath puffing from full, rose-colored lips. "Well?" he said in a monotone voice.

I rolled my eyes, dropping my hands to my sides. "I'm sorry, okay! You've been wonderful—and yes, I'm a bitch. I know it. But Lucien's like a brother. I'm a little off today."

Jules twitched a smile and brushed his thumb across the corner of my mouth. Bringing the finger to his mouth, he darted out his tongue, and the sight of it in action made mine dryer than sandpaper. "You had a bit of latte there," he said with a wink. I swallowed—Drew used to do the same thing every time I had foam on my lips. It got to the point where I would purposefully leave a little there just to feel his touch.

Leaning in, Jules placed a searing palm to my hip. The heat of his body, the smell of his peppermint scent, spun in my head. "And—apology accepted."

"As if you have a choice," I mumbled. "You're an angel. You have to accept my apology."

"Do I, now?"

There was a pause as he pulled his hand back. The absence of his touch tingled on my skin and left my hip cold. My soul empty. He dropped to a crouch in front of the desk and placed a hand to the lock. "It's a decoy," Jules said, lifting once more to his feet.

"How do you know? You an elemental, too, now?"

Jules shook his head. "No. But I can sense a lie. There might be something in there, but it's not all that important. Lucien knew that his desk is the first place an intruder would look." He glanced around the room, brushing a hand across the top of the desk. "Where's his laptop?"

"I've never seen Lucien with one. He usually just uses his phone."

"Damn," Jules grunted, and I stepped back, breath catching in my throat.

"Julian!" I dropped my voice to an exaggerated whisper. "Did you just *curse?*"

"Lucien is my friend, too." He was quiet, but his voice held traces of regret.

"I can't imagine Heaven is too keen on your friendship with an ArchDemon." I looked at him through the corners of my eyes.

"Well, they're not too excited about my alliance with you, either. But," he continued, "I think they knew it was inevitable when we—when you . . . when you fell."

The thought struck my chest like a mallet to a gong. "Could this be a Heaven versus Hell sort of kidnapping? Have any angels disappeared lately that would stir a demon kidnapping?"

He seemed to pause and think about that before bringing his massive shoulders crunching to his ears. "Could be. I don't know of any missing angels, though. I'm not about to rule anything out just yet."

There was silence as we both stared into nothing. My eyes zoned out against the cabinets lining the wood-paneled wall. "Wait." I darted over and placed a hand to the cabinets.

"I already looked through those," Julian said.

"I know—but last year, when Wills and Lexi were after me, Lucien lifted an enchantment from these drawers to give me my gun. It was almost like there was another set of cabinets *behind* these." Shit, what was that incantation he used? And would it work if I said it?

I closed my eyes, thinking back to a year ago in this very office. He had lifted both hands and it was a whisper. Barely a whisper. With a slow breath, I released my own chant. A click came from behind the cabinet, and when I opened my eyes one was slightly ajar.

Julian's narrowed eyes seared the back of my neck and all

my hairs stood on end. "How did you do that?" His footsteps against the carpet sent a shudder down my spine. "That wasn't typical succubus magic. Neither was the incantation over at Lucien's desk."

I shrugged, not looking at him. It was no use lying to an angel—the supernatural lie detectors of the realm. "I'd say beginner's luck, but you'd see right through that." After another pause, I opened my mouth to speak before Jules pressed a finger to my lips.

"I'm better off not knowing," he whispered, then turned his attention back to the cabinet. "But I think Lucien left this so that you could open it. No one else's incantation would work on an enchantment unless he ordered it to. Whatever this is, he wanted you to find it."

"Which means," I continued for Jules, "he suspected something might happen to him."

Jules gestured to the slightly ajar cabinet. "You do the honor, succubus."

15

The door moaned as I carefully swung it open. Various weapons sat organized on the shelving, and below that were a few drawers. I opened the top one, and nestled inside was a manila envelope.

It was thick in my hands, and I reached inside, pulling out a stack of papers. Julian loomed over my shoulder as he examined the papers as well.

"What do we have here?" he asked quietly.

One by one, I flipped through the pages. "They're all hit files, I think." I swallowed. "Dammit, Lucien . . . what did you get yourself into?"

"How do you know?" Jules's breath was hot, and I could feel him shift his gaze from the papers to my face.

"I saw my own file once. It looked just like this—pictures of me and everyone I knew and was connected to."

"Let me see." Jules gently took the stack of papers, rustling through them. I slid open the drawer below it, and there was another envelope with a smaller stack of papers inside. I tugged them out—also hit files.

"These are past files," Jules interrupted, leaning over with one particular sheet held up for me to see. He pointed to a date. "See? Under status, it says the job is complete. By a . . . Contenitore."

I scanned the page of the sheets I held. "And these are demons yet to be caught," I said, and shook the papers.

After a pause, Jules continued. "These are from Hell's official office. I recognize the seal."

At the top of each page was an embossed circle. Within the seal was the outline of a donkey. "I don't think they're hit files, Jules." I ran my fingers along the circle's bumpy ridge. "The Contenitore," I repeated. "Kayce was just talking about that guy. He's a bounty hunter for Hell. A new one who apparently keeps his identity very secret."

"This could possibly be the next hunter commissioned to kill you," Jules said, lowering his voice even more. "Lucien could have been getting too close—"

"—and the Contenitore took him out for it!"

Jules shrugged. "It's all circumstantial, but it's at least a lead."

The top sheet on my pile stared back at me. A demon named Grayson who is assumed to live right outside of the Vegas city limits. He was wanted for conspiring to dethrone Saetan.

"Jules—I have an idea."

He sighed beside me, stuffing his pile back in the envelope. "I didn't like it when you said that as an angel—and I still don't like it with you as a succubus."

I handed him my envelope of papers as well, which he tucked into my purse with the other.

I rifled through the rest of the drawers below, where there were a few stones—one carved into the shape of a blade. I ran my finger across the sharp edge and slipped it into my pocket. If it was locked with enchantments, it must be a powerful weapon. And Lucien wanted me to have all the weapons I could carry. "Should we take anything else?"

Jules looked over my shoulder, eyes raking across the various items. Blond hair ruffled as he shook his head. "No. We can always come back again to see if we missed anything. And you better hurry," he added. "We've got company."

I closed the doors and slid the enchantments back in place just as Lucien's door slammed open, crashing into the wall behind it.

I jumped, spinning to find Lenny's apple-shape outline by the doorframe.

Jules maintained his usual stoic stance with barely a blink at Lenny's interruption.

"What are you two doing in here?" Lenny grunted, sweat blistering along his receding hairline.

"Shouldn't we be asking *you* that same question?" I spat back.

Julian rested a hand on my shoulder, quieting me with a simple look. Damn him and that calming angel touch.

"Leonard," Jules began, "we have something to tell you. After an unfortunate string of events, it appears as though Lucien is missing." Julian's eyes glistened, eyebrows soft and empathetic. *Why, that wily little angel.*

"L-Lucien?" Lenny stuttered and his eyes darted around the room from corner to corner. After clearing his throat, he continued. "He's gone? Where?" His acting was so bad, the man couldn't have even been an extra on a soap opera.

With a quick glance at Jules, I took over. The angel couldn't physically lie. Enter: the sex demon. "I'm surprised you didn't already know." I batted my eyes, tilting my head in the most unassuming way to the side.

"What, me? Wh-why would I know? I don't know anything. . . ."

"I just meant that I thought Lucien checked in with you every day. And since he took last night off from the club, I assumed you'd be the first to realize he wasn't around."

Lenny's jaw fell, jowls pooling below his chin like an oversized shar-pei. "Well—yes . . ."

"Yes?" Julian raised a brow in his direction.

"I mean, no! Yes, I noticed he didn't check in last night. No, I didn't realize he was missing." The words whooshed out of his mouth all in one breath. Once pink lips drained of color as they pressed together into a thin line.

For a guy who hangs around the immortal crowd this much, Lenny sure didn't know much about our kind. For a guy who knew that Julian was an angel, he had some balls to lie to his face and think he could get away with it.

"Great. That's all we needed to know." Julian's gaze shifted to me and he nodded to the door. "Lenny, if you could keep mum on Lucien's disappearance, that would be great."

He nodded, skin flapping every which way with the movement.

I stared down my nose as I passed him, and he shrunk under my angry gaze. I wasn't done with that rodent of a man yet. You know what they say about rats—if you've got one, then you've got an infestation.

16

"Babe, you do not have to do this." Damien slid a glance around at the group, eyes landing on Julian's with a grunt.

"I wish that was true, but I do. I need to find Lucien."

Damien dropped his head, swiveling to look at Jules. "Tell me again why I can't be the one to go undercover? *I'm* the professional here."

"That's exactly why you can't," Kayce snapped, walking over and slapping Grayson's file down in front of me. "Quite a few people have learned your face and know that you and the angel were undercover—"

"Correction." He stalked over to my best friend, towering over her. "Adrienne was undercover. I was not."

"It doesn't matter," I offered gently. "You were partners. Those who know your supernatural nature know you're capable of this. And if they don't know, you'd be blowing your cover to all of Hell."

"And I can't do it because I already work as a bounty hunter for Hell," Kayce added.

"I *want* to do this, D. It makes the most sense . . . as a succubus who used to be an angel, it makes sense that I would team up with a rogue creature trying to take Saetan down."

"And you're sure this Grayson guy is up next on the bounty list?"

Kayce nodded. "I'm certain of it. He is gunning to take down Saetan—he is absolutely priority. I heard through a contact that the bust was happening today."

"Really? You expect us to trust your 'contact'?"

"As much as I hate to admit it," Jules interrupted calmly, "I agree with Damien on this. Who's your source?"

Kayce rolled her eyes. "The woman who handles the paperwork for our assignments. We alert the paper-pushers when we plan to make the bust so that they will be expecting the prisoner."

"When did Contenitore make contact?" Damien's hands tightened around his hips.

"Just a few hours ago."

Kayce directed her attention back to me. "Get a peek of the Contenitore. And if possible, a picture. Try to lie low, keep your reasons for being in the vicinity vague. Stay invisible and mask your powers."

I yawned, glancing over this Grayson dude's paperwork again. "Got it. If I get taken in, the evidence against me will be circumstantial. I could just be a case of wrong time, wrong place."

Damien's jaw flexed and clenched. "Right. Because Hell is so known for its just legal system," he growled.

"We'll be just a second's teleport away," Kayce said with a lowered glance at Damien.

"And what do I do if I'm too late? What if the capture's already gone down?" I glanced at my clock—Kayce had called the meeting almost immediately upon getting the news of Grayson's impending capture. It was almost midnight, and each of us had spent our respective day coming up empty-handed—except for this Grayson thing.

"I doubt it," she said. "Typically, you don't make a capture that quickly after reporting in. You want Hell to have a few hours to prepare."

I nodded. "So . . . I go to Grayson's house. Snoop around and just follow him until something happens. Right?"

"Right."

"All right." I tossed my head back, swallowing the rest of my coffee in a gulp. "Wish me luck."

"Someone should go with her, right?" Damien cut in, urgently.

Jules's crystal eyes regarded me with concern. "We can't. Both the Contenitore and Grayson will sense anyone else." Jules leaned against my doorframe with one knee bent, foot kicked up resting behind him, and arms crossed. His biceps bulged, and despite his calm exterior, he was clenching—everything. Every muscle rippled with tension.

"You're telling me that you can't mask your powers, too, angel?"

Jules's gaze shifted from me to Damien. "I can mask my powers, but I can't interfere so much with demon investigations as to join Monica on this. Not without permission from the counsel."

"Bullshit," Damien spat, stalking over into Jules's personal space.

"It's okay, D. I'll be fine."

Kayce snaked her arm into mine, pulling me in for a rare hug. "Damn right, you will. And we should see you within twenty-four hours."

I took one last look at the address. "Well, here goes nothing." With that, I closed my eyes and teleported to Flower Avenue in North Vegas.

17

New Jersey, 1776

The dark tavern was adorned with candles, torches, tables, and benches on ebony wood floors. Outside, November's freezing rain and wind whipped against the windows. Normally, I would be able to count the stars in the sky, ignoring Lucien's blatherings, but storm clouds and a curtain of rain prevented my mind from drifting off. Besides, I finally had a purpose for being out with my ArchDemon. Jack, according to his compatriots, came every Tuesday evening to Bear's Tavern—the notorious Tory haunt. Once he arrived I was to cuddle up to him and his group, introduce Lucien, and discover all that I could about the Loyalists' plan.

"You will point this Jack person out to me when he arrives, right?"

I nodded and sipped my pot of beer, glancing around the tavern. The men were loud and the clanking of mugs even louder. One voice shouted above the rest. "As if a hundredweight of sopping wet tea would stop the most vigorous army on earth!"

A chorus of "hear, hear!" rang out. Lucien's arm straightened with the rest, saluting. Beer sloshed over the edge, splatter-

ing my shoe. "Aye, my friends! Man was created to obey! Obey their Kings and their God without question!"

"Ah, yes," I sneered, raising my glass begrudgingly. "It makes such perfect sense for a King three thousand miles away to be dictating our laws and getting rich off our taxes."

Lucien darted a glare in my direction. "Keep your tongue civil, my love," he managed through gritted teeth.

"You're full of swill, Lucien." I held his fiery gaze. His mouth twitched in anger and he grasped my elbow, pulling me in close so that his breath, hot and moist, fell upon my face.

"Listen. We are here because of your vision. Undercover. Act like a damn Tory or we'll both be hung for treason." He released my arm, tossing me to the opposite side of the table, the bench beneath me wobbling with the sudden movement.

"As if you're afraid of a few Lobsterbacks," I grunted. I said it quietly enough so that no human ears could hear us. Lucien's face reddened all the same.

"No. But I am afraid of our cover being blown and me getting demoted. What do you plan to do then, dear sister?"

I didn't answer, but looked on Lucien's hard face with cold eyes. The olive skin of his face was set in a scowl, large eyebrows shadowing his already dark eyes. His long black hair sat in a coifed ponytail with curls around the crest of his head and ears.

I opened my mouth to throw back a retort when the tavern door swung open with a blast of frigid air and even colder rain. Plates rattled on the tables, and there, standing framed by the outline of blackened sky, was Jack.

"Close the damn door!" someone yelled from the back.

"Aw, shut yer hole!" Jack shouted, but with a good-natured smile on his charmingly lined face. He spun and, with the weight of his body—a body I'd come to know quite well—slammed the door closed. With a few jovial greetings, he headed to the bar, slapping a palm down. "Get me a cider, will ya?"

I smiled at Lucien. "That's our man," I whispered.

With a surreptitious glance over his shoulder, Lucien rolled his eyes at me. "Of course it is. I remember that one now."

"Do you think he is married?" I glanced around the tavern again. Only one other woman sat at the bar—also a prostitute. But not a succubus one, just your average, run-of-the-mill tavern whore.

"At his age, it's rather likely."

"I didn't see any wife in my vision."

Lucien drained the rest of his beer, slamming the empty glass down onto the table. "Now's as good a time as any to find out."

After a deep breath, I stood, wrapping my shawl tighter around my shoulders but tugging my dress lower off my voluptuous breasts. The lace edging of my bodice accented the swell of flesh there. I wanted to appear desirable but not downright like a lady of the evening. It was a fine line to be respectable enough to be seen among friends and yet lascivious enough to stir desire in the loins.

With a few bits in my palm, I moved one person down from him at the tap. "How much for another cider, please?" I opened my hand, making a show of counting my money.

His breath quickened to my left, and I knew he'd taken my bait. I stared at my palm, waiting.

"Well, well, well." I heard the rustle of his coat being removed beside me, and I smiled inwardly. "Good evening to you." When I raised my gaze to his, I mocked surprise, forming my mouth into a perfect circle. He tipped a triangular hat in my direction, his smile a seductive invitation.

I flushed as his gaze brushed the length of my body. "Jack!" I tightened my palm around the coins. "Oh, how embarrassing this is." I fluffed my curls with fingers and immediately moved to take the shawl off, positioning myself in an intentionally awkward but alluring position. "I wasn't on duty tonight—b-but, of course, I could be."

His smile deepened. "No need for any of that, my pet." He

gingerly wrapped the shawl around my shoulders, his knuckles brushing the bare flesh above my breasts. "It's far too cold to be shedding oneself of layers. In fact"—he lifted his coat from the back of the seat and nestled me inside—"take mine, too. You're dreadfully cold." His amber eyes twinkled with his smile, and another pang of regret tugged my core. He was nice. It was hard to believe such a man could be so evil. Maybe my visions were wrong? I was still new at auras and visions and the like—could I have been mistaken?

He curled his hand around mine, fisting my hand around my money. "Keep your coins, dear girl." With a gesture at the barkeep, he motioned for another cider. "What brings a sweet thing like you out to the tavern on such a cold night?" He lifted a leg to the bar, leaning closer to me.

I lowered my chin demurely. This man loved his women sweet and innocent. "I just had to get away from the other girls." I gestured to Lucien. "My brother took me away for the night."

Jack threw a glance at Lucien over his shoulder before looking back to me. "The women there—do they treat you well?" Concern sloped at the corners of his eyes.

I shrugged in response. "Well enough, I suppose. When your brother is the owner of the place, they have to keep up appearances."

He cleared his throat. It had been a handful of days since I had seen Jack. Not too long—but for a prostitute, long enough to lose one's virtue and then some. "And I assume business is prosperous?" He pulled back, taking a slug of cider.

The barkeep placed another mug in front of me, and I, too, lifted it to my mouth, making a show of taking a dainty sip. "Oh, indeed," I answered. "For most girls, very."

His brow lifted. "I wasn't asking about most girls, was I?"

I shook my head. "No, but I cannot speak to you of such things."

His breathing was deepening; each inhale–exhale heaved his well-defined chest. "Why is that?"

"It would be dreadfully inappropriate." I lowered my voice, allowing a natural huskiness to take over. I flicked a glance to his trousers; they were tighter around the center, and he snuck a hand down to adjust himself. I turned away, shyly. "I apologize."

He grabbed my hand, squeezing with urgency. "You don't ever have to apologize for that. Not to me." He swallowed, neck muscles tense. "Now tell me—it's only been a couple of days since I saw you last. Have you . . . have you been busy?"

I shook my head. "I've had many offers, but since you . . . since we . . . I can't stop thinking of you." Through my nostrils, I released my pheromone, and his pupils dilated as he unknowingly breathed in my scent.

"I can't describe to you how happy that makes me," he whispered, more to himself.

I offered him a sad smile, pulling my hand back and placing it on the splintered wood bar top. "A man such as you must be spoken for already."

Clearing his throat, Jack took another drink of his cider. "No." His voice was rough, raspy, and clenched with the threat of sorrow.

"No? You mean to tell me you're not wed?"

He stared into his mug, refusing to meet my gaze for what felt like ages. After a long pause, he lifted his gaze to stare straight ahead—still not glancing at me. "Widowed," he answered quietly.

I didn't press anymore. There was no need to. "Well, I'm certain my brother would be none too happy with the thought of losing my business. Or should I say, your business."

Jack's face split into a smile that didn't quite reach his eyes. With peek over his shoulder, he nodded in Lucien's direction. "What's yer brother's poison?"

"*Whiskey.*" *I grinned.* "*And women.*"

"*A man after my own tastes. Shall he and I get acquainted, then?*"

I shook my head, looking to the floor. Though Lucien's eyes stayed straight ahead with his back to us, I knew he was hanging on to each word. "*I'm afraid my brother's only language is that of money and the King.*"

Jack's hand splayed on my hip, the heat from his fingers burning through the layers of my skirts. "*Then he is in good company, my pet. I've got plenty of money and even more Loyalist influence.*"

Ordering a whiskey, he linked his fingers in mine and tugged me toward my boss.

Thirty minutes and three drinks later, Lucien and Jack's bond was a kinship. A brethren of sorts. I watched, in awe of Lucien, both admiring and despising him for his impressive deceit. Glasses clinked, voices sang, and arms embraced him as one of their own. All the while, Jack sat with me, his hand circling my knee higher and higher until his fingers caressed between my legs.

"*Lucien,*" *Jack said, sending me a wink and squeezing my thigh.* "*I must confess, I've grown rather sweet on your sister here.*"

"*Aye,*" *Lucien said, slurring his words and swaying in his seat.* "*She's a regular slice of apple pie, that one is.*" *His body circled, and Jack caught his shoulder just before he fell off the bench.* "*Thank you, my friend.*"

I turned my torso in Jack's direction, brushing my bosom against his elbow. His breath hitched and he slid me a scorching gaze. A smirk twitched at the corner of his lips.

Jack patted Lucien's shoulder. "*Now, about this beautiful flower you've got here . . . what can we do to arrange it so she is available exclusively to me?*"

Lucien hiccupped, convulsing his shoulders with the high-pitched noise. "Not much, I'm afraid." He fell forward on his elbows, leaning in to Jack. "She's my most requested lady. Only wish she was more bloody experienced." He lifted the empty glass to his mouth and dropped it back to the table with disappointment when he realized it was already drained.

"What if she gained experience? With me? I will pay generously."

"Believe me." Lucien's eyelids dipped, cutting his eyes in half. "You can't afford her."

"You might be surprised. I will double her normal rate weekly to be with her as much as I like."

"You need to add another double to that and you'll get her twice a week. And in exchange she sees no one else," Lucien stated, suddenly not slurring nearly as much.

"Now, now, don't try to take me that way. Double. For twice a week, but never in your facilities. She must be available as my escort and in a way that no others in town know she is a strumpet."

I sharply inhaled—bloody Hell, I hated that word.

Lucien paused, and the two held each other's stare in a showdown. "Double does not come close for all of that."

Jack swallowed, glancing around the tavern. A group of his comrades sat at the table next to us, one by one descending into drunken mishaps. It was about that time of night that the tavern crowd begins to dwindle. "Very well." Jack dropped his voice to a husky whisper, eyes still darting around the room. "I have it on good authority that Trenton will be getting quite a few visitors from . . . overseas." He cleared his throat, inspecting that no one was listening in.

Lucien leaned closer. "Go on."

"They will without a doubt be . . . looking for some jolly times. For it will not only be a holiday, but I certainly believe they will have reason to celebrate. Do you follow?"

"When will this be? And for how long can you guarantee me business from these . . . soldiers?"

"They will be here just before Christmas. And will likely be in town for quite a while. I can personally ensure that they go nowhere else for their needs."

Lucien's eyes twinkled, and he grasped Jack's hand in a firm shake. "You arrange the soldiers on top o' your double wages and you've got yourself a deal, sir. My girls would be honored to serve the King's men."

18

Despite its pretty-sounding name, Flower Avenue was a rough part of town. My powers were already masked when I turned myself invisible. And thank Hell for that. I appeared right in front of a handful of prostitutes who appeared to be coming home from work. A massive man followed them, shouting for his portion of their earnings.

The women clung to each other; one's eyes were clamped shut and an older woman held her elbow, dragging her down the sidewalk.

"Listen, bitch," he shouted, speeding up after them. "I know you made more than this tonight. You're not trying to pull a fast one on your daddy, are you?"

Across the street, the lights were on in this Grayson guy's house—but all seemed quiet. "Seemed" being the operative word here. Closing my eyes, the prostitute's chattering teeth and sniffles were thunderous in my ears. I darted for the pimp, taking him out at the knees until he fell face forward onto the concrete sidewalk.

"What the fuck!" he shouted, and I was certain that if any of his buddies had been around to witness how squeaky his voice became, he would have gotten his ass kicked by them. I jammed a knee into the small of his back until I felt his spine against my kneecap. "Who's there?" He reached around with a flailing arm, which I caught with my superhuman strength and pinned behind him until I heard his shoulder pop.

"Your worst nightmare, fucker," I growled in his ear.

He whimpered. "I wasn't doing nothin'—"

"Don't you even start that shit! You will leave those girls alone. You will let them conduct their business and not lay a hand on them. Do we understand each other?"

He didn't answer immediately. I shoved his shoulder higher to his ear, digging my knee into his kidney. "Ah! Yes, yes!" he screamed.

"Good." I pushed off of him to my feet and crossed the street, leaving him writhing in the middle of the sidewalk. I glanced at Grayson's house, then rushed back to the hurt pimp. Picking him up by the collar, I brought my mouth to his ear. "You're coming with me. You're going to talk to a friend of mine and tell him you need help. And that one of your girl's clients dislocated your shoulder. You will not mention me." I dragged him to Grayson's doorstep, and he shouted the entire way. As I let go of his shirt, he crumpled into a sniveling heap at my feet. I rolled my eyes at the pathetic sight and kicked at the door.

"Cry for help . . . get him to open the door or so help me Saetan, I'll give you something to really cry about."

"Help! Please help me!" the pimp shouted.

The tiniest rustling of noise came from the other side of the door and near the window to the side. "Go away." A deep voice called through the door.

"I-I can't. Please help. I'm dying out here."

A pause. "You're fuckin' high. Get outta here."

"N-no, I'm not. I'm clean, I swear it."

The door cracked open and a shadowed eye peered out of the shadows at the man in a pile on his stoop. "Shit," he muttered. "C'mon, man, get up. I can't have this kind of spotlight on my place."

"C-call an ambulance, please."

Grayson didn't answer. "You live around here?"

The pimp whimpered, clutching his shoulder. "Not far."

Grayson opened the door a little wider. I was met with long sandy brown hair flowing to his shoulders, and hazel eyes. A trimmed beard framed full lips. "Shit. Okay, okay. I'll call someone for you. You got a roommate or someone who can pick you up?"

He nodded and Grayson pulled out a cell, leaning against the doorframe, dialing as the pimp fed him some numbers. With the door open, there was just enough room for me to slide inside. I sucked in, thinking small thoughts, and ducked under Grayson's arm into the dark one-story house.

Just as my nose ducked under his forearm, he shifted to lean his back against the frame instead. I held my breath and dodged him, tugging my foot in, just shy of perfect timing. The toe of my chucks brushed his heel. He yelped and swiveled, eyes narrowing with the focus of Sherlock Holmes eyeing the scene of a crime. He whipped a .38 from his back waistband, clicking the safety off.

The pimp shouted, covering his head as best he could.

"Who's there?" Grayson whispered, narrowed gaze burning into his home's darkness. I held my breath and pressed myself against his coat closet in the foyer. Bluish moonlight gleamed off the barrel of the gun and winked in my direction.

"Man! Ain't no one there. Call my damn roommate already!" the pimp shouted from the cement stoop.

With one last scan of the foyer, Grayson nodded and pressed the phone to his ear. Within a few minutes, a black Buick screeched to a halt, and two men huffed their way over to the pimp.

"Get 'im to a hospital," Grayson said quietly to the men.

"Oh, yeah?" The larger of the two climbed the stairs, so full of piss and arrogance, his eyes might as well have been yellow. "You do this to my brother?"

The tiniest flick of a smile tweaked Grayson's mouth. "No. But there's no doubt in my mind he deserved it."

The pimp grunted. "Let's go, J. I need a doctor bad."

His brother moved into a fake punch—as if he were going to head butt him, but Grayson didn't even flinch at the threat. He held his ground at the entrance to his home, arms crossed and gun tucked safely back into his waistband. I kind of liked this guy, I thought with a smirk. He was rogue, refusing to play by Saetan's rules. Something that I, of all people, could respect.

The guys finally drove off, but Grayson's body language was no less tense as he closed the door behind him. He moved swiftly from room to room, darting between furniture and checking under beds and couches. The house was furnished okay—nothing special, but it was no crack house.

Finally he landed in the kitchen, placing his gun on the table and lowering himself into the chair at the head of his laminate, faux-wood table. "I know you're in here," he said, not shouting but also not whispering. It was almost like he was talking to me as if I were sitting right in front of him. "I'm not sure what you're waiting for, but I prefer to get this over with."

Part of me wanted to turn visible right there before him. Show myself and tell him to make a run for it. But then I would never learn who the Contenitore was; and I would never find Lucien. And Lucien meant more than this guy ever would.

I bit my lip and moved out of his line of vision. His eyes stayed where they were and I mentally breathed a sigh of relief. He couldn't see me.

He leaned forward on two elbows, still staring straight

ahead. "I can't sense you—it's strange. You must be something like me, but there's no aura connected." He fingered the handle of his gun, and I noticed the safety was still off. His eyes lifted once more to the wall in front of him. "But I can smell you," he whispered. "And I've got an awfully good nose, my friend. I'll be able to trace that scent anywhere you go." He closed his eyes and on a deep inhalation snapped them back open with a smile.

"Plum blossoms," he said with a rasp. "And vanilla. With a hint of . . ." He put a finger in the air, rolling his eyes to the ceiling. "Yes, a hint of lavender. You switched perfumes recently, is my guess. Maybe three months ago. From lavender to plum blossoms." His eyebrows shot up and, using his palms pressed to the table for support, he rose to his feet, taking the gun with him. "I assume you're not in a chatty mood, my invisible friend. Why the change in scents? A new beau? That's what you women do, isn't it? Get a new man and switch the little things about yourself that you think defines who you are?" He filled a teakettle and put it on the stove. "Probably changed your shampoo, too."

Knots twisted in my stomach like wringing laundry, and I ran a hand through my hair. He was spot on—plum blossoms switched about four months earlier. "I knew there was a lady assassin working for Hell—checked her out myself." He spun and retrieved two mugs from a top cabinet. "You're not her, my friend. She smelled of jasmine."

Silence hung in the air, and he tucked his thumbs into the front pockets of his jeans. His accent had a Texas drawl to it that would probably cause most women to melt at his feet. "No? Still not up for a chat? Okay." He shrugged and grabbed two teabags from a different drawer. "I hope you like mint tea. I love this brand. They use only real mint leaves, and it's great if you need to get some sleep."

He moved around the kitchen with a prowling grace and

though he appeared relaxed on the outside, every muscle was rippled and tensed beneath his clothes. "So, the way I see it, I doubt you're a threat to me. Chances are, you would have ripped into my throat by now if you were taking me in." He stopped, chuckling, and wrapped a teabag around the handle to a mug. "Or—I should say you would have tried." Only it came out "traaahd."

The teakettle whistled, and he poured steaming water into each mug. After an added teaspoon of sugar he sipped, looking up and around the kitchen from the lip of his mug. "So," he said as he hopped into a seated position on the counter, "the way I see it—you're either gaining some sort of intel about me. Or you're madly in love with me." He smirked, and the deepest dimple formed on only one side of his cheek. He inhaled. "No, no . . . I don't smell any arousal. Intel it is." His smile was one that no doubt got him his way every time. I crossed my arms and thought of anything but what those muscles would look like on top of me. "It's a shame, too; it is. You smell purty."

Maybe I should come clean. Open myself up to the guy. Maybe we could help each other?

"You should really drink up before it gets cold. Sugar's on the counter if you take it sweet."

I really didn't count on him pinpointing me so damn quickly. It was infuriating and admirable all at once. He drained the last of his tea, hopping off the counter and dropping the empty mug in the sink. "Well, if you change your mind, I'll be going to bed in a few." He glanced out the window into the night sky. "You should be safe tonight."

He headed for the bedroom, which was behind the kitchen.

"Wait—" The word was out of my mouth before I could think twice to stop myself.

"Well, well, well," he said, spinning in place. "The invisible lady is not a mute. How interesting."

"Put your gun down. Away from you."

He grunted a chuckle, rolling the gun in his hand. "And how do I know you're not armed?"

"Would a promise suffice?"

His response was a lifted eyebrow.

"Yeah, I didn't think so." I sighed. "Do you promise not to shoot?"

"I don't make promises I can't keep." His voice was suddenly harder than marble.

"I'm not here to hurt you. If anything, I think we can help each other."

"Well, then." He set the gun down on the counter between us. "I promise to shoot only if I believe you to be a threat to my freedom."

I could live with that. Of course, up until thirty seconds ago—I *was* a threat to his freedom.

With a deep breath—because I couldn't believe I was actually friending the enemy—I turned visible again, still masking my aura. "I have reason to believe Hell's bounty hunter is coming for you. Tonight."

Grayson's face fell into a scowl, lines and shadows turning him from a cute and shaggy man to an angry beast. "And you thought I needed an audience for it?"

"No," I continued, ignoring the annoying implications of his words, however true they were. He nibbled the inside of his cheek, and from behind his lips his tongue ran across his teeth. "Okay, fine. Yes. But I do actually admire what you're doing. I'm not exactly the most obedient follower of Saetan myself."

"Okay." He crossed his arms, blue veins protruding from massive biceps. "Then show me your entire nature. What sort of demon are you?"

Just as I was about to drop the rest of my mask, the kitchen window blew open. It was just the distraction the Contenitore needed to bust in through the sliding back door. Glass shattered, sprinkling my skin like a biting shower, and a man balled on the floor slowly rose.

His eyes, beginning at my toes and slowly lifting to my legs, torso, and chest like a rising tide, widened as they met mine. Emeralds colliding with sapphires, all breath expelled from my lungs and I couldn't breathe. Stars encroached my vision.

"Monica." His whisper was rough and oozed lust with a sprinkle of bitterness.

"Oh, my Hell," I panted. "Drew."

19

Grayson lunged for his gun, and just as quickly I snapped out of my trance, reaching the handle first with a fumbling grace.

Grayson growled, his sneer flashing newly glistening fangs. "Well, well, well. The prospect of an alliance faded fast, now, didn't it?"

The gun trembled in my hand, and I pointed it to the floor. "Th-this—this isn't the bounty hunter. I-I don't know how he got here, but he's a friend. Drew . . . are you okay?"

"What are you doing here, Monica?" He didn't sound angry, but he didn't exactly sound happy to see me, either.

"Are you fucking kidding me? What am *I* doing here? What are *you* doing here? You're supposed to be in Alaska."

"I was. For a while. And then I was summoned to duty. You telling me you didn't get my postcards?"

I swallowed, not answering.

Grayson hissed from behind me. "I'm not going in alive, man."

Drew's gaze drifted beyond my shoulder to Grayson. "I don't kill. It's my one stipulation. But I am obligated to get you there."

Grayson lunged for Drew, and I dove at his body, rolling on top of him. I straddled the rogue Hellion, my thighs flanking his torso, pinning his arms.

A lazy smile slid across his face and his eyebrows twitched. "Now, darlin', I know you're sweet on me, but now just ain't the time."

Drew's shout startled me enough for my grip on Grayson to slip, and he flipped me over as Drew barreled into him, knocking his body against the wall.

I rubbed at the knot forming on the back of my head and darted to my feet as well, stumbling and dizzy. I shook myself out of the daze and back to the present, where Drew and Grayson were punching and wrestling. Grayson managed to get a large arm around Drew's neck in a headlock.

"Wait! Just fucking wait!" I cocked the gun, pointing the barrel between Grayson's eyes. "Don't think for a second I won't use this."

Grayson released Drew and held up his palms.

I gestured with the gun to the other side of the kitchen. "Get over there."

"As you wish, sugar pie." Grayson sneered.

"And you," I said to Drew. "Get your ass over there." I gestured to the opposite side of the kitchen. "Are you the Contenitore?"

"You got it." His voice was hoarse—whether from sadness or anger, I couldn't be sure.

"You know this Ken doll?" Grayson growled. His grin was anything but pleasant.

Drew's eyes flicked to Grayson's long sandy brown hair, hazel eyes, and tan skin. "You're one to talk."

Grayson flinched in an attempt to attack again. I fired the gun at the now-cold mug of tea he had prepared for me. Grayson froze, his eyes locked on to me. "That's what I thought," I whispered. "Now stay the fuck there until I say otherwise."

Heat prickled my skin and all my hairs raised as I directed my attention back to Drew. "Your escape from Hell—it wasn't really an escape, was it."

"Monica, this really isn't a good time." He gestured in an exaggeratedly polite way to Grayson. "As you can see, I have work to do." I gnashed my teeth together and narrowed my eyes until finally Drew nodded. "Fine. Yes, I found a way out of Hell. Though I wouldn't exactly define it as an 'escape.' In exchange for *not* spending an eternity in Hell, I was sentenced to indentured servitude. For the next twenty years."

"Twenty years," I repeated.

"Twenty years is a helluva lot better than eternity." His eyes swept back to Grayson's, and he raised an eyebrow. "But I refuse to take a life. Even a demon one."

"Who you calling a demon, errand boy?" Grayson chuckled, and I recognized the forced casual gait from our exchange earlier. He leaned against the counter on an elbow.

"Drew, where's Lucien?"

Drew's gaze cut to me. "Your boss?"

"He was closing in on you—and now he's missing."

Drew considered this a moment and concern softened his features. "I don't know, Mon."

"You really think Heaven's gonna let a servant for Hell through their pearly gates?" Grayson snorted and shook his head. "Dumbass. You're just as screwed as the rest of us. Saetan don't make bargains he can't win."

Drew's breath was steady, and he took two steps closer. "I've heard it all, cowboy. You're not getting out of here."

"Well, I suppose you could be right. But y'all gotta catch me first." On a snarl, fur sprouted from his spine and he curled onto all fours. Hands turned to paws, nails to claws, and his nose grew into a snout. Hazel eyes flashed gold, and before I knew it, Grayson was an animal snapping his jaws at each of us.

"Grayson, stop!" He lunged at Drew, who, amazingly, instead of running in the opposite direction, fell forward onto the beast. The two bodies collided and morphed into one, becoming some sort of jellylike substance. Their combined bodies writhed on the floor, screaming. Drew's form quivered, becoming Grayson, then back again to Drew.

I stood with shaky knees and back pressed against wood-paneled walls. The gun trembled in my hand. "Drew?" I whispered.

He crawled to his feet, stumbling back with his hand to his head. "Get out of here, Monica," he rasped.

"What? No . . . I just got you back. I'm not leaving you aga—"

"I said leave!" he shouted, and his eyes snapped to mine. They were black. And not just a darkened shadow sort of black. His irises consisted of dilated pupils only. Gone was the set of sparkling green eyes I loved so dearly.

Fangs snapped from his teeth, fur sprouting on his knuckles and he threw his head back, neck muscles bursting through his skin. And for the second time in less than a year, the ground swirled below Drew, into a black tunnel, and swallowed him whole.

"The vessel," I whispered to no one.

20

Filling everyone in on what happened was certainly not an easy task. And I actually really liked Grayson. I didn't *want* him to get caught. Then again, I didn't want Drew killed, either.

Kayce's olive face drained of color. "Who's going to tell Adrienne?" she whispered. Silence hummed and all eyes darted around.

I squeezed my eyes shut, issuing a little prayer that someone else would step up. Of all the people to tell her, I am the last person she would want to talk to. Adrienne was human not too long ago. Not only human, but a witch who was Damien's partner and Drew's girlfriend. When she died saving me, she became Julian's angel mentee.

One by one they all landed on me. "Oh, c'mon," I said with an exacerbated sigh. "Why not Jules? He's the mentor!"

Jules's crystal eyes tilted down, sad lines creasing around his mouth. "I will tell her. But I'm not sure she will believe it from me."

"You're an angel! You can't lie! Besides, what makes you think she'll find me so trustworthy?"

Jules swallowed. "Because you saw him with your own eyes. And she'll see that you're not lying."

"Fuck," I hissed. "Adrienne is going to—"

"Adrienne's going to what?" The bells above the café door jingled together like a heavenly choir trumpeting the angel's arrival.

The group stilled into one collective statue garden. After what felt like a lifetime . . . but was actually closer to a few seconds, I hopped to my feet, shuffling behind the barista bar. "You want your usual? Chai latte?"

"Umm, sure." Adrienne's gaze narrowed and she lowered herself into a seat. "I'm thinking I'll probably need it, based on everyone's faces." With flared nostrils, her eyes flitted from one face to the next, landing finally on Jules's. All color drained from her normally overtanned cheeks. "Oh, no. Please no . . . it's Drew, isn't it? He's—he's . . ."

"No," Jules cut in as though he could read her very thoughts. "He's not dead."

I finished steaming the milk, sprinkled some nutmeg on top, and dropped a cinnamon stick in as a stirrer. The ceramic mug billowed steam out the top and warmed my clammy palms.

Adrienne took the mug from me and exhaled. Pinching a silver cross around her neck, she twisted the clasp. "Oh, thank goodness. Then what is it? Did you find him?"

All eyes once again turned to me. Well, here goes nothing. "We did find him—er, I found him. But Adrienne, he didn't escape from Hell. He was released."

"Okay . . ." Her eyes were steadied on mine. As though if she stared at me hard enough, she could gain all the answers to the underworld. "Isn't that a good thing?"

I cleared my throat and continued. "Mostly. But in exchange for his freedom, Drew had to commit to twenty years of servitude to Hell. As a bounty hunter."

Her head snapped to Kayce. "You!"

Kayce's hands flew up, surrender style. "I had nothing to do with this! Drew's become one of the most notorious bounty hunters. No one knows him by name—only as Contenitore. The Vessel."

"He can absorb demons and bring them to Hell within his body . . . without killing or harming them."

"No," she whispered. "He's allowing himself to be possessed?"

I nodded. "I don't think he knew what he was getting himself into."

"His soul would be better off if he just annihilated the demons!"

Jules's hand squeezed Adrienne's shoulder. "Let's not get carried away. Murder of any sort, even of our Hell-ridden counterparts, is not condonable." His voice was understanding but still stern.

"How would you know?" she snapped. "And when did you start caring so much about the lives of demons?"

"Adrienne . . ." Jules hushed, rubbing her back in slow circles.

"Any chance of a loophole in his contract?" she asked, her platinum hair flipping off her shoulder as she looked at each of us.

Kayce shook her head. "Not a chance. Those things are airtight."

"Fine. His soul would have been better off if he'd just died then." There was nothing behind her eyes. They were void of emotion as she stared into her chai latte.

"You don't mean that," I offered gently.

She stood, setting the barely touched latte down. "I really do," she said. "There's a lot I can overlook as an angel. But a man who allows himself to be possessed time after time by demons?" She shook her head and the sentence faded. "Drew is dead to me."

"He didn't know any better," I offered quietly. "I can't imagine Hell is a comfortable place for a demon—let alone a human. He would have died down there."

"Yes, but then Saetan would have had to release him to Heaven. With how clean his soul was, not even the devil himself could have kept Drew immersed in flames."

She was right—but I was certain Drew had no idea of that. And I couldn't help that queasy feeling in my stomach that if we had all revealed ourselves sooner, his soul could have been spared.

Kayce's eyes widened. "That's exactly why Saetan offered him the release. He knew Drew couldn't survive in the depths of Hell for long. And once he perished, he'd no longer have a hold on his soul."

Damien's eyes narrowed. "So? What does Saetan care about keeping a random dude's soul?"

Kayce shrugged, clicking her long fingernails against her coffee cup. "I dunno. But it makes sense, doesn't it? Now with Drew released and working for him, there's a fifty-fifty chance that when Drew dies, his soul will go to Hell."

"So the question is, what does Saetan want with Drew's soul . . ." I pressed two fingers to my temples, rubbing in circles.

". . . and what the Hell does Lucien's disappearance have to do with any of it?" Kayce finished my thought.

Adrienne smoothed her linen blazer and matching pants before tilting her chin just a tad too high to be believable. "I don't know. And Lucien is certainly not our concern, Jules." With one final, pointed glance at her angel mentor, she walked to the door. "You should have nothing to do with this case, Julian." With that, she exited, letting the door slam shut behind her.

21

New Jersey, 1776

*S*now crunched beneath my feet, and Jack's hand was frigid against mine. *"How are your hands so impossibly warm in this bitter winter?"*

His skin was chilled and rough as he raised my knuckles to his lips.

"I'm always steaming when in your presence, Jack," I answered with a grin.

There was a primal purr beneath his breath. Using my hand, he tugged me closer to his side. *"More of that talk, my pet, and we will both have chapped backsides from this snow right here."*

I had more powers than I'd ever had in my existence. I didn't know what to do with myself. I could appear in any form without so much as losing breath. It was glorious and empowering and yet was a constant reminder of the cheap trollop I was. Though Jack wasn't the strongest fix I'd ever received, he was the most constant. Lots of little meals will certainly keep one's belly full.

And I was helping the Patriots, Lucien reminded me. So each bit of his life was not taken in vain. They needed every bit of help I could offer.

Jack and I had been together now three more times. Each vision was stronger than before, and I wasn't sure I could trust my other sight. The visions of Jack—with young soldiers—children, really, who were merely fighting for a cause they believed in and killing them in cold blood, smiling as his bayonet pierced their tattered Patriot uniforms. Could my tender lover be such a cold-blooded killer? Lucien claimed that the visions don't lie . . . but he was one to talk. How many lives had the demon taken without so much as a second thought? He had no right judging Jack. Not yet. Hell, maybe not ever.

"Oh, Jack, I wish you would." I eyed the snowdrift. "You could have me here. With the snowflakes dropping tiny kisses to my body."

He chuckled, sliding his tongue along my ear and nipping the base. "You devilish little thing, you. And to think just a few days ago, you were an eye-batting virgin." His palm ran the length of my torso until it finally found the heavy cup of my breast. He kneaded my swollen flesh through the layered fabric of my dress. Using two fingers, he rolled my firm nipple. With another glance around the area, he tugged me forward, his hand returning to mine. "Come," he commanded. "My place is not far."

We walked a bit more until we came to his home. He opened the door for me, and as soon as I was over the threshold, I wrapped my legs around his waist, pressing my needy body against his firmed trousers. His lips ran the length of my neck.

"Father!" A young man's voice at the base of the staircase shouted.

"Bloody Hell," Jack rasped, pushing away from me in haste. He straightened his clothing, and I did the same. "Tom, what are you doing home from school?"

I examined the boy from the top of his head to his toes, narrowing my eyes. It was the boy from my vision—I was certain of it. The boy I saw Jack stabbing, enjoying the kill.

He couldn't have been older than eighteen. And he wore a

Patriot uniform. Jack sneered looking over the clothing choice as well, his eyes landing on the gun in Tom's hands. "Planning to steal my musket? After I pay for your education at Yale?" He advanced on his son, voice booming, eyes fiery. "After everything I have done for you—you betray me, nay, your King this way!"

Tom's eyes darted from his father to me and back again. "And this must be your latest betrayal to mother, yes?" He rolled his tongue around his mouth as if chewing something invisible. "Welcome to the family, whore."

Jack was upon his son in seconds, fisting his jacket collar and slamming his head into the wall behind them. "It is a sin to disobey your father!"

A knock at the door caused everyone to freeze. Jack threw his son back to the wall, releasing his jacket, and stalked to the door, throwing it open wildly. I shrunk back into the corner. "What?" he growled.

It was one of the other Loyalists I had seen around the tavern. "Meeting at Bear's. Now."

Jack grumbled to himself and, with closed eyes, scratched the back of his neck. "I'm coming." Spinning, he faced his son and held up a finger to his face. "You are going back to school, boy. You will not be participating in this sorry excuse for a war."

Tom's smirk was cold and barely lifted. "You can keep paying all you want, father. I will not be returning."

Jack's jaw ground to the point I could hear his teeth scraping against each other. With a hiss, he turned to me, anger melting with the swivel. He cupped a hand around my jaw. "I'm sorry, my pet. Tomorrow?"

I nodded and managed a squeaky reply. "Tomorrow."

His kiss was barely a brush of his lips across mine. He left, slamming the door behind him, and I peered out the window, watching him walk away.

I cleared my throat, stealing a quick look at the boy. "Does he do that often?"

Tom's chuckle was bitter. "Upon every visit home. I got what I came for." He held the gun up, shaking it in my direction. "And I look forward to the day I use this exact gun on him."

"Tom, no—that, that's a terrible sin. One that is difficult to atone for—"

His cackling laugh cut me off midsentence. "Really? The whore teaching me the ways of the Bible?"

I shivered despite the crackling warmth of the fire and rubbed my hands across my upper arms. "You're right." I nodded. "You're right. I am a hypocrite. But that doesn't make me wrong." I held his gaze; his eyes were the same honey color as his father's, but with fewer wrinkles framing the corners.

"And I suppose you're a Tory as well? Believing that this tax is nothing?"

I licked my lips. Could I tell him? Perhaps find a way to spare his life and have someone on the Patriot side to report my findings back to? "And what if I said I was not? What if I told you I was the same as you?"

He snorted. "I'd say you had a lot to prove. Firstly, just exactly why are you spending your evenings with my Tory father?"

Did it matter if I told him? He would die in a matter of weeks anyway at his father's hands. "I am gathering information. For the Patriots."

After a moment, Tom shook his head, brushing past my shoulder. "What a load of sod."

"It's true. I can bring you to meet my partner. We don't know exactly our role in this, but your father—he's an arrogant old sow. He's apt to have a slip of the tongue sometime."

The butt of the musket clattered against the floor. Using it as a cane of sorts, Tom sauntered over to me, stopping just in front of my nose. "Arrogant?" A smile curved on his lips. "I think I like you."

I returned his smile. "Just don't like me too much." I nar-

rowed my eyes, pulling him out of focus in an attempt to read his aura. I couldn't be sure—but I thought it was a robin's egg sort of blue. The color itself reminded me of Heaven.

"What?" He glanced down at his uniform, checking it for stains and missing buttons.

"I'll bring you to Lucien on one condition."

His nostrils flared.

"You are not allowed to utilize the services of any of our women. Myself included." I held out a hand, suspended, waiting for his answer.

His smirk returned, and he grabbed my hand in a firm shake. He raised an eyebrow. "Done. Unlike my father, I don't need to pay women for their time."

Arrogant. Just like his father.

22

I had just gotten home from opening the coffee shop, and I fell into my favorite spot on the couch, throwing my feet up on the ottoman.

A heavy knock on my door echoed through my home. I closed my eyes, letting the back of my head rest on the couch and rubbing my fingers to my temples. Maybe if I was really quiet, they would just go away.

The next knock was less courteous and more of a pounding fist. I rocked myself forward and onto two feet. "Coming, coming!" Jeez. Impatient assholes.

I peeked an eye through the peephole and froze when I saw Drew standing on my doorstep. He glanced over one shoulder with a sharp turn of his head. Then, a second later, he looked over the other shoulder. "C'mon, Mon. I know you're in there. Let me in." Then he added, "And don't call anyone else."

"Let me see your eyes," I said through the door.

His smile was soft and his sigh was one of relief, not annoyance. "I'm glad you asked," he said with an approving nod. Widening his eyes, he moved them closer to the peephole. They were their normal sparkling green. I unlatched my door and opened it to him. My friend. My Drew was finally home. I hoped this time for good.

"Hey." His grin warmed me, sending spiraling tingles down to my knees.

"Hey back at you," I whispered, and ran a thumb across his lips, taking extra time to trace the paper-thin scar on his top lip. "I'm a little surprised to see you here."

"Yeah," he said, and followed me into the kitchen.

There were dark, purplish bags under his eyes that hadn't been there before. His shoulders slumped more, and he had less of a bounce in his step. But his body—wow. He had twice the muscle I had seen on him a few months ago. Where he once bore the lean, but powerful, body of a soccer player, he now practically busted out of his white Hanes T-shirt. His size easily rivaled Damien's. His forearms were littered with veins like various highways to his heart.

There was so much to say and yet nothing to say all at once. "Can I get you something? Coffee . . . tea?"

He smiled. "If it would make you feel better."

"I think it would." I filled the coffee filter and got the machine brewing. "Drew—have you talked to Adrienne?"

His head dropped, and he suddenly became focused on my kitchen tiles. "I tried calling. She shouted something into the phone about me being dead to her and hung up."

It wasn't necessarily funny, but part of me wanted to have been there for that.

He shrugged, stuffing his hands into his pockets. "It's okay. I really didn't know what to say to her anyway."

There was another long pause as the coffee finished brewing, and I fixed us each a cup.

I chuckled, passed him his mug, and dropped into the chair across from him. "Is this you as a conversationalist? 'Cause otherwise I'd say you don't exactly have much to talk to me about, either."

He chuckled, but it was quiet. Tired. "I suppose. But you never minded a bit of silence."

The steam from my cup billowed up to the ceiling, and I blew on the top. Not because I needed to, but for lack of anything else to say. "Are you—are you okay?"

Drew nodded. "I'm alive."

"But for how long?"

Another moment of silence swallowed the conversation. He shook his head. "I couldn't stay down there another minute, Monica. I couldn't do it."

I nodded. "I understand."

"But I did learn some stuff down there."

I raised my eyebrows. "Oh, yeah?"

He pressed his lips together and nodded. "Yeah. You're quite the talk of the town. Angelic past, rocky historical start to being a succubus . . . and now. It's—it's why you would never . . ." The words faded, and he cleared his throat. "It's why we never worked out, isn't it?"

I didn't answer at first—how could I? Instead I sipped my coffee, letting the bitter brew wash over my tongue. After swallowing, I finally spoke. "Not because I didn't want to. But you deserved better."

He nodded, then leaned back in the chair, leg bouncing as though it was separate from his body. He chewed his cuticle until he realized he was doing it—at which point, he lowered that hand back to his lap. "I get it. I do." A sharp breath exhaled through his nose—part breath, part chuckle—and he ran a hand through his hair, landing behind his neck. He stayed in that position, kneading his neck muscles. "It just makes me love you that much more for it."

Everything inside of me tightened with that four-letter word. The absolute best word you could hear coming from a guy like Drew. My heart slammed against my ribs, like a creature with a mind of its own, throwing itself at a cage to be released. And my blood—my heated blood rushed through every vein with an urgency that wasn't there moments ago.

His knee stopped bouncing and his eyes landed on mine—he was still for the first time since his arrival. "My status now—as the bounty hunter for Hell—does that change anything?"

I swallowed. "As in . . . does that mean I can no longer steal bits of your life with my poisonous vagina?"

One eyebrow arched over a jade eye and he laughed, shaking his head. "Some things don't change."

"And unfortunately, one of those things that doesn't change is my nature. As long as you're human, I can never be with you." I frowned, regretting the statement, despite how true it was.

"But if I was—"

"No. Don't even say it—"

"—like you. Or your boss. Then we could?"

I closed my eyes, willing the tears at bay. "Drew . . . I know this is horrible to say. But if you were like me, I'm not sure I would love you in the same way. Part of what I love about you is how good you are."

"Monica," he whispered, and covered my hand with his. "George is still good. Kayce, Lucien—they're all good souls, even though they're damned. And you—" He chuckled, eyes crinkling with the smile. "*You're* a demon . . . and you're still good."

I snorted, refusing to make eye contact. "Am I?" My response was so quiet even I could barely hear it.

"Yes."

"What about Adrienne?" I slid my hand out from under his.

"She said it all already, didn't she? I'm dead to her."

"Well, yeah, but she doesn't mean that—"

From his back pocket, he slipped his phone out. "This is the message that made me call her in the first place." Placing it in the center of my table, he hit a button and Adrienne's voice boomed from the speakerphone. "We're done. You and me. I could accept your friendship with Monica. I could get over you ignoring me for months. I could even get over that stupid tattoo you got when you were eighteen." Her voice broke and there was a quiet sniffle. "But you work for the devil. And that's something I cannot forgive."

The line clicked off, and my jaw dropped. "She broke up with you in a voice mail?"

Drew shrugged. "To be fair, I haven't exactly been answering my phone much lately."

"Are you okay?" I looked him over—he seemed okay. Emotionally speaking. Physically, he looked like Hell. But that's what weekly demon possession will do to a guy, I suppose.

His mouth tilted a fraction. "I am. She's right, too. I'm not good enough for her." He paused. "I'm not so sure *she's* all right, though."

I nodded. "I'll check on her later."

Drew rolled his eyes, his grin widening. "Oh, I'm sure *that'll* help. Maybe see if Jules'll do it."

"Hey!" I slapped his shoulder and grinned. God, it felt good to smile. A bit rusty, but good all the same. "Adrienne and I have come a long way since you left."

Drew's smile was a lungful of fresh air after being in a smoky room. It was genuine and the boost I needed these days. And it made his chin dimple look that much more pronounced. My stomach flopped, remembering the time we had made love right here—on my kitchen table. I had nipped that chin dimple until he sighed in submission. Actually, he nipped me into submission, though I didn't like to admit that to many.

"What are you smiling about?" He eyed me from over the lip of his coffee mug.

"Oh, just the usual." I accidentally glanced down to his crotch—honestly, not meaning to. He laughed, a loud and abrupt outburst that I was helpless to resist joining. My face fell forward into my hands. "I'm sorry! I'm terrible, I know!"

"Such a tease." His voice lost the playful chuckle and took on a new tone. A rasp that was dark and sexy. He stood, walking around to my side of the table, kneeling with a hand on each knee. My legs fell open with the gentlest guidance.

"Drew, no . . ." I ran my fingers through his hair as he pressed his lips to the inside of my thigh. His fingers traced up my other leg until his hand was covered by my skirt. He hooked a finger into the string that rested on my hip and slid that same finger down until he brushed my clit. I gasped and clenched my hand in his hair, grasping his hand.

"No," I said harder this time. "I mean it. I can't. And not just because you're . . . you. I'm with Damien still."

His hand brushed that sensitive spot once more—whether intentionally or not, I wasn't sure—nor did I want to know.

He fell back onto his heels, and I snapped my legs closed. Heat burned my cheeks, and my arousal flared in every part of my body. "Well, that's a damn shame," he rasped.

My throat was dry, but Hell if I wasn't wet everywhere else. "Drew, back away. I'm not sure I can stop myself if you don't." I gnashed my teeth together and brought my mind to cats. Lots of cats. And the smell of a litter box. And, um, and a ninety-year-old man getting a sponge bath. But even with these awful thoughts, the raging itch for not just any life force, but Drew's life force, flared through my body. It was painful, like how I would imagine swallowing poison ivy would feel. A burning, ripping sensation from the inside out.

"Even more reason for me to stay." He climbed to his feet but leaned over above me, his hands on the back of my chair.

I clamped my eyes shut, but I could feel, hear, and sense his breath just above my lips. As his mouth met mine, a vibrating buzzed from my purse, hung on the back of the chair. I jumped and Drew straightened. "Damn. I *wish* I was that good," he said with a wink.

I scrambled in my bag and, checking to find Kayce's name

lighting up my screen, answered. "Hey." I stood and signaled to Drew that I needed a moment.

"Girl, where are you?" Panic strangled in her throat.

I slipped into my bedroom, shutting the door behind me. "I'm home. Why?"

A gush of air was so loud in the phone, I was surprised my hair didn't blow with the breeze of it. "Good. Stay there. I'm coming over. You alone?"

"No, Drew's here."

There was silence on the other end.

"Kayce? What's going on?"

Her voice dropped to a whisper. "Get out of the house, Monica. Go."

"But—"

"The woman who manages my assignments called me just now. *You* are Drew's next bounty. He's there to take you in."

23

I hung up, numbness taking over my body. There was no way Drew was here to drag me off to Hell. Especially not when he had just attempted to seduce me! *No, no.* There must be an explanation.

My bedroom door creaked open, the noise reflective of my creaky heart. When I peered out the door, Drew had resumed his seat at the table, leaning back with his arm stretched out resting on top.

With a forced bounce in my step, I headed back, sliding into the chair next to his. Drew's head tilted. "Who was that?"

I opened my mouth to speak—but then realized Kayce would tip him off to my knowledge of the bounty. My voice cracked as I answered. "Ju-Julian."

"Ju-Julian?" He repeated with a twitch of his neck and a smile that didn't reach his eyes.

I cleared my throat and tried again. "Yep, Jules."

He laughed, shaking his head and falling forward with two forearms rested on his knees. "For a demon, you are one terrible liar."

"I don't know what you're talking about."

White knuckles clasped his knees, and he used his weight to push off of them into a standing position. "Well, c'mon. Let's do this." He flipped his hand, gesturing for me to join him on me feet.

"Do what?" Suspicion now raged in my body, and I hated that feeling of dread; sick dread that rose like vomit from my stomach to the back of my throat.

"You know." He twitched his head to the floor. "Don't worry. I looked over your file closely. It's not a banishment— I'd never take you in for that," he added quieter. "They just need to ask you some things. I promise that no harm will come to you. And I'll have you home by dinner."

"*They?*"

"Yes, they. Fuck, Monica, c'mon. Don't make this any harder."

Drew spat the F-word and it was like a bucket of icy water being splashed onto me. Sure, I'd heard him use bad language now and then, but never so casually.

My forced cordiality hardened to marble and cracked around the edges along with my trust of him. "Fuck you," I hissed, backing into my kitchen. If I could just get to the knife drawer I could maybe defend myself. "What exactly was your plan here? Screw me and drop me to the depths of Hell with the forceful jet stream of your cumshot?"

His movement was equally calculated as he took a single step forward. "I'm sorry for that. I lost my head a little in your presence. You have that effect on men, you know."

I wasn't sure if the latter was meant as a compliment, but judging from the deep set scowl on his face, I doubted it. "Uh-huh."

"Believe me. Don't believe me. It's your choice. But coming to Hell? That's not." He held a hand out for me to take. "Not this time, at least."

Without thinking, my fingers twitched, almost reaching for

his out of habit. Instead, I managed to hold firm, hands balled into fists at my side.

His curved in a *come hither* movement. "We can do it the fun way or the hard way."

Narrowing my eyes, I glanced at him through the corners. Long lashes created a haze around his body and distorted Drew into a sort of ethereal fuzziness. "What's the fun way?"

"Come find out." His eyebrow twitched and, for all of a moment, I thought I saw a hint of a smile.

"The funny thing about that? I'm a demon, Drew. You're still a mortal." I closed my eyes and imagined myself in Kayce's living room. Magic shimmered around me and where there would normally be a blast of power teleporting me elsewhere, all I got was a faint static. I opened my eyes, still in my own kitchen—only in that split second, Drew had managed to move directly in front of me. Barely an arm's length away. "Shit," I whispered.

"It is funny, isn't it? You Hellspawn are so predictable. Luckily, I didn't leave Hell without a few tricks of my own." His eyes were sharp and his smile pointier than the tip of a knife.

I darted for the bedroom, but his arms snatched my waist before I could move even an inch. His muscles were rocks around me, but I pressed forward regardless. Spinning in his grasp, our noses smashed together and I headbutted him. Blood spurted from a fresh gash, forming a scarlet river down the side of his nose. I took the moment to knee him in the gut, but still he held firm around my waist.

I threw a punch, but he caught my wrist. I tried again with the other hand—he caught that one, too. I writhed in his grasp, unsuccessfully twisting my hands to get out of his grip. He threw me against the pantry door, and his weight on mine was hot. In so many ways.

He pinned my wrists above my head. "C'mon. Don't make me take you forcefully," he said, eyes dipping at the corners.

"If I recall correctly," I grunted, "you like it forceful." I trailed my nose along his jaw, the five o'clock shadow scraping my skin.

With a light brush of my lips across his, he parted his mouth and met me halfway with an open mouth kiss. For all of a second, I closed my eyes and just as I felt the black magic taking grip on my body, I bit down onto Drew's lip. Blood pooled on my tongue.

He screamed, letting go of one wrist but still holding firm on the other. He lifted his hand to his bloody lip, shouting. Leveraging his own grip on me, I threw him over my counter. Various pots and plates shattered and clanked onto the floor. But not even that momentum could get him to let go of my wrist, and I went spiraling over the counter with him.

He groaned and with his one free hand reached around, pulling a frying pan out from under the small of his back. "Sonuvabitch," he groaned.

A shattered piece of one of my plates rested next to me, and I stretched, grasping it so tight in my hand that hot blood spurted from my palm. With a grunt, I swiped at Drew's chest, and he dodged the hit, rolling me onto my back and pinning me beneath two massive thighs.

"Say uncle?" His breath heaved, and sweat poured along his bloody nose.

But he made a grave mistake—he left my hands free. With all the force I had left in me, I threw a punch at his balls, locking my own grip and squeezing until he had his second case of blue balls for the day.

A man's junk—it's a target that will never fail you. I pulled myself to my feet, dragging my twisted ankle behind me. If I could just make it to the front door I could get away from Drew and teleport elsewhere.

"Monica!" he shouted.

But I didn't look back. It sounded close—too close to take the half a second to see. Large hands landed on my shoulders and spun me to face him yet again. I hit him once more. And then again. And again. Pounding my fists into his chest, but it was my own that hurt. Sobs rose from within me, and before I knew it, my nose was buried between Drew's pecs, my tears drenching his shirt.

He brushed his fingers though my hair, the heat of his hand finally resting on the back of my head. His chest rose and fell in large, heaving breaths.

"Please don't take me there, Drew. Please. I'll do anything."

"I promise this isn't permanent. I'll be taking you home within an hour. Two, tops."

"Why didn't you just force the magic on me? Like you did with Grayson?"

He smiled, brushing a fallen piece of hair behind my ear. "I told you. I didn't want to force you." Both eyebrows arched and he examined my face, eyes flitting back and forth between mine. "Ready?" He held a hand out, despite the fact that I was cradled into his body.

With one last, deep breath, I dropped my hand into his palm. The floor was wobbly beneath me like I was suddenly standing on top of Jell-O. Only, I was pretty sure it was my shaky nerves and not anything supernatural. Yet.

I rolled my shoulders back and stood taller, meeting his eyes with a daring look. "Well?"

His tongue darted out to wet his lips, and he dipped his body to mine. Heat radiated off of him like some sort of furnace that, combined with the Vegas summer, caused a trickle of sweat to glide down my temple immediately. I shifted it away, getting rid of my dewy skin while I was at it.

Drew chuckled and rolled his eyes. "If you think *this* is hot . . ." His lips parted against mine, moist, warm . . . delicious. And suddenly I wasn't sure if he was referencing Hell or his lips being hotter. My tongue ran the length of the seam at his lips, and I gasped as his tongue found mine, nudging my mouth wider. The cut from my bite moments before didn't seem to hurt him, but I carefully avoided it anyway.

He took my hand, holding it out at our sides. Palm to palm, it felt as though my hand was going through his. Like we were one entity swirling in space.

God, I love her. Please let her be safe.

Drew? Was that Drew speaking? The words echoed in my mind, and though I could still feel his lips, something was different.

I blinked and my apartment was still there, but—but it was different. Two coffee mugs sat on the table. My purse still hung on the back of my chair. Pots and broken plates were scattered on the floor. My pantry door was broken, hanging off its hinges. I moved to grab for my purse, but nothing happened. My arms were lifeless, unmoving.

You don't need your purse right now.

Drew?

It's okay, Monica. There was a sigh. Mine? Drew's? I wasn't sure.

A swirling blackness wrapped my body—our bodies—like a silk scarf and twirled us in a gentle dance. My feet landed on dirt that squished beneath me. Air expanded in my lungs, even though I had not been the one to take a breath.

Step forward, Monica.

I did as he said. The movement was foreign, like trying to walk on the ocean floor. But as my foot extended forward, landing on the ground, it was like I was thrown into a wind tunnel, moving ninety miles per hour. Reality whooshed back to me.

Red clay dirt squished beneath my toes. But it wasn't the usual clay dirt—it had a consistency like moss. But red. An oppressive, stagnant heat sat on top of me. And a feeling of dread bounced in the pit of my stomach.

I was in Hell.

24

I looked down at my naked body—it was different. I was different. Different than the shape Drew knew as Monica, though I still bore many similarities. I was younger. In my teens with stringy blond hair that fell past my breasts. And speaking of breasts—these were not nearly as impressive as the ones I shifted. They were perky, but at least a size smaller.

My eyes shot up to Drew's, and I immediately covered myself with both hands.

Drew was entranced. Eyes not on my body but on my face. With trembling fingers, he reached over, brushing the dirty hair from my face and tracing my jaw.

Drew was also naked, only not nearly as ashamed of his body as I. He swallowed visibly and reached for something hanging on a ratty wall next to us. He passed the cloth to me, and I quickly scrambled to shove my arms inside, wrapping the satin fabric around my body.

"Earthly possessions can't pass through the gateway."

I nodded and licked my lips. My throat was suddenly parched even though I knew rationally that I was not a being that needed water to survive.

He studied my face another moment. "This is you," he whispered. "Your human form. It's . . . it's almost exactly the woman I know, but—but . . ."

". . . younger?" I finished for him.

He nodded. "Everyone so far who is a shapeshifter looks massively different than they did as a human. You—"

I nibbled the inside of my cheek, shifting my eyes away from him. "I didn't want to forget where I came from."

The heat was not only sweltering but thick and heavy, draining my body of any moisture or coolness it could maintain. The humidity sat on me like a wool blanket in the middle of summer.

"C'mon." Drew gestured to the one-room cottage beside us. "I require an area for me to get water while I'm here. It'll be the only reprieve you get for a while."

I followed his lead as he opened a heavy door, holding it open for me. "You take all your bounties here?"

He winked, but his smile wasn't exactly full. "Only the beautiful ones."

After some cold water and dampened cloth around my neck, we set out. "You know what I'm here for?"

Drew shook his head and opened a door leading into a pitch-black hallway. Hell was a mystery—with twists and turns. One minute you're walking outside, the next you're in a dungeon, then you turn the corner and it's as if you're in a drab office building. The whole thing is one big illusion set to each individual's Hellish standards.

I paused, glancing through the doorway to blackness. Was there any way to delay this? Dread dropped to the pit of my stomach, rolling around as if my belly were an empty playground.

Drew shook his head. "All I know is that they need to see you."

"Who's they?"

Drew shrugged. "Not sure. But considering I work for the, uh, main guy . . . he would be my guess."

"Fuck. Me."

"You've never met him before?" His eyebrows knitted together.

I flung my hands in the air, feeling suddenly panicked. My breath shortened. "I've never even been to Hell before, Drew! Lucien used to handle this shit for me!"

"Well," Drew said. "No Lucien now."

"Yeah. Thanks for nothing," I grunted. "You coming?"

"No. I have to wait here to take you back home."

Home. Thank Hell. If I wasn't going home, they wouldn't bother having Drew stick around.

His hand jetted out, fastening onto my elbow just as I lifted my foot to cross the threshold. "Leave the towel with me. They'll annihilate us both if they see that."

As if they don't know already. They can probably see everything down here. Shit, they can probably see everything up at home, too.

I tossed him the towel, which he swung around the back of his neck. "And, Monica?"

I raised my eyebrows, not trusting my voice to answer him.

"Don't believe what you feel while you're here. The dread— the hopelessness; none of it is real."

"I don't feel hopele—"

"Not yet." He nodded to the door. "Once you step foot in there, it will be overwhelming."

I swallowed. "Well, here goes nothing."

"I'll see you soon." He squeezed my elbow in a way I was certain was meant to be reassuring. But it simply acted as a reminder that I should be afraid. Very fuckin' afraid.

25

The long corridor of Hell was dark, and the path was lit with candled sconces. The door slammed shut, the sound bouncing off the walls and playing tricks on my oversensitive ears.

Even though the heat was sweltering, there was a cold feeling of dread tingling in my bones. Hopelessness didn't even begin to describe it. My feet were heavy, like two cement blocks had been affixed to them. I trudged along.

Placing a palm to the stone wall, I expected it to be cool to the touch. Only it was scorching. Like cement on a sunny summer day.

"Shit," I hissed, and cradled my hand with the other.

I suppose you could consider me lucky for never having to experience this until now. But in this moment, I felt anything *but* lucky. I shivered despite the heat and ran my hand over the pebbled gooseflesh rising on my arms. If I squinted, I could see a door ahead—the only door anywhere in front of me. Tired of this feeling, this emptiness, I ran for the door, taking off at a sprint.

Though I knew it was irrational, I checked over my shoulder. Was someone following me? Blackness morphed into shapes and shadows looming over me, and I slammed into the door. I pulled the knob. Then pushed. Something groaned from over my shoulder, and I frantically tried the door again.

It didn't budge. What the fuck?

Monica.

The voice stilled my panicked body. Lucien?

Monica . . .

"Lucien!" I called out, turning and pressing my back to the locked door. The shadow morphed into the shape of a man. Little by little, color drifted into the shadow, creating the most opaque version of Lucien. What was that that Drew had said? None of it was real?

I could just barely make out Lucien's eyes and ponytail. The smoky hand lifted for my face and as it brushed my skin, the smoke swirled around my head in a thick fog. The creature's touch left an icy chill. It would have been a nice reprieve had I not felt it in my bones, down to the marrow.

The door behind me clicked open with no fanfare. I pulled away, the dim light inside crooking its finger.

Monica . . . do not leave me . . .

Shit, it felt so real. It was Lucien's voice; it had to be. Was he here? Banished to Hell?

The door creaked open more, and I snapped my head back and forth between the shadowy figure and the reason I was actually here.

As I stepped toward Lucien, a scream came from inside the chamber. When I looked back to Lucien—the shadow—he was gone. I was left standing alone in an almost pitch-black hallway.

I sprinted across the threshold to find Grayson, hung on the wall. Nothing and no one was around him. He was nude and screaming bloody murder, body flinching as though something were striking him. He tensed once more before his head fell forward in nearly silent sobs.

"Oh, fuck. Grayson!" I ran to his side to help, but as I reached to undo the knots around his wrists, fire licked my skin. Below his feet, I saw snakes, jaws unhinged and snapping at his toes. I screamed, falling back onto my hands and ass. Scooting myself away from him, the slithery creatures disappeared. A shiver danced down my spine and his golden eyes lifted, momentarily catching mine. Fear jumped behind his eyes before he tensed, rearing his head back with yet another yelp of pain.

Only Grayson's pain looked higher—around the torso. Not where I saw the snakes snapping at his feet.

"Fascinating, isn't it?" a smooth voice said behind me.

I scrambled to my feet, searching the room for something—anything that could be used as a weapon. Air heaved in my chest with every breath I took. No matter how many times I inhaled, I swear I couldn't breathe.

"Hushhhh." Wiry fingers raised in my face with a gentle gesture that left me more unnerved than comforted. "You are safe. You are not here for any sort of torture device like our lycanthrope here."

"Wh-why snakes?"

The man chuckled, and I wondered if he even understood humor. His lack of empathy chilled me. "Hell is in the eye of the beholder. It's different for everyone. You see snakes. He sees his father tearing him to shreds."

I snuck another glance at the man before me. He looked . . . normal, for lack of a better word. He wore a robe similar to mine, but it was black with pockets and a hood. Not a creepy monk-looking robe—just your average silky bathrobe. He had ginger-red hair that was long, and a wiry beard sprouting along his jaw line.

"Are you Saetan?" I asked with narrowed eyes.

Amusement crinkled his eyes. "Is this how you picture Saetan?" He gestured up and down. "This is, after all, *your* version of Hell."

I didn't know. How did I picture Saetan? "Why is Grayson in *my* Hell?"

Again, the man didn't answer me, simply stared ahead, eyes

traveling around from me to Grayson and to space in between. "He must have left quite the impression on you."

"You're the one who brought me here . . . let's get this over with."

"Rather brazen for a girl brought to Hell by her human love." After another moment, he shrugged. "Very well. Have a seat."

I glanced behind me as a chair appeared from nowhere. I lowered myself into it.

He did the same, folding his hands in his lap. "We would like to know where the man you call Lucien is."

My heart dropped. "You don't know?"

"If we knew, do you think we would be asking you? Saetan does not like to be kept in the dark." His eyes flicked around the low-lit room, a smile cracking his face. "Figuratively speaking, of course."

"I-I honestly don't know."

His eyes narrowed, and though demons can't gauge lies as well as angels, we can usually see a shift in aura or something to help us along.

"Then to your knowledge, he is not rogue?"

"No!" I gasped. "He would never. He loved his job!" And it was true. It was one of the things about him I could never understand.

"Well, we knew that. We just thought perhaps he had a change of heart since our rebellion days. Perhaps he felt it was time for a change of Kings?"

"Rebellion days?"

The man's lip curled. "Surely, Lucien's told you . . ."

"Told me what? What are you talking about?"

"Lucien was one of the original angels cast out of Heaven. One of the originals, alongside me, Lucifer, and others, to stir the war of angels into action."

I didn't say anything—couldn't. Words choked in my throat, and though my mouth opened, absolutely nothing came out.

"Well, well, well." He leaned back in his chair, and it was again one of the few moments when joy flashed across his features. Joy from my pain. "I suppose he did not tell you everything, now, did he?"

I cleared my throat. "It doesn't matter." I shook my head, clearing away the fog. Damn, it was hot. I needed more water. "Lucien's not rogue. I saw him disappear. It was not by choice. You should be summoning Buckley here. He knows something . . ."

"Don't you concern yourself with John Buckley. He has a special table reserved down here."

"Believe me—Lucien's not responsible for his disappearance."

The man studied me a moment longer before nodding his head. I pushed onto my feet, stealing a glance back at Grayson once more.

"Where are you going?"

"I assumed we were done."

He said nothing; just stared at me with one raised eyebrow.

I cleared my throat and returned to my seat. "Sorry," I mumbled.

"Very well," he continued. "It was brought to our attention that you have the ability to mask your powers."

Fear tingled through me. Fuck. How did they know *that?* "I—um, well, I just sort of found out myself recently . . ."

"This is quite significant. Do you realize *how* significant?"

I shook my head. "N-not really. I just sort of tried it one day. And it worked."

"I see. Well, typically this sort of power is reserved for those in high power. ArchDemons, Queens and Kings of their demon race, etcetera. Do you have any idea how you received this sort of power?"

"It was, um, accidental. I ingested a witch's blood just as she died. But I didn't mean to."

His exhale was audible through parted lips, though I wasn't sure I was supposed to hear it. "Fascinating."

"But any succubus ingesting power would have absorbed the power—" I added.

"Not necessarily. Many a succubus—and incubus and demon—have tried. It has to already be in you. Sure, magician and demon blood can give you lasting life. But not all ingest their powers."

"Well, what does this mean for me?" My voice was small. Afraid. And fuck if I didn't hate sounding terrified.

"For now, nothing. We will have to deliberate and discuss how to best utilize your new talents."

Shit. Hell knowing of your powers certainly meant they would find a way to use them for the worst.

He stood, the chair disappearing from under him, and I, too, rose to my feet. The chair turned to smoke behind me.

"For now, keep your magic to a minimum. Only when you absolutely need it. And—" His finger went to my nose. What normally would be a cute gesture frightened me to the core. "Do not use your masking power to ever deter yourself from being summoned here. That is treason."

I nodded and looked again at Grayson. "Is Lucien's return a priority?" My voice trembled despite my hardest efforts to keep it calm.

"One of a few, yes."

"May I make a suggestion, then?"

He eyes raked me from toes to eyes, as if he could read what I was about to ask in my body language. "You may."

My eyes flicked to Grayson with another deep breath. I was walking a tightrope across a fiery pit. Twenty thousand feet in the air. Lined with razor blades. "Let me take the lycanthrope with me." It came out more like a whisper, but the redheaded man heard me loud and clear.

"Absolutely not."

"But—he can help. His nose and senses are unlike anyone we have at our disposal. He can get us to Lucien." When he didn't say no again, I continued with caution. "And—and I will vouch for him. He will be my responsibility. And Drew is always near me regardless. If he does something stupid, he can be on the next trip to Hell in seconds."

"You truly believe this creature can find Lucien?"

I resisted the urge to rub my chest, where an abrasive feeling gnawed behind my sternum. "I think he can help."

Why was I doing this? Why was I risking everything for a man I barely knew?

Silence hummed and the man's tight face loosened. "Very well. He is your responsibility. Should he disappear under your watch, you will be tortured in his place." The man turned his back on me, bounding toward the door.

I wasn't sure if I was in a position to negotiate. I squirmed and spoke up regardless. "Only until he is found."

He stilled, arm reached out for the knob. "Excuse me?" He swiveled back on his heel with the grace and balance of a skilled dancer.

"I agree to all those terms. Except I want one amendment: Should Grayson disappear under my watch, I will be tortured in his place . . . *until* he is returned to Hell. Then I shall be released."

The man's mouth turned up into a hint of a smile. He twitched his head, the slightest nod in response. "Very well." He snapped his fingers and Grayson crumpled to the floor, his screams echoing in my ears.

I ran to his side, placing a hand on his shoulder. "Grayson, wake up. It's okay." I glanced over my shoulder and the room was empty. There was no *crack* sounding a teleportation. No creak of a door opening. But the man was completely gone. And he left me with a quivering, naked, half-conscious werewolf to babysit.

26

———————

Grayson was finally coming to. We had him dressed in some of Drew's spare clothes and lying on the couch covered in blankets. Despite the many layers, he shivered. Blinking eyes cracked open, and a hand darted to shade them from the incoming light. "Where—where am I?" he rasped, and immediately placed a palm to his throat. Drew handed him a glass of water. The journey back from Hell hadn't been nearly as bad, but having the dead weight of an unconscious body sort of diverts your mind from wandering too much.

Grayson's eyes landed on Drew. I could see the gears churning in his mind, fitting the puzzle pieces together to form the memory. On cue, he bolted to a standing position, kicking the blankets off. He wobbled on his feet, bracing his palm against the wall.

"Calm down," I whispered, not daring to come too close. Touching a frightened wolf was as dangerous as . . . well, as touching a frightened wolf. "You're okay. We saved you. Brought you back from Hell."

Drew snorted. "She brought you back. She's taking the risk. Me? I would've left you there to burn."

"That wasn't a dream? That was you there? Trying to stop my father from beating me?"

"I was there . . . but your dad—that was just an illusion." I dug in my purse and tossed him a compact mirror. "Have a look for yourself. Physically, you're fine."

He stared into his reflection, moving his head about to examine the different angles. "It felt so real. How did you get me out of there?"

Drew's arms folded across his chest, and it noticeably puffed out. He was making himself as large as he could—doing his best to dominate the wolf. Fucking men. "She vouched for you. Do you know what that means, pup?"

Grayson's eyes narrowed. "Who you calling *pup?*"

Drew continued, ignoring him. "It *means* that if you leave her or run away or fuck up again, Monica will be held personally responsible." He flicked a glance at me, his brow stern. "It was a stupid thing to do."

Grayson's eyes widened and met mine. "You really did that? For me?"

"I made a promise to help you. I couldn't just leave you down there."

He watched me, nostrils twitching.

"I could've," Drew growled.

I darted him a glare. There was a time I would have called him out as a liar . . . but these days, I wasn't so sure. There was a hardness—an edge there that didn't exist before his experiences in Hell.

My door burst open and Damien leaped through the entryway, crushing me in a hug. "Jesus Christ," he hissed, cupping my face. "Are you okay? When Kayce called me, I was going crazy, worrying about you."

"I'm okay. Never want to experience that again, but still . . . I'm all right." If I thought Drew's face was hardened before, it was a downright ice sculpture now.

Damien lunged for Drew, slamming him against the wall. "I should fucking kill you, you know that?" He paused, eyes tracing Drew's busted nose, split eyebrow, and swollen lip. He smirked and released Drew's collar. "But it looks like my girl got to ya first, huh?" He chuckled, sending a smile my way. "What's the matter, Drew? That 'vessel' of yours not big enough to take on a succubus?"

Drew's smile was equally wry, but not nearly as jolly. "My vessel more than satisfies. Isn't that right, Mon?" He slid his gaze over to me.

Damien's face turned red, and his smile pinched into a scowl.

"Really?" I stepped between them. "A battle of penis size? *Now?*"

Before the conversation could continue, Kayce, Jules, and Adrienne walked in. Her arms were folded, and she stepped in beside Drew, but still at enough of a distance that they weren't touching. Her lips pursed together, and her eyes were glued to the floor. "You're back," she said.

"Yeah."

The room was silent, and even though we all knew it was rude, no one could tear their eyes away from the spectacle. "I take it you got my message?"

Drew shuffled a toe over my hardwood floor, scuffing a ball of dust around. Damn—I needed to sweep more.

Damien cleared his throat. "Why don't we give them a moment while Monica explains what happened." Just then he noticed Grayson, glancing back to me. "And it seems we've got a lot to catch up on."

Ten minutes later, Drew and Adrienne had gone for a walk, Grayson was resting in my bedroom, and the gang and I were chatting in the living room.

"Monica, you made a very dangerous deal with the devil. Literally."

"Jules, it's fine." In reality, it didn't feel fine. I was shakier than a diabetic in an ice-cream shop.

"It is not fucking fine," Damien snarled.

"Do you really think he can help find Lucien?" Kayce asked.

I snuck a sideways glance to Jules. Damn, he'd know if I was lying. "I don't know. I think he can definitely help. His nose is incredible. Maybe there's something he can sense."

"So, it'll be like having our very own Seeing Eye dog?" Kayce snarked.

"In a way . . ."

"And what if he runs? Or continues plotting against Saetan? Did you ever think of that?" Damien paced the room, fine Italian loafers clicking against the hardwood flooring. "What do you do then?"

"Then we'll have to track him down." I shrugged, but my fingers trembled despite the relaxed facade I presented.

"Son of a bitch," Damien huffed, glancing at the bedroom where the werewolf rested. "Literally."

"Well, then." Jules was still calm. His voice was the equivalent to catnip to our frazzled senses. "Let's get this guy working, then."

After our run-in with Lenny at Lucien's office, I didn't want to risk visiting again unless we needed to. Besides, we had a better chance of finding something new in different surroundings. We pulled up to Lucien's house—a large home on the outskirts of the city, not far from the club.

We crawled out of my Toyota like a bunch of stuffed circus clowns. Grayson stretched, and his T-shirt lifted above the waistline of his jeans to reveal a thin, happy trail that disappeared at the button. Muscles lined his hips, creating a V-like funnel directly to his—

"I didn't know you had a thing for bestiality, *babe*," Damien whispered as he brushed by my shoulder.

"I *don't.*" I rolled my eyes. "He's just interesting, isn't he? Kind of weird in a bohemian cowboy kind of way."

Grayson closed his eyes, tilting his head to the sun. The sherbet sky reflected across his tanned face. His nostrils twitched as a breeze rustled the palm trees, and his shirt billowed with the wind. It was a nice reprieve on this hot day.

Kayce groaned and looked up at the house. "Damn," she said. "I might as well cancel my date tonight. It's gonna be a long search."

I followed her gaze. She was probably right. How many rooms did Lucien have? Ten? Twelve? Even with five of us, it would take hours.

Grayson's eyes popped open, and this time they were glowing and yellow. The sight was a startling one—particularly when you weren't expecting it. "I'm picking up a scent. Do you have something of his to compare it to?"

I handed him the manila folder of bounties. "I can grab you a shirt of his as well from inside."

Grayson snatched the file from my hands and buried his nose into it. "Don't need it at the moment. But for later—we should grab one or two. Scents last longer on fabric than objects. Luckily paper is porous."

He smelled the folder again and then popped to attention, his neck elongating and his focus directed around the side of the house.

Sniffing the air, Grayson took off at a run.

"Motherfucker!" Damien shouted, bolting after him. The rest of us were only fractions of a second behind.

Damn. That werewolf could run . . . and here I thought demons were fast.

Back behind Lucien's house was a shed. Grayson slowed his sprint as he rounded to the shed and dropped to his knees, nose in the grass. "Yes, this. This is where he spent most of his time."

"What?" My shrill voice pierced even my own ears. "That's crazy. You haven't even been inside yet."

"Don't need to." Grayson sat back on his haunches. "This is where he lived." He nodded his head in the direction of the shed again.

"Bullshit. If Lucien lived in a shed, I think I would have known." I folded my arms and held his gaze.

"Fine." He slapped his hands down onto his thighs. "Choose not to believe me if you want. I could give two shits if you actually find this guy or not."

"Really?" I raised a challenging eyebrow. "Because one word from me that you're not as helpful as I thought and back to Hell you go."

Grayson's face became whiter than balled-up toilet paper.

"Yeah," I said. "That's what I thought."

He held up two hands. "Fine, you're right. I surrender. But that doesn't change the fact that my nose doesn't lie. Whether or not he *lived* out here—he spent an awful lotta time in this here shed."

"Well, then," Jules cut in. "Let's go see why." With a *crack*, he teleported inside and opened the door for the rest of us.

27

Damien's palm flattened at the small of my back, and the group waited as I took a deep breath and entered. Goose bumps rose along my arms despite the oppressive heat inside the shed. There was a cluster of candles sitting on a shelf above a ratty pillow.

The scent of cedar wafted in my nose, and I inhaled it deeply. Yep, cedar and Lucien. Wood carvings of the Virgin Mary and Jesus on the cross were flanked by the candles and a rosary hung on the wall, the beads covered in dust from years of unuse. A plank of wood held up by archaic chains created the most uncomfortable cot I'd seen in decades—shit, maybe in a century. A ratty wool blanket was in a crumpled pile on top of the bed . . . if you could even call it that.

"Is this . . ." Kayce's voice trailed off before she could finish the question. Her dark eyes arched around the room. It was audible as she swallowed. "Does Lucien *pray?*"

"It sure looks that way, doesn't it?" Damien added.

On another shelf, next to the hanging beads, was a Bible, bound by hide and twine. I lifted a hand and stopped myself before coming into contact with the holy relic. Not for fear of the burn—but because I was certain the Bible would disintegrate with my touch, it was so old. "Why wouldn't he tell me?" I whispered. I, of all people, would understand the desire to pray.

"Religion is a very personal thing," Jules answered. And it wasn't until that moment that I realized he was standing right beside me. It felt like someone had taken hold of my throat and tied it into a knot. I swiped a knuckle beneath my eye and sniffed back the encroaching tears.

Grayson clutched the withered blanket in his fists, nose nestled into the folds. His chest expanded, his eyes reflecting a glimmering shadow. He tossed the blanket back onto the cot. "Yep, this is his. He slept here. *A lot.*"

The room went out of focus, and without even thinking I walked over beside Grayson. Lifting the blanket, I closed my eyes and inhaled Lucien's scent. One single tear fell into the fabric, and the wool quickly absorbed it. I sniffled and folded the blanket, draping it over my arm. The fabric was rough and scratched my forearm before I set the folded blanket back onto the wood cot.

I turned back to the group with a steadying breath. "Well? Anyone see anything of importance? If not, we should move on?"

"Mon—" Kayce stepped forward cautiously, took my hand, and gestured around the shed with the other. "This has to mean something. Right? You knew Lucien better than anyone."

"It might mean something. It might not. There's not a whole lot to be found in here, though. It's sparse. And we should search the rest of his home just in case."

Damien nodded and, with a flat hand, circled my back. "She's right. We'll have plenty of time to discuss the meaning of the shed. But we should gather as much information as we can first."

We all circled the tiny room once more, and I took note of every detail. Every carving. Every cobweb. Every nail in the baseboards. One by one we filed out of the shed until it was just Jules and me left. He held out a palm in the universal "after you" signal.

I narrowed my eyes, holding his crystal blue gaze. They twinkled, and from over his shoulder I could feel the Virgin Mother's eyes on us. "You know something," I whispered, barely able to even get the words out. "I don't know what it is—but this room. This place. *You* know what Lucien was doing here and why."

Jules's head tilted thoughtfully. "Monica, Lucien was an angel before he was a demon—"

"Yeah. I know. He was one of the original fallen ones."

Jules folded his hands in front of him. "There you go. That in itself explains this room. You, of all people, should understand that one's relationship with God doesn't end just because you fall from grace."

"I do understand that. But wouldn't you say this is a little much?" I flicked a glance around the room—partially to get another look and partially in place of a hand gesture.

"I say that everyone gets to choose how they treat their relationship with God without judgment."

"Yeah, but we're talking about a man who pimps out Saetan's whores for a living . . ."

"Yes. A job he only took upon meeting *you*. Prior to your arrival, Lucien had nothing to do with succubi."

And there it was—that was the shocker. "What?" I shook my head. "No. No . . . he-he always had other women around him."

Jules shook his head. "Maybe I'm wrong." He moved to exit the shed, and I latched on to his elbow.

"You're hardly ever wrong."

Jules smirked. "And it only took three hundred years for you to admit that." He covered my hand with his and led me outside. "Look, I only know what Lucien told me . . . but he wasn't lying. I didn't know the man back then. But apparently, he had nothing to do with succubi as a demon. He had no desire to be an ArchDemon. He was content with being a founding demon and leaving it at that."

"So what changed with my existence?"

Jules shrugged, and we followed the others inside Lucien's house. "I think it's pretty safe to say that *you're* a game changer, Monica."

28

New Jersey, 1776

"No. *It's not true—Monica, tell me that's not true.*"
Lucien had me locked in his quarters as he paced in front of the bed, wearing treads into the floorboards. "I don't understand what's so upsetting. He's a patriot. You're a patriot. And he's going to help us pull this off."

"This? We don't even know what 'this' is yet!" *Lucien's cackle cracked in his throat, and he fisted a hand in front of his mouth. For all of a moment, I thought tears would spring from his eyes. Whether Lucien quickly got them under control or my eyes were playing tricks on me, it passed too quickly to know.* "Christ, Monica. It's a marvel to me how much you don't understand yet." *He fell into a chair, seated in front of a small writing desk, and his head dropped into his hands.*

"I don't know anything, because you insist on keeping me in the fucking dark. You are doing to me exactly what Jules did in my angel days. And it was the reason for my demise. If you want me to understand something, then tell me!"

He jumped to his feet, kicking the chair behind him. It splintered, sending bits of wood barreling through the room, and I lifted my arm as a shard sliced into the skin.

The blast of power slammed into me, and for the first time since beginning this life with Lucien, I saw—no, I felt—the kind of power he had in him. It sizzled around me and thickened the air to the point that I could barely breathe. Though not a finger was upon me, he might as well have had his hands around my throat.

A blinding tunnel of blackness creeped into the edges of my vision field. Flashes of stars winked around me. "Lucien—" I choked.

The air lifted, fizzling to normal, and my vision returned to find Lucien's lined face still scowling at me. "You are barely a succubus," he rasped. "The lowest and newest in the ranks. I don't have to tell you a bloody thing—you just have to obey. That *is your job.*"

"And you wonder why we all despise you," I whispered, cradling my arm where the wood sliced and splintered into my skin. I bit back the whimper and instead gingerly tugged at the protruding piece of wood.

Lucien was over me in seconds, and he snatched my wrist, holding my arm in front of my eyes. "This is not real!" he hissed. "When are you going to learn that? You are not real. Shift the splinter away." He shook my own arm in my face as though it were a weapon that could be used against me. "Do it!"

I swallowed, closing my eyes, and my magic wafted over my body softer than a summer breeze. It tingled across my flesh like the tenderest of kisses. And when I opened my eyes, my arm was healed, though it still ached.

"There," Lucien said softer, but the fire was still in his dark eyes. "Was that so hard?" He released my wrist.

I stared at the floor, not daring to look up at him just yet. I took note of the grain of the wood, a knot in the center plank, and I couldn't help but relate to that flawed part of the structure.

There was a creak, and the bed bounced beneath me. I stole

a glance to the side, and Lucien now breathed heavily beside me. As an angel, Jules never raised his voice like that. He never once used force in that way to get a point across. Panic rose in my throat, and a sob quivered in my chest. I forced myself to swallow it down. "Lucien . . ." My voice trembled with the repressed tears.

He didn't answer, but I could feel his shoulders stiffen beside me.

"Believe me—I understand how below you in the ranks I am." Bitterness cracked in my voice. "But just maybe if you talked to me like a person and I understood why Tom shouldn't have been a part of the plan, we could have avoided the situation in the first place."

"The situation should have been avoided regardless. Because you should know your place."

"Yes," I snapped, tears all but forgotten. "We established that. But if you want to be a powerful ArchDemon, maybe you should learn you'll get further with your ladies by treating us with respect."

"Very well." He slapped his hands to his knees and stood. Pacing resumed in the room. "No humans knew of our plan. Only demon patriots. So—now, we have a human privy to our deception. And humans are unpredictable little arses." He stopped, spinning to face me. "And—the one human you chose to tell is the son of our main Tory contact. How do you not see that as a conflict?"

"Because he hates his father. I've seen the boy's death—and it is at his father's hands."

"And just how do you expect to convince the boy of that? Without revealing your true nature?" Lucien said. "We don't know where this boy's loyalties lie. Sure, he wants freedom from the crown—but typically when it comes down between your own bloodline and a fight for freedom, there's a chance he'll choose to save his father."

"So, talk to him. You can read auras better than me."

There was a crack from outside Lucien's quarters and his eyes rolled back with a deep sigh. "Wonderful. Just wonderful," he murmured.

The door creaked open, and standing in the doorway was a tall, willowy woman with raven hair that fell in a dark curtain straight to her waist. Lucien turned pale, looking the exotic woman up and down.

Within seconds, he collected himself. "You're new."

"Relatively." Her voice was raspy, and she turned her attention to me. "But not as inexperienced as some."

I folded my arms and rolled my eyes with a tut of my tongue.

"What's your name?" Lucien asked.

I inhaled and . . . oh, bloody Hell. I smelled arousal. Lucien's arousal. My stomach turned.

"Cheng."

Lucien scanned her up and down. "Not sure if you're planning on hanging around town, but we don't get much diversity around here. Townies can barely stomach the thought of the Germans coming over. You might consider changing your—appearance."

With a tight-lipped smile, she continued. "Thanks for the lesson. I don't plan on sticking around long, though. I'm here to take you down." Her gaze shifted from Lucien to me.

"Down?" I choked out, and the turning of my stomach was suddenly for an entirely different reason.

Lucien's soft, lovesick gaze morphed back into his stern scowl. "She has business to attend to." He glanced over his shoulder at me, eyes widening. "You have that good boy soul waiting for your services downstairs, aye?"

"Ah—aye, yes."

Cheng's eyebrow lifted along with the corner of her mouth. "You know as well as I that I cannot show up to Hell empty-handed."

Lucien nodded. "I do know that. You can take me instead."

"Lucien, no . . . I can go—"

His neck whipped around and his lips blanched, pressed so tightly together they bore no color whatsoever. "No," he replied curtly. "You have business here. *Or did you forget our little chat about obeying so quickly?"*

I shook my head. "N-no. Of course not."

With a nod, he swiveled back to Cheng. "Very well. Shall we?" His breath grew shallow as he stepped closer, and another smell altogether flooded the room. Pheromones—Cheng's.

Lucien chuckled, pressing his palm flat against hers. "Don't waste your perfume, neophyte."

Their forms wobbled, as though suddenly made of water, and a black hole swirled below their feet. "Lucien!" The trance broke, and he pulled his hand from hers, looking to me with concerned eyes. "Will—will you be back?" I swallowed, trying not to sound as frightened as I felt.

He snorted. "Of course. Likely within the hour." He motioned to the door. "Go on downstairs. I'll see you later."

29

The rest of the gang had split up, gone upstairs, each taking a room.

"Well?" Jules glanced around the kitchen. Dishes were still in the sink, but it was otherwise clean.

"Well, what?" I snapped.

"Well, do you see anything out of the ordinary? You've been here before, right?"

I didn't answer. Despite our relationship, Lucien and I didn't necessarily have potluck dinners where we discussed our personal lives in detail. Sure, I'd been here before. But not enough to know if something was out of place.

Julian's gaze burned into my back, and I finally turned to face him. "Yes, of course. Nothing looks unusual to me." In his sink was a martini glass with raspberry lipstick smeared on the rim, a shaker, and an empty pint glass. The martini glass was still full with almost the entire drink. "Jules—you know anything about martinis?"

"Not really. Why?"

Pinching the glass between two fingers, I lifted it from the sink and held it up to the light streaming in from the window. I took a deep breath, closing my eyes and swigging the leftover martini.

Julian's face paled. "What in the world are you doing?" He passed me a towel. "That's disgusting."

I swished the martini in my mouth before spitting it out in the sink and placing the glass back down. "Bruised. And I know of one particular martini snob who never drinks a bruised martini."

Jules crouched, opening the cabinets. "You know who was here with Lucien last?"

"Mia. She has to be behind this. She was at the theatre that night." I gestured to Jules with raised eyebrows.

"Well, yes . . ."

"And she has been meeting secretly about me with Claudette monthly."

Jules scratched his scruff. "She's definitely suspicious."

I rubbed my eyes, opening a few more cabinets. All empty. Barely even a plate. "Damn. Grayson was right. He lived in the shed. And at the club." I froze, panic gripping my throat. "Speaking of, who has Grayson?"

"I do," Kayce said, dragging him down the stairwell. "He's not leaving my side."

"Lucky me," he growled.

Jules leaned against the sink, looking at the dishes. "For all we know, Monica, these dishes could have been left from days before his disappearance."

"Maybe. But I doubt it. A martini left out for a night or two is bad enough—but a week?" I shuddered. "It would be un-drinkable."

The door slammed and Damien entered the kitchen. "Nothing's in the basement." He looked around the crowd and grunted. "Why am I always the last person to find out what's going on?"

"You're not," I said, linking my arm in his and walking him

over to the sink. "We just need you to do some elemental work. See who was here with Lucien and when?"

He placed his one hand on the counter and the other on the martini glass. The room vibrated, humming around us. After a moment, he blinked his eyes open. "There were three people here. Lucien and two others—that's all I got. The elements here didn't really give a shit about Lucien and his activities."

"It had to be Mia," I repeated.

"And Claudette," Kayce added. "She and Mia have been spending a lot of time together, right?"

Grayson tossed a pebble into the air, then caught it with one hand. "I found a little something." He tossed the rock at me. It was coarse, porous, an ashy gray carved into a blade. "It's a sunstone."

"So?" I asked, flipping the rock around in my hands. It had a similar texture to coral but wasn't nearly as colorful.

Jules stepped back, lips tightening. "Lucien had a sunstone?"

"Legend has it," Grayson continued, taking the stone from me and holding it into the light, "that the original four angels from the rebellion were thrown into the sun when they were cast out. They were left there to burn. They managed to survive, but as demons. Each of the four were embedded with these sunstones. Throughout the centuries, they've been dispersed, but the original four are the only ones who can distribute them. Supposedly, it is the only weapon in existence that can kill an angel. Granted, it can also kill any of us, too. He glanced around the room, making eye contact with everyone one by one. "Angel, demon, succubus—whatever. One stab"—Grayson jabbed nothing with a fake punch to the air—"and you're done for."

"Oh, shit," I whispered and scrambled for my pocket. I tugged the sharpened stone that I had found in Lucien's enchanted cabinet, holding it up for everyone. "It's the same sort of stone, right?"

Grayson took the blade from me with a low whistle. "Sure is," he said. "This one could do some damage. He gave this to you?"

I explained to the group how I found it the day before. Julian nodded, stepping back once more—whether consciously or not, I wasn't sure. "He must have meant for you to have it," Jules said. "Why didn't you tell me? I was there with you that whole time."

I shrugged. "I don't know. I didn't really think it was all that important. It just looked like yet another one of Lucien's weapons he had stockpiled."

"That's a dangerous little rock you got there," Grayson murmured with a head tilt. "Question is . . . who gets to hold on to it?"

It didn't take long for us to agree on Julian.

Soon after we all left Lucien's house I grabbed Grayson, dragging him to the café.

"You gonna make me a latte?" he asked with raised eyebrow.

He held the door as I entered, and for all of a moment, I saw that Texas charm folks always talked about. "Nope. You're gonna make *me* one. If we're going to be roomies, you need to earn your keep. You ever held down a job before?"

"I worked on a ranch before . . . well, you know." He rolled a growl at the back of his throat and bared his teeth with a wink. The threatening sound was softened by his playful smirk.

A ranch. I should have fucking guessed.

"Monica!" Genevieve's shriek pulled my focus back to my business. "Look who's back!"

Drew walked from the barista bar, flinging a towel over his left shoulder. "Hey, Mon. I like what you've done with the place."

"Drew . . . you're back? As in *back* back?"

He sauntered over to us, flicking a glance at Grayson before drawing attention to me. "I was just explaining to Genevieve, I'll be in and out a lot. So I'll need you to retain managerial status. But, for the most part—yeah, I'm back." A lazy grin slid across dimpled cheeks. With a nod, he lifted his chin to Grayson. "He getting the grand tour?"

"Drew—I want you to meet your newest employee."

Grayson seemed pretty good at hiding his emotions most of the time and yet . . . his eyes darkened for that split second and he sucked his cheeks in, grinding the flesh between his sharp incisors. "You're telling me my new boss is this two-timing, little—"

"Grayson," I cut in sharply. "That's no way to talk to your boss."

He glared at me, gold shimmering across otherwise hazel eyes. "You did this on purpose."

I shrugged. "I didn't know he was coming back to work."

"Monica." Genevieve skipped over, linking her arm around my elbow. "Can I talk to you a minute?" She glanced between the guys, then nudged her head toward the back. "Over here?"

"Sure. Drew—can you show Grayson around a bit?"

I liked that Drew was smiling again—but this particular smile was unsettling. "Absolutely."

"What's up, Genn?" I said, keeping one eye still on the boys. Her smile stretched the length of her face and then some. Holding my hands, she squeezed them with hers. "I don't know how—it doesn't make sense. But I'm pregnant!" she whispered, and then bounced onto her toes.

"Oh, my gosh! Genevieve, congratulations!" I crushed her in a hug.

She giggled, hugging me back, then held me at arm's length, bringing a finger to her lips. "Shh, I'm not supposed to tell anyone for a couple of months yet. But—but I just had to let you know. Especially after the other night."

"Of course." I lowered my voice. "And don't worry. I'm a great secret keeper."

"It's so weird," she continued. "You know . . . they say these things tend to happen when you stop trying, but—I mean, we *just* found out I couldn't, you know? We didn't even have time to process everything. But that night after we talked, I felt so energized."

"Yeah . . ." I trailed off. "I, uh, can have that effect on people sometimes." I remembered the small zap of power I felt with Genevieve that night. And typically after I steal power, humans feel a burst of energy. Sort of Hell's supernatural way of ensuring our conquests won't lose steam on us. But—it was different. I didn't see her death. I saw a baby.

I snapped myself out of my thoughts. "Well, whatever the reason, it's great. I'm so happy for you. And if you ever need a babysitter . . ."

"Oh, please. We'll be calling you weekly!" she said, tossing her purse over a shoulder. "Okay, I'm off. Good luck training the new guy." Then, dropping her voice, she added. "He's a cute one, huh? Looks kind of lost, though. Like a stray."

I snorted. "Oh, G. You have no idea."

"Like this?" Grayson shouted over the espresso grinder. Several patrons squinted and covered their ears. Sure, the grinder can be loud, but it was as though Grayson's presence made the damn thing scream even louder.

"Yeah, but not so long." I reached across and shut the machine off. "You only want to grind the beans you use in the one drink."

"Well, that just sounds stupid to me. Grind the whole damn thang in the morning. Then you don't have to bother with this every time someone orders espresso."

"Gray, you can't do that. The beans won't taste as fresh."

"Would people really be able to tell the difference?" With meaty fists, he grabbed the tamp and jammed it into the filter.

"Grayson, stop! Gently tamp. Gently. It's supposed to be forty pounds of pressure." I placed my hands on his, demonstrating. "And yes. People can tell the difference."

He humphed at that. "Ain't you got any cows or chickens I

could tend to instead? I'm better with livestock." He finished tamping, then placed the filter into the espresso machine. His gaze drifted to my cleavage, then back to my eyes with a twitch of his lips. "And I'm awfully good with the chicks."

"C'mon, Old McDonald. After this, I'll show you the register. Until you learn the drinks, I'll just let you handle cash."

Over the next hour, I couldn't stop thinking about Genevieve and how strange it was that she got pregnant so quickly. Especially since it happened right after I stole some of her life.

I zoned out, staring at the granite counter. What events led up to the power I got from G? I stopped by the café after working at the strip club—and that was the night Buckley . . .

"Son of a bitch," I whispered to no one. I shook my head and shut the register drawer.

"Don't talk ill of my mama." Grayson flopped onto an elbow, leaning his body weight against the counter.

"No, no . . . not you." I scrambled for my purse, which luckily I didn't bother to put away since Drew was now back and moving into his office. "Drew!" I shouted, darting for his door. I threw it open to find him looking through some files. "Drew—I-I have to go. Keep an eye on Grayson for me."

"What the hell am I supposed to do with him?"

"I dunno . . . show him how to make my favorite drink."

Drew rose from behind his desk and sauntered toward me. Flutters deep in my belly caused a chill to shimmy along my spine, and I shifted my weight from one foot to the other. "Drew," I said. "I really need to go."

He paused in front of me, newly massive muscles towering over my slight frame. "Still take your caramel mocha with skim?" And he trailed gentle fingertips down my arm, circling my hand.

I cleared my throat. "Yep." I stepped back, only my shoulder blades hit the wall behind me. A chunk of hair escaped my ponytail and flipped into my eyes.

He linked his fingers into mine and lifted my hand to his lips. One by one, he nipped each fingertip. With each grazing of teeth on skin, my breath became shorter, sharper, until I was full on hyperventilating. "Extra caramel drizzled on top?"

I opened my mouth to answer, only in place of a dignified "yes" a squeaky rasp was in its place. I yanked my hand from his and cleared my throat while straightening my T-shirt. "Actually . . . instead, teach him how to make a simple espresso. It's *Damien's* favorite."

We stared at each other before I reached behind me for the knob and made a run to my car before Drew could stop me again.

30

I barged through the back door to Buckley's dressing room to find him shirtless and pressed against one of his rogue "angels." Angels. Ugh. The thought of one of these broads being labeled as such made my skin crawl.

She was in her costume—except for the fact that her rhinestone bra was on the floor by my feet instead of covering her taut nipples. I lifted it with magic, not wanting any of her bodily fluids to come in contact with me, and waited, tapping my toe with her brassiere in midair.

"*Eh-hem.*" I cleared my throat pointedly. Neither Buckley nor the brunette showed any signs of modesty. She giggled and bounded forward, breasts bouncing with the movement. She snatched the bra from my figurative grasp and slipped out the door with one last wave to Buckley.

"Angel." His eyes lit up and chestnut hair curled around his ears. He brushed it out of his face with one hand and leaned against the counter. His lingering gaze brushed up and down my body, and I folded my arms in front of me. "Jealous? I assure you that Brittany has nothing on you, my love."

"I'm not jealous."

"I see your grasp of your magic is coming along nicely."

"I'm also not here for small talk."

Pushing off the counter, his muscles clenched with the movement, and his six-pack abs rippled. He grabbed a shirt from the floor and slipped it on, slowly buttoning it over his tanned skin. "Well, then, what can I do for you?"

That was a damn good question. I swallowed, turning my backside to him, and lifted my shirt.

He chuckled from behind me, his slow saunter clacking against the floor. His palm slipped onto my hip, gliding across my stomach. "Now, I'm always in the mood for this."

His erection pressed into my ass, and the itch flared inside of me. I needed someone's life force soon. But not his—not Buckley's. "Not that," I said, bumping him back a step with my butt. "This." I pointed to the cross scar on my back. "You never explained yourself that night. What is this? And why would someone want to rip it off of me?"

I looked over my shoulder to find him examining it with a tilted head. "It's just a burn mark, Angel."

"Don't fucking lie to me. And don't call me Angel," I said through pursed lips. "It's not just a burn mark and you know it."

He sighed as I tugged my clothes back into place. "Fine. It was part of a spell. You know they require odd ingredients sometimes."

"Oh, I know. Like the tears of an angel," I said with enough bitterness to make my voice crack.

"Well, the burn from a holy relic was needed to complete my spell."

"*What* spell?"

"That night at the club—I made it so you and I could have, well, relations. Without putting my life expectancy at risk."

An angry flush rushed my cheeks, flaming them. I closed

my eyes and, with a deep breath, continued. "You wanted to fuck me without dying. So, that's the spell you created?"

He nodded, green eyes watery and eyebrows turned down. Regret, perhaps? I didn't expect Buckley to be the contrite type.

"And? Did everything go to plan?"

"I—believe so."

I waited, tapping my foot. Catching my lip between my teeth, it took every ounce of willpower not to lunge at the piece of shit right now.

"There was one little thing . . ."

I arched an eyebrow. "Go on."

"The spell was supposed to counterbalance a succubus's life-stealing force. Only—you mentioned that night that you got energy from me, yes?"

I thought back and nodded. "Yes. I did—a surprising amount of energy considering what a piece of shit you are."

His head flopped to the side and he sent me an exasperated look. "Is that really necessary?"

I lengthened my neck, scowling. My stance was a challenge. We both knew he was a piece of shit—he just didn't like hearing the truth.

"Anyway," he continued, "I didn't lose any time off my life. In fact, according to my crystals, it looks like I gained life. . . ."

"How do you know that?"

He shrugged. "The same way I've managed to keep myself alive for centuries. Magic."

"Uh-huh. Magic you don't want to share with the likes of me, right?"

His grin was dazzling, and for all of a moment it made me forget how much I hated him. Dimples so deep, sparkling green eyes, wavy chestnut hair. My chest tightened. "You're already far too powerful, my love. I can't have you learning my secrets on top of this new magic you've acquired."

"Fine. You gained life instead of losing it. What does tha—"
I froze, lifting my gaze to the mirror. My voice rasped in my
throat, and excitement and panic rose all at once. Genevieve—
she got pregnant after I touched her. And Buckley gained years
after we had sex. "Are you—are you telling me that I gave you
life? Instead of stealing it?"

My breath was shortened, and it felt reminiscent of a panic
attack. I leaned in, resting my weight on his shoulders, and his
large hands wrapped around my waist.

"I'm still not positive. But I believe so, yes."

"I have the power to give life," I whispered. "Why?"

"You must have always had something in you. From the
start, you've been an anomaly. But, my spell—" Buckley caught
my chin between his fingers, lifting my eyes to his. "Monica,
angel. Breathe. Breathe with me." He inhaled slowly, deeply, in
an exaggerated way, willing me to mimic the breaths. My racing
heart relaxed to its regular beats, no longer feeling as though
my pulse might break out through my neck at any moment.
"There, that's better." He scooped a hand into my hair, running
his fingers through the strands. "As I was saying, my spell was
meant for a succubus. You, my angel, are so much more. You
have different origins. And I think that affected the outcome."

"And you had no idea this would happen? With that spell?"
I shoved his hand off my hair.

"None. Whatsoever. You must believe me."

And I did. Though he had never earned my trust, I believed
him. Despite my every attempt to get his hands off me, he
cupped my face with the other hand, circling his thumbs over
my cheeks. "Monica." His voice was low and husky. "You are
not safe. I know that you already know this, but angel, I don't
think you truly understand it. You are *not* safe."

I swallowed. "I do understand that. Believe me, I do. In the
past year and a half, I've been stripped of my powers, stabbed,
captured, and poisoned. Buckley—I know."

"Then start acting like you know, goddammit." He dropped his hands and turned away. He wiped his hands down his face, and in the mirror's reflection I saw his concern. I always thought his feelings for me were more selfish, but perhaps I was wrong about him. Maybe he did love me in the only way he knew how—by smothering. By controlling.

"John," I whispered, but didn't dare go any closer. He might love me in his way, but he was still more dangerous than the most venomous snake. "I'm okay."

"You're not okay." His voice cracked, and he turned to face me. "Even more so because of that fucking spell I put on you. Before this, you were a target, yes . . . but now you're a walking bull's-eye, Angel." He swallowed. "Don't you get it? You thought you were hunted before?" He snorted an ironic laugh. "Once word gets out about this, you'll be number one on Heaven and Hell's most wanted list. It's too fucking powerful. *You'll* be too powerful."

"So . . . we don't let the word get out. Right?"

His was freshly shaven, and I could still smell the sweet musk of shaving cream on his skin. He ran a hand across his jaw. "Run away with me. Between the two of us, I can keep you safe."

What would a life of running with Buckley be? Constantly using glamour and masking my power. Changing appearances every couple of decades. I traced worry lines around his mouth with my eyes, followed the downward slope of his eyes and frown. "No, Buckley. I belong here. And Lucien needs me right now."

He nodded and sniffed, wiping his nose with the back of his hand.

"Do you know anything about where Lucien could have gone? Anything at all would help."

He walked over to a wardrobe in the corner. A spell slipped quietly from his lips, and the wardrobe lifted. He tugged at some floorboards and raised a small metal box. With a flick of his hand, the wardrobe rested back on the ground.

"Right after the show," he said, setting the box on his makeup counter, "I did a little research of my own. Within the box, I found this." He scooped something out of the box and held it in his palm for me to see.

31

_____

The silver piece was dull from years of wear but still managed to glisten under the florescent lighting. "It's a Guardian's symbol—for an angel sent to Earth to protect humans," I said with a shrug.

"That's right," Buckley said, and dropped it into my palm. I gasped and pulled my hand away, but the silver grazed my palm regardless.

Nothing happened. No burning; no sizzling pain. I bent to pick it up, touching it with just the tip of my finger. "It doesn't burn me—if it's a Guardian's medallion, shouldn't it?"

I lifted it and held it to the light. Celtic knots and designs swirled in the filigree behind the main design. "And it's Irish . . ." I faded off, staring into the coin, no larger than a quarter. "It's Lucien's, isn't it?"

Buckley lifted a brow. "I assumed you would know."

I let loose with a sigh. "I'm learning that there's a lot about Lucien I don't know." The words caught in my throat and left a bitter aftertaste on my tongue. He really never trusted me with any information, did he?

Buckley cleared his throat and shoved his hands in his pockets. "Well, it's clearly no longer holy, else it would have burned you. And it was found in the box immediately after Lucien's disappearance. So, wherever he went, it couldn't follow."

"Look." I pointed to the center of the eye where the silver formed a pupil. "It's small, but isn't that a rune? And it looks like some sort of darker magic."

Buckley leaned in close as I held up the pendant. His breath was hot on my hand, and I shivered as he turned his head to me, lips dangerously close. "Yes, I think that's exactly what it is."

I swallowed, stepping back. "So, Lucien was sent somewhere that dark magic couldn't be transported. Somewhere . . . holy?"

Buckley nodded slowly. "That makes sense. If he had been sent to Hell, his clothes would have been left behind."

"Holy. Why are they summoning him somewhere holy?" A freezing thought washed over me like ice water. "Fuck. Because we can't go after him there."

"Then you realize, the perpetrator . . ."

"Must not be a demon."

Buckley paused, then shook his head and waved his hand back and forth. "No, no. We are getting ahead of ourselves. It could be a demon who hired someone to do the dirty work."

"But—but even that doesn't make sense. If it is a demon arranging it, then how would they kill him? How would they question him if he was somewhere holy?"

Buckley's eyes turned down and a frown creased his face. "I don't know. But—I know there are only a handful of magicians in Vegas who know how to summon a demon. And any Hellbound creature physically would not be able to summon something into a holy space or relic."

"What are we waiting for?"

"We?" Buckley stepped back, leaning his weight on the back foot. With a tut and a shake of his head, those pouty lips quirked up. "No, no, no, Angel. I have a show to do. Unless you want to stick around—join the rogue angels? We could go afte—"

"No, thanks," I sneered. "I can go on my own.

Lean but muscular shoulders crunched to his ears. "Very well. Have it your way." Turning to his makeup counter, he grabbed a pad of paper and wrote down a list of names, passing the list to me.

"Thanks." I looked the pad over. A few of the names were familiar—one I knew from my problems about a year ago. Rhea. The magical jeweler from the Hawaiian Marketplace.

I tucked the list of names into my purse and headed to the parking lot, where Drew was leaning against the hood of my car. I stopped in my tracks, taking a moment to absorb his new, massively muscular body. With outstretched legs crossed at the ankles, he looked casual but still guarded all at once. Moisture gathered between my legs and my sex swelled. Something low in my stomach twisted. I had the power to give life as well as take it. I swallowed. Which meant—if that was true—there was nothing to stop Drew and me from being together.

He turned, hands clenching as he saw me.

"Wow," I said, strolling over to him. "I don't see you for months and now it's becoming a twice-daily thing."

The bags under his eyes were blue and swollen. "I can't babysit that wolf, Monica. You need to find a better place for him to spend his days."

My breaths were short and sharp. And I was fully aware of how heavy with need my breasts were. "Not sure I can. What's going on over there?"

"He told Genn he could smell her baby and that it's going to be a girl." Drew dropped his head into a hand. "And then he started sniffing the customers and guessing what drinks they wanted."

I groaned. "Oh, no. Did anyone walk out?"

Drew paused before cracking each knuckle one by one.

"No." The muscles in his jaw twitched. "Can you believe it? They all loved it! Couldn't get enough of it, actually."

"That's . . . good, then, right?"

"Except that it annoys me. And *I'm* the proprietor."

"Well, you're gonna have to get over it. Grayson is here for a while. Think of him as the puppy that followed me home." I chuckled.

"That's not funny."

I unlocked my car door, scanning the lot for Drew's car. "How'd you get here?" I slid into the driver's seat.

"I walked," he grunted.

With a tip of my head, I gestured for Drew to get in. He did, and slammed the door beside him, crossing his bulky arms. My gaze landed somewhere below his seat belt, and my mouth watered for a taste of what was under that white T-shirt.

Fuck. I snapped my gaze to the steering wheel, turning the key in the ignition. Get it together, Monica. I wasn't even sure this whole giving-life thing was true yet. I needed a test dummy before risking Drew's life.

I cleared my throat, throwing an arm behind Drew's headrest and backing out of my parking spot. "Wanna help me find the summoner that stole Lucien?" I finally made eye contact and he was smirking, leaning over the console with a glitter in his eyes.

"Will Grayson be joining us?" He raised an eyebrow.

I shook my head no.

"Then, yeah. Let's go." He reached across my chest, snatching the dangling seat belt I had yet to fasten. Tortuously slow, he stretched the belt along my chest, taking his time to glide over my breasts until he clicked the belt into place. "Gotta keep you safe," he said in a voice so low, it was practically a whisper.

32

Rhea was luckily in her same spot. Near the giant soda bottle, standing behind a small Plexiglas box of handmade jewelry. I had seen her a handful of times since speaking with her a year or so ago.

She was an older woman—maybe in her late forties or early fifties. Leathery skin from far too much time in a tanning bed wrinkled around kind, blue eyes. "Rhea," I said, walking up with a smile. "How are you?"

She beamed back, hands on her hips and a giant straw hat covering brittle, brassy red hair. "Hello, my friend. It's been too long. How are—oh!" She stepped back, eyes wide, and glanced me up and down, taking extra time around my shoulders and torso.

I swallowed, glancing nervously back at Drew. "Rhea? You okay?"

"You're different. Your aura," she whispered. Finally her eyes stilled onto mine. She cleared her throat and both literally and figuratively shook the moment off. "I apologize, my friend. What can I do for you?"

"Rhea—I need to know . . . what do you see?"

She swallowed, nibbling the middle of her upper lip. "I don't know for sure. Just—something unusual. As though your purpose here on Earth has changed."

To my knowledge, Rhea didn't know what I was exactly . . . but she knew I was something from Hell that had a lot of power.

"Changed for the good? Or bad?"

She shrugged and lifted her eyebrows. "What *is* good and bad but words made by humans?"

I smiled and shook my head. See? That's what I liked about Rhea.

Drew cleared his throat from behind me. "Oh! Right, sorry. Rhea, this is my friend, Drew." I stepped out of the way, and Drew extended a hand to her.

She took it but lifted her chin, looking down on him despite the fact that his height towered over hers. She visibly shivered at his touch, and the hairs on her arm stood at attention, lifting as though we were in the middle of a blizzard as opposed to Vegas's blistering summer heat.

After a moment, she cleared her throat. "You've lost your way." She stated it simply, releasing his hand.

"Excuse me?" Drew glanced at me, then looked back at her.

"You deny it?" She folded her arms across her sagging breasts. The pastel linen dress wrinkled under her forearms. It was the sort of dress they sold at beach-hippie stores. Which fit with her, well, hippie-like personality.

Drew hooked his thumbs into his pockets and held her stare. "I don't."

She nodded. "Good. That is the first step to redemption." Snapping out of her daze once more, she turned again to me. "So. What can I do for you? This looks like more than the perfunctory jewelry buying visit you usually make."

I smiled, and on a deep breath began. "You're right. Remember the first time we met? I was with a man—an angry-looking guy with black hair in a ponytail?"

"Yes, I remember him vaguely." She tapped her temple. "The ol' memory isn't what it used to be, but the description is familiar."

"Well." I started again with another glance to Drew. "He's missing. And we believe it was a human summoner . . ." I swallowed and let the silence finish the sentence for me.

She uncrossed her arms slowly. "Ah," she said after a moment. "And you heard that along with clairvoyance and aura readings, that I can do summonings?"

"Yes—I just had some . . . questions for you."

"I did not summon your friend," she stated quickly, and turned to fiddle with her jewelry, straightening pieces that didn't need arranging at all.

"I know that, Rhea," I said softly.

"Do you?" She arched an eyebrow but didn't look up.

"Yes. I just wanted to ask you some questions about the process."

On a deep breath, she answered with the exhale. "Ah."

Reaching into my bag, I pulled out the list Buckley had given me and unfolded it. "We were given this list of names . . . people who might be responsible for my friend's disappearance."

She held out a hand. "Let me see."

I set the paper in her palm, and she slipped a cheap pair of reading glasses onto the edge of her nose. She grabbed a pen from her table and put X's next to a few names. "David is out of the country. Backpacking in Europe. Clara, too." She dropped her chin to her chest and looked at us from over the rim of her glasses. "They are a couple," she added with wide eyes. As if this were juicy gossip we absolutely needed to know. Sliding her glasses back into place, she returned once more to the list.

"Why does it matter if they are in the area?" Drew asked.

Rhea answered him without looking up. "Summonings by humans require that we be in the area of the demon. Only wildly powerful witches and sorcerers can summon out of their area and out of the pentagram. Most of us are stuck conforming to location."

"What do you mean, the pentagram?"

With this question, she paused, taking the moment to look up at us again. "You really know very little about the world in which you live, don't you?" She gestured to Drew. "I expect this from him . . . but not you."

"Hey." It was the weirdest insult I'd gotten in a while. And I didn't like that this leathery human made me feel so inadequate. "I'm very 'live and let live.' I had no use for this sort of knowledge until now."

She tilted her head, rolling her eyes. "I suppose that's as good an excuse as any." Turning the paper over, she drew an upside-down pentagram. "Summonings can take place in only one of five points for humans. If you place the pentagram over a map of the city, you will find the five locations in which a human could have performed one." She studied the list one more time, marking a couple of other names before handing it back to me.

"Here," she said. "The two that I circled are your best bets. If they turn up zero, then try the rest. The ones with X's are either out of the area or dead."

"Thanks," I said, taking the list from her dry hands.

"One more thing. You were missing a name. Maybe because he's fairly new to the circle. I added him at the bottom."

I gasped, clenching the paper in my fist and almost ripping the damn thing. The newest, last name on the list, written in a different hand than Buckley's scribble, was Damien Kane.

33

Drew's hands rubbed circles over my back as stars flooded my vision. Damien? Again? First with the whole being the son of Carman thing—and now this? He was like the world's best secret keeper. That son of a bitch! I was going to kill him!

"Monica." Drew's voice was soft, concerned. "We need that list. Be careful."

I glanced down at my fists, and balled between my white knuckles was our list of names. I unwrinkled the paper, smoothing the crinkles with my palm. "Shit. Sorry," I muttered.

"I take it that you know Damien, then?" Rhea asked.

I shook my head. "I thought I did."

"Summoners are not bad people. You think I am bad because I can call upon demons?" she whispered with a quick glance around at her peers.

I shook my head. "No, Rhea. Of course not. But you and I aren't sleeping together. And you aren't keeping information from me."

Drew tensed from beside me.

"Thanks again," I added, and turned back for the car. Drew followed silently.

The drive back to the café was pretty quiet. "Drew, do you mind if I drop you off? We can finish the list later. Or tomorrow." He nodded, clearing his throat. "Sure. Want me to take Grayson home? Keep an eye on him?"

I nodded. "Thanks."

I flopped back into my seat, reclining it just a tad more. It might not have been the most ideal time to relax, but I needed to release the tension. Both here in the car and in my heart.

With another leveled glance at Drew, I found his eyes locked on me. They glistened like the top of a lake at sunset, shimmering with emotions that I couldn't quite read. There was a time I could have discerned and interpreted that look immediately. These days, I had no idea.

"What?" I said, switching my attention between him and the road.

He didn't answer, but his already stiff shoulders clenched into a slab of muscles. "Nothing." He turned to the window, propping an elbow on the edge.

"Seriously?" I snapped, and quickly lowered my voice back to a calm state. "This can't be 'nothing.' In the past six months you discovered that your angel girlfriend died saving a sex demon and that almost your entire group of friends is immortal in some way. Add on top of that, you've been possessed by Hell knows how many demo—"

"Yes, okay?" Drew shouted. "Yes, it's something. It's something that the woman I saw myself spending a lifetime with will kill me every time we make love. It's something that everyone I care about has been lying to me for God knows how long. But this vessel thing? That's nothing in comparison to watching you with other men for years. Watching as every passing fuck in the bathroom or random date didn't work out. Watching. Waiting. And hoping for the day you'd realize that you could have more and be more than the girl who takes off her clothes for money." He panted, swallowing to lubricate a dry throat before continuing.

Betraying tears brimmed the edges of my eyes. "Well, now you know why I can't be."

"Bullshit," he growled. "You are so stuck in your box of what good and evil is, you can't step outside for one second to find a way to make this work."

I slammed the brakes, swerving onto the shoulder. Luckily, we were already on the back roads and no one was behind me. I snapped open my seat belt, curling my legs under me, and turned to face Drew.

"You want to do this? Let's do it for real, then, shall we?"

"What are you talking about?" Drew's nostrils flared.

"Stop pussyfooting around the subject. Say what you want to say!"

Drew held up his hands and looked around the car as if he had an audience. "I'm sorry, was I not speaking English? I said exactly what I meant just now. You are a coward, Monica Lamb. And it's disappointing. I used to think you were so brave."

Heat flared in my face, and my voice dropped to a dangerously low volume. "You're saying that it's not brave to ignore my feelings for you? To save you from death and a life of corruption?"

Drew snorted and unbuckled his seat belt, leaning in closer. "Again—I call bullshit. Look what good those years of chastity did us. I'm now a bounty hunter for the devil and you're *still* not able to be with me. Or so you claim. So much for living a life void of corruption, huh?"

I dropped my face into my hands, rubbing circles over my temples. "I don't even know how to talk to you right now. I don't know how else to fucking say it, Drew. I can't sleep with you. How can we have a healthy relationship without a sex life?

How can we have any relationship when you know that I'm going to have to run off and fuck other men to get power?" My throat tightened—if that was even true anymore. If I could indeed give life as well as take it, that meant I had no more excuses to avoid Drew.

Drew's face went tight. "You manage it with Damien," he whispered.

Bam. Right hook to the kidney. "That's different," I answered. "I don't kill him with each night together."

He shook his head. "You wouldn't even *try*. We could have made it work. Sex isn't everything. . . ."

"Maybe for you it isn't." The bitter laugh escaped along with one errant tear. Fuck. I wiped it with the back of my hand.

"You know what I don't understand?" Drew twisted his hands in his lap before leaning against the window once more. "I should hate you. I should never want to see you again. And yet, every morning—you're the one I wake up thinking about. You're the woman I can't wait to see. I should hate you . . . but I can't stop loving you." He ran a hand down his face with another sad chuckle. "Which in turn makes me hate myself a little." His voice was trembling dangerously—like a shaking hand holding a gun for the first time ever.

And before I knew what either of us was doing, Drew was leaning over the parking break with one hand on the console and the other on the headrest. His lips captured mine, searing my heart—branding my soul as his.

And I kissed him back. It was just Drew. And just me. Molding into one with a kiss that wasn't sweet but wasn't feral like two cats in heat. No, it was something entirely its own. And desire drilled through my core.

The kiss ended, and we sat across from each other, panting.

After a moment, I spoke. "That was nice. But I'm still with Damien. And I like Damien . . . even if he's a little rough around the edges."

He ran a tongue across his top lip, lingering at the scar there. "Yeah. I figured as much. Can't blame me for trying, though." "I do love you. And that's why I can't help but think you'd be so much better off with someone else. Someone like Adrienne."

Drew rolled his eyes. "She's made it pretty clear we're not meant to be." He met my gaze again. "And I had to agree with her. I don't love Adrienne. Not the way I love you."

I stared at him several heavy moments. "I just need to figure out what I want. And I need to talk to Damien before . . ." I trailed off, letting that thought linger between us. Before what exactly? Before we make anything official? Before we take it to the next level?

Drew slowly leaned in again, lips parted and wet. Pausing just in front of my face, he veered, turning the keys in the ignition. He smiled, then quickly turned serious again. "Then we best get going."

I called Damien after dropping Drew back off at the café to find that he was home for a few hours. I pulled in behind his truck and knocked. The door swung open, and Baxter came barreling into me, jumping on two feet and darting around the yard with a ball in his mouth. He trotted back, dropping the ball at my feet, tail whipping back and forth.

I looked to Damien, who shrugged in response. "I dunno," he said. "He's been this way for a few days now. The arthritis seems to be gone . . . shit, he even looks less gray, doesn't he?" Damien chuckled, bending at the waist and clutching the slobbery ball in one hand. He reared back, throwing it in the yard, and Baxter took off once more at full speed. "I'd like to know where he's hiding that fountain of youth." He chuckled, then wrapped an arm around my waist to pull me in for a kiss.

I braced a hand on his chest, pushing those damn sexy lips back. I was frozen, stunned. Didn't I zap Baxter like I had

Genevieve? That night I was attacked? Holy shit. I swiveled, ignoring Damien's curious gaze. "Baxter! C'mere boy!" He bounded for me again and I crouched, catching his collar before he could knock me over.

I cupped his face in my hands—it was true. The white peppered into his golden coat all but disappeared. His big brown eyes no longer bore the bluish tint of glaucoma.

I swallowed, rising slowly to my feet staring at nothing particular. "Damien—we need to talk."

His brow furrowed, but he held the door open for me, whistling for Baxter to come in, too.

I sat at his kitchen table as he put a pot of coffee on and began with my day. Buckley and the Watcher's symbol he found in the box Lucien disappeared in. Pausing, I remembered Buckley's warning—not to tell anyone of my newfound powers of giving life. I omitted that part—for now. Damien nodded, listening intently, and set a steaming cup of coffee down in front of me. It was just how I liked it—half and half and two sugars. Light and sweet.

I cleared my throat after a sip. "Buckley gave me a list of the local summoners who might have been able to capture Lucien." I paused, reading Damien's face. It stayed still—statuesque and unmoving. Not even a twitch of his eyebrows. Damn detective in him. "And after I met with one of the local summoners, Rhea—she told me someone was missing."

Damien leaned back in his chair, folding his arms with one hand clutching the cup of coffee. "Oh?" One eyebrow climbed higher. "Monica—whatever you're getting at . . . get there faster."

"Fine." I dove a hand into my purse and pulled out the list, sliding it over to Damien across the table. "Why didn't you tell me?"

He flicked a gaze down and chuckled. "Seriously? You think I'm the one who summoned Lucien into a church?"

"No—I don't think that. But why didn't you tell me? If you understood how summonings worked, that could have been really helpful to us."

"If I thought it had any bearings on the case, I would have told you."

I dipped a finger into my coffee, stirring it. "On one hand—it's me finding out you're Carman's son all over again. Yet another fact about yourself you never told me." I paused, with a deep breath, then continued. "But—that being said, I need to be straight with you, too." I raised my eyes, chin still dipped low almost to my chest. "Drew kissed me today," I said quietly. "He initiated it, but I didn't exactly stop him."

Damien tightened, and though nothing changed, his knuckles whitened little by little around his coffee mug.

When it was clear that Damien wasn't going to scream or throw anything or simply walk out, I continued. "I knew he'd be back eventually—but now that he is, I think I need some time to figure things out."

Damien closed his eyes, and his nostrils flared with an audible breath. "Nothing has changed, Monica. You can't be with him . . . not if you're still living by your rules."

I swallowed. "I'm not so sure anymore. I have some . . . things to work out." I ran a hand through my hair, the strands silkier than usual. When I lowered my hand, my nails were glossier, too. A sure sign that I was due for another fix.

Damien's gray eyes were stormy. Fixed onto mine. Under the table, I wrung my hands, forcing myself not to fidget. "Well," he said, sucking his teeth. "I'm curious to see how this all plays out." There was a forced bravado to his voice that sent a chill through me. "Can I watch?" he sneered.

"Damien, don't do this—"

"No, seriously," he interrupted. "We could have a threesome. That way you get the best of both worlds."

"Am I naked right now?" I whispered. " 'Cause in my nightmares, I'm usually completely nude."

"It could be fun." He ignored my outburst and blathered on. "The succubus, the elemental, and the vessel. No, wait, you're pretty much just a vessel yourself, aren't you?" His voice cracked as he pushed the chair back and stood. Hands clenched on his hips, and he shook his head. "Well, we'll just have to come up with another name for Drew, then, won't we?"

"Don't be a dick," I said, rising with caution as well. "I was trying to be honest with you!"

He kicked the chair across the room, and it broke into several pieces.

"You're gonna have to apologize to your chair for that one."

"You're not fucking funny, Monica. You don't get to come in here, tell me you want to take a break so that you can fuck the human you think you love, and then expect me to still be here for you!"

His face flushed scarlet and the veins in his neck protruded. "Damien," I began softly. "I don't expect you to wait around. In a lot of ways, the rational side of me knows that you and I are perfect for each other. We are both supernatural but fighting the good fight. I can't take your life or your soul. You understand my unusual needs to sustain a life here . . ." I faded off, tears catching at the back of my throat. A shaky breath cracked in my chest. "But—but, isn't it unfair to you that you don't have all of my heart?" The tears were streaming down my cheeks. I didn't bother wiping them away. They felt good. Salty and cleansing, they ran down my neck.

A single tear danced at the corner of Damien's eye, too, before it glided down the bridge of his nose. He swiped it away with his thumb, clasping his hands to his hips and looking at the floor.

"I'm sorry," I choked. "And I would rather be alone than risk lying to you or hurting you anymore."

I sobbed, grabbing my purse and flinging it over my shoulder. I ran past him to the door, but Damien caught my elbow, pulling me into his chest. He stroked a hand through my hair and tipped my head back. A tear fell from his other eye, only this time he didn't bother to wipe it away.

His fingers circled the base of my neck from under my curtain of blond hair. He dipped his lips to mine, nudging them open with his tongue. The hand that trailed a light touch at the back of my neck raked into my hair, tugging me deeper into the kiss.

The kiss ended with several smaller kisses, and through my teary eyes Damien's beautiful face was distorted. Like I was looking at him through a water glass. He closed his eyes and dropped his forehead to mine, now cupping my face with both hands.

"I'm sorry," I whispered again.

His head shook against my forehead, and I heard his sniffle. Stepping back, he looked me over from head to toe again and nodded. "Bye, Monica."

I ran out the door, not daring to look back.

34

New Jersey, 1776

*T*om and I lay next to each other on a woven rug in front of the hearth in my bedroom. The fire popped and licked the metal grate, craving to get at us. I lay on my stomach, and Tom had his head rested at the small of my back, each of us with a book in hand.

He had been secretly spending a lot of his time at the brothel—particularly with me. He glanced to me through the corner of his eyes, a smile curving his lips. He flicked back and forth between the page and me. Finally, I laughed, looking back over my shoulder. "What?" I giggled.

He shook his head, closing the book and letting it rest on his chest. "I've never met a girl who can read so well. Let alone one who . . . does what you do."

I shrugged with one shoulder. "My brother made sure I had the best education possible."

Tom narrowed his eyes, rolling onto his side and propped his elbow onto my back. "So that you could then become a lady of the evening?" He raised an eyebrow. "It sounds awfully strange to me."

I cleared my throat, flipping the page and not meeting Tom's eyes. "As you can imagine, neither of us imagined this life for ourselves. We fell on hard times and were left with little options."

Tom shook his head and pulled up to a sitting position. "Even in the hardest of times, I don't think I could ever ask of my sister what Lucien has asked of you."

I went back to my book, and after rereading the same sentence twice, I felt the heat of Tom's gaze still on me. Sneaking a glance again, I found those amber eyes burning into me. "I'm trying to read!" I laughed and smacked him across the shoulder with the book binding.

"I still don't believe it," he said through a grin. "Read me a sentence . . . prove that you are literate."

His tone was playful, and I matched his smile with my own. "Absolutely." I cleared my throat, making a show of the sentence to come. " 'Thomas,' she begged. She pleaded. 'Don't be such a dolt and throw more wood on the fire.' "

"That is not what it says!" He laughed and scrambled over me, reaching for the book. With my head tossed back, my own smile was larger than it had been in years. It stretched across my face and was more refreshing than a splash of cool water.

I slammed the book shut and tossed it across the room. "You'll never know!" I said with a smirk.

He shifted off of me, lying on his back. Our shoulders brushed, and there was a low heat in my belly. I squeezed my eyes shut and ignored the sensation. "I suppose I'll simply have to borrow the book after you in search of a character named Thomas whose job is to put more wood on the fire," he said. "Ironic, isn't it? That the passage you were reading happened to be about needing wood when our fire is dwindling as well?" He raised an eyebrow, and I shot a look to the dying embers.

"And yet—there are still no additional logs for our fire."

He rolled onto his stomach next to me. "When did you last see my father?"

My entire body tensed with the question. "Why do you wish to know?"

He shrugged, fiddling with his fingers. "Just curious."

"A few days ago. He's been busy with the preparations of the Hessians coming."

"Ah, right. The secret plan I am not entirely privy to," he cracked.

I rolled onto my side to face him. "There really is nothing more to know of the plan. The girls and I plan to tire out the garrison so that when the battle commences, they'll be exhausted. Any idea of when the Patriots plan to attack?" I swallowed, of course leaving out the part where we would drain the men of their lives as much as possible prior to battle.

"It's so treacherously cold out. It will probably be a while." Tom played with the edge of the rug, glancing back to me. "Your plan seems rather thin, I must say."

I shrugged. "We all do what we can, Tom."

An idea dawned on me, sending a jolt through my body. "How would the Patriots feel about attacking on Christmas Day? The Hessians won't expect it. They'll be exhausted, and most will likely be drunk—"

Tom cracked a laugh. "Why, that's just ridiculous! That would mean Washington's troops would need to cross the Delaware in the dead of winter to make it here in time for Christmas!"

"What's wrong with that?"

"They'll die out there! Do you know how difficult it is to cross that terrain in this weather?"

I paused. "But it's not impossible, is it?"

Tom chewed his bottom lip, regarding me with skepticism. "I suppose not."

I nodded. "This could work, Tom. This could change the war entirely in our favor."

Tom grinned and tugged on one of my spiral curls falling out of the coif sitting high on my head. *"You are an odd little bird, you know that?"*

I returned his smile. *"You think it may work, too, don't you?"*

He nodded, crunching one shoulder to his ear. *"It could."*

"Don't speak a word of this to anyone yet. I must first bring it to Lucien to decide." My grin stretched all the way to my ears. *"But I have a feeling he'll believe us to be geniuses."*

"Your children will be unstoppable someday, you know that?" he added quietly.

The comment knocked the wind out of me, and I was certain it showed on my face. Tom's immediately fell as well, crumpling from playful to concerned. *"Oh, damn. Did I say something stupid again?"*

I shook my head, offering him a weak smile. *"No, no, of course not."*

Tom shimmied his body closer to mine, and the mere proximity flared heat through my body. It tore into my core, ripping through to my limbs in a searing pain. *"Tom, no—"*

But it was no use arguing it. His hand was behind my neck and the pulsing—no, raging—heat between my legs was too intense to ignore. I groaned as he caught my bottom lip with his teeth.

A hand slid down my bodice, cupping the heavy, swollen flesh of my breast, and he kneaded through my dress. Grasping the edging, he ripped it down past my breast, springing my rosebud nipple free to the chilly bedroom air. He grazed his teeth along the peak, suckling and licking in a spiral around the sensitive nub. I moaned and tossed my head back, arching into his mouth.

"Tom—no!" I said, more forcefully this time, shoving his shoulders away. I slipped my dress back in place. *"We can't."*

He chewed the corner of his lips defiantly, a resolute look etched onto his face. *"Why not?"*

I shoved off the floor, yanking a log from the pile beside my bed. "Do you even need to ask that?" I threw the log on top of the fire and poked at the embers with the steel end of my poker. "You promised. That we would not—" I gasped as he crept behind me, his hand cupping the cleft between my legs.

He tugged the other side of my bodice and my other breast sprang free. "I did say that," he said, brushing his lips along the length of my neck. "But I'm not paying for your company." He raised his gaze to mine and pressed his lips together. "And you actually want to be with me."

He rested both hands on my shoulders and turned me to face him. "And you are far too good for my father."

I swallowed. I did like Tom. I wanted to touch him. Make him moan and cry out my name in a passionate moment.

But I couldn't take his life—it would be wrong. And detrimental to the battle. If my vision of Jack was correct, Tom didn't have long for this world as it was. The thought landed heavy in my chest, simmering low in my heart.

"You are correct. About everything. I do like you. I am too good for your father. But, you, Tom . . . you are too good for me."

His hands traipsed down my arms, and each cupped breast. He bent, kissing each budded nipple. "That's ridiculous—"

"No," I interrupted. "It's not." Grabbing his face, I pulled his focus back to my eyes.

His eyes darkened to a smoky taupe. "I hate that you are with him. I hate that he has seen you and knows how your body works. I hate that he gets all of you and I get only a portion of you."

My pulse pounded heavy in my ears. "All he has is my body. Everything else is a lie—even our intimacies are a lie. He has none of me."

"Except for what's between your thighs." Tom turned, bending at the waist and snatching his book from the floor. "I should go," he muttered.

"No, don't leave like this!" I grabbed his elbow, tugging him back to me with a little more strength than I intended to use. He barreled into my body, and we fell to the ground, Tom landing on top of me with a heavy fall.

"Christ! Are you well?" His pink tongue circled full lips, and they glistened with moisture.

"I apologize," I nodded.

"Where did you get that sort of strength?" His eyes traveled over my entire body, finally landing back on my eyes.

I shrugged, not knowing how to answer that. Thickness pushed through his trousers, nestled between my legs. My sex jumped, pulsing with the desire to feel him deep inside of me.

I held my breath. The slightest movement and I was certain my pheromones would seep out.

"Bloody hell." The words sprung from him like a leaky roof. "You are aroused, aren't you?"

My eyes sprung open, and I hoped they didn't reveal the panic I felt strangling me inside. "No," I answered quickly.

His grin widened and he rolled his hip over me in a fluid motion that made me lose my breath. "Yes, you are."

I made a noise, something between a gasp and a groan. My sex pulsed, swollen and needy. I wanted his seed inside of me. Instead, I squeezed my knees together.

I dragged my fingers down his arm until I had his hand in mine. "Please, Tom. Don't do this."

"May I kiss you?" he panted, his lips only a breath away from mine. "A real kiss. The kind that you would never give to my father."

"It's a dangerous door to open. . . ."

"I know. I need this. I need something that he doesn't have."

"You have everything of me that he doesn't, Tom."

"And yet, it's still not enough."

"Promise you will stop?" I asked the question, but knew he wouldn't. My lips would never satisfy him fully. He would never stop trying, because that's my poison. It's addictive.

He paused. "I promise."

I wet my lips, only the tip of my pink tongue peeking out to run along the seam, and Tom stiffened above me.

"Is that a yes?" His voice was deep and rich, like a plush velvet brocade, and I nodded.

His eyes grew large, and a smile twitched before it was replaced with a determined, sexy pout. His hand snaked around the back of my neck and lifted my head from the floor. Curling his fingers around my tendrils, he tugged—the movement gentle and yet completely dominant.

I rested my hands on his broad shoulders and stroked them to his upper back. Taut muscles roped through the thin fabric.

He pressed his lips to mine, gently at first, working my lips in the smoothest movement. He tasted of tea, and his tongue dipped into my mouth, gliding against mine. My nipples responded, hardening and aching for his touch.

Tom angled his head and deepened the kiss, his groan vibrating deep inside of me. Desire flared deep in my core, and the itch for his life force flared like ale being thrown on a fire. I clamped my thighs together, but the sudden pulse only made the itch worse.

Before I could stop myself, I purred into his mouth, a breathy moan, and my hips bucked against his manhood.

The absence as he tore his lips from mine was a hollow coldness. I took a moment to collect myself before opening my eyes again. His breath was heavy above me, and fire danced in his eyes. "A promise is a promise," he husked, then pushed to his feet, offering his hand to me as well.

I adjusted my dress to a more decent state, then took his hand. "But," he continued, tugging me into him once more, "if you ever change your mind about us . . . don't hesitate for a moment to tell me." He grinned, and it momentarily took my breath away. I couldn't tear my eyes from his mouth. That full, wet pout that I wanted to see between my legs.

"What?" he asked, blinking and glancing over my face.

I shook my head. "Nothing."

"Come, now. No secrets." He chucked a finger beneath my chin, forcing eye contact once more. "Tell me."

"Really. It's nothing."

He shrugged, that playful smile not dissipating in the least. "Very well. Don't tell me." He lunged for my ribs, shifting the mood from sensual to playful, tickling until I collapsed into his arms. My laugh exploded in the room, and I wrapped my arms around his belly, tugging him down onto the floor beside me and rolling on top of him. The itch cooled slightly but still stayed as the constant reminder to what I was giving up. But I didn't care. Tom's life was spared, and that's what mattered. A small period of my discomfort was worth it. I pinned his wrists above his head, and my hair draped into his face.

"Now this is a position I could get used to." He pushed a half-ready erection into me.

The door blew open and we both jumped as it crashed. "Lucien!" I hopped off of Tom, running over to him. "You're back."

Tom cleared his throat, adjusting his shirt and smoothing his hair with a palm.

He raised an eyebrow, glancing between Tom and me. "Yes."

"I-I didn't get to thank you. For . . ." I threw a look over my shoulder at Tom. ". . . for going on that trip in my place."

I stepped back, examining Lucien. His face was pale where it was usually tanned and glowing, even in New Jersey's bleak winter. His eyes drooped and sagged just a little more than I was used to seeing. "Are you well?" I asked more quietly.

"Of course," he clipped. "I see you're taking good care of our Patriot here."

"We were reading." The words rushed from Tom's mouth without any prompt from Lucien or me. When we both just stared at him in response, his eyebrows creased with worry and he shrugged at me. "Well, we were."

Lucien inhaled deeply, dropping his eyes to the moistened circle of my skirt. It fell just between my legs, and I quickly covered it with my hands. Lucien chuckled in a way that was anything but amused. "Come now, Monica. I could smell it from the other room," he whispered as he stalked farther into the bedroom. He circled the area in front of the fire where Tom and I had been.

I cleared my throat and sat at the edge of the bed. I looked to Tom, then back to Lucien with a deep breath. "Lucien—we came up with a plan. A way to win the battle. But we'd have to be ready by Christmas."

Lucien's face lit, sparked by surprise. "Do go on. I love a good battle. Especially one on Christ's birthday."

35

"Grayson! Get your potato-chip-covered hands off the map! They're leaving grease stains!" George snapped, rolling his eyes.

Grayson lazily lifted his hand, wiping it along his flannel shirt.

George watched with a curled lip and straightened his black-fitted vest. "Just because you're an animal doesn't mean you have to constantly act like one."

Grayson leaned back in the chair and kicked his feet up, crossing them onto my kitchen table. He threw a chip into the air and caught it in his mouth. It crunched loudly and he smiled, proud of himself. "Au contraire. I think that's exactly what it means." He wiggled his eyes at George. "Tell me something, incubus. Is your excalibur as magical as they say it is?"

Grayson grinned at George, chomping away at the salty snack. He was referencing George's long past and having fathered Merlin. A flush of red crept onto George's mocha cheeks.

A grin curved on my face before I could stop it from forming. "Man, I missed you, George. It's good to have you back."

George sent me a wink. Deep dimples creased with his 100-watt grin, and bouncy black curls complemented his smooth skin. He looked up, honey-brown eyes regarding me warmly. "Unfortunately, I have to go back in a couple hours. But that's the beauty of teleportation, right?"

I slapped the bottoms of Grayson's feet, considerably harder than maybe I should have. "Get your dirty-ass feet off my table. And chew with your mouth closed. No one wants to see that."

"Oh, I dunno," Grayson grunted, shifting to sit straight in the chair. "I think pretty boy there wouldn't mind seeing all of me. Even the dirtier side." He winked at George, who rolled his eyes again, shooting me a narrowed gaze.

"How long do we need to dog-sit this fool?"

"Oh, please," Grayson said through a grin. "You know you want to pound me like a slab of steak."

"Oh, for the love of . . ." I trailed off, flipping the tracing paper and popping the crumbs off of it and into the air.

"Enough," Kayce snapped. "Grayson, stand up. Put the chips down and fucking help out, already. You're part of the reason our girl is in this mess."

"Me?" Grayson drawled. "Y'all have a twisted memory."

"So!" I raised my voice in an attempt to get us back on track. The tracing paper drifted down onto the map of Las Vegas. "According to Rhea, the five points of the upside-down pentagram will show us the areas in which a human can perform a summoning." Collectively, we all leaned over the map. "From there, we can narrow it down to spiritual areas in which a black magic idol could not have transported." I tossed George a marker. "Rhea said the pentagram had to have these measurements in ratio to a standard map to be accurate."

George glanced at the slip of paper I handed him as well. "Jesus." He trailed a hand over his hair. "You realize this is not easy. Do you even have a protractor?"

"Only guys have them. Though I hear it enhances orgasms gloriously." Kayce humped the table, flicking her tongue.

"Not prostate. A protractor," George quipped. Despite his seemingly annoyed voice, a smirk broke through.

"We know, we know," I said. "I bought one earlier." I slinked over to the office nook off the kitchen and grabbed the Staples bag, tossing it to George.

He cleared his throat, turning the Sharpie and protractor over in his hands. "And just how do you expect us to get in there to save Lucien if it's blessed ground?"

Tipping my head farther down, I refused to make eye contact. In truth, I hadn't thought that far ahead just yet. "We have angels and humans on our side who can help, you know," I said quietly.

"Uh, Monica . . . I hate to be the one to point this out, but I'm not so sure Drew can go on the holy ground anymore, either." Kayce's gaze shifted between me and George.

"He's still human. He should be fine," I snapped.

"And Jules and Adrienne might not be allowed to help us," George added.

"Look!" I slapped a hand down, the map crinkling beneath my touch. "We'll figure it out later. But step one is simply *finding* Lucien in the first place."

Even though George still looked skeptical, he leaned over and, with one thick line, started the pentagram. My breath froze in my chest as I watched, gripping the edge of the table until my fingers grew numb.

"You know"—Grayson examined his fingernails in a haughty attempt to look uninterested—"while I am not in wolf form, I am for all intents and purposes . . . a human."

We all turned to glare at him. Slowly. Purposefully. "What do you mean?" I asked, narrowing my eyes.

Pushing off his knees, he stood, peeking over my shoulder at the map. "Unless I shift myself into wolf form, I'm no demon.

Werecreatures are weird hybrids of human and beast. We're demonlike as an animal, but human while—well, human. The only time we can't control it is in the full moon. And that's the only time we can create other weres. Saetan can't create us. Nor can he destroy us."

"Then why are you under his rule?"

Grayson shrugged. "Because where else were they going to put us?"

"So . . . you're a human?"

He nodded.

"And you live a human life span."

Again he nodded.

"So as long as I don't shift into wolf form on holy ground, I'm safe."

George, Kayce, and I exchanged a look. "No," Kayce stated with raised brow. "We can't trust him yet." She slid her eyes to the sides, looking at him. "He hasn't proven himself. So he can go in only if there's someone else to join him. Damien?"

A lump formed in my throat so fast, I barely had time to swallow it down before speaking. "I-I'll have to check that he's around."

"Of course he'll be around," George said. "That boy's crazy protective of you." I couldn't see George's face as he bent over the map, his nose practically touching the opaque tracing paper.

"Yeah," Kayce snorted. "A damn lotta good he is at that. If Damien were a condom, our girl would have been knocked up months ago."

"I said I'd ask him, okay? Can we just figure out where Lucien is in the first place," I snapped, ignoring the looks that passed from George to Kayce.

"Okay, okay. Jeez, calm yourself." George squeezed my shoulder.

It took roughly twenty minutes, three sheets of tracing paper, and a handful of "Fuck!"s for George to get the pentagram right. He stood, fists triumphantly in the air. "I did it! That's it, right?"

I measured the edge, eying the lines carefully. "It looks right to me. . . ." I failed to add *but what the fuck would I know* to the end of that.

"Seriously, I think that's right!" George bounced, and his curls sprung about the room with him.

"Yeah, yeah." A yawn escaped as Kayce stretched, having long given up on watching the upside-down star being drawn. "Great job, Aristotle."

"Aristotle was a philosopher," George added. "Pythagoras was a mathematician."

"Whatever."

"Okay." I leaned over the map, examining the points. "The southernmost point . . ."

"The ram's nose . . ."

I slid a glance to Grayson—a guy who just loved to inter-rupt—and continued. "Yes, the ram's nose falls just south of Paradise. Kayce, can you write down these coordinates?"

She nodded and jotted them down.

"The westernmost point falls on Oakley Boulevard."

George had his laptop out, pulling up the coordinates. "Okay, it looks like the southernmost point is some sort of empty lot. Nothing holy or spiritual. That I can determine at least."

"We should still check it out for ourselves," Kayce rasped. "You never know with shit like this."

I nodded. "Wow," I gasped. "The easternmost point falls right in the center of Las Vegas Valley." I snapped up, looking between my friends. "Could that be holy?"

"That's the annoying thing," Kayce said. "Any of these places could be spiritual or blessed in some way or another. All it takes is your precious Jules popping in and giving it a blessing and *bam!* Instant spiritual ground."

"Shit," I muttered, clamping my hands onto my hips.

George chuckled from behind his laptop screen. "Well, well, well . . . all but one place, that is. Guess what address pops up with the coordinates on Oakley? Our friendly resident succubar. Suck 'n' Swallow."

"Succubar!" Kayce exclaimed with a laugh. "Why the Hell didn't they name it that instead? That's way better."

"Kayce, please! Focus!" I scrambled to peek at George's computer screen. "Are you absolutely sure? That's an awfully big coincidence, isn't it?"

George shrugged. "Seems like it to me."

Kayce raised an eyebrow, resting her elbow on George's shoulder. "And we know Mia's gunning for you."

"But it's not blessed. Otherwise none of us could get in there. . . ."

A clatter to my right startled all of us. Grayson scraped the chair back, walking to the sink and filling a glass of water. "Let's think about this rationally, shall we? This summoning, five point business is probably relatively common knowledge, right? Your Queen is a smart lady, so she probably knew upon buying that space that it was a summonings grounds. Therefore, she was finding a way to cut back on the illegal summonings." Tipping his head back, he glugged the water, wiping the excess droplets with the back of his hand. "Doesn't seem that coincidental to me."

"He's right," I said after a moment. "Fuck. I hate that he's right."

"Now," he continued with a slow saunter back to us, "that don't mean that someone couldn't summon Lucien into a holy relic. Any one of these five points could be where it was done . . . and it was simply the vessel—"

Drew's face entered my mind, and I snapped a glare to Grayson, a threatening hiss escaping.

Two hands shot up in surrender. "Sorry, sorry. Poor choice

of words. It could simply be the . . . idol in which they are storing Lucien that is holy."

"Like . . . a genie in a bottle?"

He put a finger to the tip of his nose, pointing at my chest with the other. "Bingo, darlin'." He knocked a fist to the table and winked at Kayce.

"Do you just hit on everyone?" I sneered.

He chuckled, scratching dirty fingers into his facial hair. "Well, now, c'mon, Ms. Kettle. Don't be calling Mr. Pot black." He held up a finger before I could throw out a retort. "One more thing. You mentioned Lucien was abducted during a magic show? That he volunteered to step up for?"

"Sorta. It was a . . . an acquaintance's show."

Grayson shrugged, using his flair for the dramatics to emphasize a point. "Did he know he was going to be going onto the stage? How could anyone have foreseen that?"

Waves of goose bumps flowed down my body. "Fucking Buckley," I whispered. "It was supposed to be me in that box."

36

"Yep," Kayce said. "Buckley came up to you, and Lucien stepped in with a cock block."

Yet again, Lucien was in trouble because he was protecting me. In the craziness of the past couple of days, I forgot that I was probably the initial target.

An arm landed heavily around my shoulders, squeezing me into a lean, muscled chest. "You can't beat yourself up about this, baby girl. Lucien knew the risk and it's why he stepped in. He preferred to be the one in trouble . . . not you."

"Besides," Kayce added, brushing a wisp of jet-black hair from her eyes. "He knows there's a lot of people looking for him. Wherever he is."

Everyone's eyes landed on Grayson, and I sniffled, looking away. Kayce chewed the corner of her lip and raised her brows.

Grayson clapped me on the back in a gesture that was not exactly comforting so much as the way you encourage a batter before he goes up to the plate. "Yeah, there, there. Let's all put on our big girl panties and go kick some ass."

A laugh exploded through my nose, and I nodded. "A for effort, Grayson."

George gave my shoulder one last squeeze before releasing me. "So, let's say we do go exploring in these places. How will we know if Lucien's there?"

Silence thrummed in the kitchen, and I became all too aware of my leaky sink dripping water every three seconds.

"I might be able to smell him," Grayson threw out.

Kayce looked doubtful. "Through an enchantment?"

"I dunno." He shrugged and tapped a finger to the side of his nose. "It's pretty damn powerful, though."

Kayce stood, walking with her back so straight, she may as well have had a rod for a spine. Ducking into a duffel bag of items we had brought with us from Lucien's house, she pulled out a T-shirt. "All right, oh mighty sniffer. I'm going to hide this. With an enchantment on it. And it's going to be invisible. Let's see how you do." She snapped her fingers—mostly for effect . . . we all knew she could just turn invisible without the fanfare—and disappeared.

Moments later she was back, empty-handed.

Grayson closed his eyes and inhaled, his chest expanding and hard nipples piercing through his paper-thin cotton shirt. George and I stared on with admiring eyes before we each caught the other. He nudged me in the ribs with a sharp elbow. "You've got the coffee man *and* the detective. Leave some for the rest of us."

I smiled softly at George, inwardly sighing. I'd have to tell them sooner or later that I didn't have either man. Later would suffice, I thought, and linked my arm through his. "You speak as if I was competition to a stud like you. Besides, I just like to look."

Grayson's eyes snapped open and they were glowing yellow. "Jesus," hissed George. "Not sure I'll ever get used to that."

He glared at Kayce and, for a second, I thought he might go primal wolf on all of us. He stared in a way that suggested he didn't speak our language at the moment. But then, he was thundering down the hall, a growl rolling in the back of his throat.

Minutes later, after a triumphant roar and a testosterone-addled beating of his chest, Grayson returned with an invisible clump of something in his hand. He tossed it into Kayce's face, and with a quick incantation the enchantment was lifted.

"Found it in record time. Even with your invisibility cloak, your enchantment, and your dousing it in the lovely lady's perfume." He looked to me with a wink that passed so quickly, one might have missed it.

"My per—what? Kayce! That shit is expensive!"

I snatched Lucien's shirt, bringing it to my nose and inhaling. Dammit, Kayce.

"Oh, calm down. You shouldn't be wasting your money on that shit, anyway." Kayce rasped. "Besides, your natural scent is so much better." She wiggled her eyebrows at me.

"I'd have to agree with the lady," Grayson said.

I clicked my tongue. "Damn, dude. You *do* just hit on anything that walks upright."

He raised an eyebrow. "And some that are on all fours, too, darlin'."

"So!" Kayce clapped her hands together. "How about we start at the southernmost point? Wolfie—are you able to teleport?"

Grayson rolled his eyes. "Did you not just hear me when I said that when I'm not in wolf form, I am human? No. I can't teleport."

George looked at the clock. "Unfortunately, you guys might have to start without me. I'll catch up with you later, though, okay?" He kissed me on the forehead before disappearing with a *crack*.

"Okay," I said to Kayce and Grayson. "Shall we go?" I shifted my clothes, and stars flooded my vision as though something had bashed me across the temple. I fell into a chair, immediately dropping my head between my legs.

Kayce sunk to a crouch in front of me, brushing my hair behind my ears. I lifted my gaze to meet hers, and her eyes watered with concern. "How long has it been since you charged?"

I shrugged. "A few days at least."

She cursed under her breath, shaking her head. "Jesus, Monica. And in those days, you've been attacked, slashed, invisible—you've probably used more energy in these days than you usually do in a week."

"You think I don't know that?" I snapped, then pinched the bridge of my nose. "I know. They're not gonna let Lucien go without a fight."

"Monica," Kayce added softly. "You have to choose a good man. Someone who will give you ample energy."

After several deep breaths, I stood. "Don't worry, Kayce. I'm trying something a little new." Her eyes narrowed so much, they almost looked entirely closed. "Trust me. If it doesn't work, I'll bang a second guy just to ensure I have energy."

Grayson raised a hand, that annoyingly sexy smirk even larger than normal. "Could I volunteer?"

Kayce spun, storming toward the door and slapping Grayson on the back of the head as she passed. "You're an idiot, you know that?" With a hand clamped around the doorknob, she turned to face me. "You have an hour and a half, Monica. We'll all meet back here at eight."

37

New Jersey, 1776

T*he Hessians had been in Trenton for a week. Their garrison was stationed right off of King Street, a convenient block away from the brothel. And many of our succubi had simply moved into their barracks. But not me. Jack was still adamant about keeping me all for himself.*

It was our first night spent at his house in what felt like ages. Even with the fire crackling in the hearth, frigid air crept in through the flimsy closed windows and crawled across my bare flesh until goose bumps covered my body.

I wasn't necessarily cold, despite the gooseflesh and tight nipples. Jack palmed my breast, squeezing and rolling my nipple between his fingers. Though the sensation wasn't exactly disagreeable, I got the sense that it was more for his amusement than mine. And why shouldn't it be? He was paying for the privilege, I supposed.

Dawn was just breaking over the horizon; orange light glittered along Jacob's Creek. All I could do was stare out that window at the beautiful, glistening water as Jack's hand dipped from my breast down my stomach and into the crook between my legs. I bucked as his fingers brushed my most sensitive area and my bottom rammed into his hardened manhood.

Despite the fact that we had just had sex less than eight hours ago before falling asleep, that blasted itch surfaced, flaring itself through my body like a hungry beast. And my body betrayed my heart, betrayed my mind, as moisture gathered between my thighs. Jack's fingers were skillful, that was for sure, and he dipped two inside, my body stiffening at the movement. A moan escaped, and I hated myself for enjoying it.

The creek glittered, the twinkling light hitting my face with the morning sunlight, winking at me as if it approved. I lifted a knee, dropping my foot behind Jack's body to offer him my everything as widely as I could. I throbbed for him. His touch, his erection, his lips, his tongue—all of him.

Snaking his hands under my body, he rolled me on top of him—only I was on my back, lying atop his nude body. His erection cradled between my buttocks and I curled my feet under, bent at the knees. I spread for him. Open. Wet. Needing.

His lips found my neck, nipping at the top of my shoulder while he inserted three fingers, drowning them inside of me. My breath caught, breasts bouncing as my body clenched around his fingers. Oh, how I wanted to hate this. I wanted to hate his touch; but he was too damn good. My back arched into his hand and his thumb circled the mass of curls between my legs while his palm added pressure to the nub above my opening.

A cry echoed in the room and my body exploded, clenching and curling around his knuckles.

He scooped my hair to the side, taking my ear into his mouth and suckling at it. "Sit up, my dearest. I want to see those tight prats of yours," he said, and trailed his hands to my buttocks, squeezing and slipping a finger from my slit to crack. The other hand gently pressed the top of my shoulders, aiding in pushing me to my knees, facing away from him atop his erect rod.

Lifting myself, I held him firmly at the base and impaled myself on him. His course leg hair scratched the insides of my thighs, and his wiry hair brushed my backside. The itch slashed low inside my belly, and I cried out at the rush of him inside of me. Tears welled, and while I would normally need to swallow them, watering the seeds of self-loathing, I let them fall free this time. One by one they dripped down my face onto my breasts and down between my legs.

I rode Jack. Soft at first, reveling in the feel of his soft head gliding in and out. Then faster, his tip hitting the delicious knot deep inside of me. His hands started on my hips, rotating them in circles as well as up and down—as if I didn't already know just how he liked it. I fell forward between his legs onto my hands, and his finger brushed my bum. The other hand spread my backside as his finger explored into my tightest pucker. I gasped as he entered a finger, and I tightened all over. My body went rigid. How could something so unusual feel so bloody good?

"Don't stop," I whispered, my tears long forgotten.

"Never," he husked, pushing deeper inside. I gasped as both penetrations touched inside of me.

I was teetering on the edge of another explosion. On a wall, several stories into the sky, ready to happily leap over the other side.

He pumped into me harder and harder, but all the while keeping his finger in slow, controlled movements.

"Jack—I'm so close. I-I'm going to . . . I'm going to . . ."

"Oh, my pet," he groaned, lifting his own backside off the bed in a final thrust. His hand gripped my hip bone while the other wiggled against my hole. His fluids spurted hot and sticky inside of me, and I screamed as the rolling waves of orgasm slammed into me at the same time as his life force.

With every climax he had, I saw the reel of his life. Saw his life thinning before my very eyes. He would still kill Tom. But he would die minutes after the battle thanks to a gunshot to his temple. I smirked to myself. All it would take is once or twice more with me. And then he would be dead before he could even place a hand on his son.

38

"Curious seeing you here." Jules's golden blond hair whipped around his neck with a breeze from a ceiling fan.

"Don't start with me, Julian." I snapped the book shut and placed it back on the shelf with others, glancing around the bookstore. "What are *you* doing here?"

He chuckled. "Oh, you know . . ." he said, holding up a book as well. "Just finding a purpose for driving along this life. Like you."

I rolled my eyes. "Exactly the ambiguous answer I'd expect from you."

I turned, stomping in the opposite direction, and in the blink of an eye, Jules was standing before me. I slammed into his chest, bouncing off of him. He caught me around the shoulders, steadying me. "Monica—why are you in the spiritual section of the bookstore?" His smirk was gone, replaced instead with rosy lips thinned into a line.

"Leave me alone, Julian. I mean it," I said through gritted teeth. "I have business to attend to."

"In the religious studies section? An angel should do anything but cramp your style here."

"Fine," I snapped. "Stay. Watch. You'll regret it, though."

He paused, raking assessing eyes down the length of my body, taking in my cardigan sweater over a pink A-line dress. "You're not about to do what I think you're going to do, are you?"

"You're the lie detector. Does it look like I'm lying to you right now?"

"Monica," he whispered. "Don't go back to this life." His crystal eyes widened. "You're better than this."

"Julian—you have to trust me." I swallowed. I don't know why I was asking him to trust me when I could barely trust myself with this. But the bottom line was that I needed to know if this whole "giving life" thing held any weight. And the only way to find out was to be with someone I didn't completely despise, like a Hell-bound asshat.

His eyes tipped and his mouth marred into a frown. Without another word, he turned to leave just as I grasped his elbow.

"Wait—"

Hope sparked across his features.

"Jules, I know that angels of death exist. Like the Banshee—and I'm sure there's many others. Are there any . . . I don't know . . . angels of life? Or something?"

Furled eyebrows marred his beautifully chiseled face. "No. God is the only being that can give life. Though many can take it away. Humans included." He glanced down at my clenched hand, still grasping his elbow. "Why?"

I swallowed, knowing there was no way to lie to him. "I was curious. There's so much I never bothered to learn about both angels and demons." I looked away, knowing the statement was absolutely true. "It was stupid. Always depending on you and Lucien to take care of me. I guess I'm just regretting my ignorance now with Lucien gone."

Jules narrowed his eyes at me again, eyes flitting around my hair. Reading my aura. Fucking angels. After a moment, he nodded, one side of his mouth twitching to his eyes a fraction.

"It's not the whole truth—but at least it's something," he said, that smile cracking a touch larger.

I exhaled. He could have grilled that a lot harder, that's for sure. With a *crack,* he was gone.

Forty-five minutes and three religious men later, I still hadn't managed to land one of them for even a make-out session. Shit, maybe I was setting my standards too high. Spiritual guys needed time to trust you, know you, maybe even love you. I looked at my cell phone. I had less than an hour. There was no time to fall in love.

Flopping onto the wall behind me, I slid into a crouch on the ground.

"Can I help you find something?" A young man with plastic, black-rimmed glasses, rumpled brown hair, and a golden aura looked down on me.

I climbed to my feet and inwardly smirked. He was cute. More than cute, in a smart, *I read a lot* kind of way. He wore corduroys with a tiny rip on the knee and a fitted Ramones T-shirt that hugged a trim torso. "I think I found it, actually."

"Oh. Okay." He shrugged and turned to leave.

"I was going to grab a coffee in the café. Are you almost off your shift?"

His eyes assessed me from head to toe, stopping only momentarily at my breasts. He glanced at his phone. "No, but . . ." He trailed off, then shook his head. "No, not for a while," he finished with a smirk.

I nodded, catching my bottom lip between my teeth. "Okay. What's on the agenda for work today?"

He looked at me curiously and gestured to a rolly cart of books and a printed list. "Moving last week's releases from the front to the back."

I exhaled, my pheromone seeping out from my nostrils to his, and as he sniffed, his pupils dilated.

"You're telling me *that* can't wait thirty minutes?" I glanced at his name tag. "Elliot?" I ran a finger along the edge of the tag, making sure to brush his chest in the process. "Are you the manager?"

He ran a hand through his already mussed hair, and his hazel eyes surveyed me. I did the same, brushing my fingers through his soft strands until I reached the base of his neck. Gripping the long curls there, I tugged, pulling him into me.

He smirked, a quiet confidence lurking just below the surface. He nodded. "I'm actually the owner."

I broke character for a moment, stepping back. "You're Elliot Allen? I've been trying to call you for months!"

"Uh, what?" He glanced to the side, adjusting his glasses with pinched fingers.

"Sorry, sorry—I, uh . . ." Shit. "I'm Monica. Over at the GrindHouse. I've been trying to set up a meetup for local business owners."

He narrowed his eyes, then nodded. "Oh, right. Drew's main girl, right?"

"Drew's—what? His . . ." I snorted, shaking my head. "I mean, we're friends, but I'm not his . . . his anything. Least of all, his gi—"

Elliot chuckled, sliding his hands into his front pockets. "I meant, you're his manager. The main barista, right? But it's nice to know where you two stand." He held up one hand, palm out to me. His grin was annoyingly haughty.

"Well, it was nice to finally meet you, Elliot," I said, slapping my hands to my outer thighs as I walked past him. I guess I was resigned to another night with low powers. I'd done it before—I could do it again.

He snatched my elbow, looking down over inky eyelashes at me. "Where you going, Monica?"

"I-I, uh, I thought—"

He licked his lips with a quick glance around the bookstore. "The stockroom is empty right now." He leaned closer, the tip of his nose brushing my cheekbone. "And even if it wasn't, I'm sure I could clear it out for us."

Wow. The sparkly souled beta-boy was surprising me with each turn.

"You sure about this?" I batted my eyes at him, and he rolled his eyes with a snort in return.

"Does that doe-eyed shit usually work on guys?"

I bit back my smirk. I kind of liked him. Sarcasm and all. "Elliot—you'd be amazed."

His grin widened and a nod bobbed his head while he glanced around his store. "You realize how weird this looks, right? You sitting here for an hour, barely looking at any books. Then suddenly coming on to me?"

"You've been watching me?" I put a hand to my chest with delicate fingers and dropped my mouth. "Besides, you stopped *me* from leaving just now."

He unsnaked his hand from mine. "Hey, if you want to go, no one's holding you here." He put both hands up in surrender before hooking his thumbs back into his pockets and leaning on the doorframe to the stockroom. A challenging eyebrow arched over a sparkling hazel eye.

A pregnant pause hung in the air, and I shook my head, leading the way to the back room. "You're a lot of trouble already, you know that?"

"But worth every minute of it," he whispered, shutting the door behind him.

His hands were immediately cupping my ass, and he tugged me into his body for an embrace. Our noses bumped as we got our bearings in the dark, and soon his lips were everywhere. On my lips, my neck, my ear—and damn was he good with that mouth. Tingles ran like rapids through my body. He ripped open the cardigan, raining little pink buttons all over the cement floor.

The itch flared through my body like a raging fire, and I drank in his kisses. With some help from Elliot, he lifted me onto a counter and flipped my dress up around my waist. His fingers circled my silky thong, the moisture pooling between my legs. I groaned, my head falling back on the wall behind me.

He hooked a finger into the panties, pushing them to the side, and he glided over my clit with skilled but gentle movements. My body clenched with desire.

"You are so wet," he whispered, claiming my mouth once more and nibbling on my bottom lip.

"Wet for you," I panted. "Please. Now . . ." I couldn't even formulate a full sentence, I was so wrought with need.

He chuckled and plunged two fingers deep inside, continually adding pressure to my clit with the heel of his hand. "You didn't even know who I was ten minutes ago . . . and now I have you begging for it." He withdrew his hand, placing the wet fingers into his mouth and sucking me off of them.

I tugged at his pants, pulling the button free and unzipping the fly. His boxers were covered in bright yellow smiley faces. "Really? Smiley faces?" I smirked and raised an eyebrow.

"Really? A cardigan?" he countered.

"Touché." I pushed his boxers to the floor, and his erection bounced free.

I gripped him with one hand, pumping him until he was solid steel in my palm. He grunted and smacked a palm to the counter. "You gonna make *me* beg now?"

"It'd be nice. . . ."

He lifted his gaze to me, holding eye contact for so long that it made my hair stand on end. Lowering his lips to mine, he took me in another kiss, the kind that you watch in movies with envy. He cupped my jaw, running tender fingers down my neck to my breasts. When he pulled away, his eyes blinked open, meeting mine once more. "Please," he whispered.

I wanted to laugh and cry all at once. I could count on two hands the number of people with whom my sexual experiences had been meaningful. Pleasurable. And with someone whose company I actually enjoyed. I closed my eyes and thought a prayer to whatever God would have me that Elliot would keep his life. Keep his soul. And not perish at my vagina.

With a firm hand gripping his dick, he positioned himself at my opening. The itch burned, and I winced as the beast spiraled down, like a fiery drill tearing through my guts. Elliot pushed inside, and I stretched around his girth. I moaned, and he placed a finger to my lips with a quiet "Shhh." The other hand palmed my clit, applying pressure to the sensitive nub.

His grin widened as he purposefully attempted to make my moans louder. I squeezed myself around him, and he echoed my moans.

"Not so easy to keep quiet, is it?" I panted, and trailed my thumb across his plump bottom lip.

He nipped the edge of my nail. The sliver of light from beneath the door caught a glint of perspiration on his temple and at his hairline. He pumped into me faster, alternating between pulsating pressure and light flicks to my clit.

Wow, was he good at this, I thought, and studied his face. Pressure built, and beneath the painful itch an even more pleasurable sensation swelled. With each thrust, his glasses slipped farther and farther down his nose, and with a finger I pushed them back up just before they slipped off the edge. His lips tipped into another smirk, and with his free hand he scooped my hair back away from my shoulder and pressed a kiss to the crook of my neck.

Our bodies rocked in unison, and the swell of pleasure burst through the itch, exploding, convulsing around his erection.

He groaned, and his strokes slowed as the heat spurted inside of me.

It was a high like no other, the sensation no less shocking each time. Pins and needles pricked all over my body; it was like jumping into an icy river.

A burst of white light blinded me. The reel of his life was fast: images of him and a girl having coffee at the GrindHouse. Elliot, a few years older at what looked like a meeting of local business owners, sitting across from Drew and me holding hands. The final part of the vision was an older Elliot . . . in his early seventies, maybe. He grabbed his chest, falling to the ground, and a woman—his wife, I assumed—ran to his side to help.

For all of a moment, I thought hope was lost. I'd taken his life—the life of a man who was to become my friend, apparently. But then, the vision continued—and his seventy-year-old eyes popped open. He sat up, breathing heavily.

The present rushed back to me like a frosty gust of wind. I blinked, staring into Elliot's eyes. For the first time that I could remember, one of my visions hadn't ended in death. Had I given him his life back? It seemed that way. The smell of rose water and hibiscus filled my nose. I knew that scent . . . but from where?

I gathered up my sweater's remnants and tossed them into an industrial-size trash bin as Elliot situated his pants. "About that meetup . . ." he said.

"Um, can we discuss that another time?" I interrupted. "No offense, it's just . . . I'm not feeling at my most professional right now."

"No worries," he said, though his smile wobbled.

I grabbed my purse off the floor. The corner of a white note-card poked out the top like a steeple. Slipping out the stock-room door, I tugged on the note, flipping it open.

Midnight at the Suck 'n' Swallow. Come alone. Enter my back room invisible and with powers masked.

P.S. It's good to see you are finally embracing the good-souled men.

My back room. That meant only one thing. Mia was calling a meeting between us.

39

New Jersey, 1776

*T*he stairs at Jack's home were creaky. With each step, they moaned their displeasure at my being awake at such an hour. But sleep was simply nowhere near, and my lying beside Jack's lightly snoring body wasn't going to make a difference.

A cup of hot tea, however, just might. A few glowing embers were left amidst the ash in the hearth; the faint orange glow cast a warm hue through the nearly black room. The steel poker was like ice in my palm, and I shifted the embers around while throwing a log on top. The embers caught, and soon the fire blazed.

The room smelled of apples. As it always did. The pot still had some water in it thankfully, and I hung it over the flames. They licked the black bottom, dancing around the base.

"Is there enough water in the pot for two?"

I yelped, swiveling and covering my mouth with a palm. "Tom!" I shushed, with a quick glance up the stairs. "I didn't realize you were here tonight."

"Obviously," he grunted.

"Thomas, don't be like this. You know I have to . . ." I swallowed. ". . . to do my job."

"Don't call me Thomas as though you're my mother." He turned away, staring out the window.

"Sorry. Tom," I corrected.

We sat in silence while the water heated. Until you have to wait for a pot to boil in agonizing discomfort, you don't realize how long it actually takes. I grabbed two noggins from the cabinet, as well as Jack's teapot, and ladled the hot water into them.

"Please," he whispered, and the desperation in his voice reverberated down to my stomach. "Don't do this anymore. Everything is almost in order . . . there's only two days—"

I rushed him so quickly, it felt as though my feet were separate from my torso, and I clamped a hand over his mouth. My lips pressed together so firmly that I could feel the wrinkling in the corners, but I did not care. With violent movements, I put a finger to my lips, then pointed upstairs. "He was sleeping when I came down. But that's not to say he still is," I whispered.

Tom swallowed and, despite the anger flashing in his eyes, he nodded.

Tom was the first man whose company I'd actually enjoyed since Buckley. Since Julian. And that terrified me. Because love never came without its price.

"Tom—the other night was fun. Amazing, even. But I have a job to do."

He stayed seated, and even though it would have been nice to join him, it just didn't feel right at this point. When I finished the tea I would, without question, be rejoining Jack upstairs.

I crouched in front of the fire, staring at the flames. Fire was an enchanting thing. Beautiful and graceful with each lick.

A sigh came from behind me, and though I knew I should have ignored it, I snuck a peek over my shoulder. Tom sat reclined in his chair, one foot propped on his knee and his cup of tea clenched in one hand.

His eyes examined my face. "You look sensational in the firelight." His mouth curved with only the tiniest hint of a smile.

"*Thank you,*" *I managed to choke before swallowing a gulp of steaming tea.*

Tom pushed off the table and with a slow gait walked until he stood just above me. He sank into a crouch as well, the firelight catching in his eyes. "*I know you have to do this,*" *he said softly.* "*But that doesn't make it any easier.*"

Smoke billowed from the fire, and the scent of burning wood mixed with Tom's personal musk was intoxicating. If only he knew that with each night I spent with his father, I came that much closer to saving his life. But he couldn't know that. There was no way to reveal such information. Not after seeing the trouble I could have gotten into simply for inviting Tom to be part of our rebellion. Bloody Hell—if they sent Lucien to the underworld for that, imagine the response for revealing my nature to a human!

With a light touch, I ran my fingers through Tom's hair, brushing the strands at his temple behind an ear. "*It will be worth it. I promise you that, Tom.*"

He grabbed my hand, bringing it to his lips, and he pressed a firm and lingering kiss to my palm. It tingled up my arm and sent a shiver down my spine. I finished my tea, and Tom gently took the cup, placing it on the table next to his. "*I'll tidy up,*" *he said.*

"*Thank you.*" *I stood, straightening the skirt of my dressing gown.*

Then with no warning, he took my lips, claiming them with his. His muscular thighs framed mine. His lips molded against mine in a kiss so vibrant that for all of a moment our bodies, our thoughts, were one. I could taste his lust. His daring move blazed something torrid inside of me, and my nipples flared with the desire to be touched.

His fingers tunneled into the mass of curls piled on my head, and he haled his lips to my chin and down my neck. Despite my better judgment, I yielded to the moment, a low purr humming at the back of my throat, and I melt into him.

Finally, I placed a palm to his chest and gently pushed him away. "Enough," I panted in a breathy voice. "Good night, Tom."

I slid away from his grasp, not only on my body but on my heart, and ascended the stairs, not daring even one more look down at his boyish face. I reached the last step, and as I turned toward Jack's bedroom, my nose hit a sculpted shoulder.

I gasped, jumping. "Jack!" I barely recognized his face; newly hard lines framed a scowling mouth and slanted eyes.

A wry grin slid along his face in a way that suggested anything but a normal smile. "Coming back to bed, my pet?"

I swallowed with a nervous glance back down the stairs. "Y-yes. I couldn't sleep."

Jack nodded, the scowl melting into yawn. "Very well. Was that Tom I heard down there as well?"

I nodded. "Yes, Jack. I suppose he couldn't sleep, either. I made us each tea."

"How very . . . maternal of you." A smile twitched at the corners of his lips. "Let us get back to bed now."

I followed Jack into the bedroom, but that uneasy feeling still gnawed in the pit of my stomach.

40

Eight o'clock had come and gone long ago. The first location was someone's home, and with a quick walk around the perimeter, it didn't appear to have any sort of spiritual connections. Nor did Grayson smell any hint of Lucien.

The next locale was an empty lot—same thing. No scent. No religiosity.

The third was a cemetery. Though it was obviously spiritual, Grayson couldn't smell Lucien at all. He sniffed around the headstones and grass for a while, stating after that a lot of people had been through there, and though he could smell the sulfur of past summonings, still no Lucien.

We arrived at the Valley a little after eleven. Kayce had her phone out with the coordinates plugged in—luckily there was an app for that. GPS led us directly to the entrance of an old mine.

Grayson stiffened, the half-full moon shining a blue haze along his hair. "There was a summoning held here," he said, inhaling the night air. "More recently than any of the other places, though I can't be sure when."

I gripped his elbow. "Lucien. Do you smell Lucien?"

Grayson's eyes fluttered closed, and after a moment's thought, he shook his head. "I think so," he said. "But it's very faint. And I smell someone else . . . someone new."

"Just one other person?" Kayce asked, tucking her phone into her back pocket.

Grayson nodded. "The smell is equally as strong as the sulfur. I'd say the scent is the last person to hold a summoning."

Kayce nodded. "That's good. That's a good start."

"So . . ." I trailed off staring up into the entrance of the mine shaft. "Do you think he's being kept inside the mine?" My voice was small as I looked around. "I mean, if you faintly smell Lucien out here . . ."

Kayce led the way, followed by me and Grayson. The darkness inside the shaft was blacker than any night I'd ever experienced.

From behind me, there was a *thunk* followed by an egregious curse.

"You all right, wolf?"

"Yeah, yeah," Grayson grumbled.

"Dogs aren't quite known for their vision, huh?" Kayce snickered.

"No," Grayson said. "But we are known for our noses. And I'm telling you that Lucien's not here in the mine. The smell I'm picking up was outside, and even that was barely discernible."

I paused, running a hand along the rock wall, and Kayce stopped walking, following my pause.

There was a crank sound and then a flick. A dull light flickered on, and in Grayson's hand was a lighter. "That's better." He paused, mouth pressed into a line while his eyes roamed the mine. "I don't think they expected you to have a wolf helping. And based on the lingering smell of a summoning and this random person, I think it's possible that the faint smell I'm picking up could be his scent contained in a vessel. It would be significantly lessened as opposed to his shirt from our experiment before."

"So, basically, Lucien's not here now. But he might have been summoned here." Kayce tutted and rolled her eyes. "I said it in one sentence, dude. Let's get going, then. We're wasting time."

I reached into my purse and my hand brushed the note card Mia had given me. A chilling reminder of what the rest of my night entailed. My Queen was a terrifying woman, and there was little I wanted less than to be in her presence with no one knowing where I was. The time was passing quickly. It was almost midnight.

I cleared my throat. "Hey, guys—I'm gonna go ahead to the Suck 'n' Swallow. I forgot . . . I told Damien I'd meet him there at midnight."

Kayce's eyes narrowed. "Okay," she said. "I'll teleport with you. The dog can drive himself."

"No," I answered quickly—perhaps a little too hastily, because her gaze narrowed even more. "We can't leave Grayson alone, you know?"

Kayce inhaled deeply, and the leather tank she wore creaked with the movement. "Fine. We'll be right behind you."

I nodded. Perfect. I sure hoped this meeting wouldn't take more than thirty minutes.

I teleported outside the Suck 'n' Swallow, changing my looks with my newly abundant power, thanks to Elliot. I used the same small, brunette girl persona as last time and slipped past the bouncer easily, shifting my eyes, the pass code to enter.

I cruised the bar, and standing at the edge in a black tailored suit was Mia. She looked up from her martini, immediately catching my eye and raising a brow.

I scurried behind the jukebox where I shifted invisible, cloaking my powers.

Mia stood slowly, tapping the bar to get Ink's attention. "Bring my visitor to the back room when he arrives."

Ink gave one sharp nod, collecting some empty glassware from the bar.

"And Ink?" Mia's voice lowered, but despite the quieter sound, she managed to hold his attention. He lifted his chin, meeting her eyes. Though Ink was a large man, I could smell the trepidation on him. "The martini is good today. About time." Her mouth quirked so slightly that one might have missed the miniscule tip if they hadn't been watching.

She turned for the back room, holding the door open long enough for me to slip in with her.

The room looked exactly the same; just as unsettling. Mia didn't speak to me. Didn't even acknowledge that I was standing there in front of her, though we both knew she was fully aware of my presence.

After several agonizing minutes of silence, Mia glanced at her phone and spoke. "You're late," she said quietly. "I would think you'd know by now how much I detest tardiness." She clung to the double *s* of the last word in a snakelike hiss.

I cleared my throat. "I'm sorry."

Her hand jerked up to a halting position. "Don't speak," she snapped. "My guest will be here soon." Reaching into her bag, she pulled out a bottle of Chanel No. 5. "Dab this on your pressure points. You should learn that if you plan on masking yourself, you must do something about that scent of yours. Anyone with a good nose will know your presence from your smell alone."

She tossed the bottle of perfume at me, and I just barely caught it in time. After dabbing a bit behind my ears and on my wrists, I placed the bottle onto the glass coffee table.

"What's this about?" I asked, hiding the tremor in my voice.

"Shhh," Mia cooed. "He's here."

The door creaked open and Ink stepped forward with a bow. "Your highness." He gestured for someone behind him to enter.

Peppermint slammed into my nose, and I could taste him on my tongue. Cool and fresh. Julian stepped inside with a nod to Mia.

41

New Jersey, December 25, 1776

"Now bring us some figgy pudding—and a cup of good cheer!" The massive group gathered at the garrison singing in a circle, and Lucien had an arm draped around my neck, swaying us both in time to the tune.

He clinked my cup, his eyebrow snaking higher and smirked. "Good tidings, sister."

"Good tidings, Lucien," I answered, staring into my ale as though it held tea leaves that could predict the future.

Lucien had arranged for the local bar to bring barrels of ale and cider to the garrison along with as many of his succubi as he could scrounge up. Women straddled the men, right in front of the crowd. Some were penetrated by more than one as there were not enough women to go around.

"Victory or death." I whispered the code words into Lucien's ear, and he raised eyebrows in my direction. "I thought our additional . . . rations were to have arrived by midnight."

Lucien swallowed with a glance out the window. "Yes. With this weather, the goods might not make it until morning."

Panic swelled beneath my calm exterior. "Or not at all."

*Lucien paused. Then nodded. "That was always a risk."
Worry lines etched deeper in his face before he finally relaxed,
patting my leg. "You worry about your job. Keep the men enter-
tained."*

*I nodded, but I still couldn't shake the trembling fear in my
gut. "Lucien—have you seen Jack?"*

*Lucien studied my face momentarily, then shook his head.
"Hours ago. He's around somewhere."*

"I have to be with him once more before . . ."

*"Before Christmas is over?" Lucien cut me off with a pointed
look.*

*Honestly. As if I would have slipped with something that big
just before battle. I stretched my neck in an arrogant way. "Pre-
cisely. I must give him his gift. Tom's life depends on this gift. . . ."*

*"There will be plenty of time for that. In the meantime,
there's a very important man who wants to meet you." Lucien
pushed off the floor, taking my hands and pulling me to my feet
as well.*

*Dragging me to a strapping man of about fifty with a white coif
of curls and ponytail tied tightly at the nape of his neck, Lucien
presented me with one hand. "Colonel Rall . . . this is Monica. The
most beautiful woman in Trenton."*

*Tucking one foot behind the other, I offered the commander
a curtsey. "Colonel Rall. It's a pleasure to meet you."*

*"The pleasure's all mine." Colonel Rall lifted my hand, drop-
ping a feathered kiss to my knuckles. "And please, call me Johann."*

*Jack appeared from nowhere, standing on my other side. His
grin was tight as he planted a kiss to my cheek. "Ah! Commander," he said, taking Johann's hand in a firm grip. "I see you've
met Monica. I heard you had your eye on her."*

"Y-you don't mind, Jack?"

*"Mind? Not at all . . . not for Colonel Rall. He deserves the
best. I knew I couldn't keep a girl such as yourself forever."*

I swallowed. Nothing he said was overtly bad . . . but the timbre in his voice was on the edge of fury. "Jack," I whispered. "Maybe we should talk . . ."

"About what, my dear?" Jack's lips clenched, and his face twisted from friendly and smiling to burning with rage. The transformation was instant and terrifying. "About how you betrayed me?" I stole a glance over my shoulder at Lucien, who was entertaining the colonel for the time being. "How you kissed my son in my own home?" His grip on my elbow tightened, squeezing the flesh between his fingers.

"Jack—it's not what you think—"

"I think nothing," he rasped. "It matters not to me. You two can have each other." He spun, stalking in the other direction. He froze after two steps, looking over his shoulder. "Merry bloody Christmas. My pet."

"Colonel!" A man in uniform burst through the garrison doors, rushing Johann. "Colonel, we just got word. A note from General Grant—Be on your guard."

I darted a look to Lucien, unease settling in my chest. But Lucien's face remained marble, watching the conversation.

Rall took the note, flicked an eye quickly over, and stuffed it into his pocket. "We've been liable to be attacked at any moment since our arrival." He draped an arm around the soldier's shoulder, directing his gaze out the window. "Look out at that sleet. That snow. No man will attack in this. Not on Christmas. Not any day." With a slap on the soldier's back, he gave a nudge toward the barrels. "Now, get some cider! And let them come . . . we will go at them with the bayonet!"

He turned back to Lucien and me with an exasperated look. "These boys," he grumbled. "We were attacked by locals just earlier." He patted the note within his pocket. "Certainly that's what this late warning is for."

Lucien rolled his eyes with a puff of his lips. "Boys. They never know when to have a good time." Slipping his arm into *my elbow, he guided me toward Rall once more. "Now, you, Colonel. You know a good time, aye?"*

A predatory gleam flickered in Rall's eyes, and his smirk climbed higher. "I certainly do."

By sometime after seven the next morning, I had still not slept. And Washington's troops still had not arrived. I slid out from beneath Rall's arm, draped across my breasts, and slipped my various layers of dress over my head. In my vision of Rall's death, it was obvious the battle would happen. Soon, before the snow melted from the ground.

Puddles of questionable fluids covered the floors. No matter where I stepped, it was nearly impossible to avoid. A draft of something rancid flooded my nose, a combination of sweat and booze, leaking out of all the men's pores. I covered my face in an attempt to swallow the retching. A job well done by the succubi. The men were guaranteed to be hungover. Some likely still drunk.

There was a throbbing ache between my legs. Never before had I had relations so many times in such a short period.

From outside, voices grew louder and something jumped in my belly.

"Der fiend! Der fiend!"

The voices grew louder. Panicked. And movement stirred within the garrison. Men jumped from their inebriated states, scrambling for bayonets and britches all at once.

There was a plethora of guns and weapons for the taking. One thing about the European armies—they were not at a loss for funds. I rushed the table, grasping a gun in my hands.

A firm grip on my arm pinched and twisted me around. Standing in my face was Jack, reaching around my body for his own weapon. "What are you doing?"

He gripped the barrel of the gun, wrenching it from my hands, but I held firm in a tug of war.

"*I want to fight. I want to help.*" *I swallowed. Bloody Hell, I hoped he couldn't see through my lies.*

"*You want to help?*" *he sneered, letting go of the bayonet and shoving it into my chest.* "*Very well. Get yourself killed. See what I care.*"

He stomped passed me, grabbing his own weapons and racing out to King Street where battle, blood, and death awaited.

42

Jules entered the back room with one last glare at Ink. "I didn't realize you had humans working in your establishment."

Mia shrugged slowly, with intent. "You'd be amazed at how many humans want to bow down and worship Hellish creatures." She sent a smirk to Ink, who winked and closed the door behind him.

Jules crossed the room, hands relaxed into the pockets of his ripped jeans. They were casual and yet he managed to make the look worthy of a billboard ad.

My heart clenched.

"What's this all about, Mia? My superiors would not be happy that I'm having a secret meeting in the back room at a succubus hangout. They despise the fact that I'm as connected to the demon world as it is."

"You mean to say that they're mad you're as connected to a succubus as you are." Her plump, scarlet lips lifted into a feline grin. Julian didn't take the bait and continued to look upon her with quiet command.

"Fine." She took one more sip of her martini before placing

it back onto the table. A satisfied *mmm* hummed from her lips. "I know I am the main suspect—not only in Lucien's disappearance but in Monica's hit."

A breath caught in my throat, and I had to swallow the urge to cough.

Mia held Julian in a stern glare. "Read my aura, Julian. I am not involved in any of this. I do not want to kill one of my daughters. Nor did I have anything to do with Lucien's disappearance. Am I lying?" She tilted her head.

Julian looked on, eyebrows softening, and he brushed a hand through his silky, gold locks. My own fingers twitched to touch him, as well. "You are not lying."

Mia floated to the couch in a seated position so elegant, Princess Caroline would have a thing or two to learn from it. "Please, have a seat." She gestured to the other end of the couch, and Julian lowered himself, much more cautiously. Tensed.

"I know that you and Lucien were close," Mia continued after another sip of her martini. "As close as an angel and a demon could be, that is. But I know Lucien better than you ever will. And there are some things that perhaps you don't know?"

"Quit with the games, Mia," Julian growled, and it was the first time in a while I had heard him so angry. "Tell me why you brought me here."

Mia rolled her eyes. "Very well. You really are no fun." She crossed a thin knee over the other. "Before Lucien fell from Heaven, he was a watcher . . ."

"I know," Jules interrupted.

"Patience," Mia purred. "When he and the others lost the rebellion, they formed a counsel of demons to head up Hell. Lucien is among the higher ranked originals. Lucien was given his Earthly position as a watcher as well—but for Hell. They took his angel medallion and marked it with sunstone dust."

"So?" Julian's gaze narrowed, and I, too, was wondering

what the Hell this had to do with anything. Jules's throat tightened, and the muscles in his jaw jumped. Had I still been his partner, I would have brushed a knuckle across his gritted jaw . . . a reminder to him to relax.

I forced my eyes back to Mia. That wasn't my job anymore. Not for centuries. It was up to Adrienne to keep him calm now.

"So," Mia said, "Lucien was assigned to work in Ireland back in the middle ages. Assigned to a very special human. His task was simple—get the human to sign away her soul."

Warmth tingled through my body, and I was suddenly filled with so much heat, I feared I might pass out. With an outstretched hand, I found the wall and leaned back against it.

"Monica?" Julian whispered, and I snapped my head up to look at him. "It was Monica?"

Mia nodded. "Monica was one of the many subjects assigned to him to watch and convert to the dark side. Only—he loved her."

"What?" Julian growled, hopping to his feet.

"Oh, calm down." Mia flipped a hand dismissively. "Not in the way you love her. He developed a fondness for her. And he couldn't do it. He never showed himself. If anything, he acted the opposite and protected her. She died with her soul intact, and Lucien was punished gravely for his choice."

"Was he looking to be redeemed? By Heaven?" Julian's face crunched in thought.

"I don't know. I doubt it—Heaven was just as furious as Hell. There's an order to things, I suppose." Mia sighed and finished her martini, chewing on an olive. "Lucien was punished for his choice. Severely. And on top of his torture, he had to corrupt a large number of souls to reinstate his status on the counsel."

"Why didn't they just fire him? Banish him from the counsel and Hell?"

"They couldn't," Mia answered simply. "He was one of the

originals. Without his sunstone, Hell's fortitude wasn't strong enough to withstand a battle of Heaven and Hell had it arisen."

"What exactly are you telling me, Mia?"

"I'm saying that perhaps you are investigating the wrong side." She leaned forward and hushed her voice. Not as if that mattered—we were in a securely enchanted room. "Examine your angels as much as the demons—you're more likely to find the kidnapper and Monica's hitman among your own kind."

Julian snorted and pushed to his feet. "Don't be ridiculous. Angels don't murder."

"They don't murder *humans*," she corrected. "If you think for a second they would bat an eye at killing a demon, you're in denial."

"How do you know it wasn't someone from Hell's counsel? Someone still angry about his sacrifice for Monica and looking to get rid of Lucien and steal the sunstone?"

"Because," Mia responded calmly, "if they had the sunstone, they wouldn't be ransacking his home and office. They wouldn't be hiring everyone and anyone they could to find Lucien. I'm telling you Julian . . . whoever did this is likely not from my side of the realm."

Jules's hands flailed to his sides. "Why are you telling me all this? Why not San Michel?"

Mia snorted and rolled her eyes. "*You* shouldn't even trust those guys, let alone me trust them."

"You're speaking ill of my superiors." Julian shook his head and stalked toward the door. "We're done here," he growled.

"Ironic, isn't it?" Mia called over her shoulder. "Monica was destined for Hell. No matter how Lucien tried to spare her, she still ended up there. Only, it wasn't a demon who put her there—it was an angel."

"No!" Julian shouted. "Buckley put her there. Dejan put here there. Heaven had nothing to do with it." He yanked the door open.

And Mia rose to her feet. "Are you trying to convince me? Or yourself?"

Julian's hand clenched around the knob, his knuckles white.

"Just think, Julian. Had you only done your job better—" Mia didn't get the rest of the sentence out before Julian slammed the door and rushed her. His hands clenched around her throat, and he shoved her into the wall just beside me.

She smirked, not affected by his attack in the least bit. "Yes," she rasped through the grip he had on her windpipe. "Prove my point, Jules. Angels can murd—"

Her voice cut out on a squeak, and I lifted my invisibility and mask. "Jules, no!" I shoved his arms, and he released his hold, falling back onto the couch.

"Monica!" He ran to me, taking me into his arms. "What—what's going on here?" He glanced back and forth between Mia and me.

Mia's face was red, and she shifted it back to its normal porcelain coloring. "I wanted Monica to hear the truth. And I wanted her to see that I wasn't lying. An angel was the best way to prove that."

"I wouldn't have killed you," Jules said stiffly.

Mia smirked, walking slowly past him. With a light slap to his cheek, she crinkled her nose. "Believe me," she said, "if I thought for a second you could, I would have put up much more of a fight."

Jules rubbed the front of his forehead, swiping at the concerned wrinkles there. "So, Lucien risked everything to save your soul." Jules looked to me, wetting his lips. "And you think angels kidnapped him?"

"No—" I cut in. "Whoever got Lucien we think meant to capture me."

"Though I'm sure getting Lucien was a nice consolation prize," Mia said.

"Mia," I said. "Did you realize that the Suck 'n' Swallow is one of only five places in the city where a summoning can take place?"

"Yes. Of course. Why do you think I bought it? Along with the parking garage and a series of homes near Paradise."

I chuckled to myself. "You own more than half of the summoning areas in Vegas?"

"Well, I couldn't buy the damn cemetery. And I've been searching for the owner of that mine for decades without any luck."

Julian cleared his throat and looked between us. "If an angel was behind this, they certainly wouldn't need one of the five points to get Lucien. It doesn't make sense."

Mia rolled her eyes in a manner that was still poised. "You are so naïve. The angels themselves would never do the task. Much like Ink or my lackeys, they get a human to do their dirty work with the promise that they will get through those pearly gates."

"I'm meeting Kayce and Grayson here in a few. Are you able to stick around?"

"I have a little time." His eyes flickered, locked on me, and a flush flared across my skin. The tiniest smile crinkled the corners of his eyes, and my gaze fell to his heaving, tensed chest.

"Right. Of course."

Mia opened the door for us, allowing me first, then Jules. As I exited, I set my purse down on the bar and flipped open my phone to check on how far away Kayce and Grayson were.

"Do you mind if we wait outside?" Julian asked with a sneaking glance around the club.

I nodded and followed Jules out the door, still texting. With a deep breath, I tucked the phone back into my pocket and looked up into the night sky. It was past midnight and yet our evening was just beginning. I snuck a glance to Julian to find his gaze locked on me. "It's going to be a long night," I said.

"With you?" Julian smirked, tucking his hands into his pockets. He looked to the moon as well. "It always is."

Two headlight beams caught Julian's hair with a golden light, creating a halo effect. I smiled. Damn, was he beautiful.

"Stop staring, Monica." I could hear the smile in Julian's voice. "Your boyfriend is watching."

Kayce's car pulled into the spot in front of us, and she switched the engine off, climbing out and hopping onto her hood. "Hey, guys." She gave us a bemused smirk as Grayson and Drew climbed out of the car.

Drew's swagger was confident, sexy. He stopped just in front of me. "Fancy seeing you here." His grin widened, and he twirled a stray curl around his finger before tucking it behind my ear.

"I should have fucking guessed." A growl came from behind me, and I twirled to find Damien's hard gaze cemented on us.

43

New Jersey, December 26, 1776

The frigid morning winter air blasted me in the face as I ran out to King Street. A formation of men was lined in a V, and the entire town was blockaded, stopping any escape to Princeton or beyond. A pair of eyes I recognized glistened as they connected with mine. Tom! I wanted to run to him, but I had to be covert in how I fought. Though gunshots could not kill me, the locals would surely burn me at a stake if a bullet to the heart didn't kill me instantly.

Colonel Rall walked the line in front of his men across from the Patriot artillery, outnumbered by at least double. Fear rattled in his watery eyes. "Fall back!" he shouted in German. "Take cover in homes! Taverns!"

Gunshots mirrored his orders, blasting through the quiet morning. And the onslaught of bloodshed began. Jack loaded his musket, firing the line. He froze, and I followed his gaze to where it landed directly on Tom. A smirk rose, crinkling his eyes. Tom's head was down as he was reloading.

Jack raised the hilt to his shoulder and, squinting an eye, took aim at his only child. His blood. His legacy.

"*No!*" *I screamed, charging Jack and managing to knock the gun from his hands just in time.*

"*You traitor!*" *He curled back and spat in my face. Yanking my hair, he threw me to the ground. I looked around King Street. Some Hessians had already taken cover in other establishments. Others surrendered and were being taken in as prisoners of the Patriots. Rall lay on his back, a giant bloody hole in his gut, lifeless eyes directed to the sky.*

Jack pulled me to my feet, holding me in front of his body as a shield. Using me as a hostage, he backed toward Assunpink Creek—the only area not guarded by Washington's men.

His gun was shoved under my chin, pushing the skin up and into my tongue. Blood filled my mouth as my teeth came down on sensitive tissue.

Tom watched on, a horrified expression marring his beautiful face. I shook my head at him as he twitched to charge his father. I squeezed my eyes shut. Please, no, Tom. For once, don't be chivalrous. Don't be the hero.

If only I could have told him my nature. Warned him that no matter what, I'd be fine.

But of course, he had no way of knowing such things. And as his fellow Patriots took prisoners and invaded homes and Bear's Tavern, Tom took off at a sprint, following Jack and me. Though Jack had no way of knowing just yet, I could hear Tom's footsteps several yards behind us. I could smell his perspiration. Hear his pounding heart and staggering breath.

Jack swiveled around, gun cocked, knocking the barrel into Tom's knee and sending him spiraling to the icy ground.

"*No!*" *I shrieked. "Jack, no! Don't kill your son!" The sobs clenched my chest, and my tears fell to the snow, heating tiny holes into the ice.*

"*Quiet!*" *he shouted back. "Thomas, drop your weapon."*

"*You won't get away, Father,*" *Tom panted, catching his breath. "The town is surrounded."*

"*I'll get away,*" *Jack sneered.* "*I'm just a civilian.*"

"*You think the Patriots won't know your involvement here? You think I haven't already given them your name and all your mates?*"

"*Why you ungrateful little sod!*" *Jack's hold on my hair tightened.* "*Throw me your weapon!*" *he shouted again, and Tom did as his father asked.*

Jack chuckled and kicked the gun away. "*You're a stupid little thing, you know that?*" *He looked to me, yanking my head back, exposing my neck.* "*And you, you whore. You two thought you could pull one over on the likes of me?*" *He chuckled in a bitter way that brought bile to my throat. He looked back to Tom, the metal barrel colliding with his son's temple.* "*You love the whore, son? You think she will make a loving mother to your future bastard children?*"

"*On your knees, streetwalker,*" *he gritted through clenched teeth, undoing his fly.* "*Watch closely, son. And tell me if after this, you still want to make this whore your wife.*"

He pushed himself into my mouth, and when I slid a glance to Tom, he was crying. Steady streams of tears flowed past his cheeks.

Panic swelled in my chest—the tree behind him—the snowfall. It was the scene from my vision. Tom would die soon if I didn't act quickly.

I took Jack all the way into my mouth until he hit the back of my throat. Then I bit down. Jack cried out with a curse and slammed his boot into my nose. Stars flooded my vision, and I could taste the blood as it flowed into my mouth.

I blinked open, barely registering the feel of steel against my sternum. A blast of pain ripped through my chest—the most pain I'd ever felt. In the distance, I could hear Tom's screams. Felt his arms cradling my body.

And with a sudden windstorm, life entered me again with a

deep breath. I blinked, coming back to life, and shifted my gaping wounds closed, pulling myself to my feet.

Tom and his father were in a full on fist-to-fist battle, rolling in the snow, throwing punches. I ran for Tom's gun Jack had kicked away. The two fought, and I could barely discern who was whom in the scuffle. "Tom!" I shouted.

The men froze, each of their faces paling to the same white as the snow. "What . . . it's not possible," Jack stuttered.

Tom scrambled to his feet. "Darling—Monica, how is it possible?" He rushed to me, grasping my face with his hands and planting a firm kiss on my lips.

"Tom, run!" I shouted, pushing him from me just as a blast cracked through the air. Blood splattered onto my face, and Tom swayed before falling into my arms, his short breaths sporadic at best. A puddle of blood seeped from beneath his body, absorbing into the snow.

From behind us, Jack panted, musket in hand.

I fell to the freezing ground with Tom, cradling his head in my lap. With the palm of my hand, I brushed his sweat drenched hair from his eyes. "Breathe, my love. Breathe." I squeezed my eyes shut as my tears fell one after the other onto his face. Though he was looking directly at me, I didn't think he could see me. His hand trembled, lifting into the air, and each breath was a labored wheeze. I grasped his hand and brought it to my lips. "I'm sorry, Tom," I said through my tears. "I'm sorry. Where you're going, my love—you're so much better off."

With one final breath, his empty eyes rolled back into his head. I wrapped my arms as best I could around his heavy, limp body and embraced him one final time.

When I finally looked up again, Jack had the musket aimed between my breasts. A terrified frown tilted on his face and hatred burned through me. "What are you?" he said, aiming the gun at me once more. "Are you the devil?" he shouted, firing off another round.

The bullet burned once more, ripping through my flesh and my organs, and I fell to the snow beside Tom. Only my heart didn't need to pump in order for me to exist. I didn't need to take oxygen into my lungs to survive. I lay in the snow, watching the white powdery flakes fall to my face. One landed cold and wet on my nose. And despite the burning pain, I slid my palms under me and pushed to my feet, Tom's gun still in hand.

"You are a stupid man. If a bullet didn't kill me once, did you think it would the second time?"

I was unsteady for a moment. The pain was there, but bearable. The wooden butt of the gun was coarse against my palm, but also a calming reminder of revenge.

He shot again, only this time I was ready for it, and I steadied myself for the hit. I dug a finger into the hole and pulled out the steel ball, throwing it at Jack's feet.

His breaths were shorter, sharper, and he scrambled to reload.

I walked toward Jack at a steady and controlled pace. "You killed your son," I whispered, stopping just in front of his body. His chin bounced as he looked for a retort, but only silence came from him. "You killed your son!" I said again, louder, and slammed the butt of the gun into Jack's nose. Blood spurted like a geyser, raining droplets of red onto the snow. "You killed your son!" I screamed this time, bashing the gun into his eye socket.

He stumbled back but managed to stay on his feet, shouting with each hit and cradling his face in his hands. "How—how are you alive?" Jack asked. His fear was tangible on my tongue. It was bitter and popped in the back of my mouth along with his coppery blood.

"On your knees," I said with a peace that I couldn't explain.

Jack obeyed, falling to the ground before me with his hands up, palms out. "P-please. Monica . . ."

"Do not speak to me. Don't you dare speak to me right now."

Tears caught in my chest, and I wanted to simply lie there, spooning with Tom's body.

I cocked the gun and pressed it between Jack's eyes. "I'd tell you to tell Tom I love him—but I don't think you'll see him where you're going, Jack." I paused. I knew what I had to do. I had to pull the trigger. A shiver ran down my spine. I'd never before taken a life this way. Not at my very hands. But of all the people I had come across in my existence, this was a man who didn't deserve to live. A tear welled in my eye and fell down my cheek. With a final deep breath, I whispered, "I'll see you in Hell, Jack."

A gunshot blasted through the air, and Jack fell to his side. I looked down at my gun—only, I hadn't pulled the trigger. Pieces of Jack's skull were splattered in my hair, and with numb fingers I wiped his blood from my cheek.

"Monica!" Lucien ran to me, and I fell into his arms. He took me by the shoulders, forcing eye contact. "You can't murder. Not like this. Not out of spite." He crushed me into an embrace, his hand flanking my cheek.

"But you did," I whispered, and I could feel his nod within the embrace.

"There is no redemption for me," Lucien whispered. "But there's still hope for you."

44

"Not even twenty-four hours we've been broken up and you're already in his arms." Damien chewed the corner of his mouth. His fitted polo was clinging to clenched muscles, and his hands were clutching his hips with tight, white-knuckled fists.

"What?" Drew pulled back, examining me.

"What?" Kayce chorused.

Well, shit. "What are you doing here, Damien?"

His badge was clipped to his black pants pocket and he fiddled with it, puffing an exasperated breath through tight lips. "I don't know about coffee man there, but Kayce called me. She said you needed help."

"Same here," Drew said. "She picked me up on her way over."

I shot her a look, to which she responded with a shrug. "How was I to know you just broke up? You didn't say anything!"

She was right. I knew that. "Look, I don't think we're going to find anything in there," I said. "I just talked to Mia, and it was made very clear that she has nothing to do with any of this."

"Listen, y'all. I don't frequent these demon bars much." Grayson stepped close, lowering his voice. "But something here smells different. I can smell the summoner who was at the mine. He's in there . . . and I'll bet the ranch that if we find him, we'll find Lucien."

Ink barreled out the door to the bar, rushing toward me. "Oh, good. You're still here. You left this on the bar." He waved my clutch and handed it to me. Flipping his long inky braid over a shoulder, he huffed back into the bar.

"Um, y'all . . . I hate to break up this fun," Grayson said. "But, that guy—the one who gave you your purse back? That's our summoner."

45

"Ink?" I whispered, careful to keep my voice down.

"How do you know?" Kayce asked.

Grayson's response was an exaggerated eye roll and a tap to his nose. "Y'all have seriously got to stop questioning the schnoz."

"So," Damien growled, sending me one last hatred-filled glare. "Ink is the human responsible. But that doesn't lead us to the main suspects."

I stole a glance at Jules, who seemed lost in thought. "Mia had an interesting theory." I cleared my throat and proceeded to fill the gang in on her ideas about Heaven perhaps being responsible.

"It's preposterous," Jules whispered.

"Look," Damien said, swiping his hand through dark hair. "If we watch him, we can follow him and maybe he'll lead us either to someone of importance—or to Lucien directly."

"There are way too many of us for a stakeout. We'll stand out to him in seconds." I stated the obvious, and the group fell silent.

"We'll split up," Damien said quietly. "The most pertinent parties in the stakeout are Monica and Grayson, right?" He scanned the group, and everyone nodded. "Fine. Monica, Grayson, and I will follow this Ink guy. The rest of you stay close, but not too close. We'll be in touch at each place."

"What about George?" Kayce interjected. "He'll want to be here for this."

Damien nodded. "Give him a call and let him know we may need his help."

"Why do you get to go with Monica and Grayson?" Drew asked, eyes darkening.

"I'm sorry," Damien quipped, bitterness cracking at the back of his throat. He looked back to me and Grayson. "Either of you ever done a stakeout before?" We were both silent, and he continued. "Either of you know how to follow someone without being spotted?"

Again, silence. Damien nodded, looking back to Drew. "Just as I thought."

Kayce lifted a finger, quietly adding. "I have a suggestion . . . one that's probably not going to be popular."

Damien raised an eyebrow at her. "Let's hear it."

"George and I can both teleport anywhere. As can Julian and Mia. Drew cannot . . ."

"So?" Damien snipped.

Oh, shit. I knew where this was going. "So, it makes sense that he goes on the stakeout with the rest of you. Otherwise, if you need backup, it'll take us twice as long to get to you."

Damien was quiet for a thoughtful moment before he grunted something that sounded vaguely like "Fine."

Two hours later, four of us were tucked into my Toyota with Damien at the wheel. It was apparently less conspicuous than Damien's monster truck. A couple of times, I slid a glance to Drew in the backseat. He twitched a smile back to me; that same little half smile I'd grown to love so much through the years. Excitement pulsed through me—Drew and I had a chance at a real relationship now. One not hindered by my stealing pieces of his life. Or constantly needing to sleep with other men. We could be faithful. I could get my energy from him and not risk his life in the process. The thought still made me tingle. Tingly and nervous and excited all at once.

But neither of us dared to speak. Not with Damien right here—it just felt wrong.

"Man, it is quiet in here," Grayson finally blurted out, stretching his lean, muscled body in the backseat. "I mean, I thought things were quiet on the ranch, but at least there you had the sounds from the animals." He paused, glancing between everyone. "I mean, it's clear the three of you have somethin' to work out."

"We have nothing to work out," Damien grumbled.

I looked at my lap, fiddling with my cuticles. This was the last conversation I wanted to have with both guys right here.

"It's obvious," Damien continued, hands gripping the wheel at ten and two. "Monica's done with me. And she's moved on to you. That was always kind of the plan, wasn't it?" He shot me a glance, and though his face was hard, the slightest sheen of moisture glassed over his eyes.

"Oh, Damien," I whispered. "For once in my life, I was trying to handle things the right way. Coming and talking to you first instead of just running away or acting rash." I swallowed, my chest tightening. "I'm sorry I hurt you. But you can't be mad at me for being honest with you."

"Honest? Is that what you call it?" Damien swallowed a harsh laugh. "How long have you been fucking him?"

"Oh, come on, man!" Drew finally exploded into the conversation. "We haven't done anything. The moment you saw just—"

"Shut up!" Damien said.

"Don't tell me to shut up—"

"No, I mean it! Shut up!" Damien was rasping a whisper. "Ink's right there! Sure he's human, but he still might have good hearing."

The car fell silent for what felt like the millionth time in the past two hours. He walked directly in front of the car, eyes glued to his phone, and we all ducked down.

"Oh, yeah," Grayson whispered. "That's the scent from the mine. I'm sure of it."

Ink stopped in front of a yellow Pantera and pressed his phone to his ear.

"Now, how in the Hell can a bartender at a Suck bar afford such an expensive car?" I asked quietly.

"Look, I can't find it!" Ink shouted into his phone, then looked around the parking lot with a quick glance. He yanked open his car door, then slid inside, clamping the phone between his shoulder and his ear while sticking the key in the ignition. "Fine, fine. I'll check again. But I'm telling you, it ain't there."

His engine revved, and he tossed the phone into the passenger seat. His car glided out of the lot and onto the road.

After a few seconds, Damien crept onto the road. "Off we go," he said, staying two cars behind Ink.

After about twenty minutes of driving, I had to admit that I was rather impressed by Damien's tracking skills. He always managed to stay just far enough behind that it wouldn't look suspicious. "You're really good at this," I finally said aloud.

Damien snorted, a barely visible shake of his head. "Yeah," he grunted. "I'm good at chasing what I want."

After an inward sigh, I gave up on the chitchat. Another few minutes passed, and I was zoning out watching the desert whiz past us. Finally, my blood turned cold. "Wait—are we going—"

"Well, I'll be damned," Damien said. The Pantera slowed and turned right into Hell's Lair.

46

"Well, granted most of what I know about our legal system comes from reruns of *Law & Order*," Grayson said, "but this don't look good for Ink, here."

"This is perfect," I said. "It won't be suspicious at all if I'm in there!" I threw off my seat belt as Damien's hand clamped around my wrist.

"Wait," he growled. "Just hold on. If this guy meant to capture you, not Lucien, it's best if you don't rush on in there."

"Don't be ridiculous. There are a ton of people who know me in there!"

"You know where else there were a ton of people? Buckley's magic show didn't exactly stop anyone. . . ."

"I think Damien's right, Mon," Drew said from the backseat.

"Shut up." Damien shot a dagger-filled look in the rearview mirror.

"I was agreeing with you!"

"I don't care."

"Oh, for fuck sake." I rolled my eyes and hopped out of the car. "I'm going in. Worst-case scenario, I turn invisible."

Damien muttered a curse and scrambled out of the car, too. "We'll be right behind you. Three dudes off to see some strippers." He turned his attention to Grayson. "You'll be able to locate her scent even if she's invisible, right?"

His smirk widened, and he looked at me as though I were his next meal. "Oh, yeah. I've done it before. . . ."

I hung behind as Ink slipped past T and into the club. As I entered, I gave T a small wave, and he nodded in response.

"Haven't seen you around much the past couple of days."

"I've been keeping busy," I said while scanning the crowd for Ink.

"I'm not asking," T said as his lips tugged to his eyes. It was subtle, but the smile was there. Barely.

The club's crowd was thinning out. I finally spied Ink at the bar. He, too, was cruising the room, seemingly looking for someone. His gaze swept to my right, and I quickly ducked into a corner before he could see me. Again, not that it would matter. But I'd mostly rather not be spotted.

I ducked behind T and shifted myself invisible.

"Nope," T said to nobody. "I am definitely not asking."

When I peeked around the corner, I spotted Ink's jet-black hair as he was slinking into Lucien's office. I managed to slip through the door before it closed behind him.

For my vision, the blackness of the room was fine. But I saw Ink walk right into a small office chair, slamming his shin into the hard wood.

"Fuck!" he hissed, shoving the chair out of his way. After knocking over another notebook he finally reached a desk lamp, which he switched on.

Oh, shit. The Newton's Cradle, one of the few items that will react when an immortal being is present, moved with my presence. The metal balls wildly clacked, swinging from side to side.

Ink's gaze darted back and forth, eyes wide and frightened. "Who's there?" he whispered. "Come on . . . show yourself."

I tiptoed to the Newton's Cradle and placed my hands on it. It recalibrated to my powers, and the balls slowed to a stop. I held my breath, and finally Ink relaxed, puffing a breath out through his lips.

"I'm fucking losing it." He ran a hand across his face, taking a moment to rub his eyes.

He opened some drawers, rummaging around the various pens and invoices tucked in there. "Shit," he said, slamming the top one shut.

"Who's in here!?" A voice boomed from the other side of the door as it swung open.

Ink fell to the floor, rolling under the desk. Lenny stormed in, clicking on the overhead light.

Ink was a pretty large man, and his feet hung out from the other side of the desk more than a little. "Jesus Christ, man. Get up," Lenny snarled in his nasally voice, shutting the door behind him. "What the hell is wrong with you?"

Ink pushed to his feet, brushing some dirt off his pants. "Sorry—they're on my ass to find that stupid stone," he grunted. "I didn't think people would notice me slipping in."

"Lucky for you, no one did. But how stupid can you be, turning on the light in here? Use a flashlight, dumbass."

I'd never heard Lenny be the alpha. He was always the sniveling little lackey, never the brains behind the operation. Something here wasn't sitting right.

"Besides—I told you. I checked everything. It's not here."

Ink folded his muscled arms. "I can't believe what a little Houdini this succubus is. I swear—she's either a genius or the fucking luckiest demon I've ever known."

"Believe me," Lenny snorted. "She's no genius. She's a bitch whose luck is about to run out."

My stomach rolled in my belly like a cold, dying fish. There was no way Lenny was smart enough to be behind all this.

"Call the girl. Arrange a meeting with the big guy," said Lenny.

"But—he only wants to see me if I can provide the sun-stone. . . ."

"Don't argue with me!" Lenny snapped, and ran a hand across his shiny, balding head. "We need more time. Lucien's not giving anything up. And he's the only one who can provide the extension. I'll go check the theater again; maybe it was on him at the time of the summoning. You go check the mine once more."

Ink tugged his phone out of his back pocket and muttered a few choice words to Lenny as he dialed. "Hi," he said. His voice was lower than normal and took on a more menacing tone. "I need to arrange a meeting with you know who. At the mine. Yes . . . tell him to meet me there in thirty."

When I snuck out of Lucien's office with Ink, I found the boys sitting at the bar. Grayson inhaled, eyes blinking. "She's back," he said. They all swallowed their drinks in a gulp, and together we rushed back to our car.

After a minimal time spent arguing, we decided to stay on Ink's tail instead of half of us breaking off to follow Lenny. Since we knew where Ink was going this time, we could let him get ahead of us without concern. Finally, once we arrived at the Valley, we parked and walked up to where he had done the summonings.

"Does anyone have a plan if we find Lucien?" Grayson asked.

"We fight like Hell and save him," I said.

Grayson shot me a glance that was more than a little doubt-ful. "There's only one way to get Lucien out of his imprison-ment. And that's to summon him."

I raised an eyebrow at Damien. "Well, then, it's a damn good thing we've got a summoner here with us."

Damien rolled his eyes and threw his hands up. "I need salt. A circle. Fire . . . how do expect me to just do these things without talking about it first? Communication. It's one of your biggest problems," he grunted with a condescending head shake.

"Look. We can draw a circle in the dirt. I've got a lighter on me. . . ."

"Salt?" Drew asked doubtfully.

My heart plummeted.

"Oh. Right," Grayson said, and tugged a fistful of something from his back pocket. "I always steal these from fast-food joints. I like my fries salty with ketchup." He opened his fist to reveal a few packets of ketchup and three packets of salt. My grin sliced across my face, and I raised my eyebrows at Damien.

"Will that work?"

He took the salt and my lighter, rolling the items over his fingers. "I don't know. But it's worth a try if it comes to it."

We were almost to the mine, and up ahead I could see the circular glow of a flashlight scanning the perimeter. "I should call Kayce," I said. "Let her know that we're here. She should probably join us sooner than later."

Drew nodded and pressed his phone to his ear. "I got it," he said. "Might as well be useful for something."

I tilted my head and offered him a half smile. A snort from my right broke the spell of the moment, and I withdrew my hand, stopping myself before I squeezed Drew's hand or offered any sort of affection that Damien might take the wrong way.

"Kayce got to George, and they're teleporting in at the parking lot so no one hears them," Drew said, hanging up. Within a few minutes, they were walking up behind us.

George had his arm slinked around Kayce's svelte waist, and she draped hers across his shoulders. "What do you say we go kick some ass?" she said with a grin.

As we walked closer, I saw Ink on his hands and knees,

looking under rocks and such. A *crack* sounded through the air, and I gasped at the noise, freezing. Everyone in the group heard it as well, and we all crouched behind some rocks. There, walking up to Ink, was Adrienne.

Her platinum blond hair was twisted into a sophisticated bun, and she wore a flowing white skirt with a blue tank. She folded her arms underneath her breasts. "You called?"

47

"Oh, God, no . . ." Damien whispered, clamping his eyes shut and shaking his head. "No, no, no. Adrienne is not a part of this."

"I didn't call for *you* to be here," Ink said, raising his gaze to meet hers. He stayed on his knees in a bowed position. "I called to speak with—"

"Yeah, yeah. He'll be here shortly," Adrienne said, her voice saccharine. "They sent me to keep you company until then. In the meantime, can I help with anything?"

Grayson inhaled deeply, then finished the breath with several small inhalations. "I think . . . yes—I think I smell him. Lucien." He darted a glance to me, and I shivered as those glowing, yellow eyes connected with mine. "I need to get closer, but I think he's here. The scent is stronger than when we were here earlier."

I twirled to Damien. "Can you get a salt circle started?" He continued staring at Adrienne, a sad, lost look in his eyes. "Damien!" I whispered more urgently, and he snapped his gaze to me. "We don't know that she's a part of this yet. Can you build the circle?"

He nodded. "I forgot—I need something of Lucien's to put in the circle. Otherwise, I'll just be summoning any demon."

I reached into my pocket and pulled out the medallion Buckley had given me. "Here. Don't let anyone else have this." I dropped it into his palm.

"Can I help?" Drew asked.

After a tense moment of holding each other's stares, Damien nodded. "Yeah. Grab a rock and draw me a circle."

Grayson and I pressed forward, careful to walk as silently as we could.

"I'm not supposed to talk about this with anyone else," Ink said, glaring at Adrienne.

She shrugged, dropping herself to a seated position on one of the larger rocks. "Very well. Have it your way. Can I at least help you look for whatever it is you're digging for up here?"

"No," Ink grumbled, and tucked his flashlight under an arm. The ray of light caught the silver cross Adrienne had around her neck, and it gleamed across the valley.

Grayson's breath cracked, and he clasped my wrist. "It's the necklace," he said. "I'm almost certain."

"Grayson, I don't think she had anything to do with this. Ink made a call to someone, but his request was for others higher up. . . ."

I cleared my throat and straightened at full height, walking directly to Adrienne and Ink.

"Monica!" Grayson whispered, grasping to catch my arm. "Son of a bitch," he said, then finally stood as well, following me into the middle of the scene.

"Hey, Adrienne," I said, putting my hands to my hips. "What's up, girl?"

"Monica?" She shaded her eyes from the bright flashlight beam directed right at her face, and Ink scrambled to his feet. "Monica—is that you?"

"I hope to hell you know what you're doing," Grayson whispered, but it came out more like a pant.

"What are you guys doing out here?" I asked casually. As though it was perfectly normal that I was also in front of a mine a few hours before dawn.

"Us?" Ink growled, the predatory edge tangible in his voice. "What the fuck are *you* doing out here?"

"Now, now," I chastised. "I asked first."

"We're just having a meeting." Adrienne answered. "You know . . . angel stuff."

I cocked a head. "You're telling me this guy is angelic?" I shot him an exaggeratedly sweet smile. "I bet Mia would love to hear all about that."

"Monica, really." Adrienne rolled her eyes and brushed a hand through her side-swept bangs.

"Where'd you get your necklace?" From the corner of my eye, I swore I saw Ink stiffen.

Adrienne fingered the cross, pinching it between two fingers. "My boss gave it to me."

Panic flooded my chest. "Julian?" I whispered.

Her brows creased. "No. San Michel."

My exhale was audible in the silent Nevada night. "We're going to need that cross, Adrienne."

"What?" She flattened a palm to her chest and drew back. "Why?"

"Because," Grayson said, "I'm certain that's where Lucien is trapped."

"What? You guys are ridiculous."

"Yeah? Then let us see the necklace. We'll give it right back. I promise."

Grayson stepped forward with an outstretched hand. Adrienne shrugged and rolled her eyes. Reaching behind her neck, she undid the clasp and held the necklace above Grayson's hand.

"No!" Ink shouted, and lunged for the necklace.

"Now, Damien! Now!" I screamed, and turned. The fiery circle blazed in the night.

Adrienne stood there stunned. "Is that Damien? And . . . and *Drew?*"

I only had a second's glance, but I saw Drew on the phone and Kayce and George charging us at supernatural speed. George was on top of Ink in a heartbeat, tearing him off of the wolf with a force I rarely saw him unleash. Ink thrashed around beneath George's grasp, and a scream echoed in the mine as George fell backward, clutching his neck. The smell of singed flesh permeated the air, and when Ink scrambled to his feet he held the cross out as though the mere sight of it would keep us off of him.

"Keep back," he panted. "I warn you!"

Kayce snickered. "Or what? You think we can't handle a little burn?"

From his back pocket, Ink pulled out a vial of water. He bit the cap off. "Or I will drop your friend into this holy water. You think it's painful being trapped in a holy relic? Try drowning in it. I doubt he'd survive it. . . ."

We all froze. Even Adrienne stilled.

"San Michel's behind this, isn't he?" I finally asked, and Ink panted, eyes darting from person to person. He was a caged animal with no way out. Caged creatures had a greater tendency to be deadly.

"Y-yeah. I-I wasn't really a part of it. I swear to you."

George rubbed the burned skin on his neck. "Yeah, right."

"Okay, fine. I did the summonings part. B-but that was only because I was looking for redemption. From some stupid dark magic in my past."

"And the ArchAngel agreed that if you captured me, you'd be redeemed?"

Ink nodded, his hand trembling above the holy water. "Yeah, but then Lucien went and fucked it all up. Lenny told me you all were going to the show. Buckley had told his ensemble women he was going to pull you up for that trick. Lenny watched from the audience and texted me at the right moment to summon you. Only—it wasn't you that appeared in the circle."

I smirked. "How pissed at you were the angels?" From the corner of my eye I could barely make out Damien's fire circle growing in size, and so I paced around Ink, turning him so that his back was to the summoning.

"He wasn't happy. But said he could use this, too. That Lucien had it coming, and if I could find the sunstone, he would offer me redemption."

"But they still want to kill me?" I narrowed my gaze, and my voice grew so brittle that with one little change it could break any moment.

Ink swallowed and nodded.

"Why?" I shouted. "Because some stupid mistake Lucien made when he didn't corrupt me years ago? Who cares!?"

Ink's eyebrows lowered in confusion. "What? No . . . you have a gift. One that they never saw in a demon before." Ink licked his lips and glanced nervously around.

I looked to Adrienne, who simply shrugged. "Don't look at me. This is all news. All I know is I got the necklace as a gift from Michel a few days ago and that I've been the liaison between Ink and San Michel." She held up two hands. "That's it. I swear."

"I have . . . a power?" I thought back to Genevieve. To Elliot. A power to give life.

Ink nodded. "That's all I know." He opened his mouth to add something just as the cross started swinging in circles in his hand. It trembled, and he looked down at the idol. It gave us just enough time to jump him; I slammed my body into his massive wall of muscle. Grayson did the same, pawing at the necklace, and Ink went spiraling to the ground, landing with a thud.

He struggled against my hold, but I was too strong for him. Wind picked up all around us, and from the left I heard a *crack*.

Then another and another; in the confusion, several people showed up at once.

The necklace finally stilled in Grayson's hand, and when I looked over, lying in a heap in the middle of the summoning circle was Lucien.

Unmoving, blistered, and bloody.

48

"Oh, Lucien." Tears flooded my eyes and my throat tight-ened as I swallowed them down, running to his side. I fell to my knees beside him, the red clay dirt staining my pants. "Are you okay?" I asked, and immediately regretted it upon looking his body up and down. He was certainly *not* okay. "Someone get him water!" I shouted into the night. Within moments, Kayce was beside me, running her hand along Lucien's leg.

"Here," she said, gently handing him a bottle. He drank the entire contents, then finally managed to prop himself onto his elbows.

"Thank you." He held Kayce's eyes for a moment, a heated exchange passing between the two.

A sheen of moisture flashed across Kayce's almond eyes, and she pressed a knuckle to hold back the tears. Giving Lucien a light tap on the leg, the tears were gone in a blink. "Don't dis-appear like that again. I'll kick the shit out of you."

Lucien's chuckle was raspy. He licked his dry, cracked lips and nodded. "I'd never dream of leaving you again." His head turned back to me, and he squeezed my hand with what little strength he had left. "Thanks for finding me."

I nodded. "I never would have stopped." Then, leaning in, my lips tugged into a smile. "There's still hope for you, Lucien."

He laughed again, a bit louder this time, and his eyebrows arched. "I'm not so sure about that. But thank you all the same."

"Uh, y'all..."

"Grayson, not now," I snapped, not even bothering to look back at him.

"Monica, you're gonna want to deal with this," he continued, his voice uncharacteristically shaky.

"Fine." When I looked up, San Michel was standing with one hand fisted around Lenny's one-size-too-small shirt. Lenny squirmed, doing his best to wriggle away from the sheer blast of power the ArchAngel exuded. Adrienne stood a few feet behind them, looking from side to side. And somewhere along the way Mia, Julian, and Buckley had shown up.

"Well." The word gushed from my mouth on an exhale. "Looks like we've got ourselves a little party here."

Mia still wore her perfectly fitted suit, and her fiery scarlet hair cascaded in shiny waves down her back. She moved beside me, as did George, Kayce, Damien, and Drew. "You can see you're outnumbered." Her words were a practiced melody, and if my Queen was the least bit nervous, she certainly didn't show it.

"Are we now?" Michel's eyes glided across my friends, finally landing on me with a cold gaze. His dark skin would have been swallowed by the inky night, except for his glorious luminescent wings, which arched over his towering frame. The lack of humanity in the angel's eyes sent a chill through my body.

"Why do you care about my powers? Great or not, they come nowhere close to anything you possess," I said.

Julian stood to the side, his head darting back and forth between his ArchAngel and me. When Michel didn't answer, he finally spoke. "San Michel had nothing to do with this. Right?" Jules's voice cracked, and Michel turned to look at Jules slowly.

"Naïveté turns my stomach," he said. "Only one can give life—and that is our God. No demon, no succubus, not even an angel should be able to interfere in giving back life to a human," he spat the words, enunciating each syllable.

"What?" Kayce asked. "What are they even talking about. . . ."

Michel's face registered surprise. "You didn't tell them, then?"

I shook my head. "No. I didn't tell anyone—how did you know?"

He smirked. "We've known your potential for some time. You were never meant to be one of us." Michel tilted his head. "We wanted you out of Heaven—only as soon as we placed you in Buckley's hands, we realized our mistake. Sorcerers always make such a mess out of things."

A grunt came from behind me, and Buckley glared at the angel, hands fisted at his sides.

"The very fact that you became a succubus instead of a vampire was the result of some botched spell, isn't that right, Buckley?" Michel clung to the letters in his name, overenunciating them purposefully.

Buckley shrugged, the movement itself seemingly casual, but it was done with a tenseness that suggested anything but a relaxed motion. "Magic's tricky sometimes."

I bit my tongue and somehow managed to hold back a biting retort. After a deep breath, I looked back to San Michel. "So, why now? I've been a succubus for centuries."

"There was a change in you a couple of years ago. We saw that you were not able to fully control your powers. You would touch people, kiss people, and feel electricity, yes?"

I nodded.

"That was the beginning of the turnover," Michel continued. "And we knew it was just a matter of time. Then when the sorcerer linked that final spell to you, that's what pushed it over the edge."

"So naturally you had to kill me? You could smite me down at any moment. Why go through such a process?"

"Well, we tried to keep it under wraps. Such a blatant killing would very likely begin a war between Heaven and Hell."

Lucien coughed and spat blood onto the ground while pushing himself to his feet. "You son of a bitch," he grunted. "Nothing changes, huh? You preach about love and forgiveness. And yet you had a soul in need of redemption, and even as an angel you couldn't grant it to her." He wobbled a bit and steadied himself on George. "And you wonder why the four originals rose up against your regime. It wasn't your God we were against. It was *you*."

Michel held Lucien's glare. Finally the silence broke as Michel held a hand out to his side. "Bring me the tattooed human."

Adrienne darted a glance at me, then Jules, before she stepped forward, dragging Ink behind her. Michel grasped his arm, yanking him the rest of the way.

"You and the short human failed. You neither captured Monica nor successfully gathered the sunstone." Michel placed hands to the tops of Ink's and Lenny's heads. Their shouts echoed through the night as flames shot to the sky. Their bodies were engulfed in one quick flame, leaving nothing but two piles of ash in their wake.

"No!" Julian screamed, and rushed forward, but he was moments too late. He fell to his knees in front of the ash, and ran a hand into the charcoal.

I covered my mouth, suppressing a whimper. Sure, I never loved Lenny. And he and Ink were the reason we were all here tonight. But I didn't wish them dead.

"Now," Michel continued. "If it's a fight you desire, then a fight you shall have. But while there may be more here on your side, keep in mind an angel's power far outweighs a demon's."

Jules's head hung slumped. Michel shifted a glance down at

him and through clenched teeth ordered, "Get up. Stand beside me, brother."

Julian slowly rose, head still bowed in thought, or maybe prayer, beside Lenny's ashes. He finally looked up into Michel's eyes. He stood beside his angel brethren, a lost look in his crystal blue eyes.

A tear slipped down my cheek, and I twitched a smile in his direction. "It's okay," I mouthed to him.

The stones crunched beneath his feet, and Julian walked over to me. He placed a kiss on my forehead, the feel of his cool lips tingling against my skin. His peppermint scent embraced me in the summer evening. Turning, he stood beside me, taking my hand in his. "They are no brothers of mine," he said.

"Have it your way," San Michel hissed.

"Adrienne?" Julian held out a hand.

She was quiet a moment, looking down at her hands. Finally, she looked up, meeting Jules's eyes first, then mine. She shook her head, then dropped her gaze once more.

Michel smiled triumphantly. "Come now, Monica. Do you really want to put your friends through this?"

I swallowed and stepped forward. "No," I whispered. "I don't."

Voices rose behind me all at once, and I held out a hand to silence them. "Guys—enough." I walked until I was right in front of Michel, my nose coming just below his chest.

His hand fell to my forehead and I closed my eyes, whispered an incantation. The fire rose from my feet, and I pushed my palms forward as the flames did my bidding and landed on Michel's wings. The feathers sparked, and he screamed as they flared orange and red. Michel was on top of me in seconds, the smell of burned feathers hitting the back of my throat.

"That was a mistake, succubus," he said coldly.

There was a commotion of feet running toward us. "Do it quickly," I rasped as his hands closed around my throat.

Mia shoved me aside, and I fell hard to the red clay ground. The flames swallowed my Queen along with her screams. Damien ran full speed at Michel, and the wind picked up around his twirling fists. Adrienne jumped in front of him, and he halted with a gasp. "What're you going to do? You going to kill me?"

A pained expression twisted on her face. "No—but I can't let you hurt my ArchAngel, either."

Damien moved to pass her, but she followed. He moved the other way, and she blocked him again. Just as Damien moved to jump again, Drew barreled into Adrienne from the side, the two forms morphing together as one. He stood, wobbling, eyes dilated cloudy and white.

Michel smiled at me. "Let's try this once more."

Before he could get his hands on me, George landed on the angel's shoulders. With one hand at the base of his wings, he tore one off. The cracking sound was worse than any bone breaking. It echoed in the mine along with Michel's screams.

Julian pushed me aside, holding the carved sunstone in his hand. George twisted Michel's arms, bracing them behind his back. The wings, or what was left of them, fluttered behind, and with each brush against George, steam sizzled and rose.

"This is what you were looking for, right?" Julian held the stone up, eye level to Michel. "This is what you wanted? What you were willing to annihilate the only woman I ever loved for?"

Michel swallowed. "Julian, listen to me—it isn't like that. Only God can give life. We can't let an abomination—"

Jules shoved the makeshift knife against the angel's throat, and I could feel everyone still around us. All fighting halted. "One flick of my wrist," Julian growled. "That's all it would take."

"Julian, no!" I screamed, lunging for the sunstone. My hands clutched around his; the sharpened edge of the stone sliced into my palm and blood cascaded down my wrist. Shifting wouldn't result in the wound closing—I knew that.

I pried his hands away and Julian fell to the ground, his hands covering his face, blond hair flopping into his eyes. Michel wrestled out of George's grasp, slamming him into one of the giant rocks twenty feet away. He moved faster than I'd ever seen a creature move in my life. Faster than any vampire, succubus, or demon. He darted for me, and I lowered into a crouch, arm extended. I looked to Julian, and though it was all moving so fast, in that instant time slowed to crawl and I held his blue gaze.

"There's no redemption for me," I whispered. "But there's hope for you."

With one lunge, I plunged the sunstone into Michel's chest.

49

New Jersey, December 26, 1776

"What do you mean there's still hope for me? I'm a sex demon . . . How can you even say that?"

Lucien tilted his head, a half smile lifting one corner of his lips. He tucked a frizzy curl behind my ear. "Trust your master and commander."

I shook my head. "I don't believe you. I can't. Even when I tried to do this in the most Heavenly way I knew how, good people still died." My chest quivered as I looked down at Jack and Tom, bloody with gaping angry holes in their bodies. "I really fancied Tom," I whispered.

Lucien nodded, curling his hand around the back of my neck and pulling me in for a tighter hug. "I know," he answered. "And you're right. No matter what we do, good people will die. That's a part of life."

"Then what's the point!?" I sobbed, clinging to his jacket.

His sigh lifted my cheek, and I rose and fell with his exhalation. "I don't know. All I know is, you are a good woman. You deserve better than this, and I hate that this life is so miserable for you."

"*If good people die. And bad people die . . .*" *I faded off, pulling back from Lucien's embrace and staring into his eyes.* "*. . . then why am I even attempting to be good? Why am I sacrificing my energy and happiness to spare them?*"

Lucien swallowed. "*Because that's what you do, Monica. That's who you are.*"

I shook my head and stepped over Jack's body. "*Not anymore,*" *I whispered.* "*Hell wants souls? I'll give them souls.*"

"*This is a normal feeling you're having.*" *The snow crunched beneath Lucien's boots.* "*And while you are in your rebellious phase, I will make a promise to you. I will not take the souls of any Heaven-bound women while you are acting out. That way, the balance is still right.*"

My stomach fluttered and relief filled my chest, though I didn't want to admit it. "*Do as you wish,*" *was all I could say in response.*

"*And Monica . . .*" *He stopped, grabbing my elbow and turning me to him once more.* "*There is hope for you. Always. Your angels aren't the ones who forgive sins—remember that. There's only one who can pardon your indiscretions. And that is yourself. Learn to forgive yourself and you'll never be more than a stone's throw away from redemption.*"

I sniffed and wiped my arm across my nose. "*Then how come you say there is no hope for you?*"

Lucien's face fell and grew very serious. He looked down at Jack's body.

"*Because I don't want forgiveness. Not from Heaven.*"

He tilted his gaze to the sky, closing his eyes.

"*I have no desire to join their ranks again—though I never stopped loving God.*"

50

The stone slid in easier than I thought it would, and my eyes widened as Michel's blood flowed down my forearm to my elbow. "Oh, God," I whispered to no one but myself. I had not taken the Lord's name in vain for as long as I could remember. But if ever a time warranted it . . .

The entire battle had frozen, with everyone staring at the sight of the dying angel at my feet. A trickle of blood dripped from the corner of his mouth as he wheezed a breath.

The sunstone fell from my trembling hand, and red dust billowed as it hit the ground. Lucien was beside me within seconds, limping and wheezing. He pocketed the sunstone and wrapped an arm around my shoulders. The smell of his blistered flesh brought bile to the back of my throat and I gagged, bending at the waist and losing what little I had eaten that day.

"What have I done? Mia—" My Queen's name strangled in my throat, and when I lifted my gaze to Lucien's, all he could do was shake his head.

I heard a *crack* from directly beside me and a low growl from Grayson. The redheaded man from Hell towered above.

Every muscle in my body trembled at the sight of the man again, and Lucien held me tighter. "Levi." Lucien nodded in his direction.

The redheaded man—Levi, it seemed—nodded as well. "Brother Grigori." His eyes trailed down Lucien's various wounds. "I'm glad to see you are well—of sorts." He scanned the crowd, resting his gaze on Grayson. "He was of help to you, I see?"

I nodded, somehow managing to find my voice. "Y-yes. He was."

"Nor did he run."

Grayson choked a bitter laugh out. "Who'm I gonna run to, now? The angels?" He curled a lip, looking to San Michel, still gasping for breath at my feet. "Even if they would have me, that's not a family I want to be a part of anymore."

"You and me both," I whispered.

Levi's eyes widened at my comment. "Lucien—was it this angel that was responsible for your capture?"

Lucien nodded. "Yes. San Michel." His eyes landed briefly on Adrienne, and she stiffened. "To my knowledge, that was all."

Levi sauntered to San Michel, towering above the dying angel. His singed wings sat lopsided beneath his body, crushed on the ground. "I make no apologies," Michel rasped, licking his parched lips. "Lucien was caught in a crossfire battle. But it was the succubus we wanted."

Levi nodded, slowing to a stop in front of the angel. "So I heard. And in the battle, my Succubus Queen was murdered."

"An accident."

"Seems to me you've been having an awful lot of accidents lately."

The two were silent as they stared with hard, lined faces. Michel's chest heaved violently with each pained breath.

"We cannot have a demon with the ability to give life."

"And I cannot have you terrorizing my subjects whenever

you damn well please." Levi's voice darkened and left a coldness in the pit of my gut. "A bounty on my succubus will create a battle between the Heavens and Hell. Is that what you want?"

There was no answer from the angel.

"Very well," Levi continued. "Kayce Cheng—"

Kayce lifted her gaze, still with bowed head, her way of respecting her boss.

"Ever killed an angel before?"

Levi raised a hand, and before his mouth could open, I ripped my arms free from Lucien's embrace. "No!" I shouted. All heads turned to me. I ran to where they stood, and Kayce's eyes met mine with a panicked tenseness.

"If I promise to use my powers to give life only in extreme cases, can we end this? Can we all walk away if I make the promise not to go around intentionally giving life to people?" I swallowed, darting a glance between Levi and Michel. "Please!"

Levi's head dropped to a tilt. "This angel will likely not live as it is. . . ."

Michel grunted, speaking as quickly as he could manage. "If you can hold that promise and confer with the counsel before using the power to give life, then yes. I—Heaven—will submit to that."

"I want permission to use it on one person—for me to gain life force. One person—whom I am in a relationship with." I glanced to Levi, adding with a whisper. "And he works for you, so you will be happy with the arrangement as well. If he'll have me, that is."

I ignored Damien's sharp breath from beside me. Levi didn't smile, but held a palm out to me, which I took firmly with one shake. "You are also still responsible for the wolf," he reminded.

"I agree to these terms as well." He held a hand out. I hesitated before taking it as well in another handshake. Using my weight as leverage, Michel pulled himself to his feet, still curled in pain.

With one final look at each of us, he nodded to Adrienne and disappeared with a *crack*.

Levi leaned into my ear. "We will have a discussion soon about the open position of Queen." And with another *crack* he, too, was gone.

Kayce and George rushed me, crashing into my body with a hug, and I squeezed them both tighter. "Holy shit!" Kayce squealed. "It's over! It's over . . . I mean, it is over, right?"

"I-I think so," George whispered.

Lucien limped over, cupping my face in his large, calloused hands. "Thanks for saving me, kid."

I swallowed, my throat feeling thicker than usual, and looked to where Michel's blood stained the dirt.

"You did what you had to do. Redemption begins when one forgives themselves," said Lucien.

I nodded. "I know . . ." My voice trailed off as I found Damien, Drew, and Jules standing side by side—each lost in their own way. "I need a minute." I met Damien's eyes first, and he immediately dropped his gaze down to the ground, shuffling his shoe into the dirt.

"I'm sorry, again—the giving life thing was secret, and I wasn't sure—"

Damien shook his head with pursed lips. "Please stop," he said, and there was a catch in his voice. "Just stop apologizing. Please."

I nodded, saying nothing more. He pinched his nose between his thumb and knuckle.

"I'm glad you're safe again," he added quietly. Looking over to Drew, he chewed the side of his cheek. "You be good to her." Then with one resolute sigh, he turned for the parking lot, pausing as his shoulder brushed Drew's. "And—I expect my espresso in a to-go cup tomorrow morning." The tiniest smile twitched at his lips before he continued walking away.

Kayce grabbed my keys. "George and I will give him and Grayson a ride home." She turned to Lucien. "C'mon, you. You should wait until you feel better before teleporting."

The four limped toward the car, and I was left with Drew and Jules. Julian's crystal gaze locked on mine; every muscle in his face tensed with a sadness—no, a hopelessness—I had never seen before in him. Well, maybe once—long ago, when I fell.

"Julian," I whispered. He walked over to me, grasping my upper arms with a firm grip. He pressed his lips into my forehead. "Your side—it's still . . ." It's still what? Good? I couldn't finish the sentence.

"Don't say it." He shook his head, and his voice scraped me in a way that left me on edge. There was a sad lilt that broke my heart with each syllable. "We will both know what a lie it is."

Julian turned, walking into the night. "Jules!" I cried. "Where are you going?"

He stopped, pausing before turning to face me once more. His hands were stuffed deep into his pockets, and he shrugged. "I don't know. I just need to leave here." His eyes fell to the blood staining the dirt, and he swallowed, blinking rapidly. "I never would've guessed it. . . ." he said, fading off.

"What's that?" I managed to choke out despite the knot in my throat and the tears blurring my vision.

A sob heaved in Jules's chest, and his face twisted as he looked to the sky. "All this time, I was trying to teach you to be angelic. But even as a demon, you're still twice as good as everyone I put my faith in." Jules pressed his thumbs to his leaking eyes. In the space of a breath, I crossed the distance between us, throwing my arms around his neck. He lifted me off the ground in a crushing hug. My salty tears flowed into his hair, and his large palm cradled the back of my head.

He kissed my temple once more before pulling away. "You be good, which I know won't be hard for you." He sniffed and then jerked a nod toward Drew. "And don't let that guy corrupt you too much." I clutched his hands in mine, not wanting to let go. Never wanting to let go. "Close your eyes, Monica."

I shook my head. "No," I whispered through a ragged breath. I felt shattered; undone.

He ran his fingertips down my face, beginning at my hairline and brushed over the tops of my eyelids as they shut with his movement. A light brush of lips skimmed mine and then I heard a *crack*. And just like that, my angel, my Jules, was gone.

"Jules?" I shouted into the desert, with no answer. "Julian!"

"Monica." Drew's voice caused me to whirl around, nearly crashing my nose into his massive chest.

"Drew—he's gone! Julian, he—why—"

"He'll be back, baby." Drew curled his body around mine, his tender arms a wild change from the man I saw battling to save my life. "We all know these guys can't stay away from you." His lips curved into a grin.

I huffed a laugh, blowing my side-swept bangs into the air. "You say that like it's a good thing."

Drew chuckled, too, wrapping his arms around my waist and tucking his hands into my back pocket. He flashed me one of those amused half smiles I loved so much, and his dimples deepened with the grin. "So this whole 'giving life' thing . . ."

"I'm all yours. For as long as you want me." I ran my thumb over Drew's scar along his top lip, and his eyes wandered the landscape of my face. I felt the weight of the world with that one simple look.

"Is forever an option?"

I laughed and tugged the hair at the nape of his neck. "That is an awfully long time, Romeo."

"And yet, it's not long enough."

Drew's fingertips traced a path up my neck, stopping at my jaw. His breath was hot as he sloped his lips across mine. At first, the pressure was so light, I barely felt it. I opened my mouth to him as he increased the pressure and delved his tongue into my mouth, stroking mine with a soft, smooth motion. His strong arm curved entirely around my waist, crushing me, deepening the kiss. His mouth was cool and tingled across my lips despite the desert heat.

Desire, passion, love, and anticipation swelled within me. I didn't need to see a flash of his life to know that it would include me.

My body clenched as heat flared in every area, and despite my best efforts, my moan buzzed at his lips. He smiled against my mouth and I pulled back, ending the kiss, daring a look upward into his eyes.

"I love you, Drew."

His inhale expanded his chest and he closed his eyes, a serene smile splayed on his lips. "I've waited years to hear you say that."

There was a pause. "And?"

He blinked open, grin widening. "And I love you, too, Monica Lamb." He tilted my head back, hands clasping either side of my jaw, and kissed me again. I fell into his lips, hoisting myself onto his waist and wrapping my legs around him. The kiss ended with several more peppered onto the end.

I panted as his hands cupped my ass. "Well? Now what do we do?"

He lifted an eyebrow. "If you have to ask, you're not much of a succubus."

"Awfully presumptuous, wouldn't you say?"

He closed his eyes, a smile lifting his lips to his eyes. "Woman, I've waited years for this night. You're coming home with me whether you like it or not." With my legs still wrapped around his midsection, he began to clomp toward the parking lot, tightening his hold around my waist.

I laughed and nuzzled into his neck; the smell of coffee and soap was overwhelming and yet I thought that I could never get enough of it. "I require at least a date before I go home with you, you know."

"Lucky for you, I know the owner of a café near the city.

He's pretty handsome, too, you know." He winked, dropping a kiss on my nose.

A rare Nevada breeze caught my hair, flinging it around us, and I shivered. I had Drew. A lifetime—shit, with my new-found powers, we had as many lifetimes as we wanted. I felt my face turn serious, and I ran my fingers across his features, along those chiseled cheeks and sharp chin. His stubble rasped along my fingertips as I brushed over his dimples.

He stopped walking, lowering me back to a standing position in front of him. "Monica?" Concern filled his voice.

"I never thought I'd find love. Not in a way that I could attain." I swallowed as tears sprung again, and I glanced behind him to where the battle took place. "So many lives were lost and . . . and for what? For *me?*" Despite immortality, life—existence felt so short. When I looked back up at Drew, his green eyes twinkled in the moonlight.

"I don't want to wait. Ever—not with you."

Drew glanced around the valley, a chagrined smirk on his face. "So . . . coffee? Or sex?"

I smirked and shook my head. "If you have to ask, you don't know me well enough." I leaned into him, my nipples piercing through my tank top.

Drew claimed my mouth with his, and his palm found my heavy breast. As his lips trailed my throat, I looked to the sky. I had found my soul—my life.

"Right," he said against my lips. "Coffee it is."

Don't miss Katana Collins's

SOUL SURVIVOR

*With immortality comes a craving that can't be satisfied,
a need never fulfilled. . . .*

Once an angel, now a demon, Monica is still a succubus with
an insatiable desire for sex. The more the better. Soul-stealing
orgasms beat out dealing with her broken heart any day of the
week. Monica has no interest in being near both her ex-lover
and his new girlfriend, so she's not thrilled when she's asked to
join them in investigating a string of murders that are clearly
beyond the pale. But when she sees that one of the victims has
her Celtic family crest carved on his arm, she realizes she may
finally find the answers to her past she's been searching for all
these years.

An Aphrodisia trade paperback on sale now!

1

The neon-colored lights were blinding as they swooped around the club like laser beams. First purple. Then green. Now blue. It felt like I was in the middle of a lava lamp, watching them spin around me. With the little straw stirrer, I sipped my Long Island iced tea and kept dancing. Sweaty men bumped into me from all angles, each attempting to brush my ass or breasts, in the hopes I might look up and give them even the slightest bit of attention. If only they knew just how deadly my attention could be.

Kayce, my best friend, grabbed my elbow and swung me around, our noses almost bumping in the process. Even with immortal hearing, I could barely make out what she was saying over the thumping of the bass. Grabbing the back of my head, she pulled me in closer, her lips on my ear. "I think I found two!" she yelled.

For normal girls on the town, this could mean anything— two seats, two bucks, two drinks. For two succubi on the town? It meant victims. We prey on the local men and women here in Las Vegas to satiate the raging itch between our legs and sustain our immortal souls on Earth.

With her hand still wrapped around the back of my neck, she turned me toward two college-aged guys who were staring at us, transfixed, while their clammy hands clenched plastic cups spilling over with cheap beer.

My head snapped back to Kayce. "They're so *young*," I said, noting their auras, silver and sparkling. These two were Heaven-bound for sure.

"I thought you didn't care anymore?" Her gaze narrowed.

My stomach twisted, guilt trying to gnaw its way out as if some little animal had burrowed into there. I pushed the feeling aside. "I don't," I shouted over the music with a nonchalant shrug. I was bluffing. If Kayce knew I was lying, then she chose to ignore it.

"What do you say we give them a little something to look forward to?" she said as a devious grin crept its way across her face. She nestled her body into mine, pulsing to the beat of the music. Running her hands through my shoulder-length blond curls, she sent a wicked glance to the two guys watching, their mouths hanging agape. "C'mon, girl," she whispered. "It's show time."

I moved to the music with her, running my fingers down her open, bare back. We turned in rhythm so that I was looking directly at the leaner college kid; he had surfer blond hair that flopped to one side and full lips. An itch surged through my core, shooting between my legs and my mouth went dry. A droplet of sweat tickled its way down the side of my face along my hairline and I quickly shapeshifted it away, making sure to settle my makeup, yet again. Drinking was making me sloppy with my appearance—and I had it much easier than most humans. With one hand, I swept Kayce's curtain of jet-black hair to the side and ran my lips ever so gently up her neck to her ear. My eyes stayed on the college kid as I darted out a tongue that barely grazed her earlobe.

Her fingers splayed against my scalp, weaving into my hair

and she tugged my neck back. "Which one do you want?" she whispered. With my eyes closed, nose aimed at the ceiling, I could feel her kisses as they trailed down my throat. When I finally opened my eyes again, I turned around, still on the beat, dropped myself down the ground, and swiveled my hips back to a standing position.

"Surfer boy. We've been staring at each other," I answered as though I were ordering mustard on a sandwich.

"Okay, then," she answered. "That leaves me with the mocha candy."

The crowd on the dance floor had parted, and there was now a group of people circled around us, watching. Men gazed hungrily and women scowled, eyes red and angry. Their jealousy surged a bolt of energy into me. Even though I used to be an angel, that bad-girl side wins out every time. An angel turned succubus—I was a creature no one in the demon or angel realm could explain. The succubus with a soul.

The song ended and Kayce took my hand, leading me to the two guys. "This is Monica," she said, running a fingernail down the length of the other guy's bicep, which bulged beneath his Hollister polo shirt.

Surfer boy took my hand in his. "I'm Paul," he said. His palm was sweaty and after the handshake ended, I wiped my hand on my slinky, sequined dress, not caring if it stained. That's the beauty of shapeshifting. It took a lot of my focus not to slink away, hoping that none of his other body parts were *that* sweaty.

Kayce already had a leg wrapped around the other guy, pressing herself against him to the beat. I grabbed Paul's hand and pulled him off the dance floor. I wasn't quite the exhibitionist Kayce was. The bathroom was an extremely modern design with clear glass walls that fogged over as soon as you locked the door, so that no one could see in. I tugged Paul inside, locking the door behind me. The glass fogged, encasing us, and making it look as if the entire club on the other side of the glass had filled with mist instantaneously. He grabbed me from behind and turned my hips back to him, his hands squeezing my waist in a way that suggested a carnal need. Our lips rushed to find each other's and his hands cupped my jaw. Bright blond hair flopped forward into his face and I brushed it back, my fingernails running through the silk-like strands. My tongue found his and they twisted around each other.

With my eyes closed, it was easy to pretend for a moment the hair belonged to Drew—my human manager at the café where I worked during the day. I pretended that those lips were fuller with a tiny scar slicing across the top. Pretended that this college boy's hands were more calloused and weathered from years of hard work as they circled and caressed my body.

An apelike grunt pulled me back to reality. Cool air tickled my puckering nipples and it wasn't until that moment that I realized he had pulled my dress down over my breasts. A raging erection poked through his jeans against my belly and the contact sent a jolt of electricity through my blood. I needed his life to survive—this wasn't about passion or even sex; it was survival. Never mind that I had had sex the night before as well. Never mind that I had chosen Paul because he had a slight resemblance to the man I loved but couldn't have. Never mind I probably could have gone two weeks without another conquest with all the Heaven-bound men I'd been seducing lately. Right now—all that mattered was the life force in front of me. A morality so strong that its power pushed on my gut causing the air to gush out of my lungs, leaving me breathless.

I shoved Paul against the opposite wall, wrapping my legs around his waist. As I propped myself on his hips, the dress slid up above my ass and I shapeshifted my panties away. One of the glorious things about having more sex than I need—I have plenty of power for superfluous shifting.

A finger slid inside me and I tensed my sex around him.

Again, I captured those pretty-boy lips in mine and drank him in. His soul was glistening, shimmering. He was going to be an amazing fix—the high would be electrifying. Much more so than the assholes and Hell-bound men I used to sleep with. And what's a week off their life in order for me to not be condemned to Hell? A week off their life so that I could maintain a human body and not be a drifting soul in the bowels of Hell. And in exchange, they get a night with me—sex extraordinaire. It's an even trade.

Okay, maybe not even, but it's the closest I can get to justifying my actions. Besides, my broken heart is still on the mend. Anonymous sex speeds up the healing process. Not only had I discovered Drew was working things out with Adrienne, but now she was the apprentice to my Julian. My old mentor back when *I* was an angel. I'd lost both the loves of my life to the same woman.

I shook the memory away, concentrating again on the fix that stood before me. I wasn't against falling in love—but I was against getting involved with humans or angels *ever* again. Demon dates only from now on. And the biggest downside to dating demons—they're a bunch of fucking assholes. But Paul was here in front of me. He was hot. And he wanted me. My job is to corrupt souls for Hell and steal their life force. I used to fight my duties . . . but these days, I was becoming friggin' employee of the year.

His arms, which had been holding me up by the ass, released me back to the ground. We both scrambled to get his pants off. I tore the pale blue polo shirt over his head and threw it on the floor. His hands wound through my golden, soft curls and just as I thought he was going to pull me in for another kiss, he grunted and pushed me to my knees.

Under normal circumstances, this sort of overt lack of regard for my sexual needs wouldn't fly. If I was training him to be a consistent lover at my beckoned need, then I would have taken the time to fight it. But for now, fuck it. I flicked a tongue out and ran it along the tip, then up and down the length of his shaft. His fingers still twisted in my hair, tightening their hold on me. He pulled my face closer to his cock. Done with the appetizer, he wanted the entree.

I grabbed his balls, squeezing perhaps a little too tightly, to where pain turned into pleasure. A gust of air whooshed from his lips, the sudden change from gentle to rough proving too much for him. Amateur. I took his entire length into my mouth, wrapping my lips tightly around his girth. My teeth just barely grazed against him as he fucked my mouth. With the skill of an expert, I used my other hand to grip the base of his dick, rotating my head with a swirl as I reached the tip. His head slammed against my throat.

"Fuck me with those stunning sucking lips, gorgeous." He was growing in size; getting bigger against my tongue. There was no way I was letting him get away with not doing any work. I lowered his hands from my hair and placed them on my breasts. His thumbs rolled over my pebbled nipples sending shock waves through my whole body. The ache between my legs grew and I pulled my mouth away before he could finish.

He groaned and tried to pull my head back towards his cock. Slapping his hands away, I stood, bending over the sink. I flipped my dress up past my hips. "Don't you want this instead?"

His eyes grew wide and licked his dry lips before approaching. Two large hands wrapped around my hips and the sides of my ass. The tip of his finger teased my opening, wet and slick and ready for him. The same hand traced around the curve of my ass and spanked me. It wasn't a hard slap, but I gasped in an exaggerated way. Finally, he pushed himself into me. Reaching around front, he flicked at my clit. My knees buckled with the small, but effective motions. The tension was building and I gripped the sink, body trembling, as an orgasm rolled over my body. The itch between my legs was fierce, reminding me that though it was pleasurable, this fuck was a necessity. I could come a hundred times for him, but until he spilled his seed on me, his soul—his energy—was safe.

Thanks to my succubus senses and inhuman reflexes, I saw him unlock the bathroom door before the fogged walls cleared. Within those milliseconds, I shifted my face to look like someone else. Just because Paul was an exhibitionist, didn't mean I had to be. Modesty might seem silly—being that I corrupt souls by fucking countless men each week—but I didn't like my Hellish duties to cross over into my day job. And even though most of these people here in the club were visiting from out of town, I didn't want to be known and recognized as the girl who was publicly getting it from behind. I did the same thing with my night job as a stripper—shift my looks slightly so that most people wouldn't necessarily recognize me during the day.

The walls around us cleared. See-through. "Oh yeah," Paul grunted and slapped my ass, squeezing it hard enough to leave a mark.

Grabbing a fistful of my hair and yanking my head back, he pushed into me with one final thrust. Sliding out just in time, he came all over my ass. It dripped down into my folds and the rush of his life force was like walking into an air-conditioned room after sweating outside on a hot summer's day. It momentarily took my breath away. His life reeled before my eyes, like I was watching an abridged version being projected before me. He'd graduate cum laude; move to Chicago; work in a boutique marketing firm before marrying and settling down in the suburbs. And lastly, he'd die of a heart attack.

Finally, I released the breath I'd been holding, thankful that I hadn't stripped too much of his life. I pulled my dress back down over my ass and looked into the mirror above me. I was glowing, radiant with the new life force. Paul's life force.

I turned to face him, not bothering to shift back into my original features. He was so drunk on cheap beer, he wouldn't even notice I looked slightly different from before. I glanced quickly out at the line of people formed to watch our little performance, then touched his cheek, running a finger down his jawline. "Thanks, Paul."

His pupils were dilated, eyes wide, ready to party some more. Just a side effect of my poison. He was high on me. "Who says it has to be over?" He grabbed me around the waist, pulling me in for another kiss. The crowd of people watching outside whooped and hollered. I let him kiss me a moment longer before pulling away and handing him his pants.

"I say so," I said quietly, reaching for the door. "Oh, and Paul?" When I looked back over my shoulder, he still had the energy, but a dejected look was etched on his pretty, boyish face.

He straightened as I turned around, eyes wide and expectant. "Yeah?" he said, hopeful, zipping up his pants. Like a puppy, I imagined two floppy ears perking up.

"Never shove a woman's head to your dick without reciprocating the act yourself." His face dropped, all color draining quickly away. On an exhale, my shoulders slumped slightly. I spoke again, a tad more quietly this time. "And lay off the red meat, okay? I mean . . . it's just—it can be bad for your heart."